RESIDENT EVIL™
CODE:Veronica
BOOK THREE

Wri[illegible]

[illegible]lish Dialogue by
[illegible]ed Adams
and Kris Oprisko

Letterer
Robbie Robbins
w/Cindy Chapman for IDW

Design/Cover Design
Larry Berry

Assistant Editor
Kristy Quinn

Edited by
Jeff Mariotte

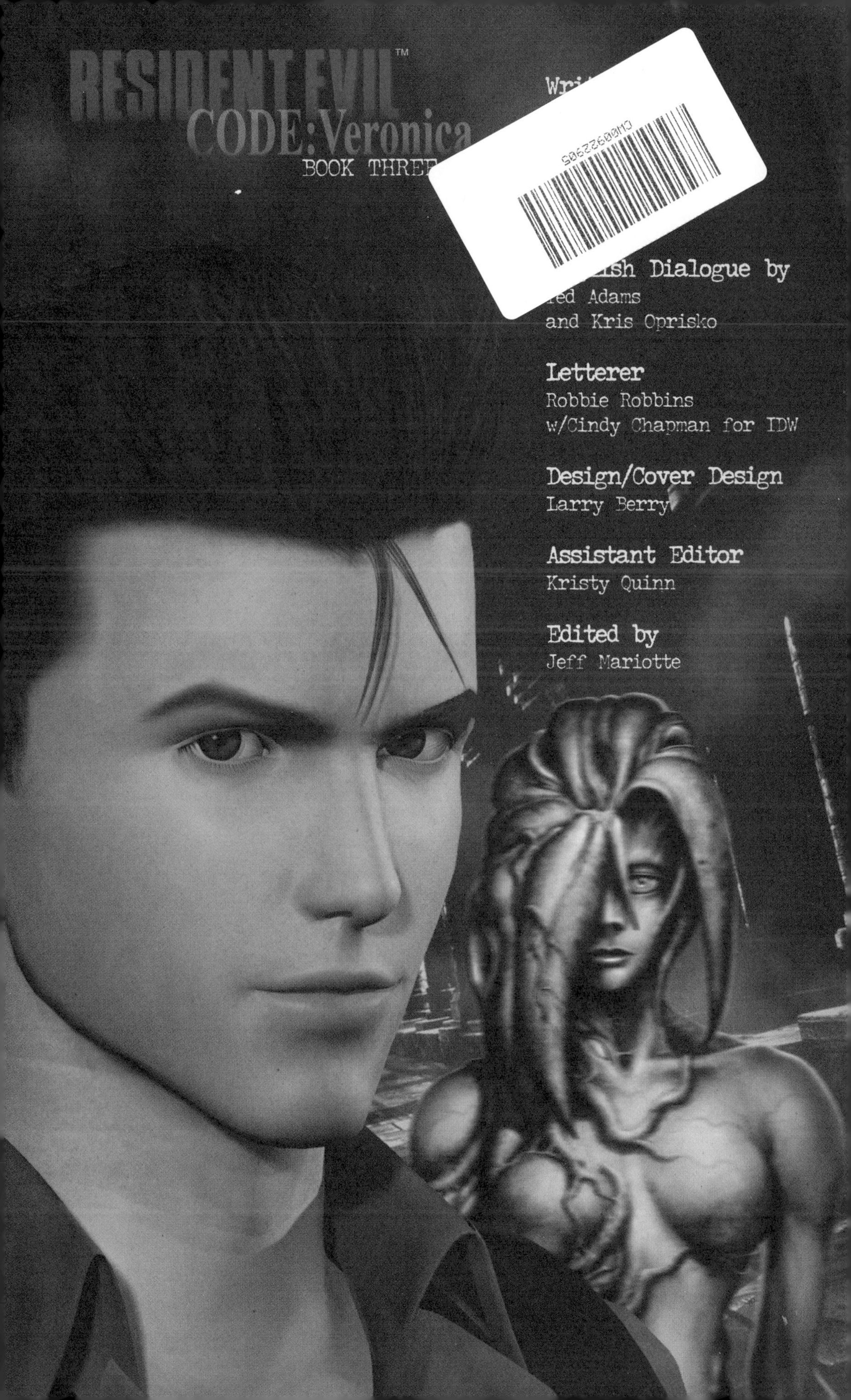

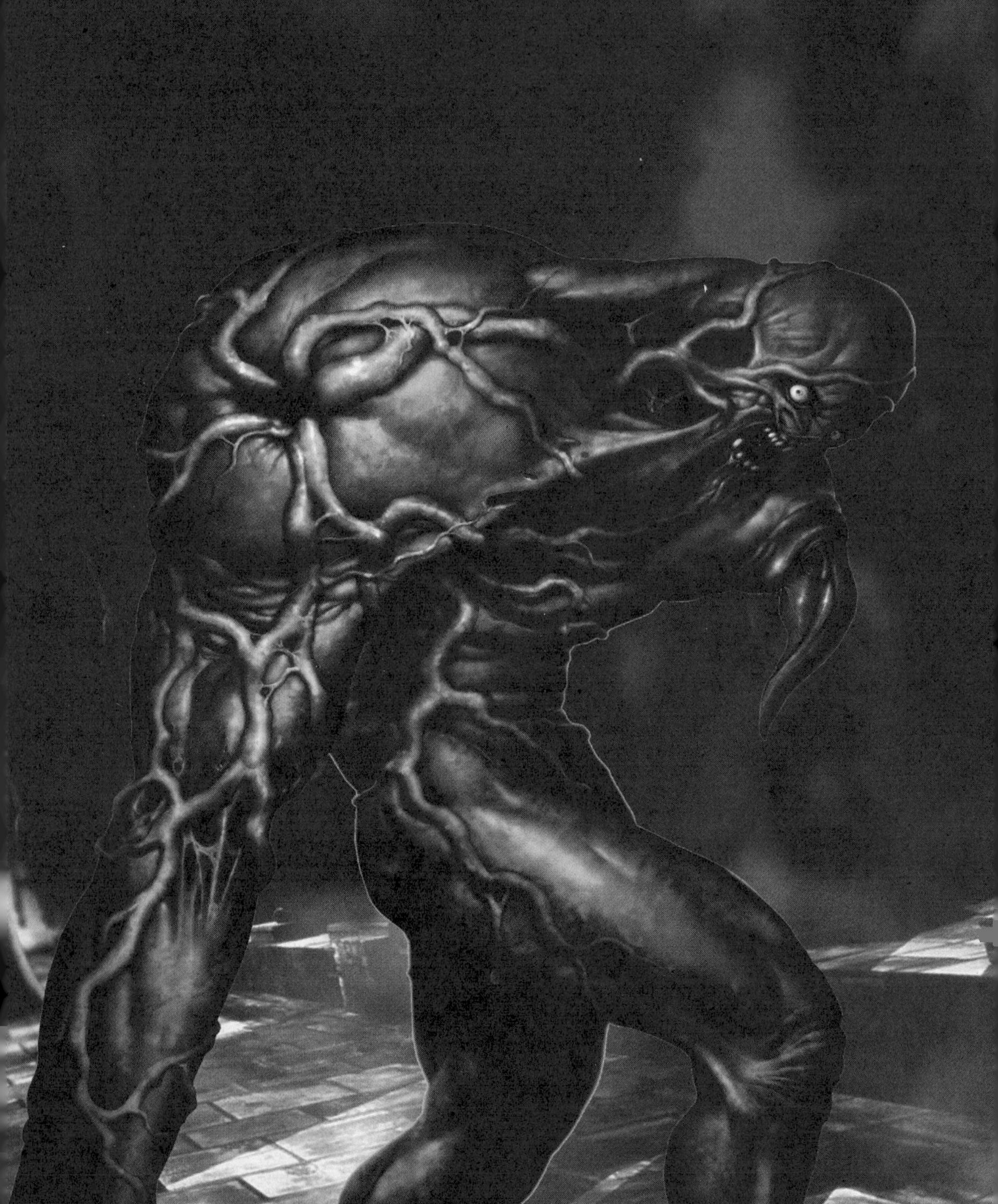

Resident Evil™ Code: Veronica #3. Published by WildStorm Productions, an imprint of DC Comics, under license from CAPCOM CO., LTD. Editorial offices: 888 Prospect St., #240, La Jolla, CA 92037. Printed on recyclable paper. WildStorm does not read or accept unsolicited submissions of ideas, stories or artwork. ISBN 1-56389-920-5. Printed in Canada. DC Comics. A division of Warner Bros. -An AOL Time Warner Company.

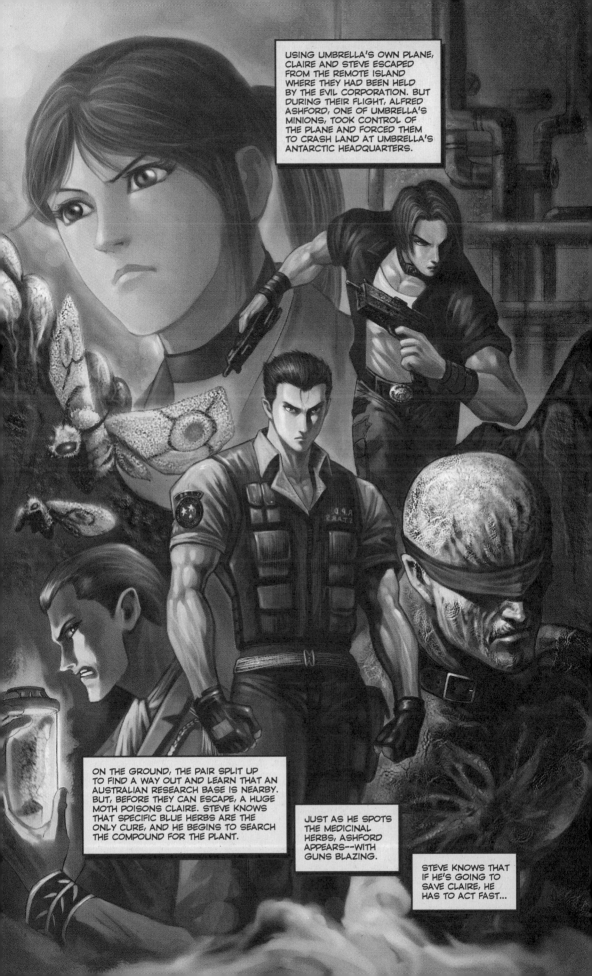

USING UMBRELLA'S OWN PLANE, CLAIRE AND STEVE ESCAPED FROM THE REMOTE ISLAND WHERE THEY HAD BEEN HELD BY THE EVIL CORPORATION. BUT DURING THEIR FLIGHT, ALFRED ASHFORD, ONE OF UMBRELLA'S MINIONS, TOOK CONTROL OF THE PLANE AND FORCED THEM TO CRASH LAND AT UMBRELLA'S ANTARCTIC HEADQUARTERS.

ON THE GROUND, THE PAIR SPLIT UP TO FIND A WAY OUT AND LEARN THAT AN AUSTRALIAN RESEARCH BASE IS NEARBY. BUT, BEFORE THEY CAN ESCAPE, A HUGE MOTH POISONS CLAIRE. STEVE KNOWS THAT SPECIFIC BLUE HERBS ARE THE ONLY CURE, AND HE BEGINS TO SEARCH THE COMPOUND FOR THE PLANT.

JUST AS HE SPOTS THE MEDICINAL HERBS, ASHFORD APPEARS--WITH GUNS BLAZING.

STEVE KNOWS THAT IF HE'S GOING TO SAVE CLAIRE, HE HAS TO ACT FAST...

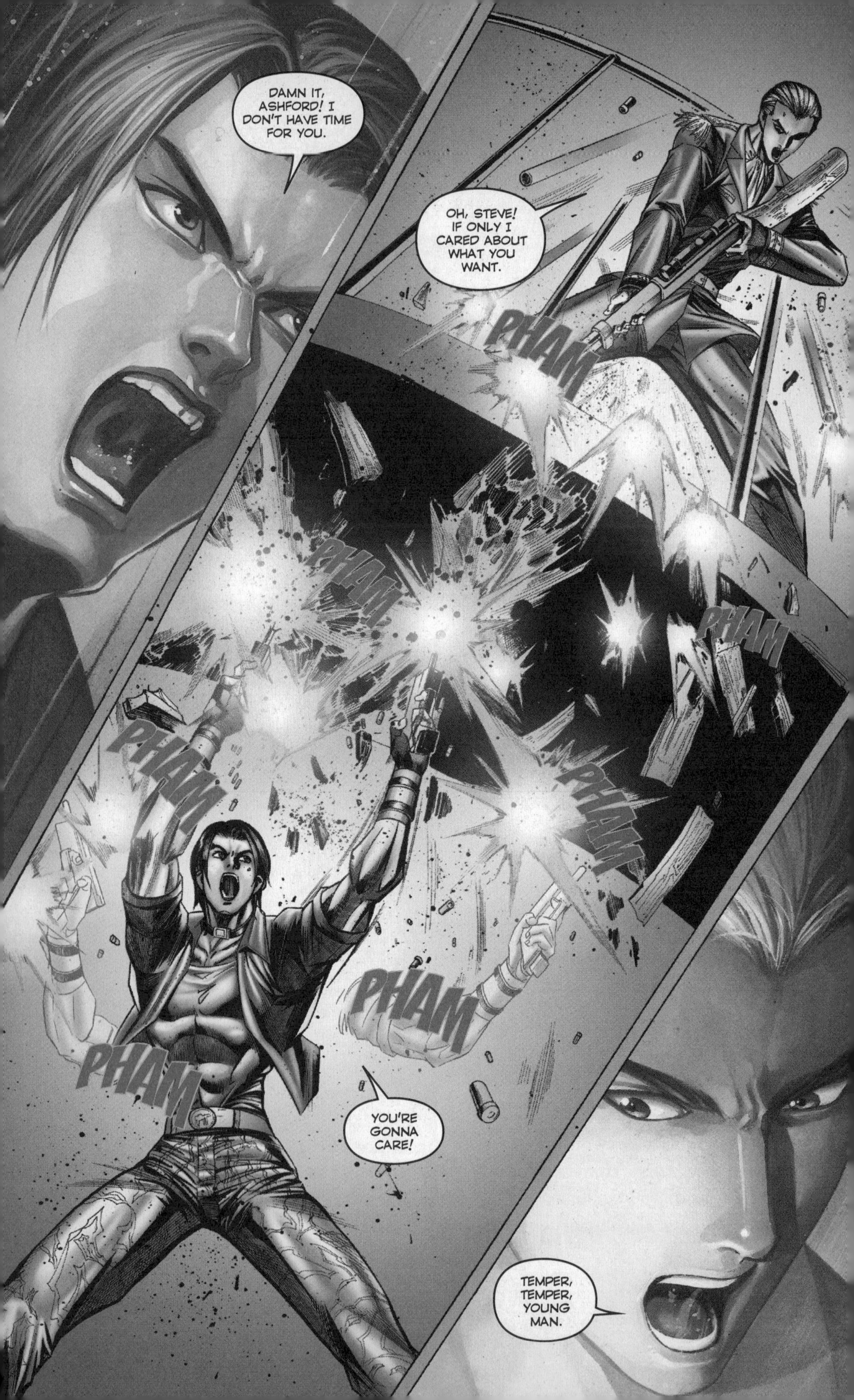
DAMN IT, ASHFORD! I DON'T HAVE TIME FOR YOU.
OH, STEVE! IF ONLY I CARED ABOUT WHAT YOU WANT.
PHAM
PHAM
PHAM
PHAM
PHAM
PHAM
PHAM
YOU'RE GONNA CARE!
TEMPER, TEMPER, YOUNG MAN.

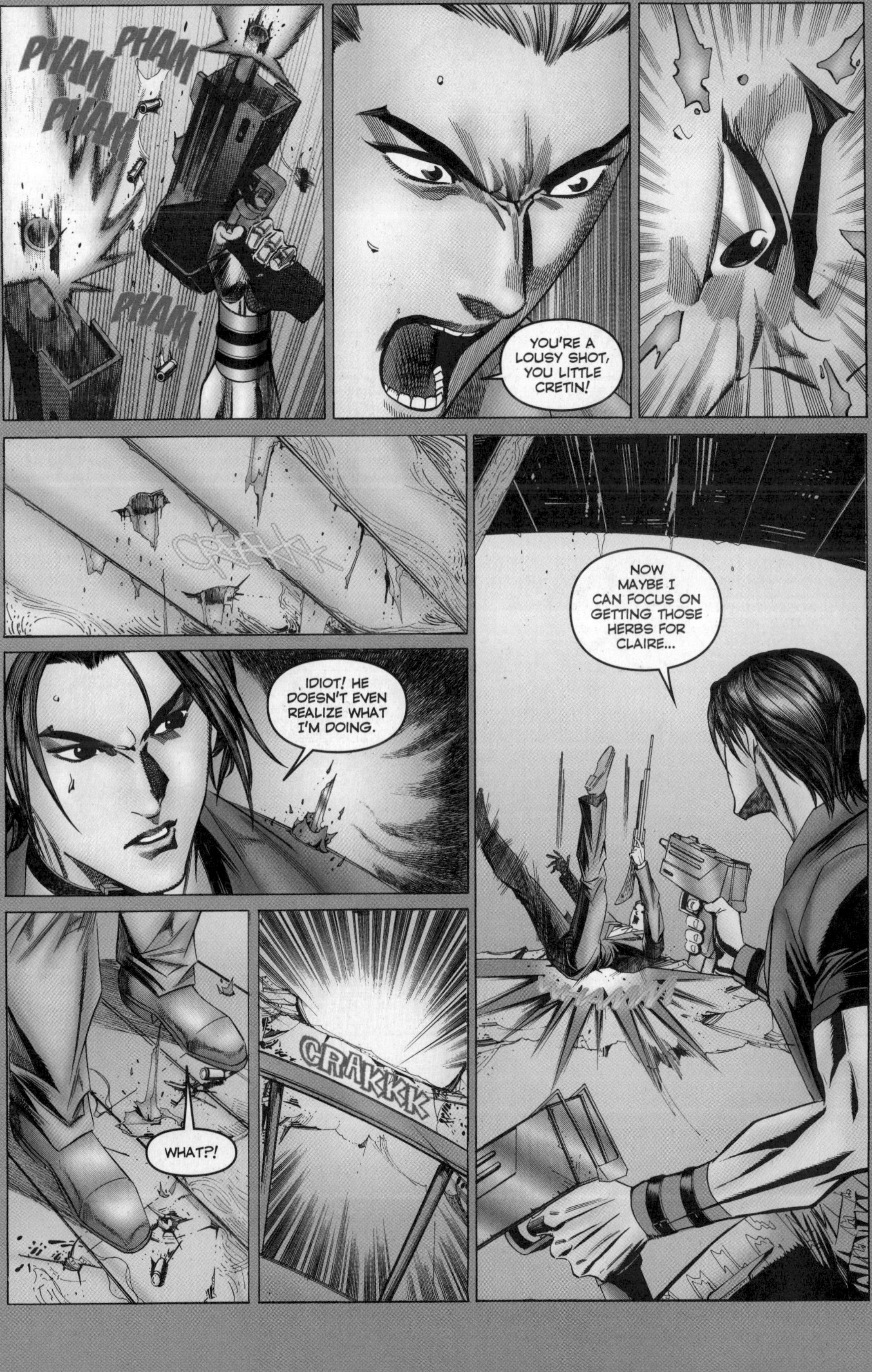
PHAM
PHAM
PHAM
PHAM
YOU'RE A LOUSY SHOT, YOU LITTLE CRETIN!
IDIOT! HE DOESN'T EVEN REALIZE WHAT I'M DOING.
WHAT?!
CRAKKKK
NOW MAYBE I CAN FOCUS ON GETTING THOSE HERBS FOR CLAIRE...

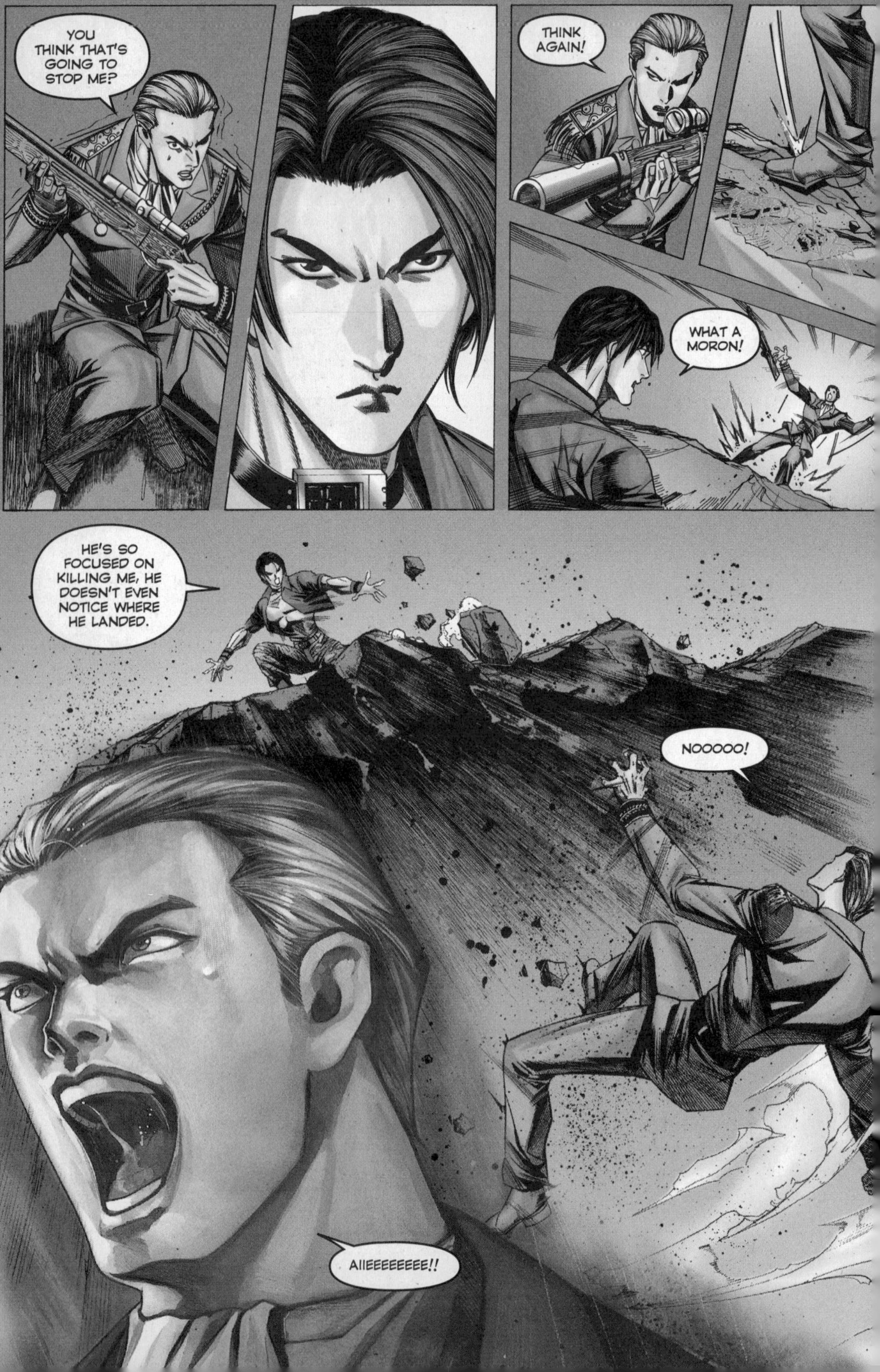
YOU THINK THAT'S GOING TO STOP ME?
THINK AGAIN!
WHAT A MORON!
HE'S SO FOCUSED ON KILLING ME, HE DOESN'T EVEN NOTICE WHERE HE LANDED.
NOOOOO!
AIIEEEEEEEE!!

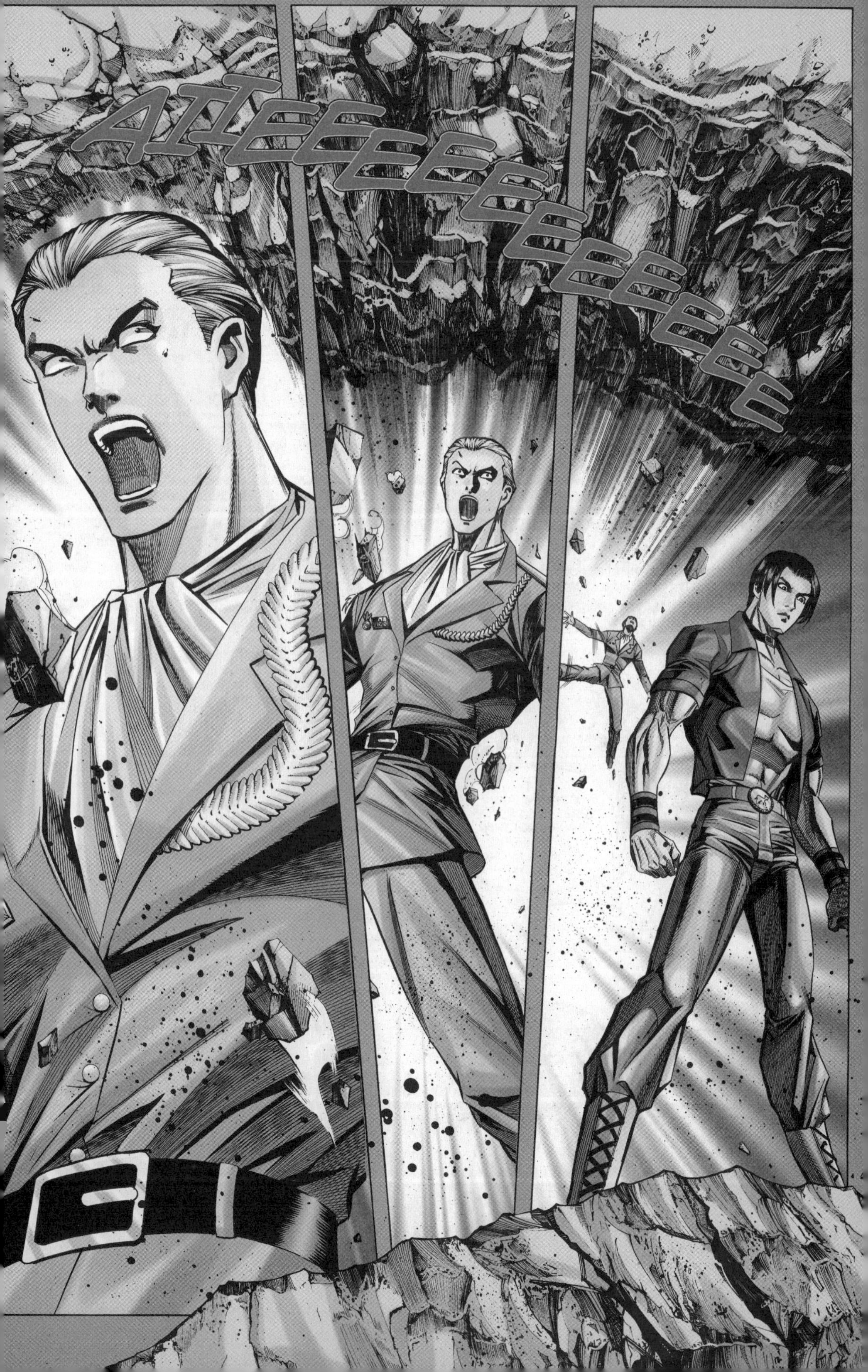
AIIEEEEEEEEEEE

GOOD RIDDANCE! GOT TO GET BACK TO CLAIRE.

STEVE... IT HURTS...

HOLD ON, CLAIRE.

I GOT THE HERBS WE NEED.

IF I COMBINE ALL THREE COLORS OF HERBS TOGETHER IT'LL MAKE THE EFFECTS EVEN STRONGER.

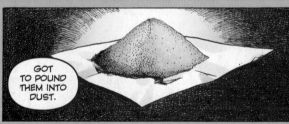

GOT TO POUND THEM INTO DUST.

CLAIRE, YOU'VE GOT TO SWALLOW THIS STUFF.

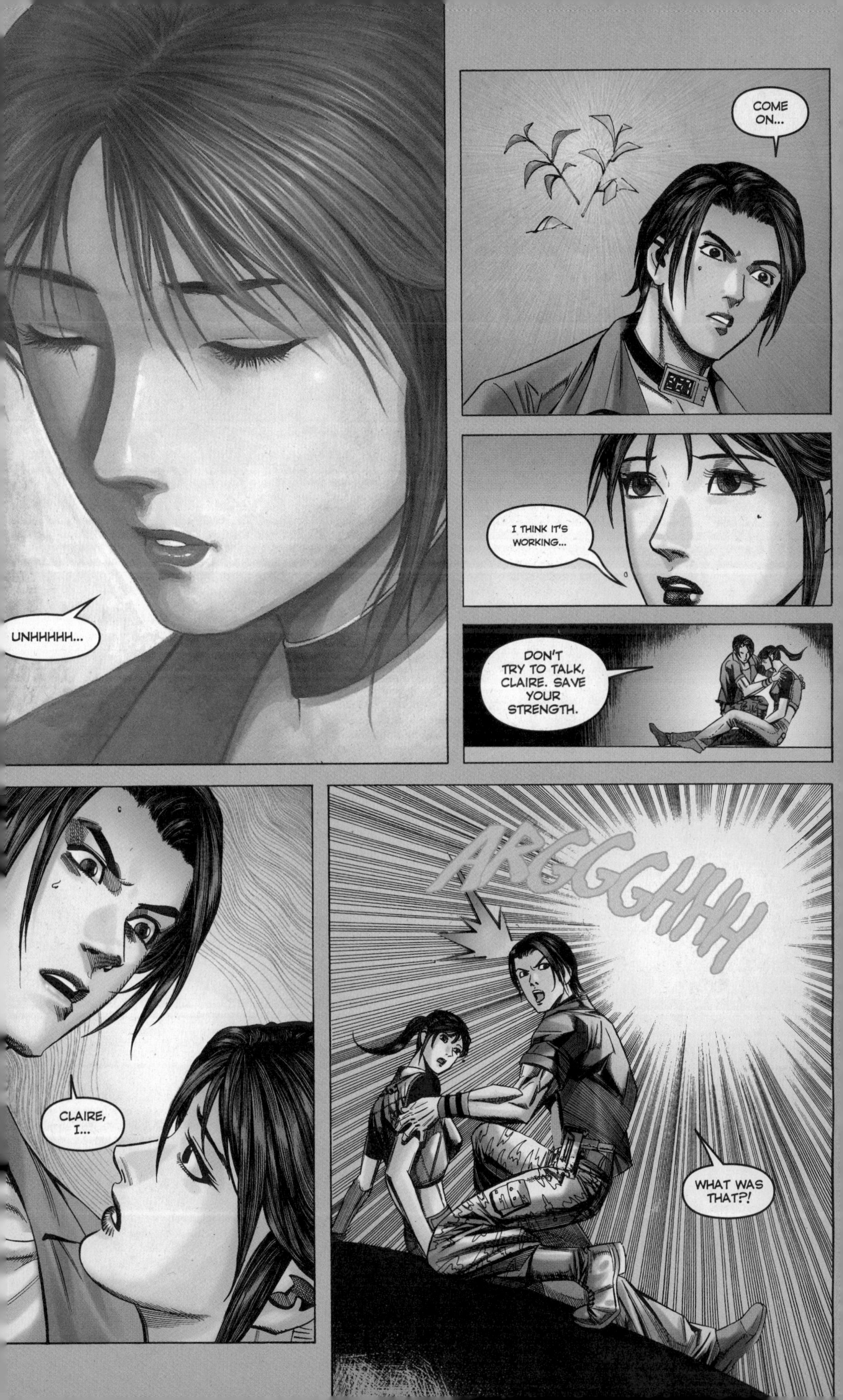
UNHHHHH...
COME ON...
I THINK IT'S WORKING...
DON'T TRY TO TALK, CLAIRE. SAVE YOUR STRENGTH.
CLAIRE, I...
ARGGGHHH
WHAT WAS THAT?!

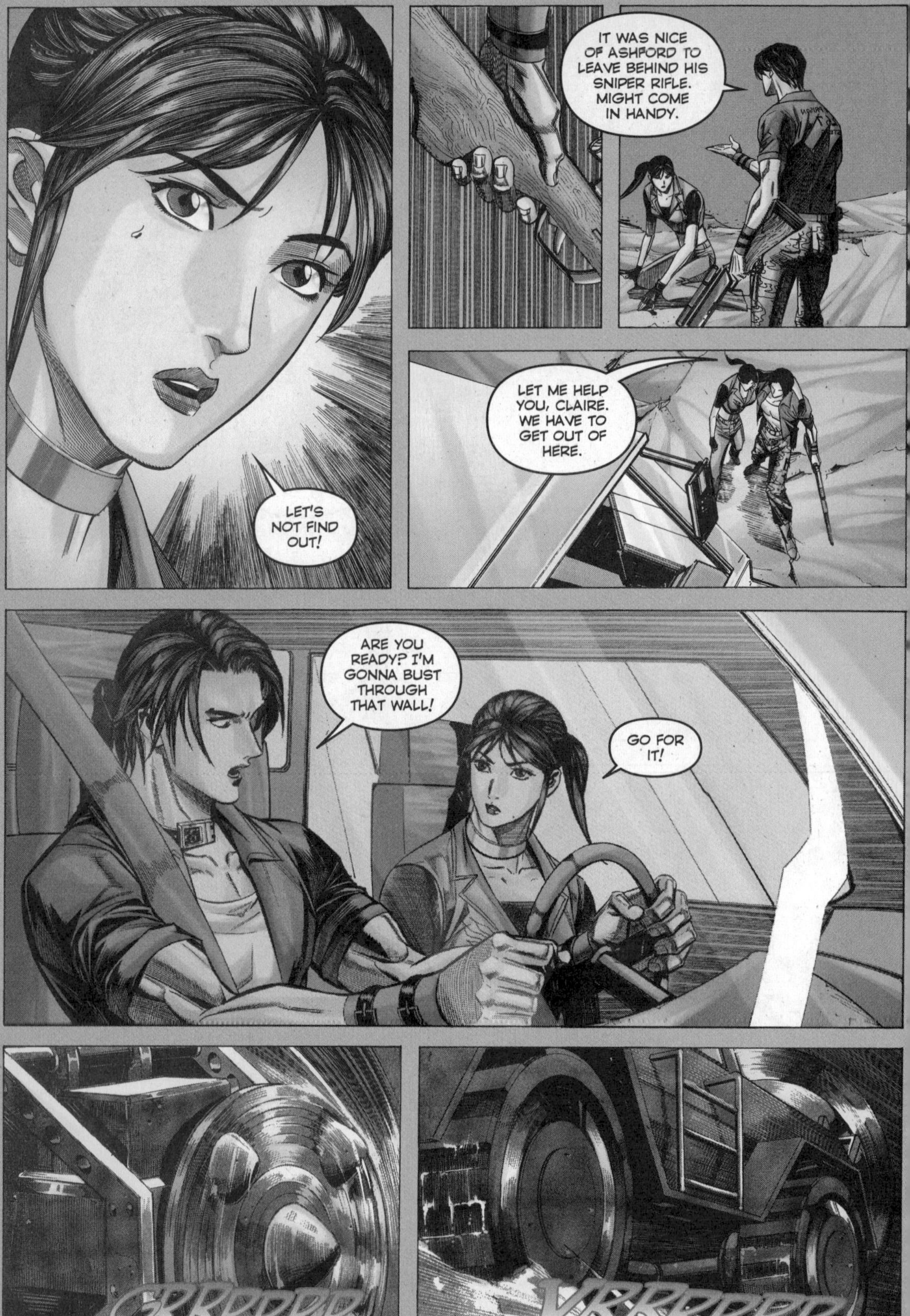
LET'S NOT FIND OUT!
IT WAS NICE OF ASHFORD TO LEAVE BEHIND HIS SNIPER RIFLE. MIGHT COME IN HANDY.
LET ME HELP YOU, CLAIRE. WE HAVE TO GET OUT OF HERE.
ARE YOU READY? I'M GONNA BUST THROUGH THAT WALL!
GO FOR IT!
GRRRRRR
VRRRRRRR

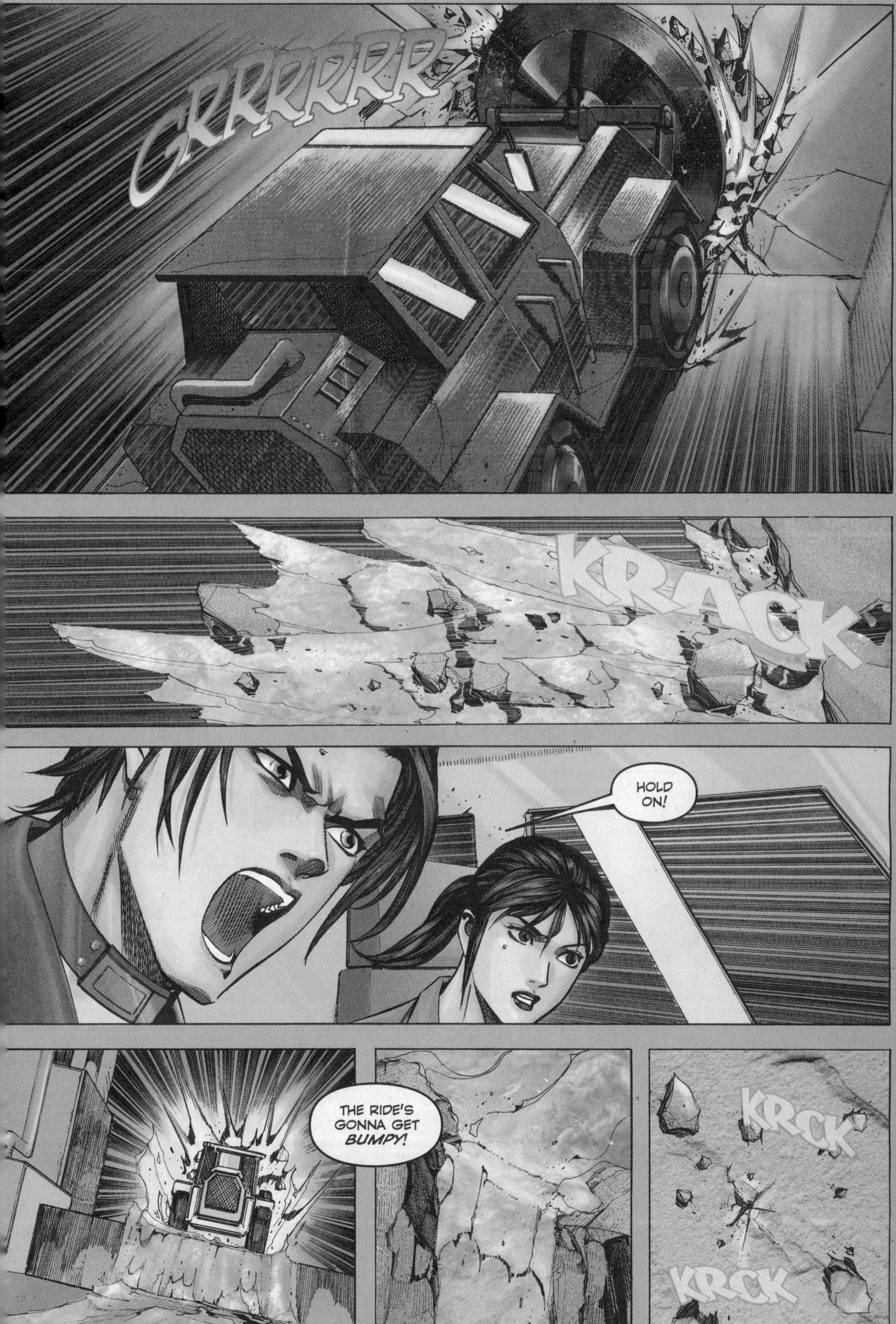
GRRRRRR
KRACK
HOLD ON!
THE RIDE'S GONNA GET *BUMPY!*
KRCK
KRCK

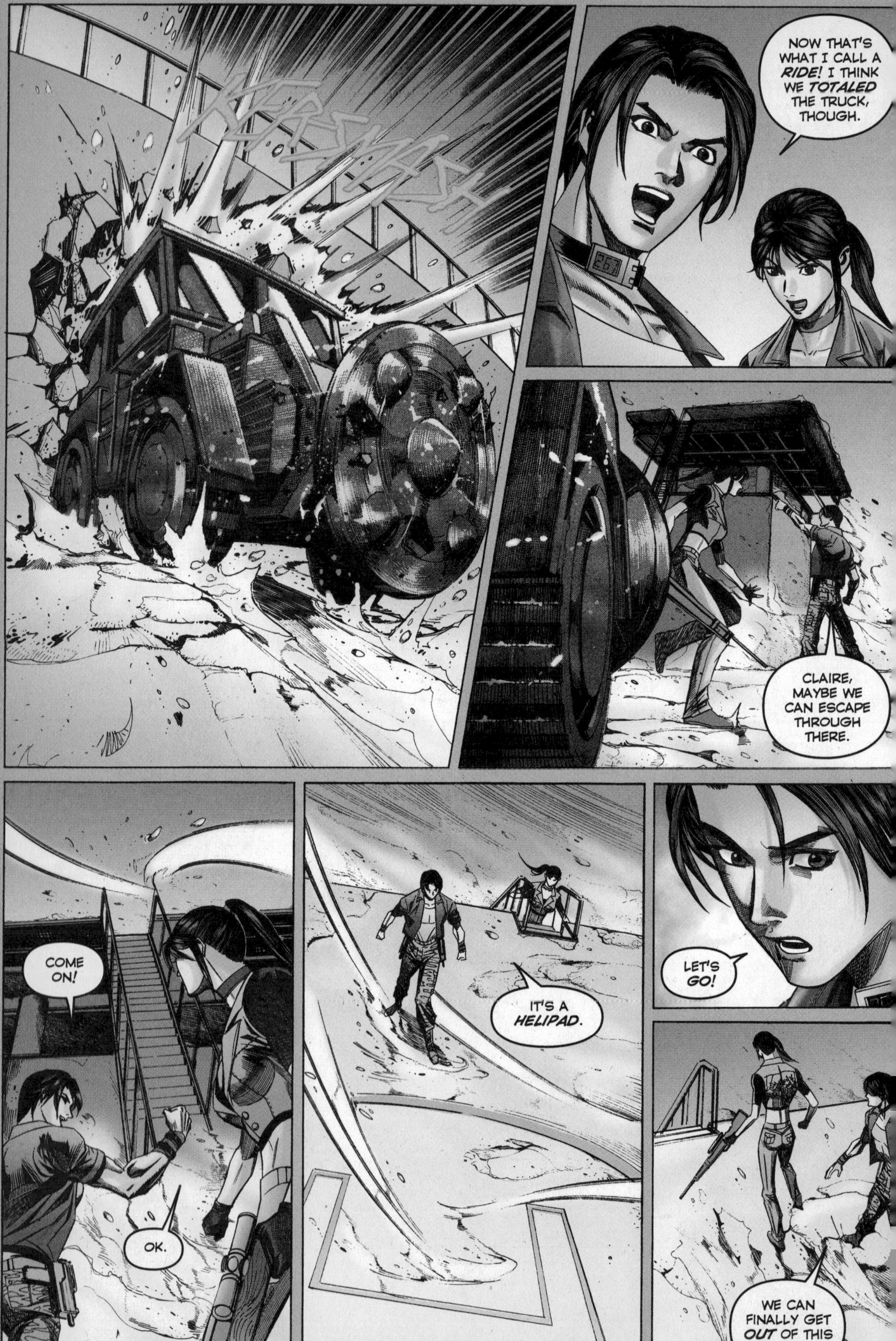
KERSMASH!
NOW THAT'S WHAT I CALL A *RIDE!* I THINK WE *TOTALED* THE TRUCK, THOUGH.
CLAIRE, MAYBE WE CAN ESCAPE THROUGH THERE.
COME ON!
OK.
IT'S A *HELIPAD*.
LET'S *GO!*
WE CAN FINALLY GET *OUT* OF THIS ICEBOX.

HUH?!

WHAT IS IT, CLAIRE?

I'VE SEEN THIS THING *BEFORE*.

WHA...?!

ARGGGHHH

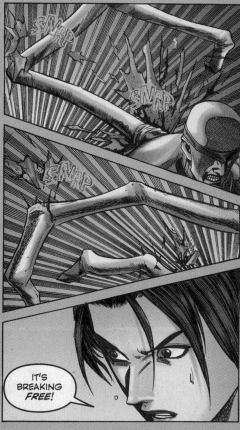

SNAP

SNAP

SNAP

IT'S BREAKING *FREE*!

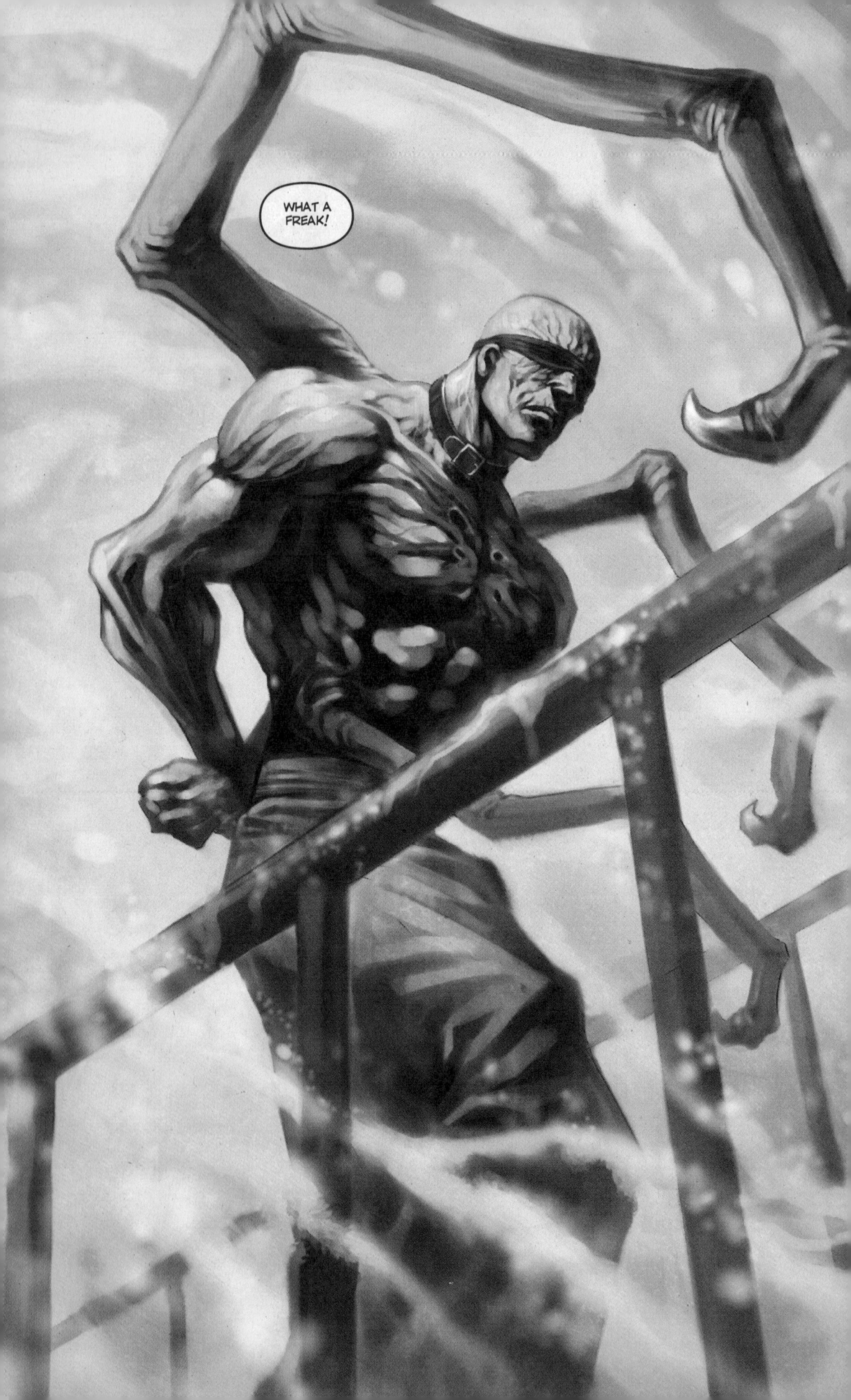
WHAT A FREAK!

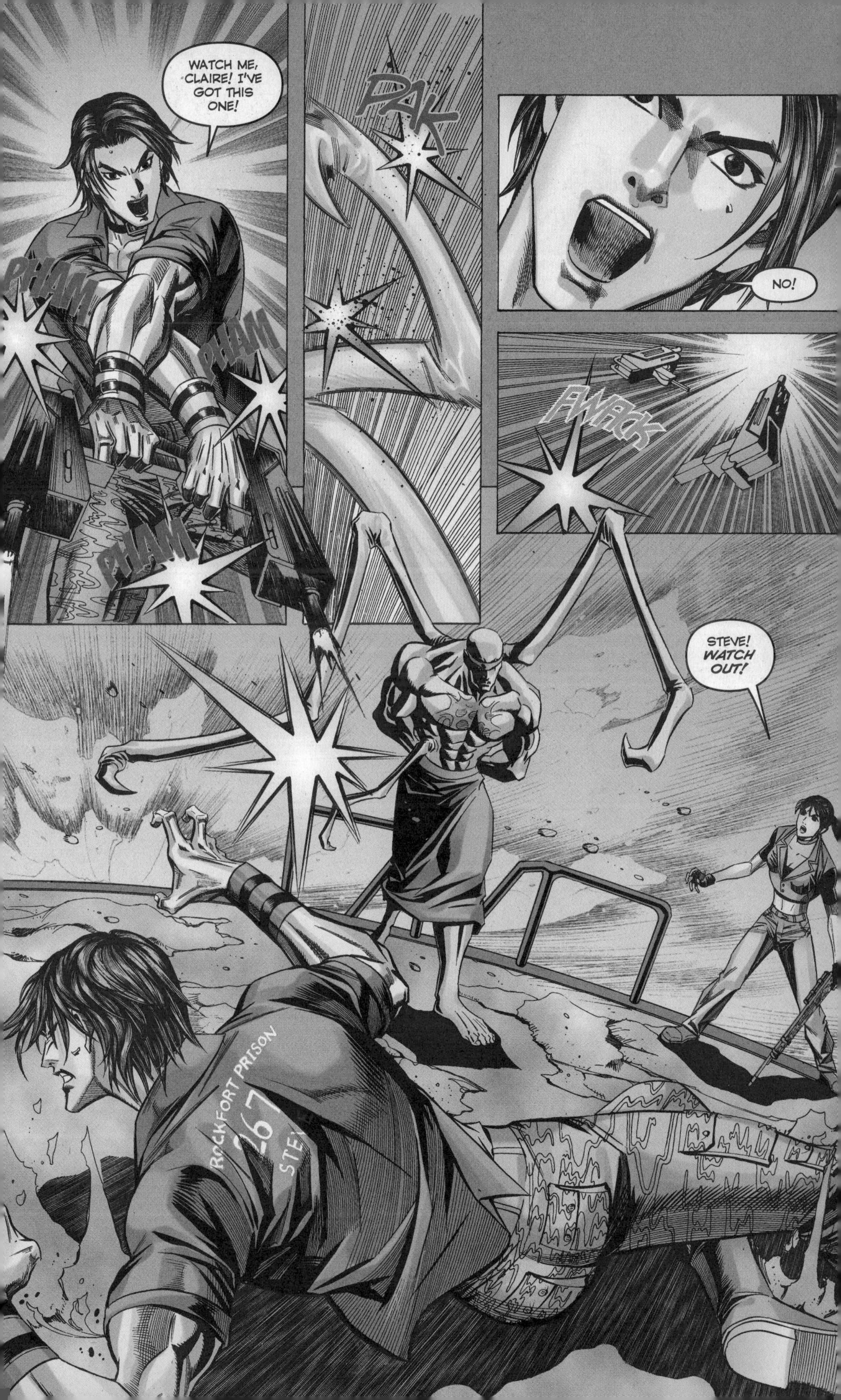
WATCH ME, CLAIRE! I'VE GOT THIS ONE!
PHAM
PHAM
PHAM
PAK
NO!
FWACK
STEVE! WATCH OUT!
ROCKFORT PRISON
267
STE

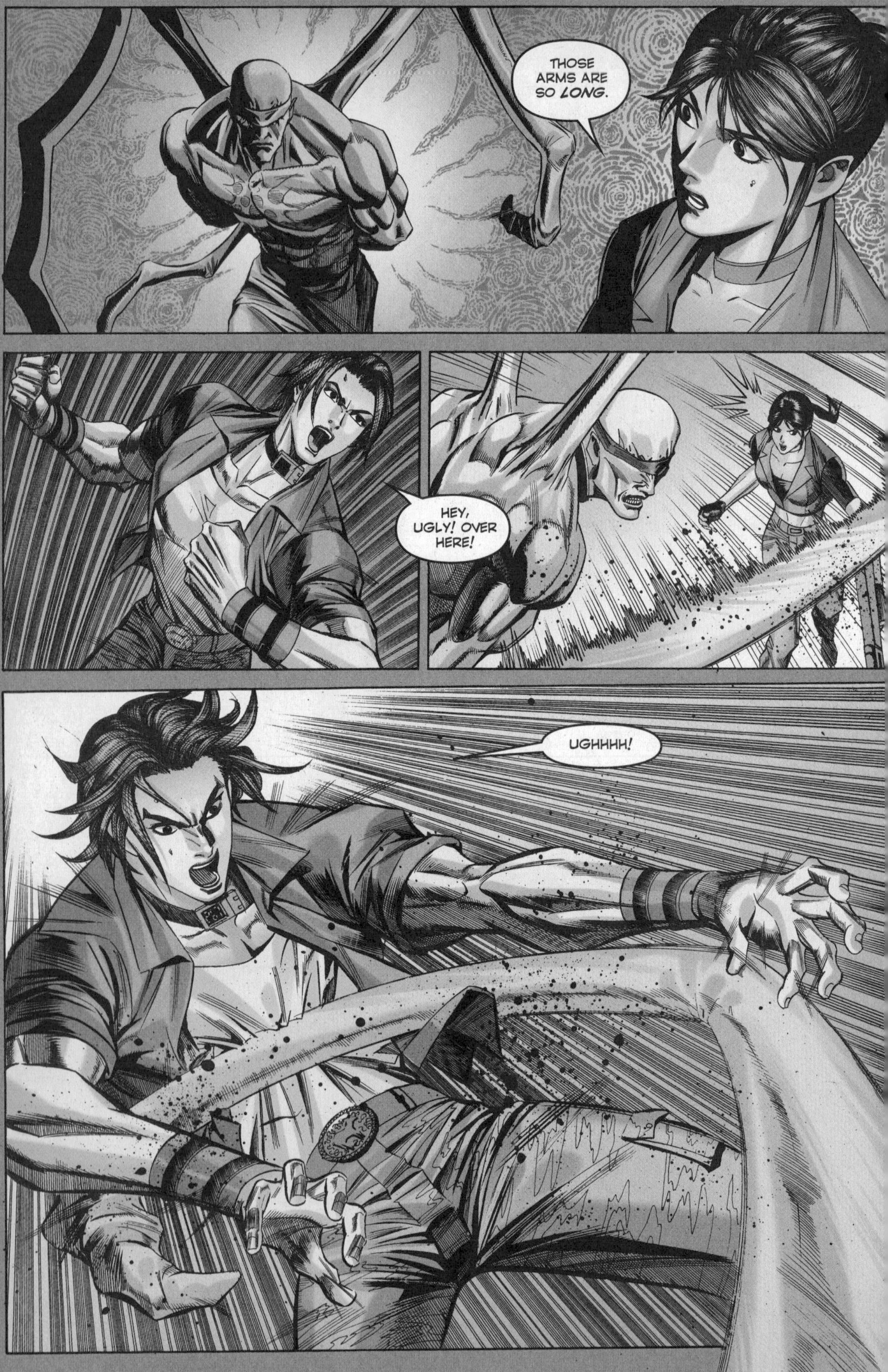
THOSE ARMS ARE SO *LONG*.
HEY, UGLY! OVER HERE!
UGHHHH!

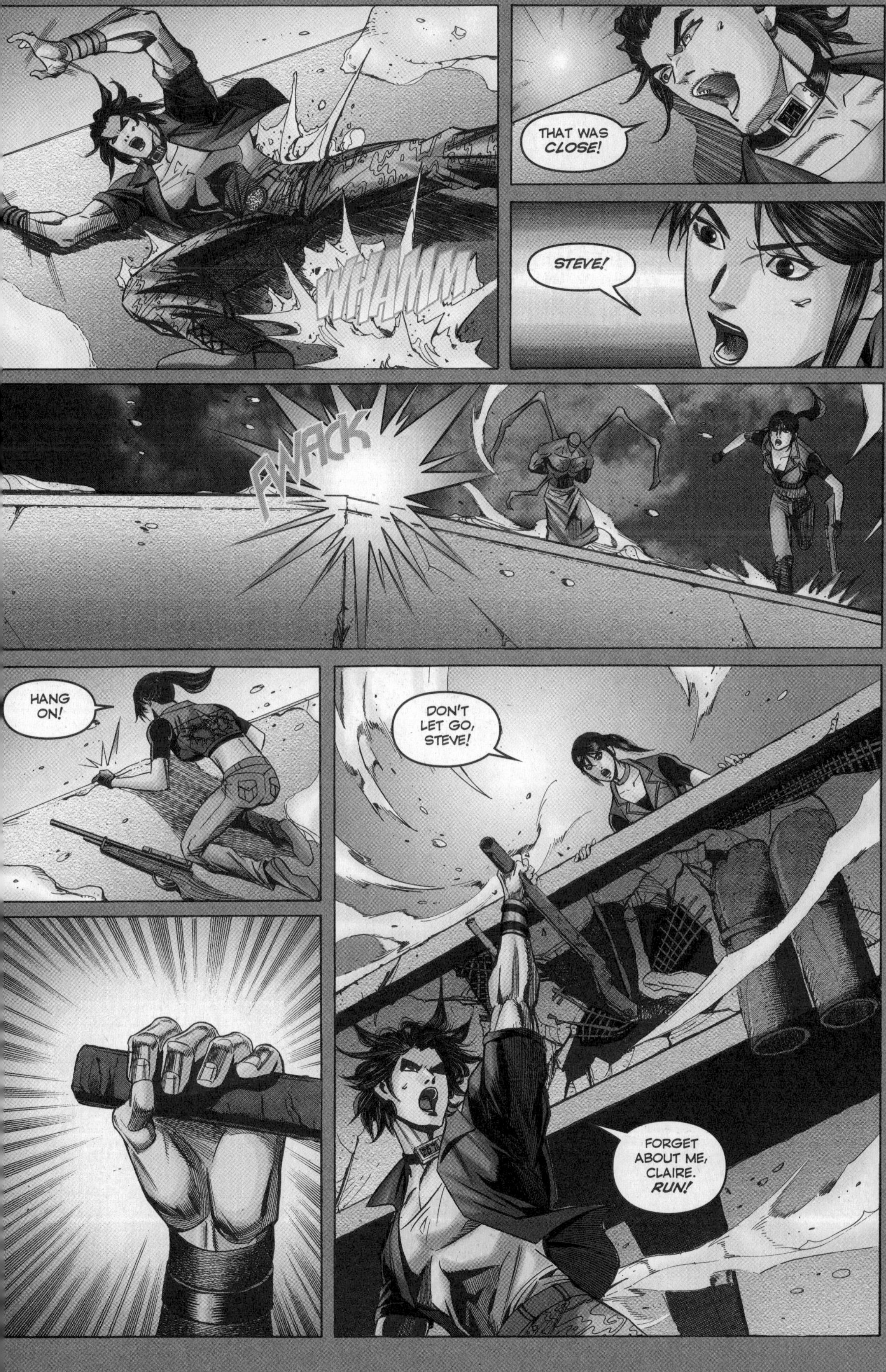
WHAMM!
THAT WAS CLOSE!
STEVE!
FWACK
HANG ON!
DON'T LET GO, STEVE!
FORGET ABOUT ME, CLAIRE. RUN!

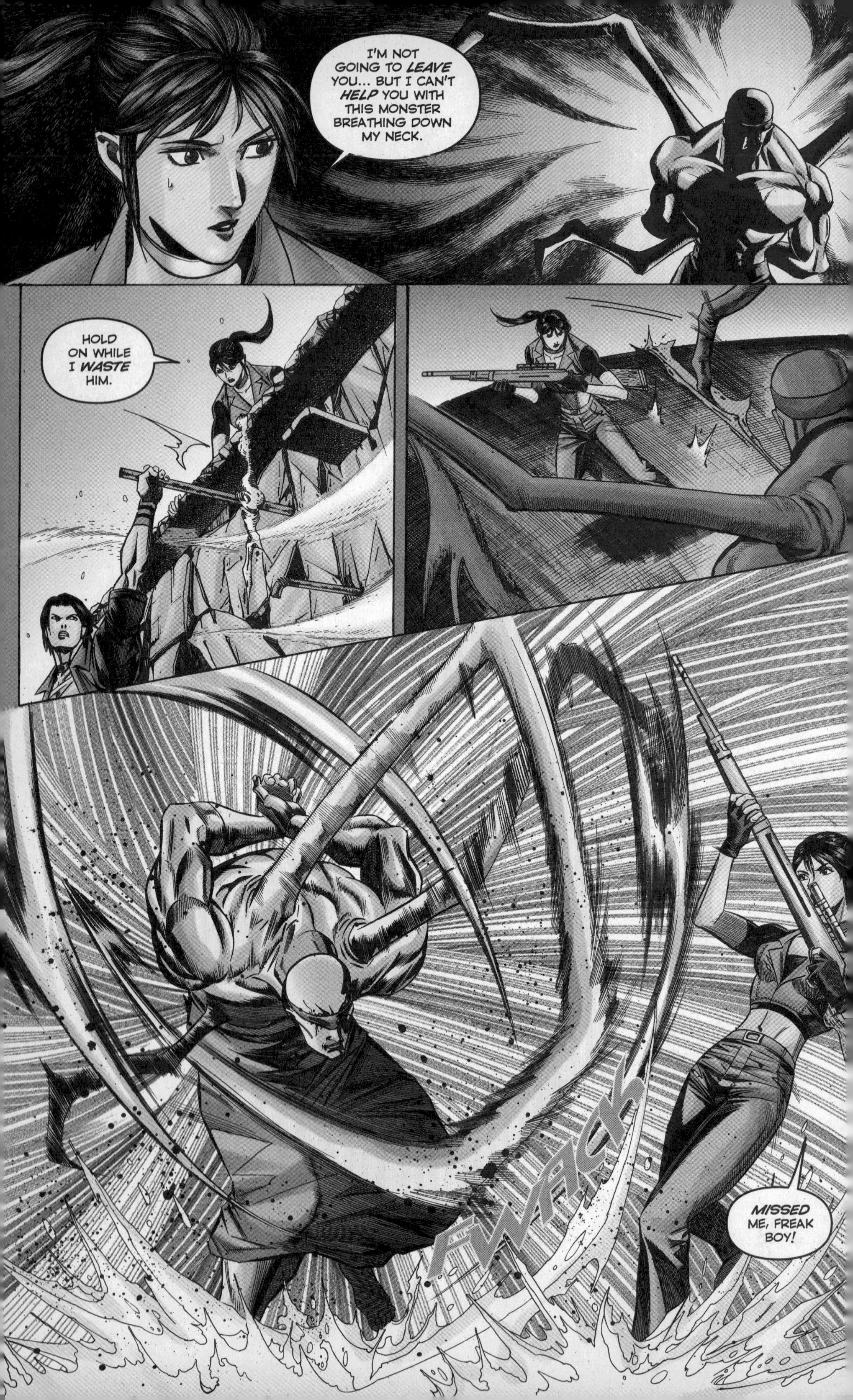
I'M NOT GOING TO *LEAVE* YOU... BUT I CAN'T *HELP* YOU WITH THIS MONSTER BREATHING DOWN MY NECK.
HOLD ON WHILE I *WASTE* HIM.
FWACK
MISSED ME, FREAK BOY!

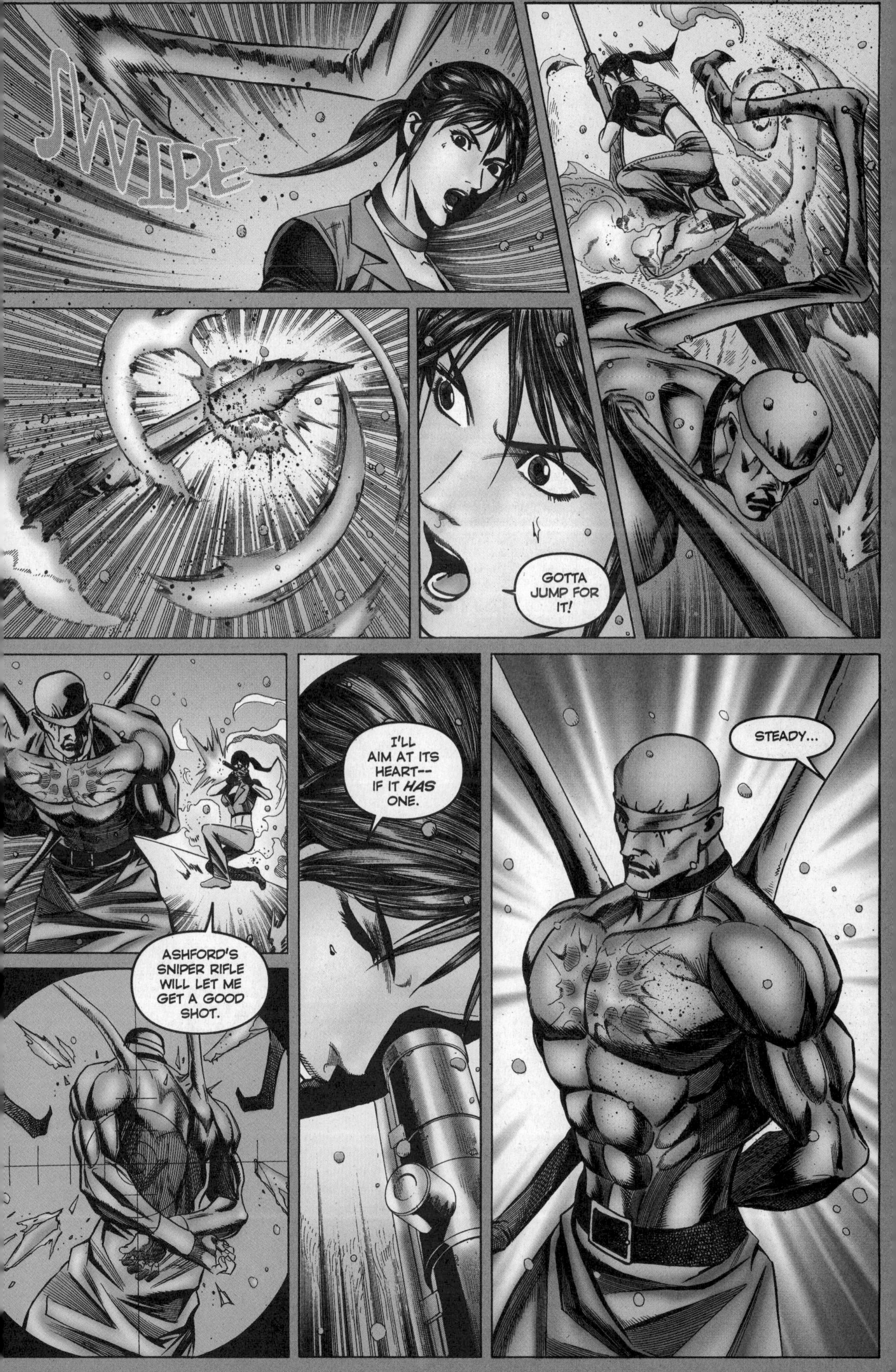
SWIPE
GOTTA JUMP FOR IT!
ASHFORD'S SNIPER RIFLE WILL LET ME GET A GOOD SHOT.
I'LL AIM AT ITS HEART-- IF IT HAS ONE.
STEADY...

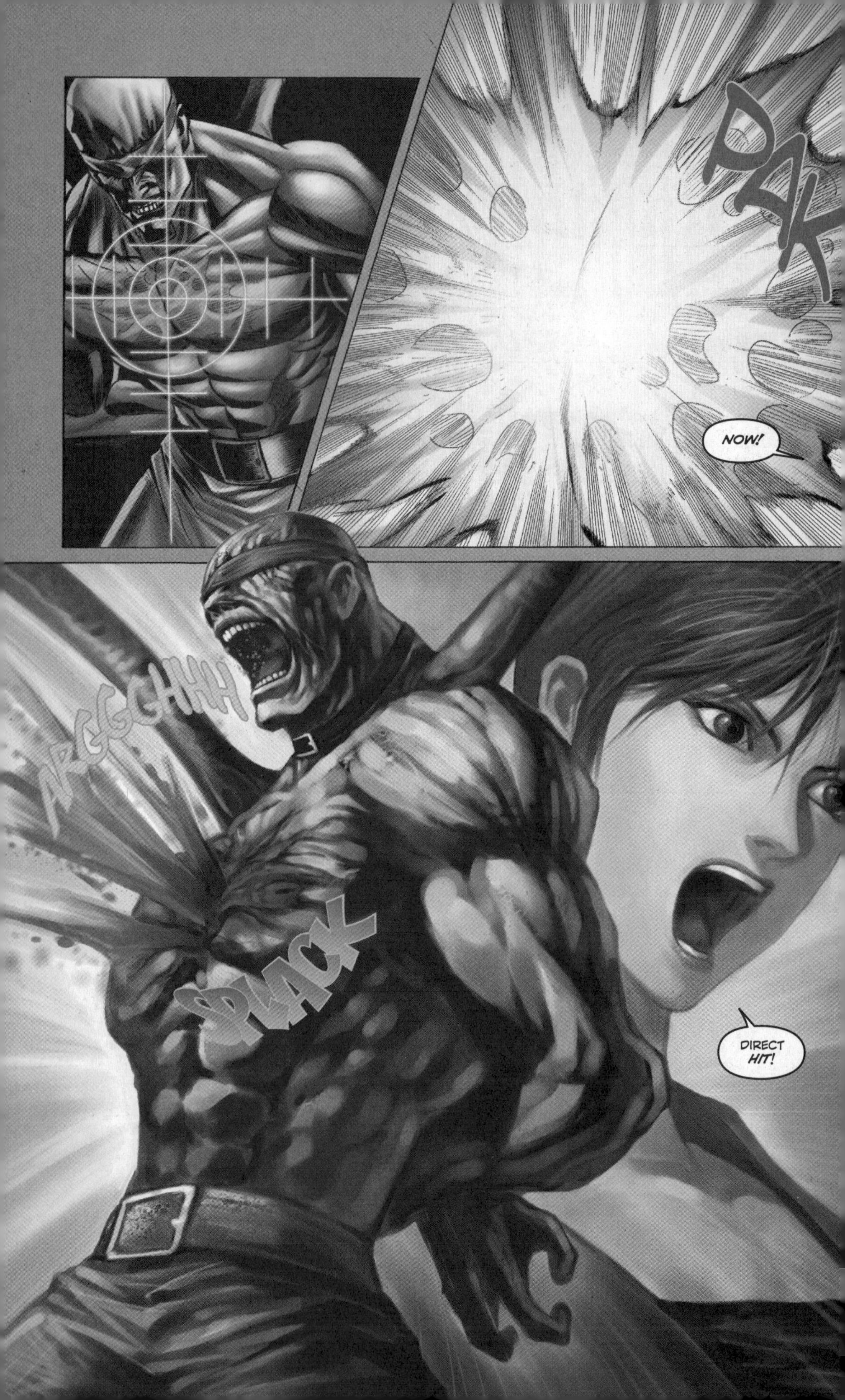
PAK
NOW!
ARGGGHHH
SPLACK
DIRECT HIT!

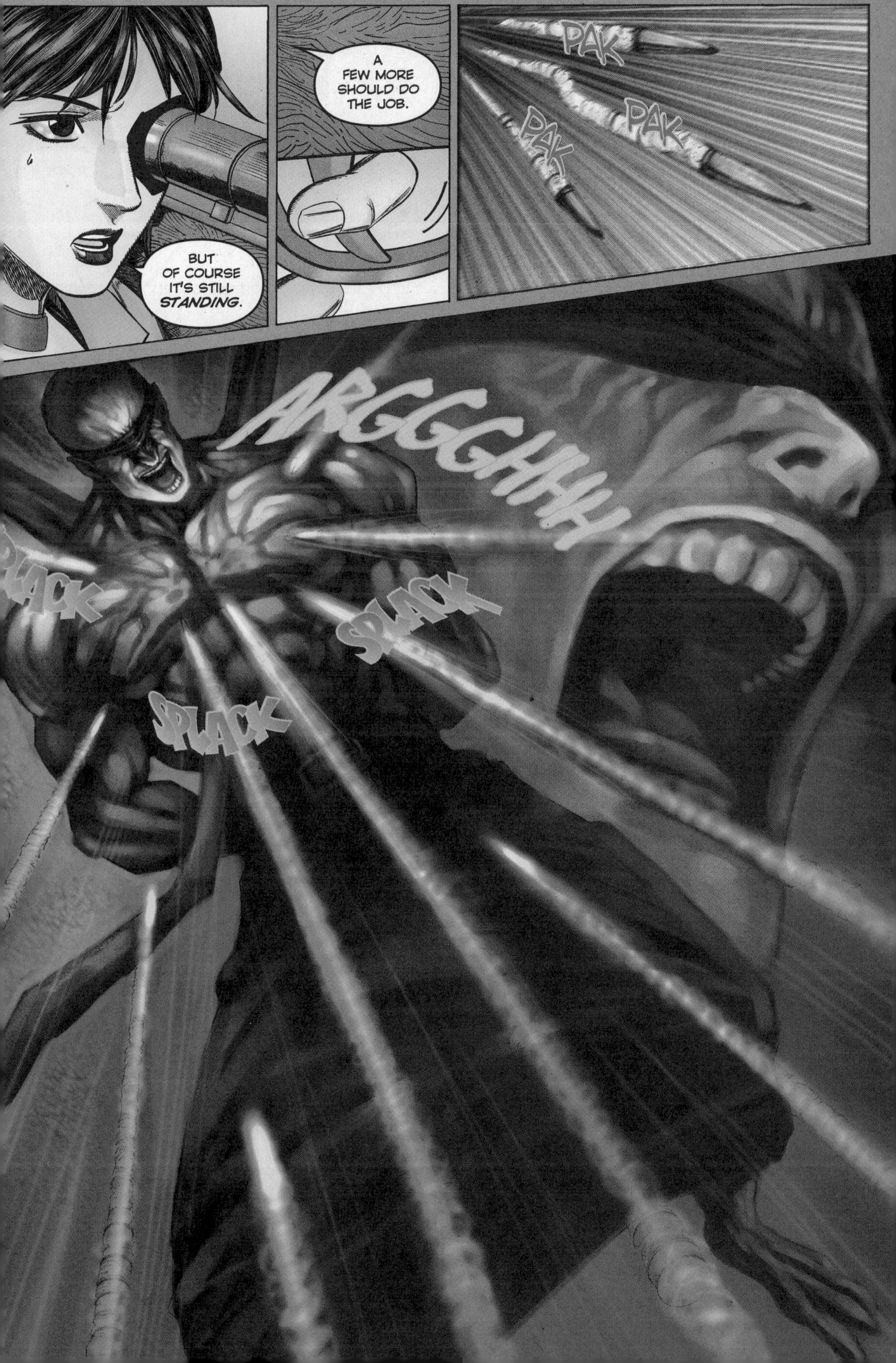
BUT OF COURSE IT'S STILL STANDING.
A FEW MORE SHOULD DO THE JOB.
PAK
PAK
PAK
ARGGGHHHH
SPLACK
SPLACK
SPLACK

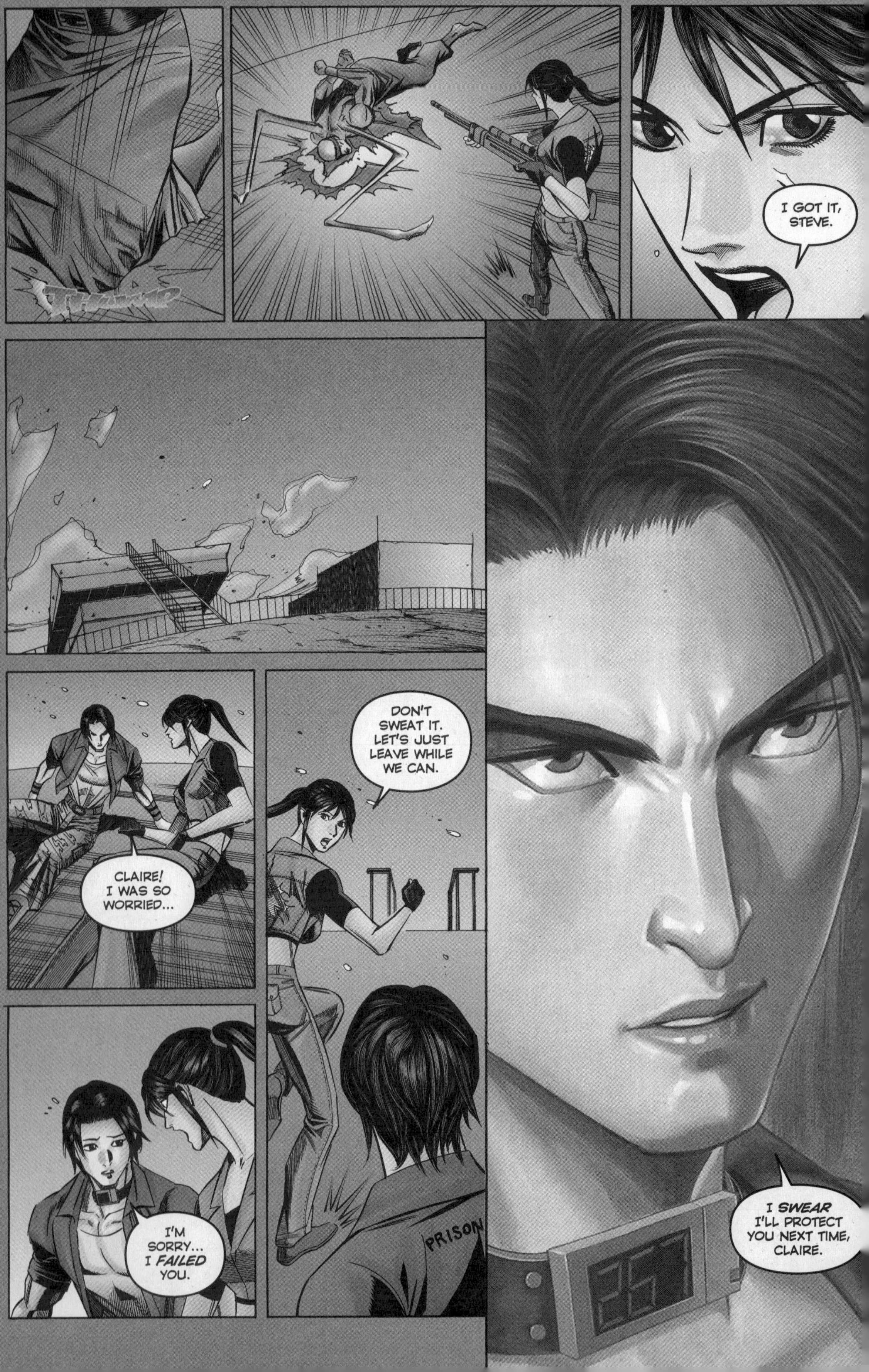
THUMP
I GOT IT, STEVE.
CLAIRE! I WAS SO WORRIED...
DON'T SWEAT IT. LET'S JUST LEAVE WHILE WE CAN.
I'M SORRY... I *FAILED* YOU.
PRISON
I *SWEAR* I'LL PROTECT YOU NEXT TIME, CLAIRE.

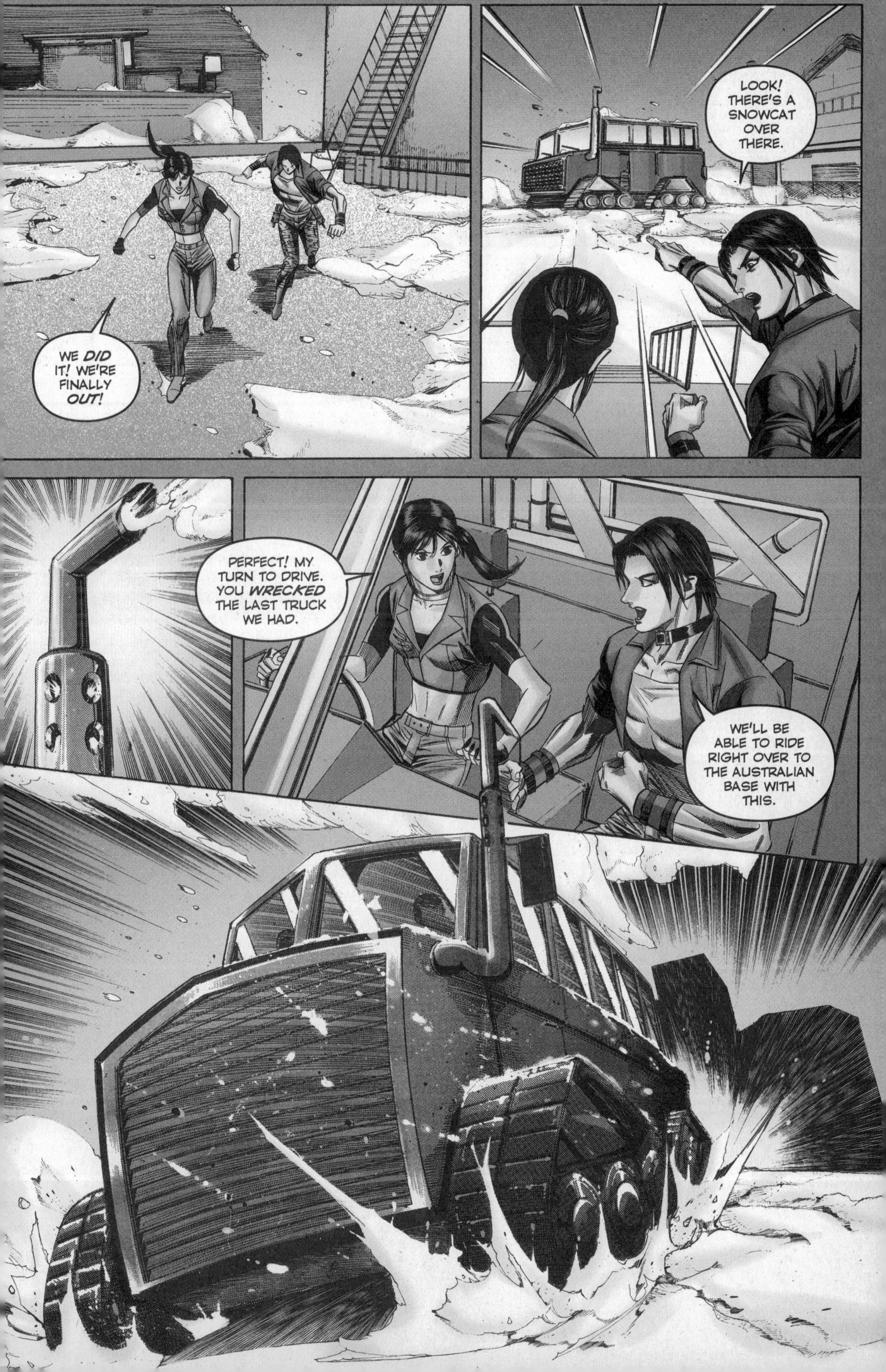
WE DID IT! WE'RE FINALLY OUT!
LOOK! THERE'S A SNOWCAT OVER THERE.
PERFECT! MY TURN TO DRIVE. YOU WRECKED THE LAST TRUCK WE HAD.
WE'LL BE ABLE TO RIDE RIGHT OVER TO THE AUSTRALIAN BASE WITH THIS.

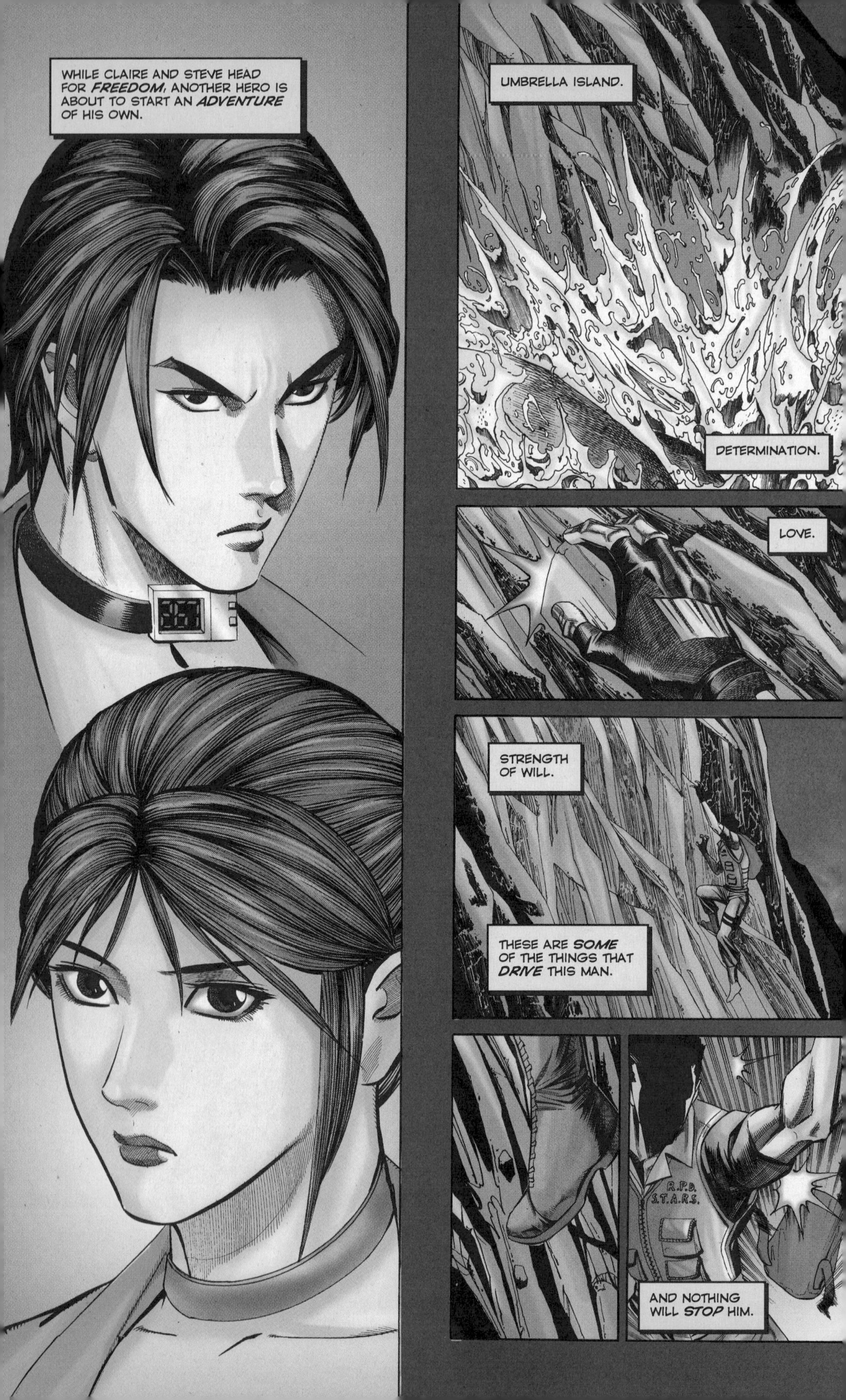
WHILE CLAIRE AND STEVE HEAD FOR FREEDOM, ANOTHER HERO IS ABOUT TO START AN ADVENTURE OF HIS OWN.
UMBRELLA ISLAND.
DETERMINATION.
LOVE.
STRENGTH OF WILL.
THESE ARE SOME OF THE THINGS THAT DRIVE THIS MAN.
R.P.D. S.T.A.R.S.
AND NOTHING WILL STOP HIM.

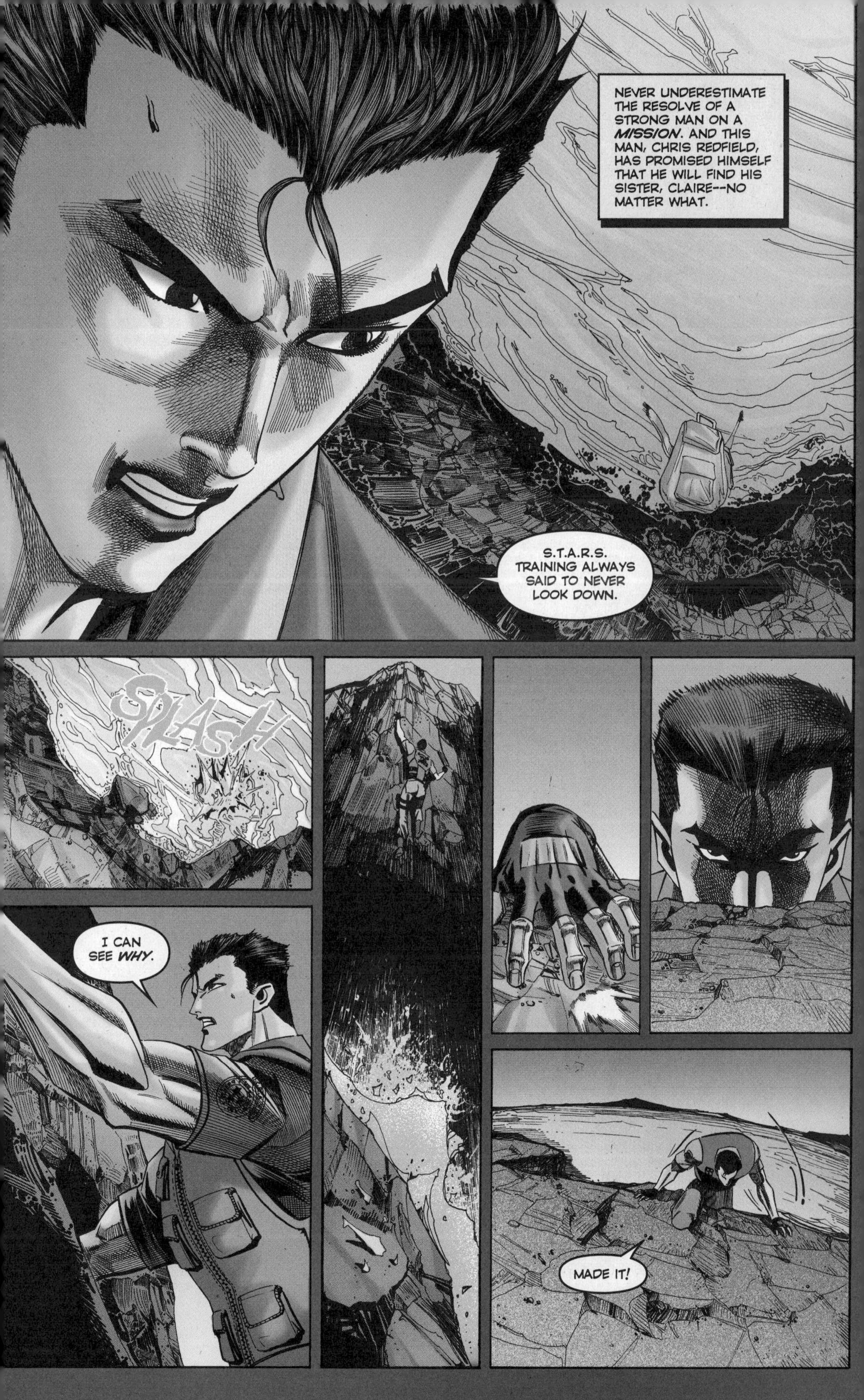
NEVER UNDERESTIMATE THE RESOLVE OF A STRONG MAN ON A *MISSION*. AND THIS MAN, CHRIS REDFIELD, HAS PROMISED HIMSELF THAT HE WILL FIND HIS SISTER, CLAIRE--NO MATTER WHAT.
S.T.A.R.S. TRAINING ALWAYS SAID TO NEVER LOOK DOWN.
SPLASH
I CAN SEE *WHY*.
MADE IT!

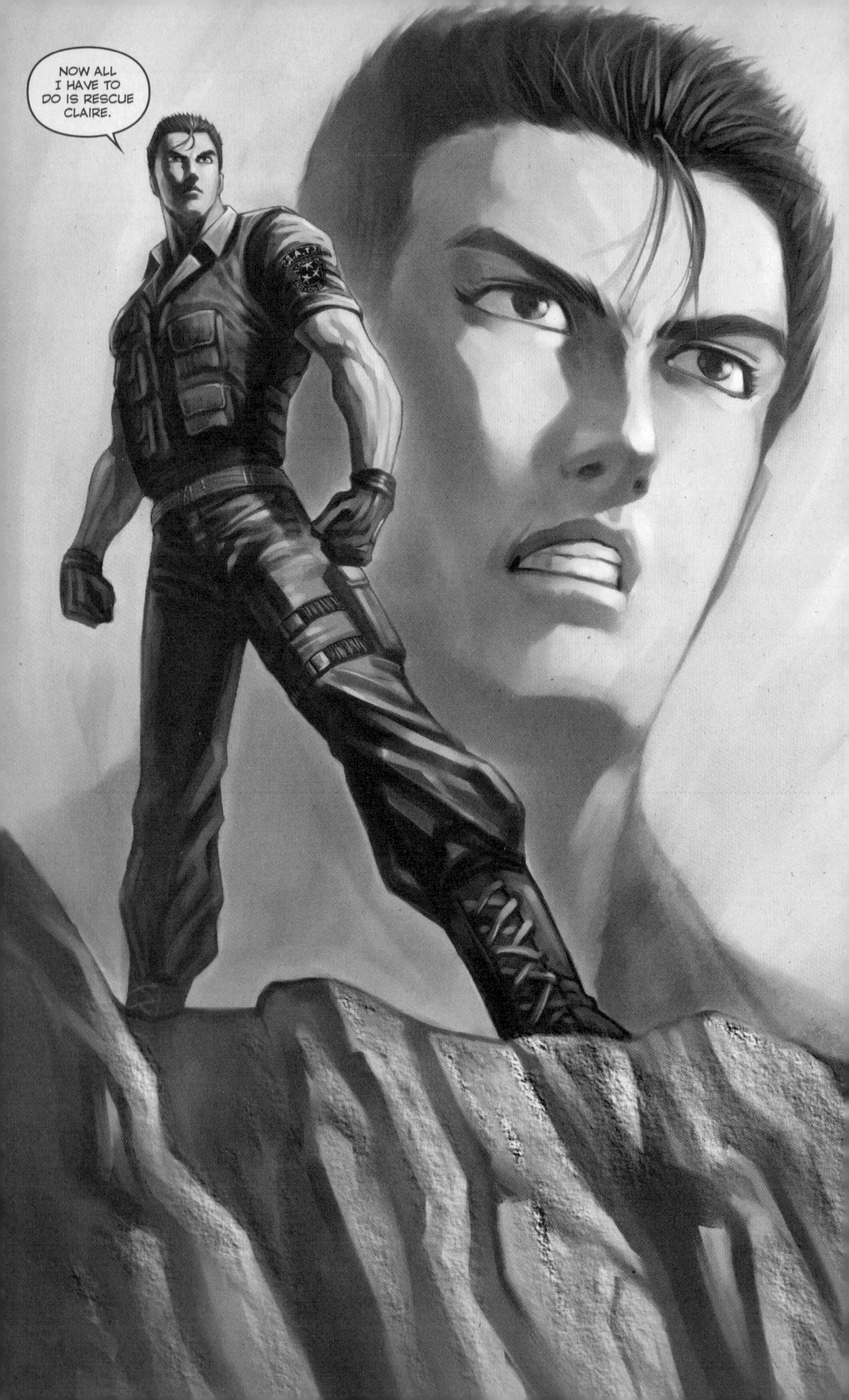
NOW ALL I HAVE TO DO IS RESCUE CLAIRE.

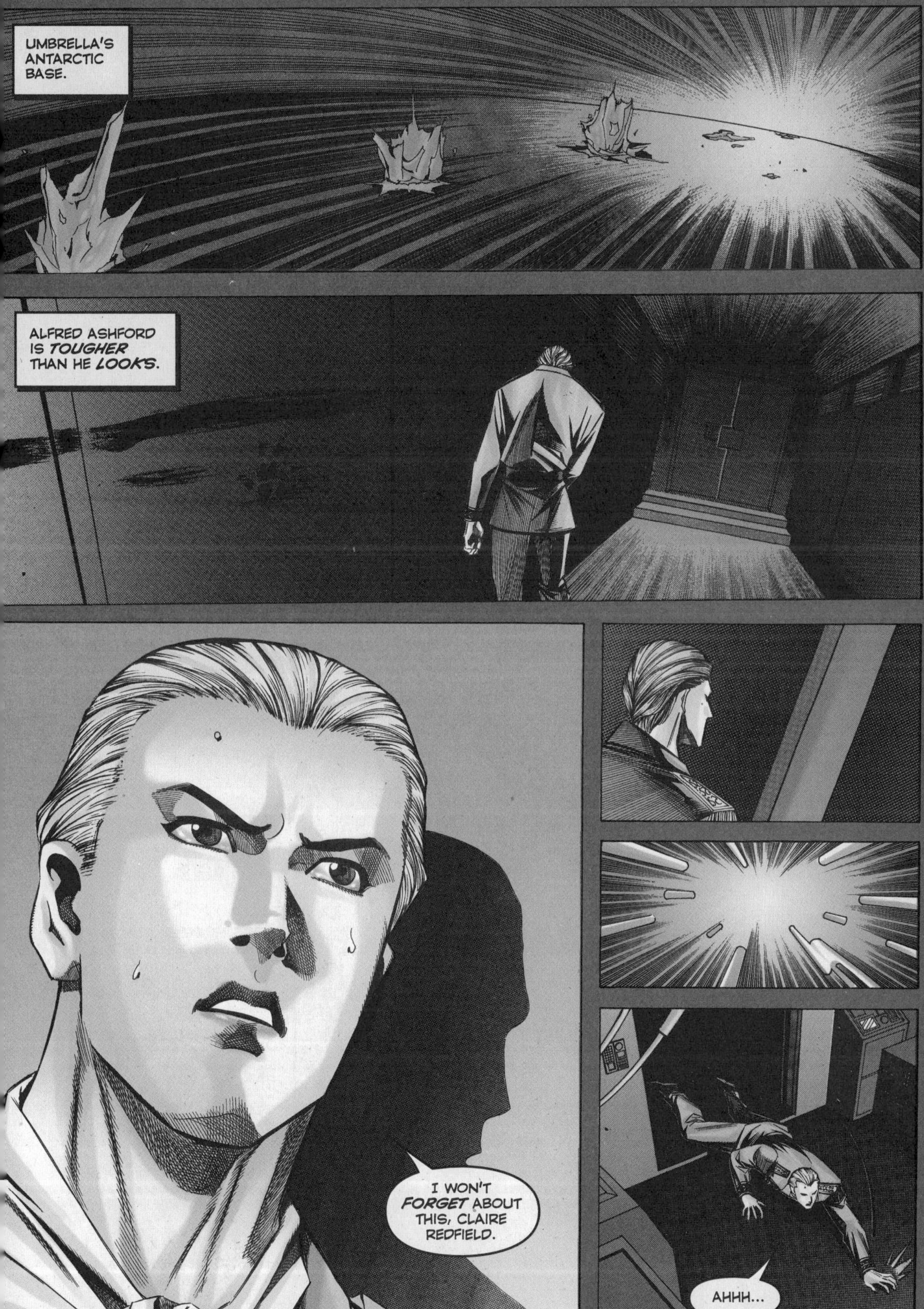
UMBRELLA'S ANTARCTIC BASE.
ALFRED ASHFORD IS TOUGHER THAN HE LOOKS.
I WON'T FORGET ABOUT THIS, CLAIRE REDFIELD.
AHHH...

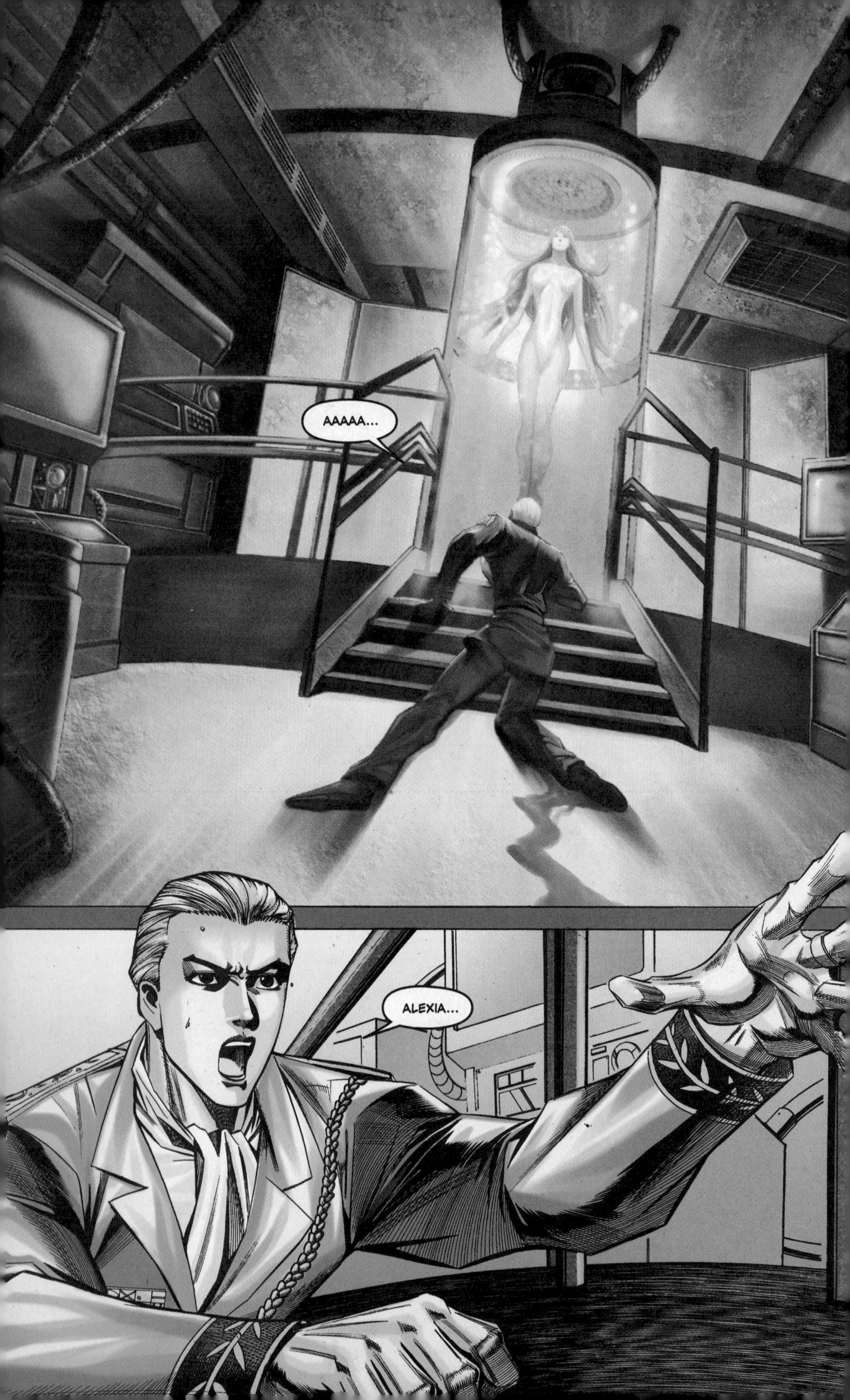
AAAAA...
ALEXIA...

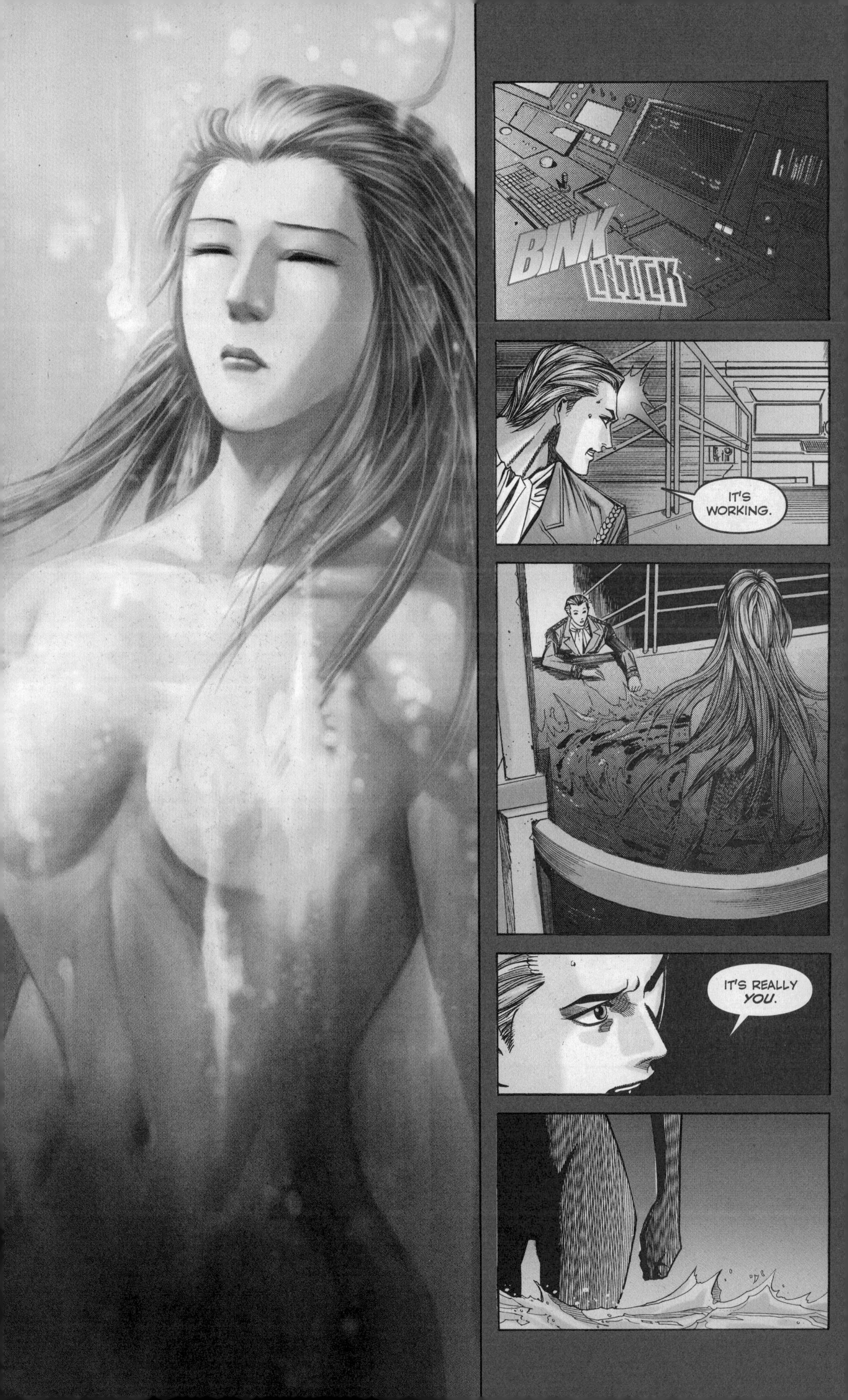
BINK
CLICK
IT'S WORKING.
IT'S REALLY *YOU*.

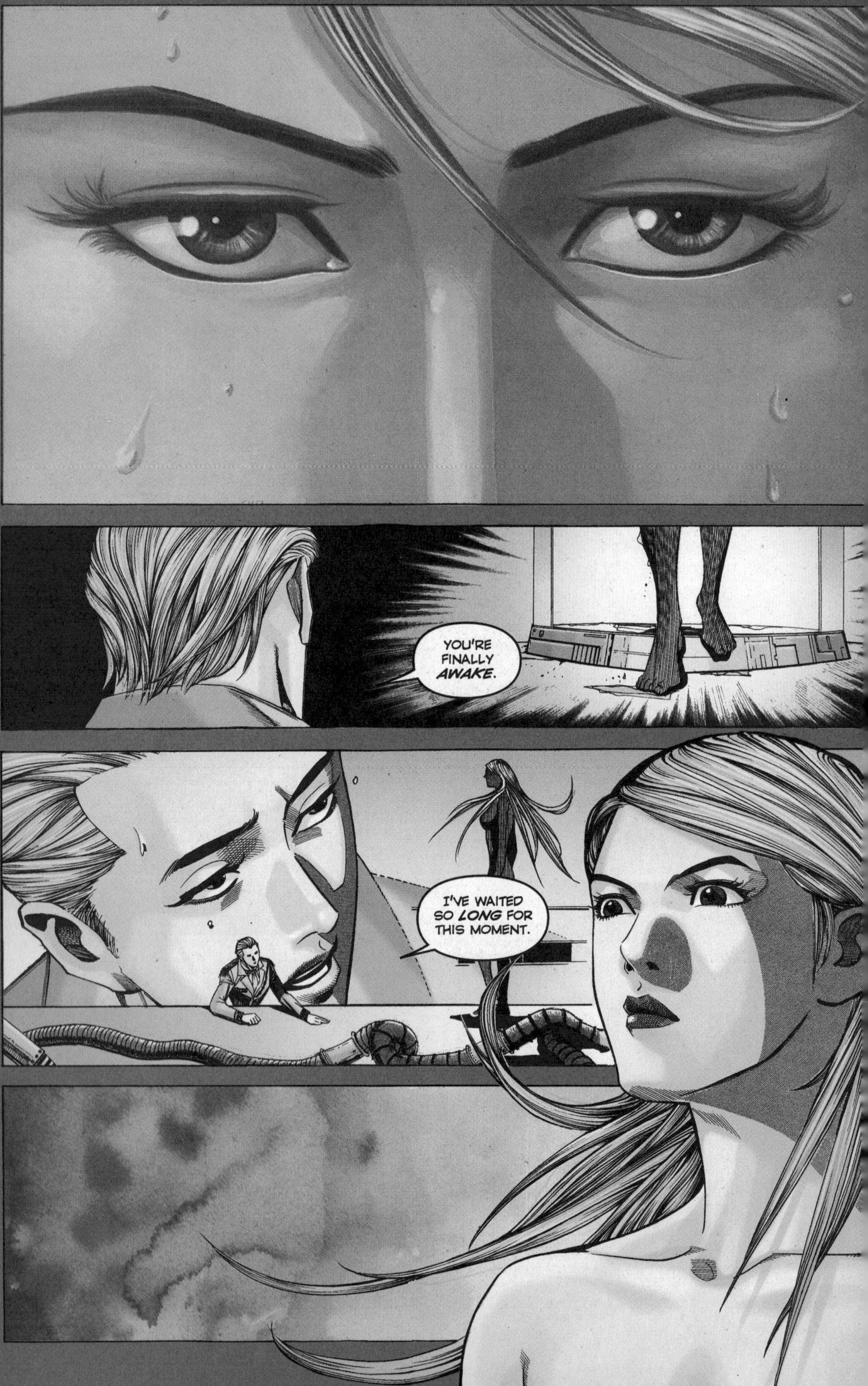
YOU'RE FINALLY AWAKE.
I'VE WAITED SO LONG FOR THIS MOMENT.

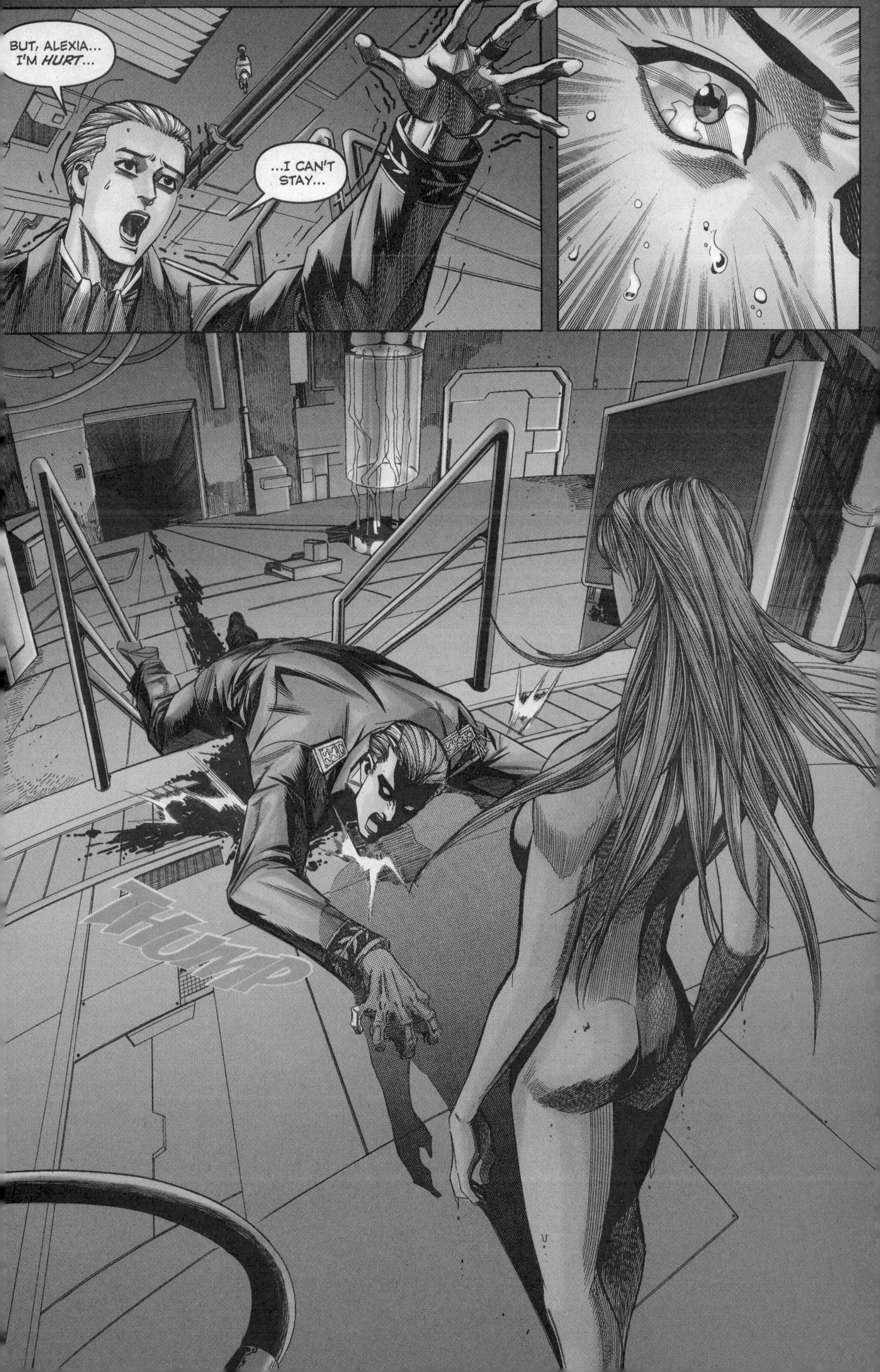
BUT, ALEXIA... I'M *HURT*...
...I CAN'T STAY...
THUMP

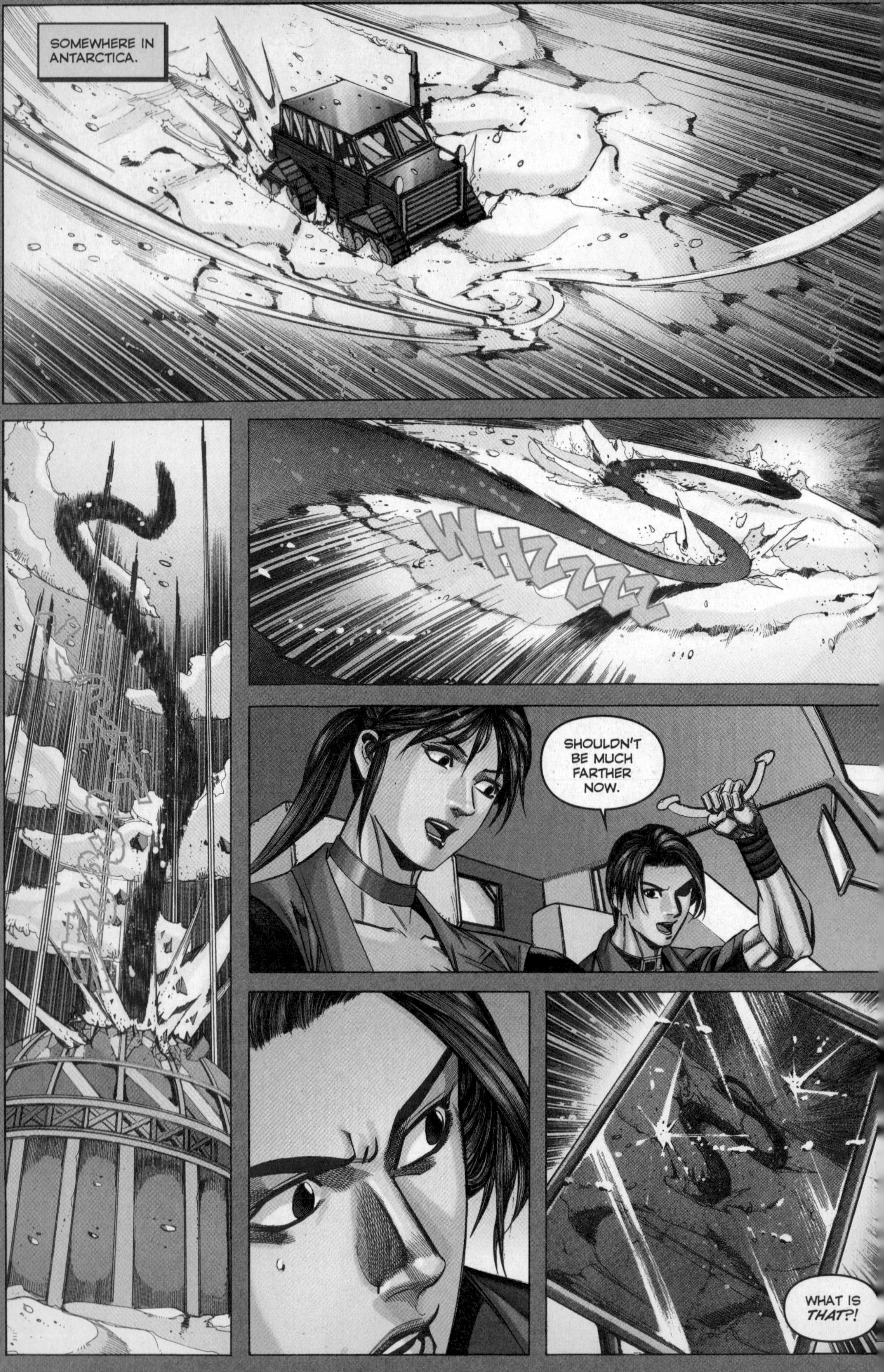
SOMEWHERE IN ANTARCTICA.
WHZZZZ
SHOULDN'T BE MUCH FARTHER NOW.
WHAT IS *THAT*?!

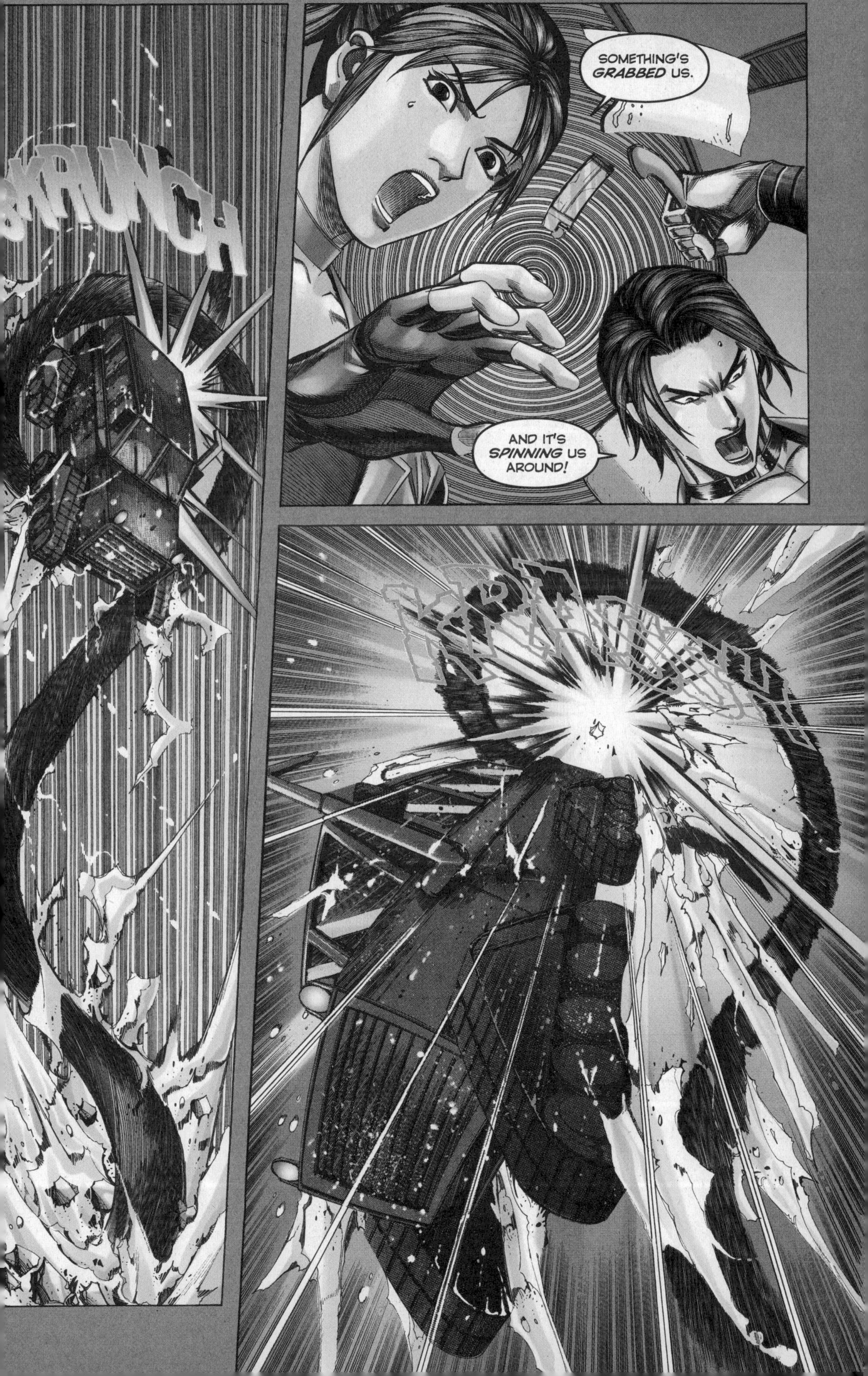
KRUNCH
SOMETHING'S GRABBED US.
AND IT'S SPINNING US AROUND!

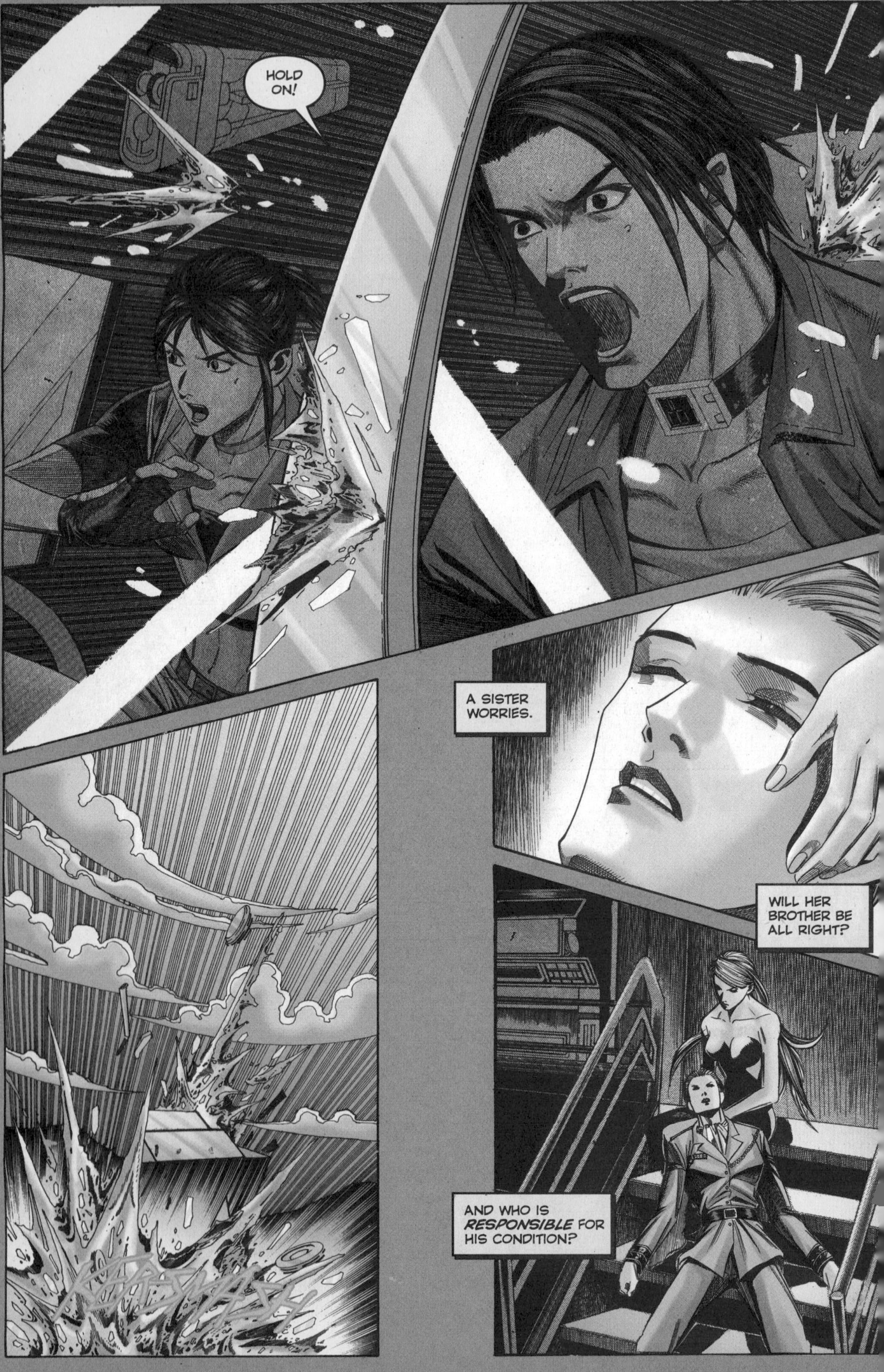
HOLD ON!
A SISTER WORRIES.
WILL HER BROTHER BE ALL RIGHT?
AND WHO IS *RESPONSIBLE* FOR HIS CONDITION?

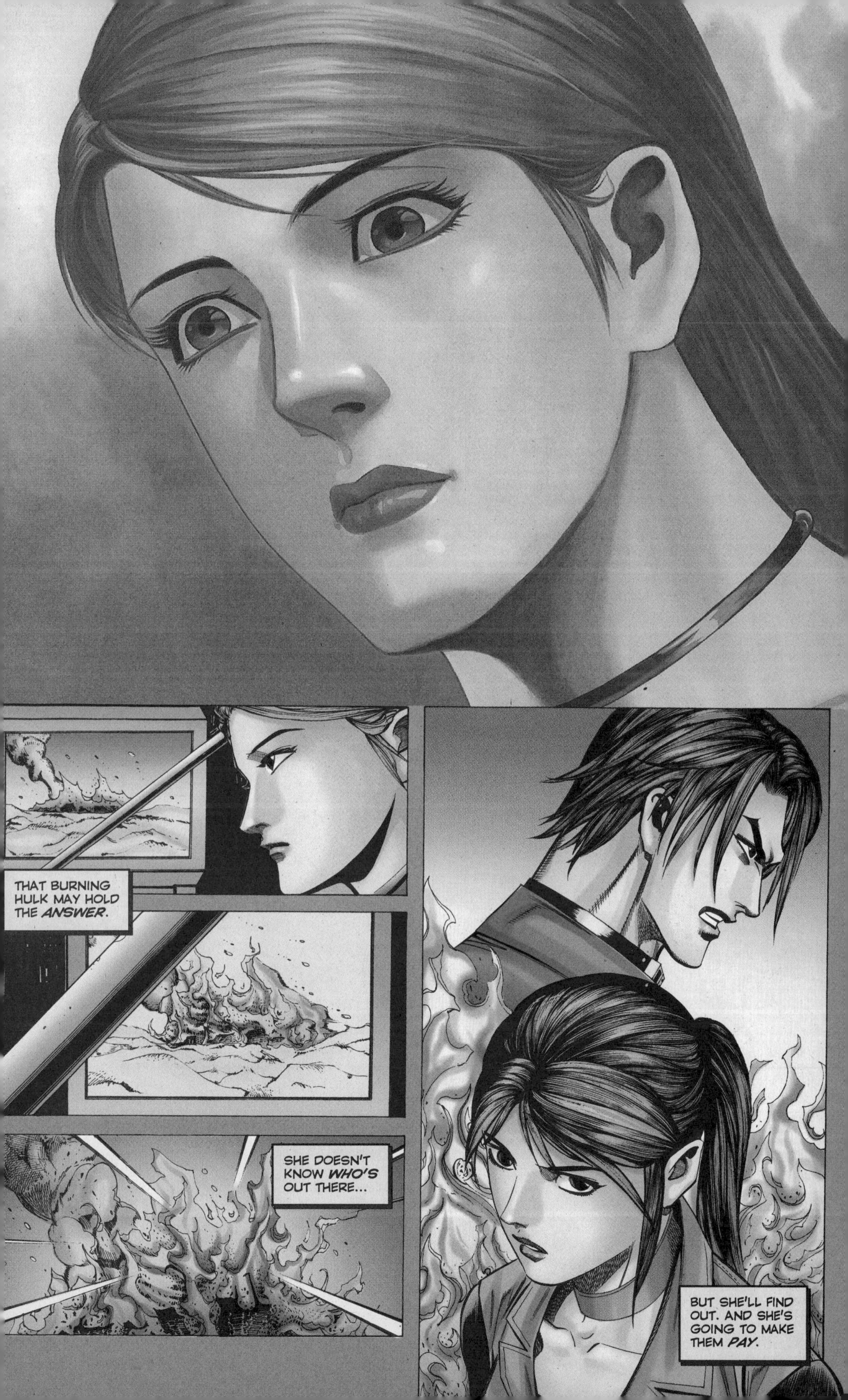
THAT BURNING HULK MAY HOLD THE *ANSWER*.
SHE DOESN'T KNOW *WHO'S* OUT THERE...
BUT SHE'LL FIND OUT. AND SHE'S GOING TO MAKE THEM *PAY*.

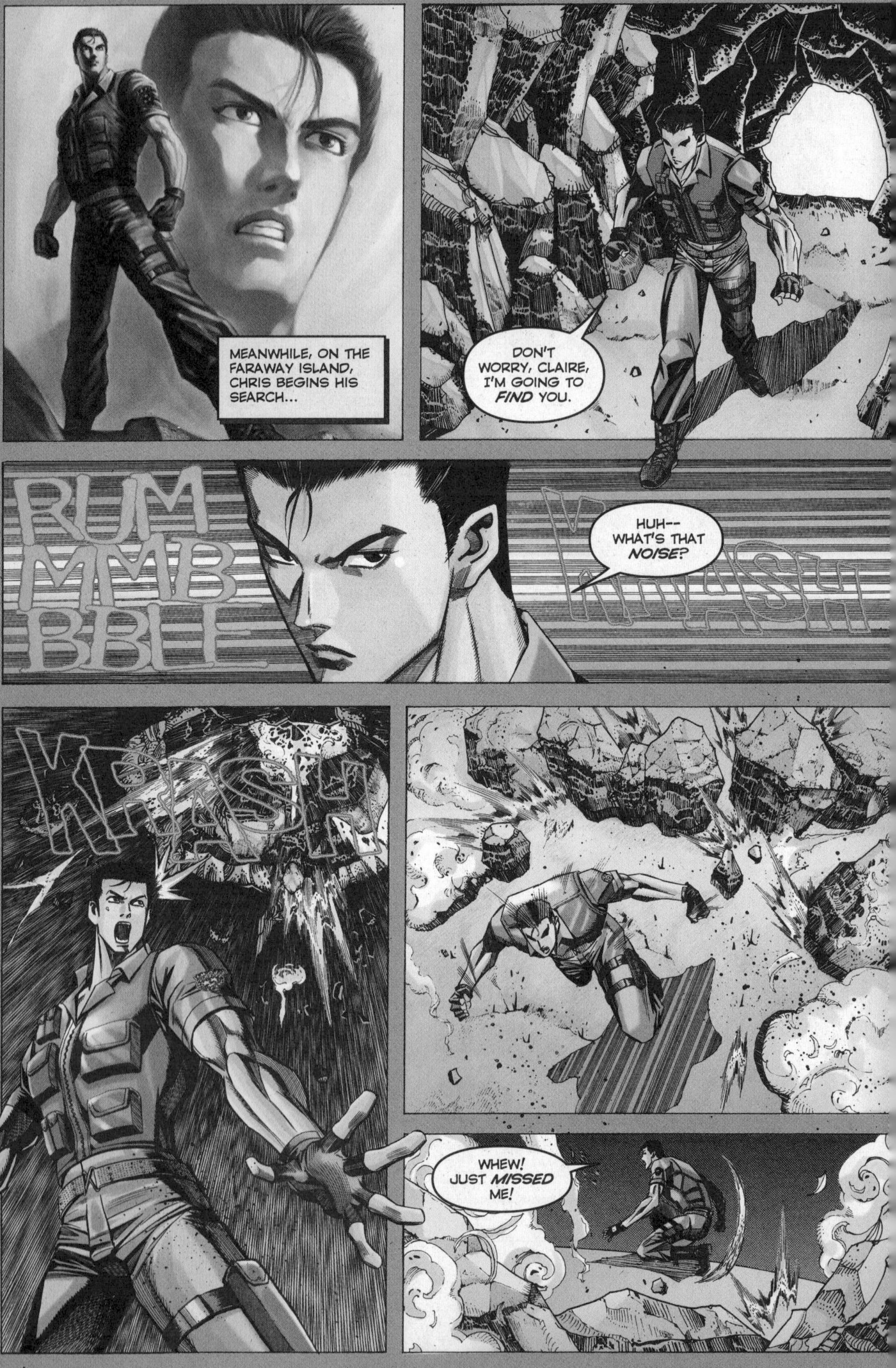
MEANWHILE, ON THE FARAWAY ISLAND, CHRIS BEGINS HIS SEARCH...
DON'T WORRY, CLAIRE, I'M GOING TO *FIND* YOU.
RUM
MMB
BBLE
HUH-- WHAT'S THAT *NOISE?*
KRASH
WHEW! JUST *MISSED* ME!

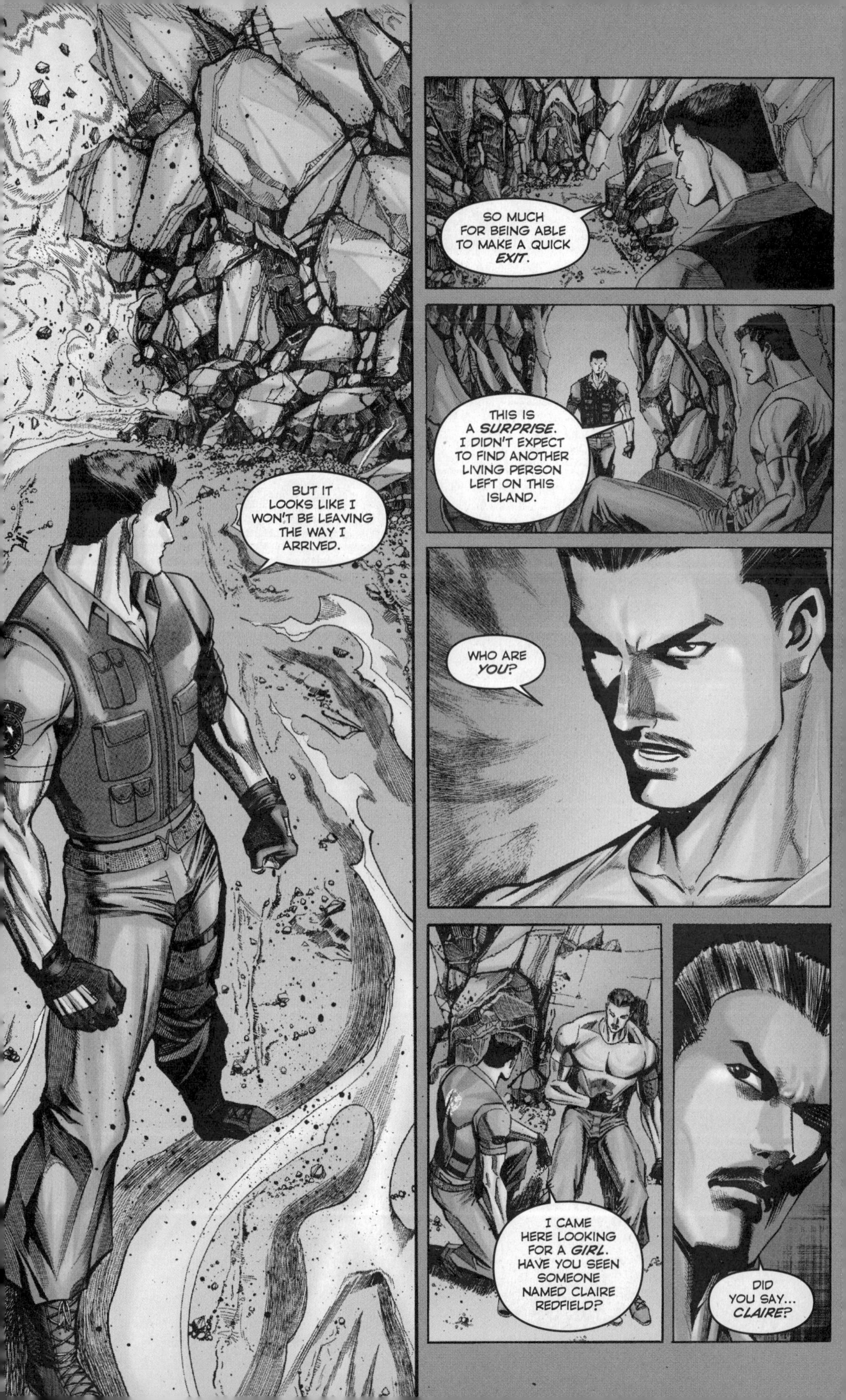
BUT IT LOOKS LIKE I WON'T BE LEAVING THE WAY I ARRIVED.
SO MUCH FOR BEING ABLE TO MAKE A QUICK *EXIT*.
THIS IS A *SURPRISE*. I DIDN'T EXPECT TO FIND ANOTHER LIVING PERSON LEFT ON THIS ISLAND.
WHO ARE *YOU*?
I CAME HERE LOOKING FOR A *GIRL*. HAVE YOU SEEN SOMEONE NAMED CLAIRE REDFIELD?
DID YOU SAY... *CLAIRE*?

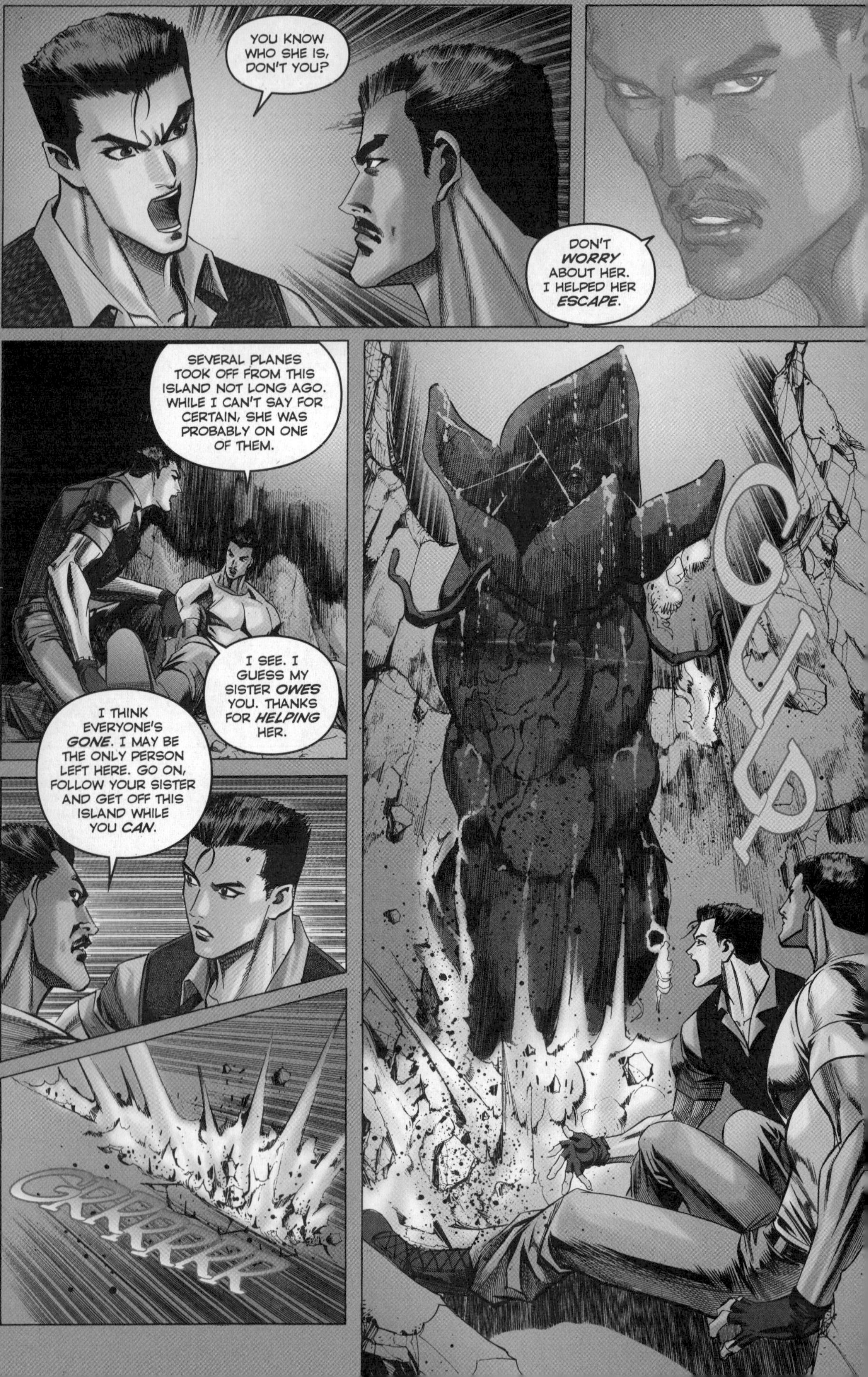
YOU KNOW WHO SHE IS, DON'T YOU?
DON'T *WORRY* ABOUT HER. I HELPED HER *ESCAPE*.
SEVERAL PLANES TOOK OFF FROM THIS ISLAND NOT LONG AGO. WHILE I CAN'T SAY FOR CERTAIN, SHE WAS PROBABLY ON ONE OF THEM.
I SEE. I GUESS MY SISTER *OWES* YOU. THANKS FOR *HELPING* HER.
I THINK EVERYONE'S *GONE*. I MAY BE THE ONLY PERSON LEFT HERE. GO ON, FOLLOW YOUR SISTER AND GET OFF THIS ISLAND WHILE YOU *CAN*.
GRRRRRR
GULP

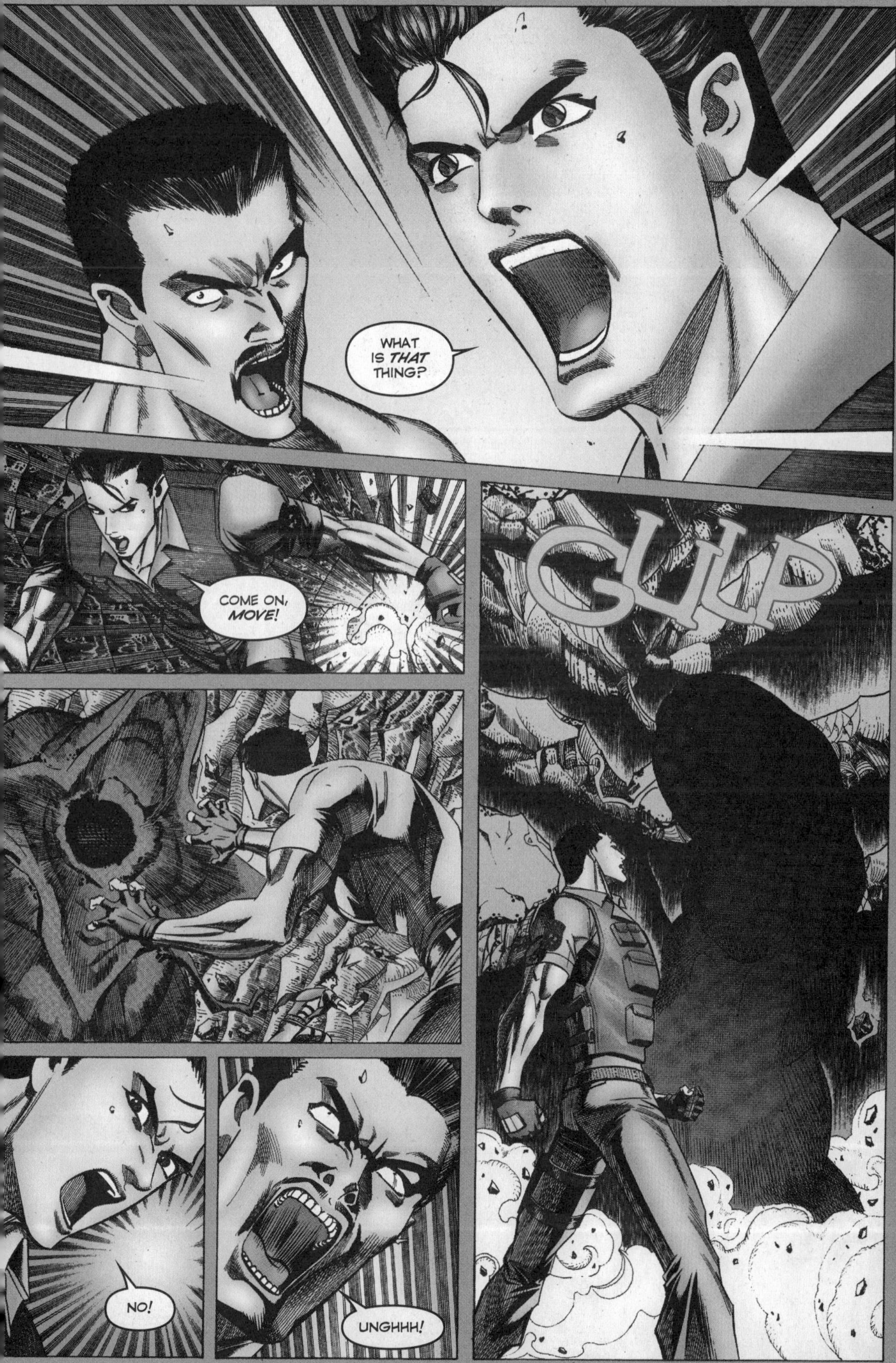
WHAT IS *THAT* THING?
COME ON, *MOVE!*
GULP
NO!
UNGHHH!

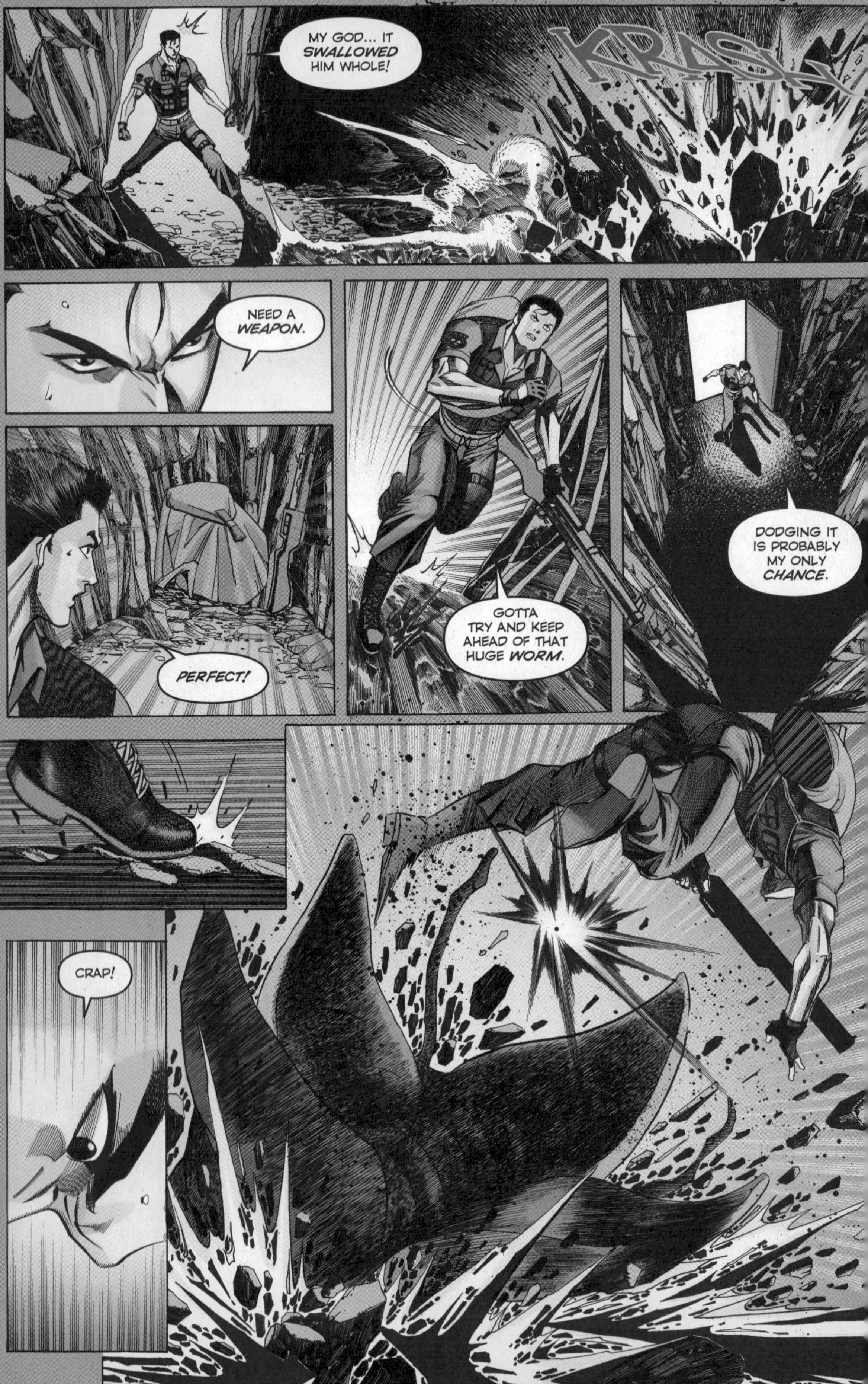
MY GOD... IT SWALLOWED HIM WHOLE!
KRASH
NEED A WEAPON.
PERFECT!
GOTTA TRY AND KEEP AHEAD OF THAT HUGE WORM.
DODGING IT IS PROBABLY MY ONLY CHANCE.
CRAP!

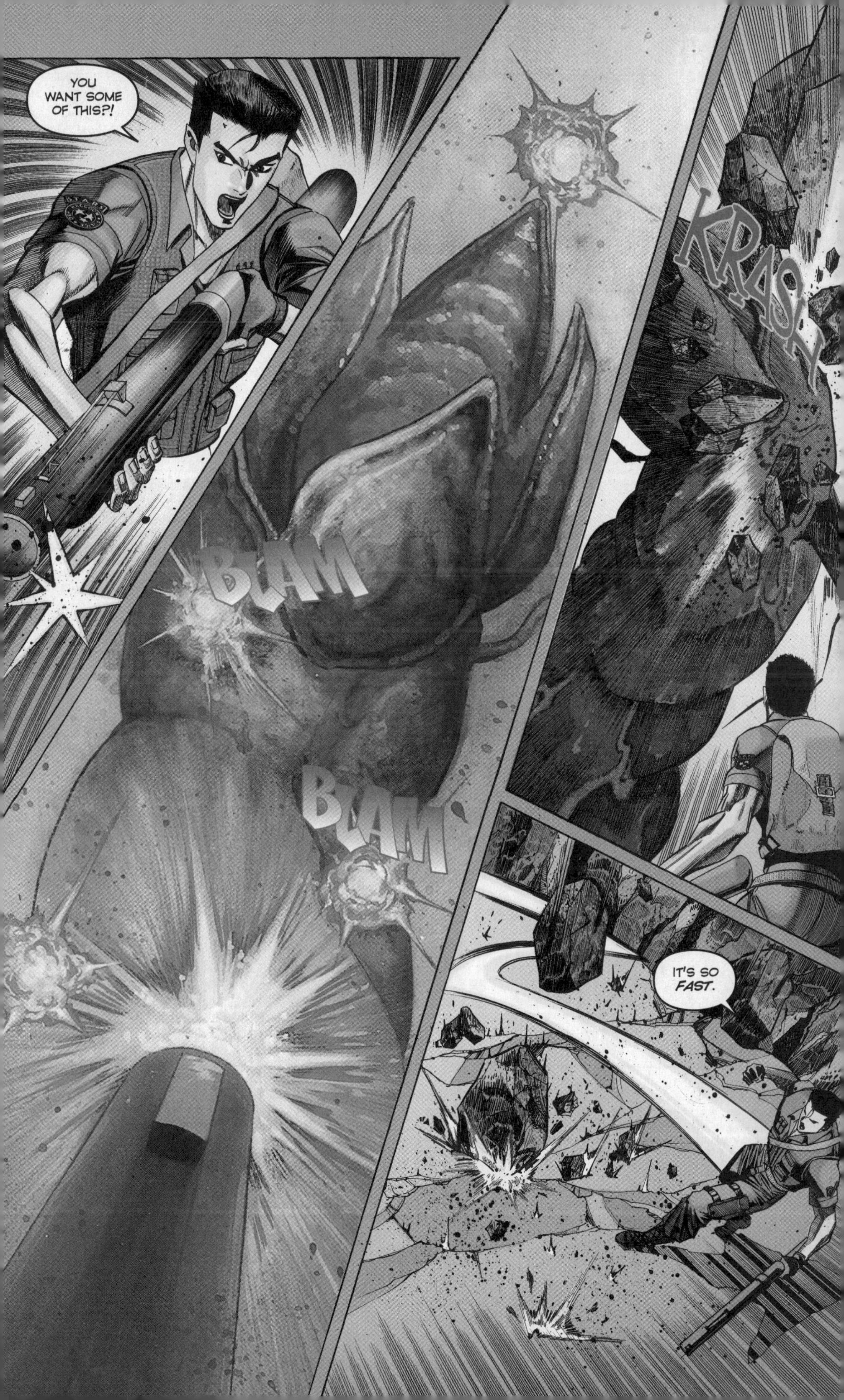
YOU WANT SOME OF THIS?!
BLAM
BLAM
KRASH
IT'S SO *FAST*.

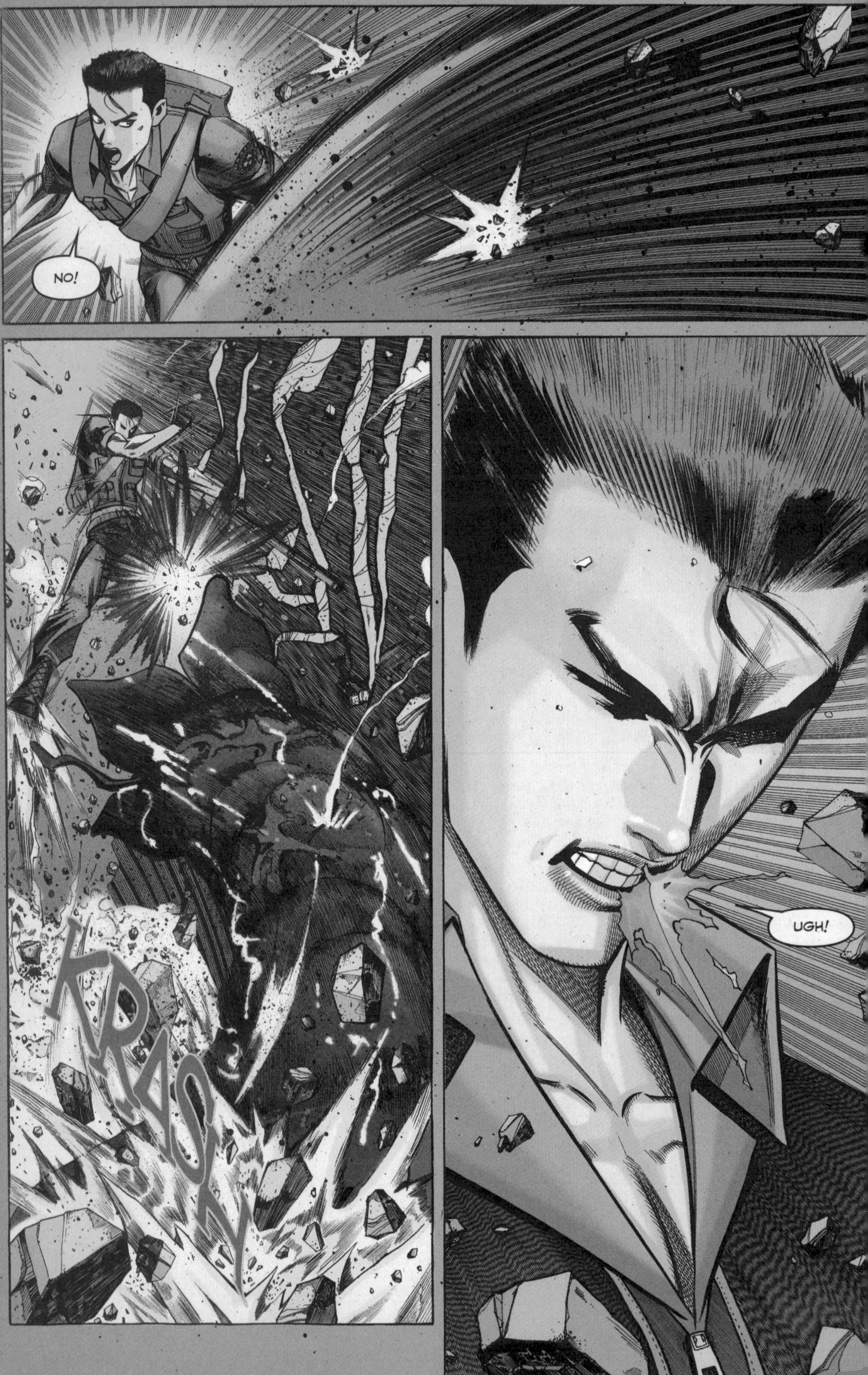
NO!
KRASH
UGH!

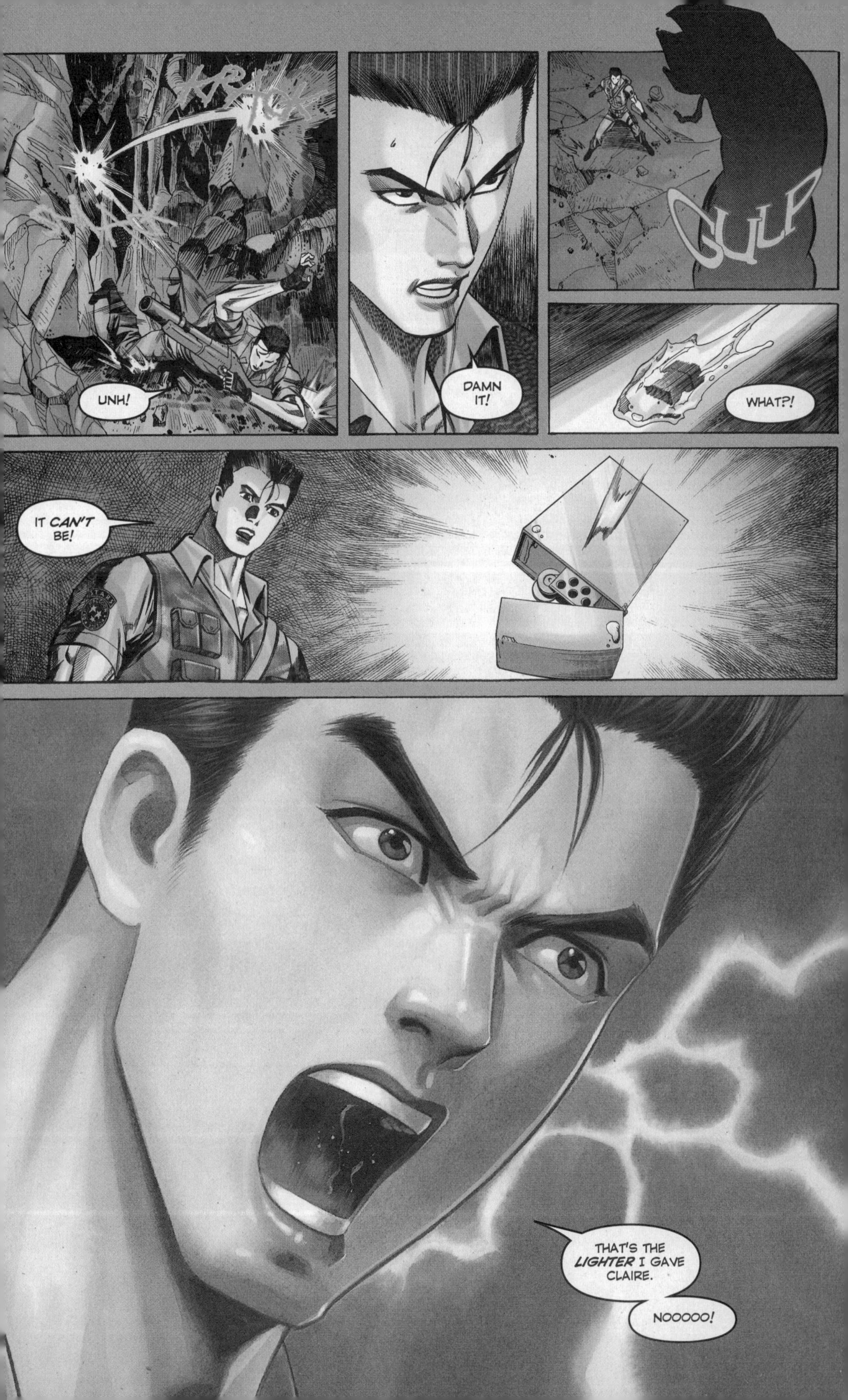
UNH!
DAMN IT!
GULP
WHAT?!
IT *CAN'T* BE!
THAT'S THE *LIGHTER* I GAVE CLAIRE.
NOOOOO!

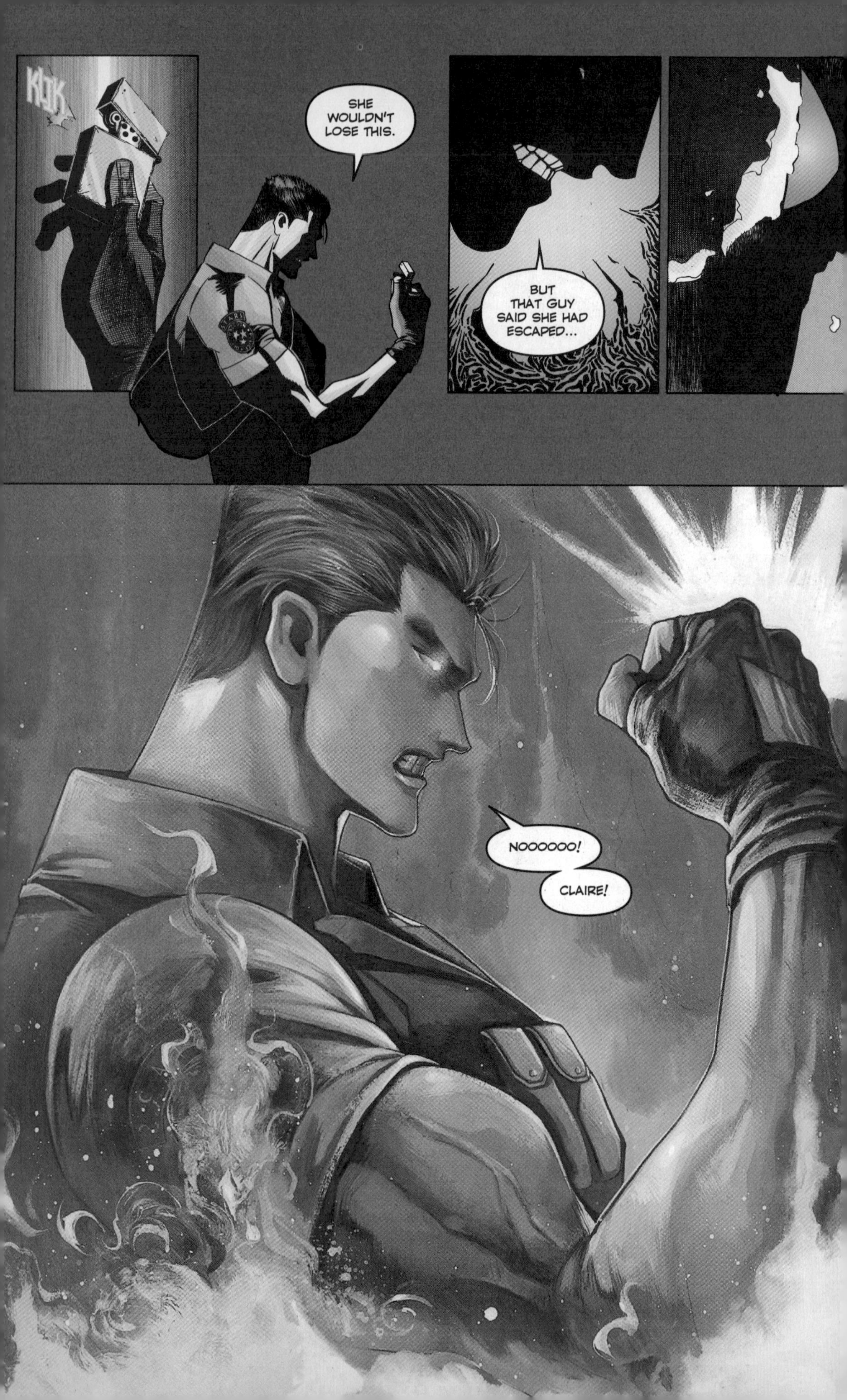
KLIK
SHE WOULDN'T LOSE THIS.
BUT THAT GUY SAID SHE HAD ESCAPED...
NOOOOOO!
CLAIRE!

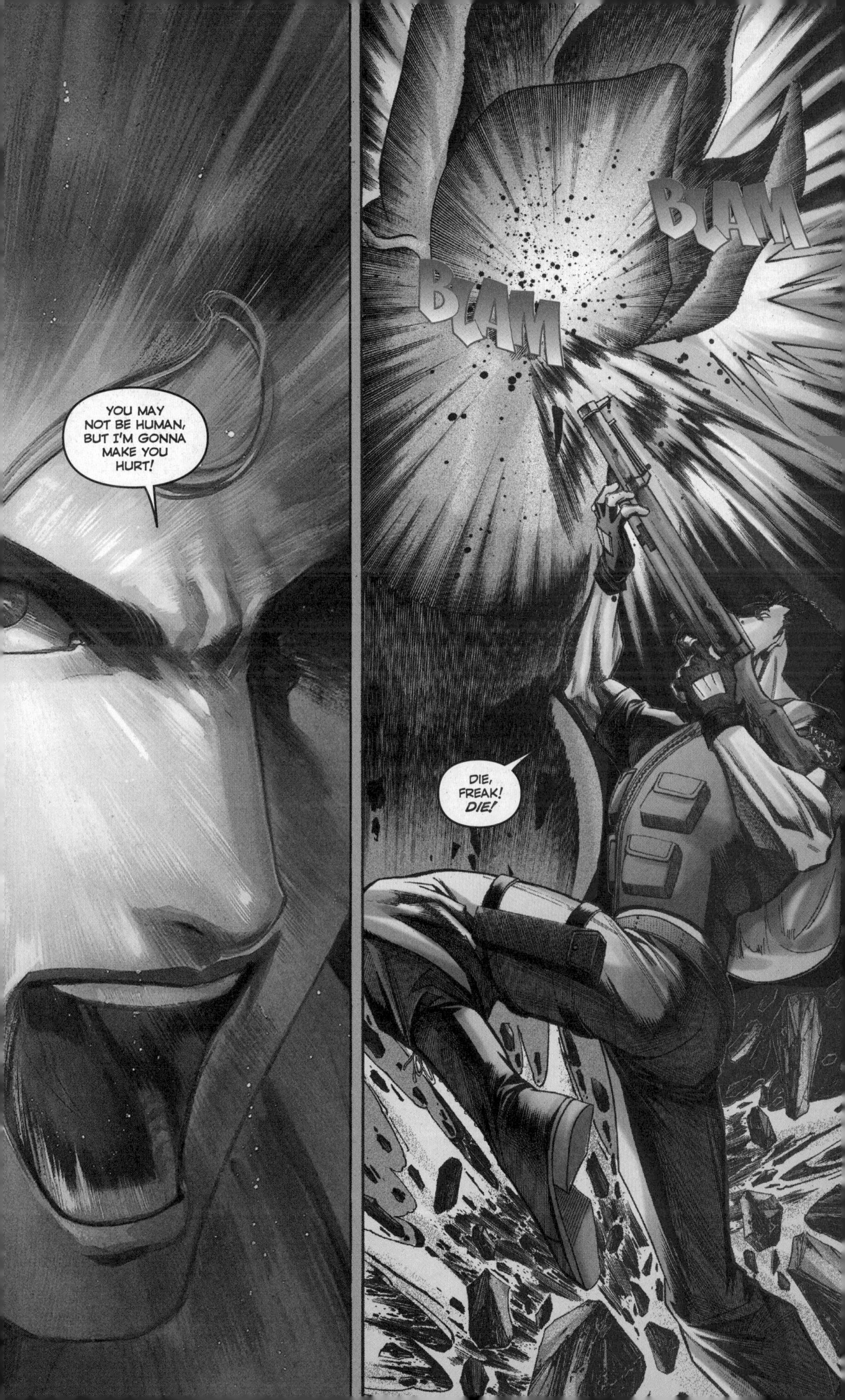
YOU MAY NOT BE HUMAN, BUT I'M GONNA MAKE YOU HURT!
BLAM
BLAM
DIE, FREAK! DIE!

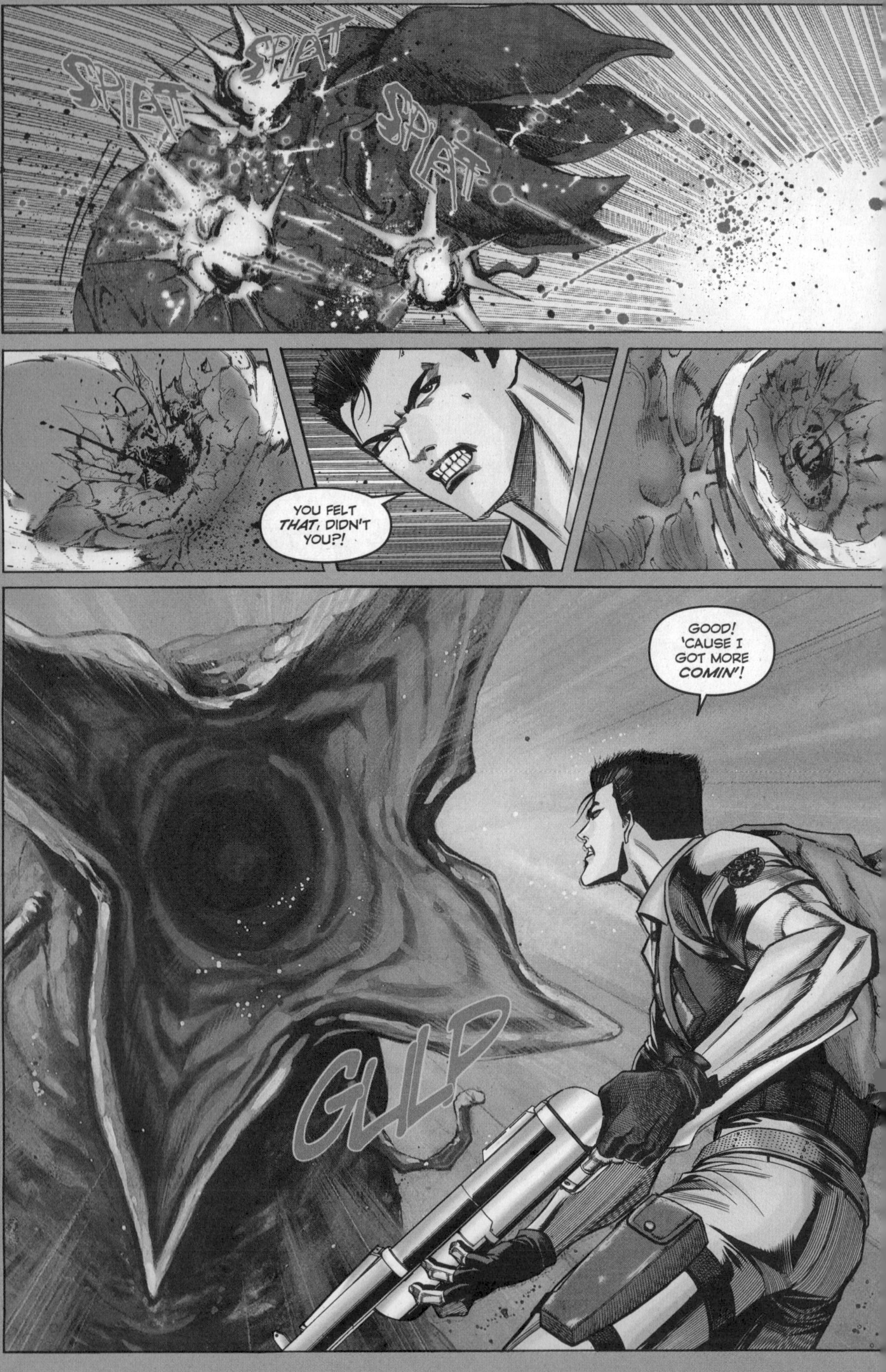
SPLAT
SPLAT
SPLAT
YOU FELT THAT, DIDN'T YOU?!
GOOD! 'CAUSE I GOT MORE COMIN'!
GULP

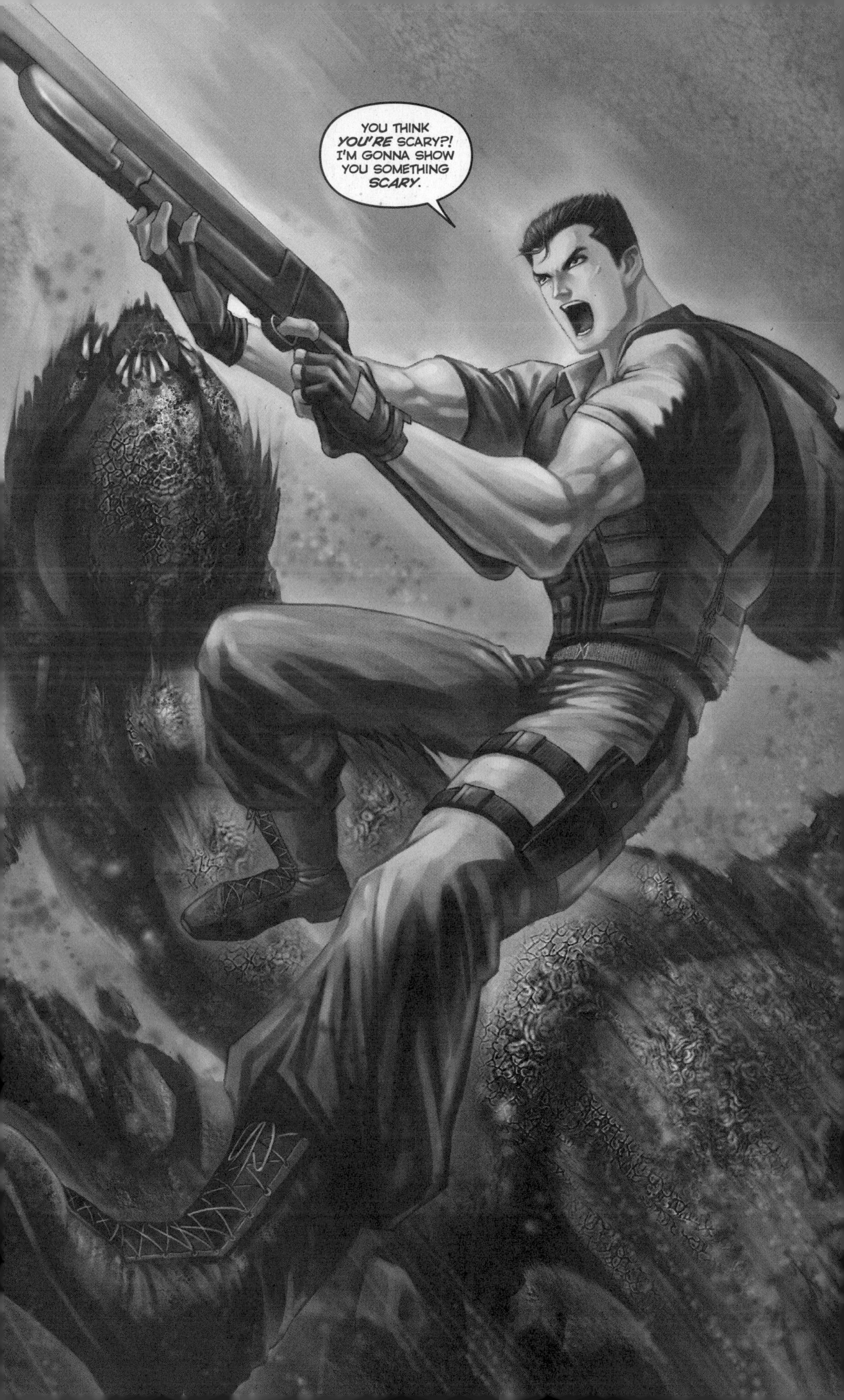
YOU THINK *YOU'RE* SCARY?! I'M GONNA SHOW YOU SOMETHING *SCARY*.

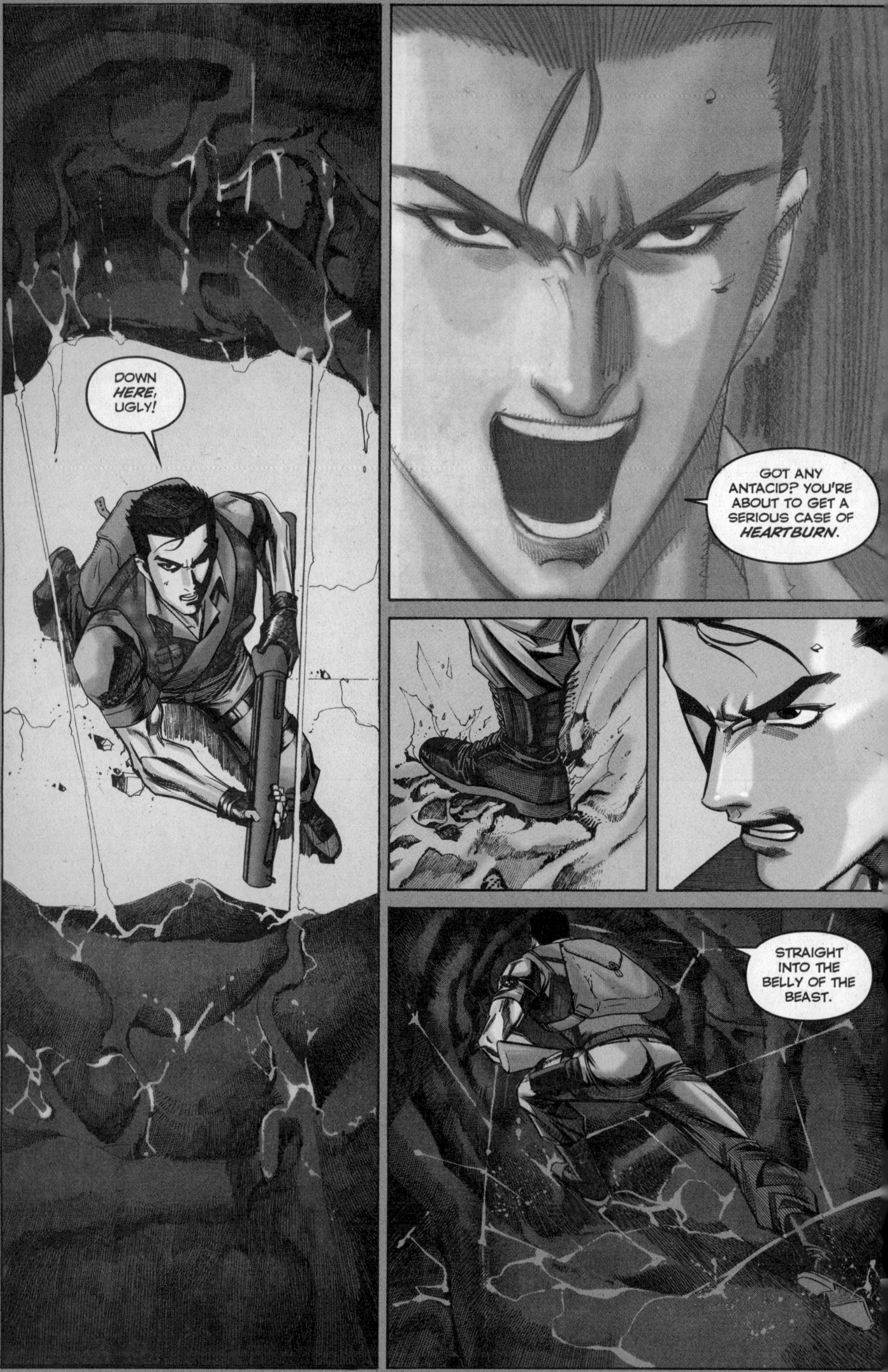
DOWN HERE, UGLY!
GOT ANY ANTACID? YOU'RE ABOUT TO GET A SERIOUS CASE OF HEARTBURN.
STRAIGHT INTO THE BELLY OF THE BEAST.

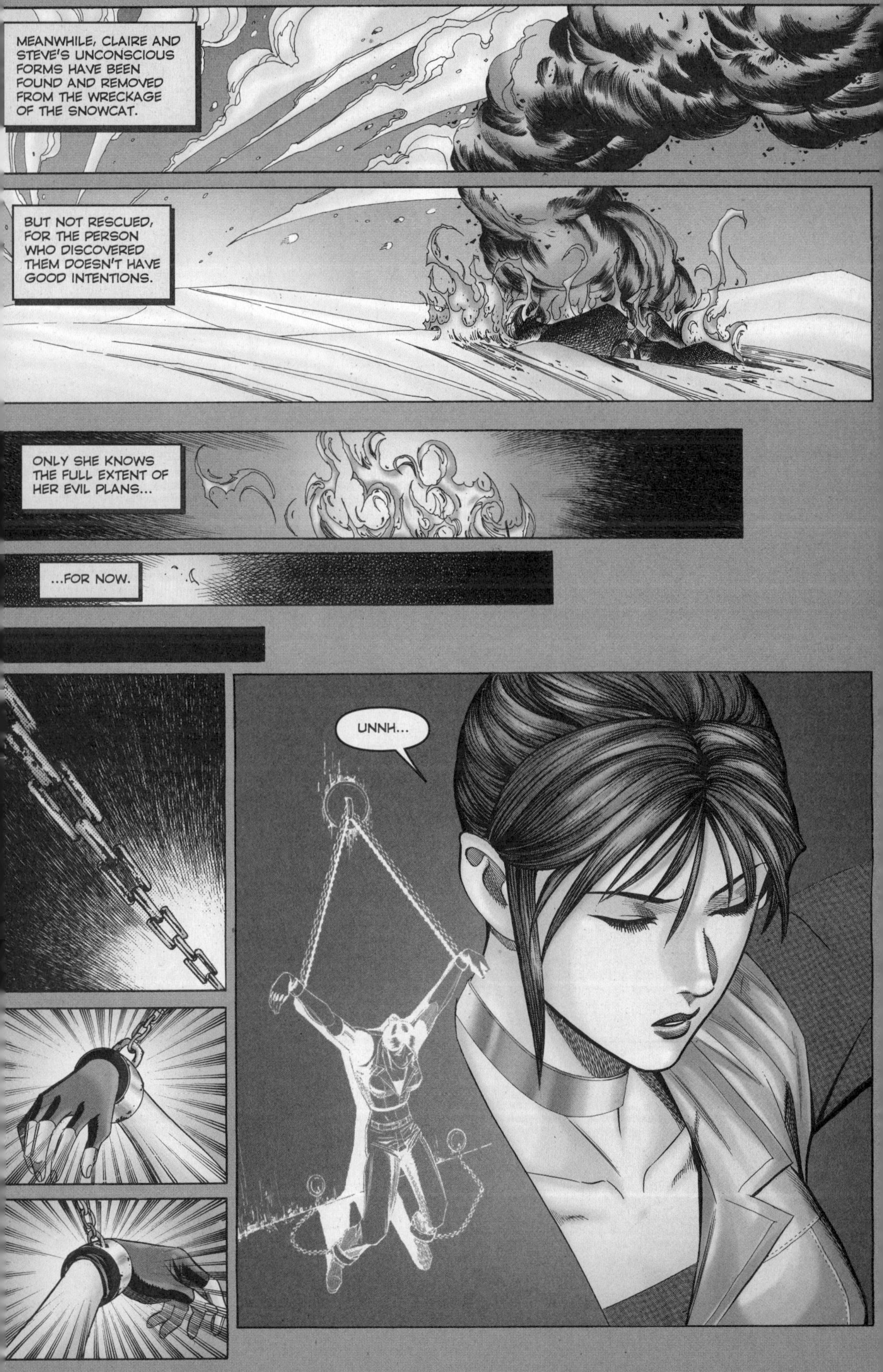
MEANWHILE, CLAIRE AND STEVE'S UNCONSCIOUS FORMS HAVE BEEN FOUND AND REMOVED FROM THE WRECKAGE OF THE SNOWCAT.
BUT NOT RESCUED, FOR THE PERSON WHO DISCOVERED THEM DOESN'T HAVE GOOD INTENTIONS.
ONLY SHE KNOWS THE FULL EXTENT OF HER EVIL PLANS...
...FOR NOW.
UNNH...

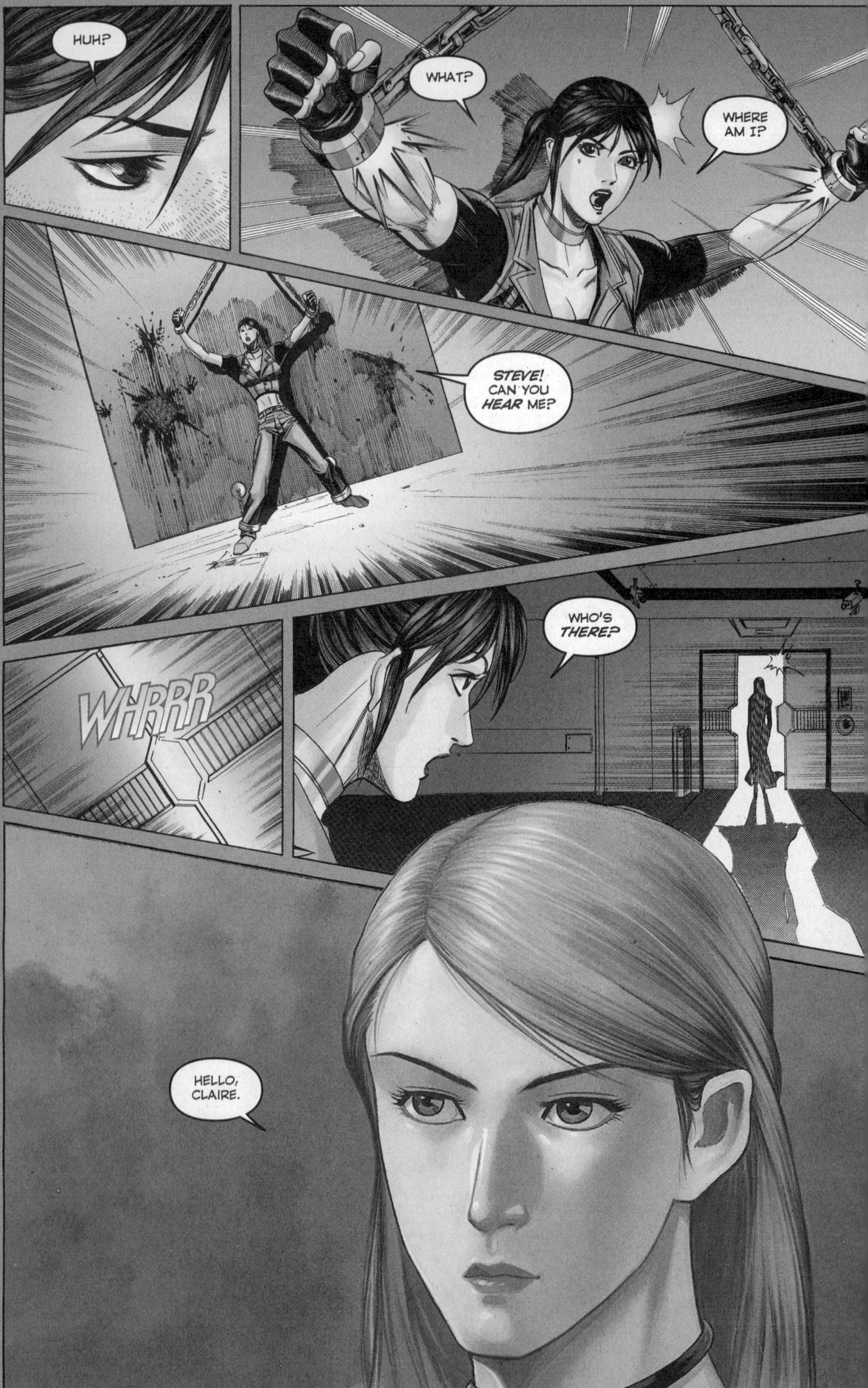
HUH?
WHAT?
WHERE AM I?
STEVE! CAN YOU HEAR ME?
WHRRR
WHO'S THERE?
HELLO, CLAIRE.

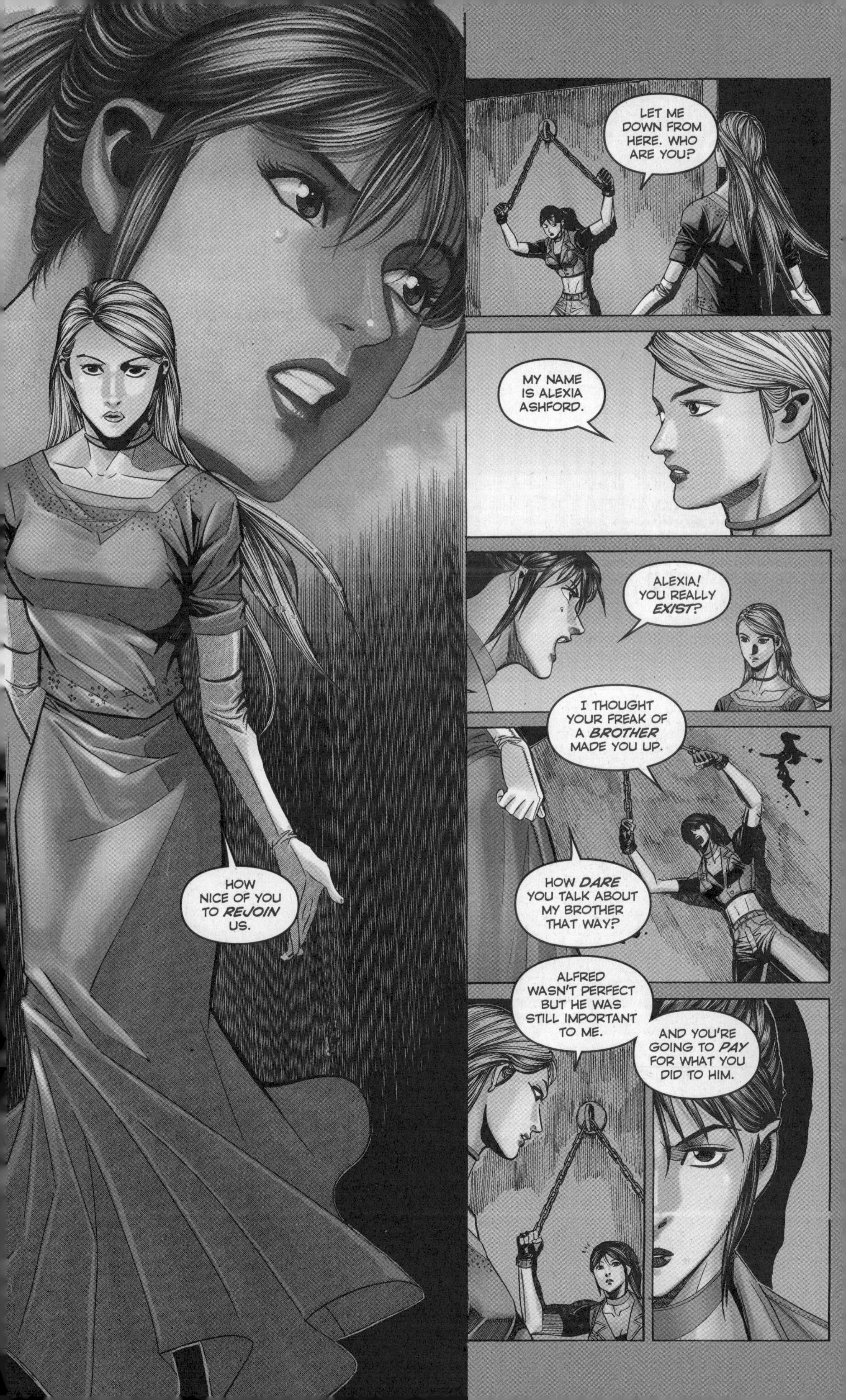
HOW NICE OF YOU TO REJOIN US.
LET ME DOWN FROM HERE. WHO ARE YOU?
MY NAME IS ALEXIA ASHFORD.
ALEXIA! YOU REALLY EXIST?
I THOUGHT YOUR FREAK OF A BROTHER MADE YOU UP.
HOW DARE YOU TALK ABOUT MY BROTHER THAT WAY?
ALFRED WASN'T PERFECT BUT HE WAS STILL IMPORTANT TO ME.
AND YOU'RE GOING TO PAY FOR WHAT YOU DID TO HIM.

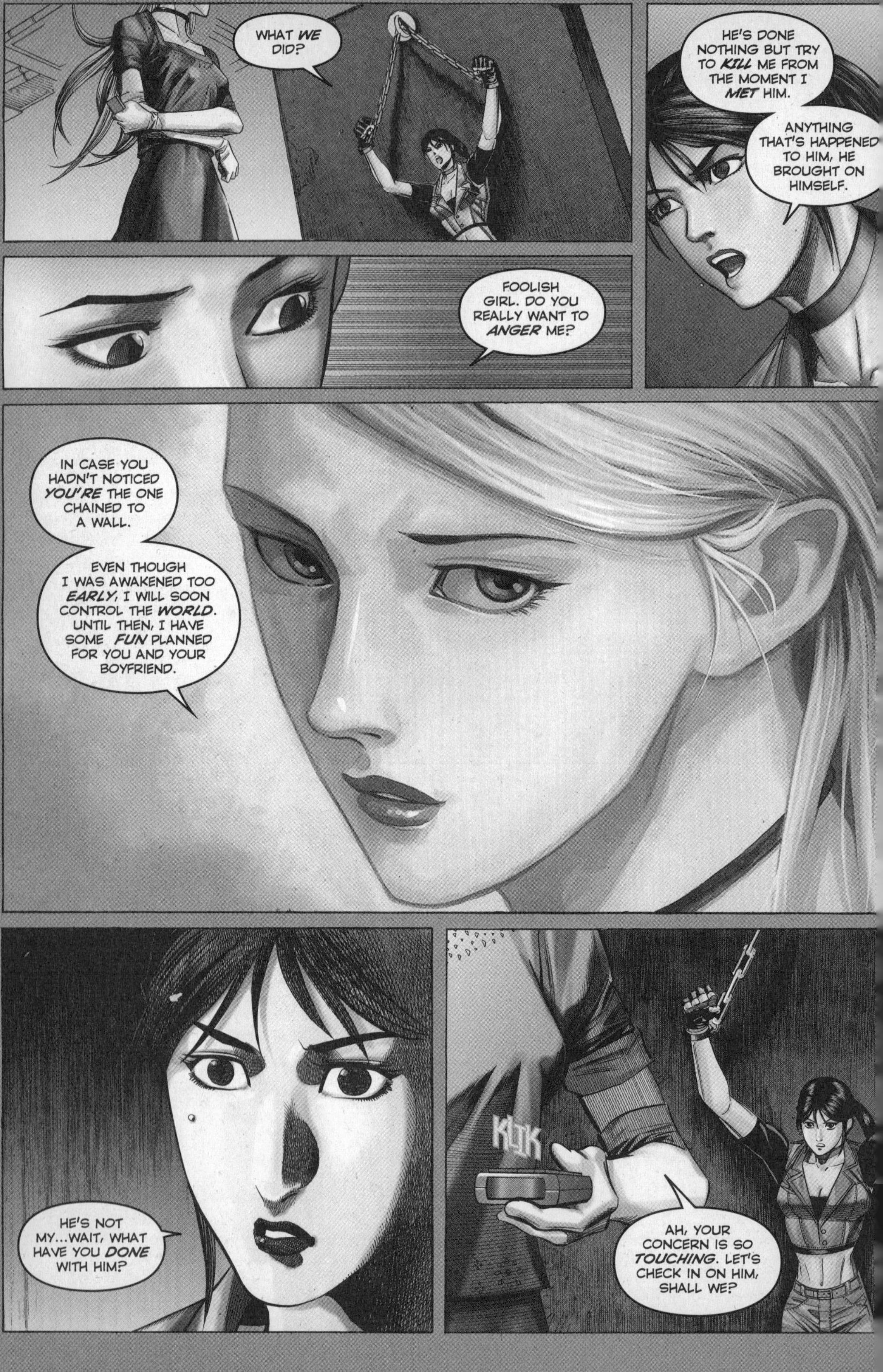
WHAT WE DID?
HE'S DONE NOTHING BUT TRY TO KILL ME FROM THE MOMENT I MET HIM.
ANYTHING THAT'S HAPPENED TO HIM, HE BROUGHT ON HIMSELF.
FOOLISH GIRL. DO YOU REALLY WANT TO ANGER ME?
IN CASE YOU HADN'T NOTICED YOU'RE THE ONE CHAINED TO A WALL.
EVEN THOUGH I WAS AWAKENED TOO EARLY, I WILL SOON CONTROL THE WORLD. UNTIL THEN, I HAVE SOME FUN PLANNED FOR YOU AND YOUR BOYFRIEND.
HE'S NOT MY...WAIT, WHAT HAVE YOU DONE WITH HIM?
KLIK
AH, YOUR CONCERN IS SO TOUCHING. LET'S CHECK IN ON HIM, SHALL WE?

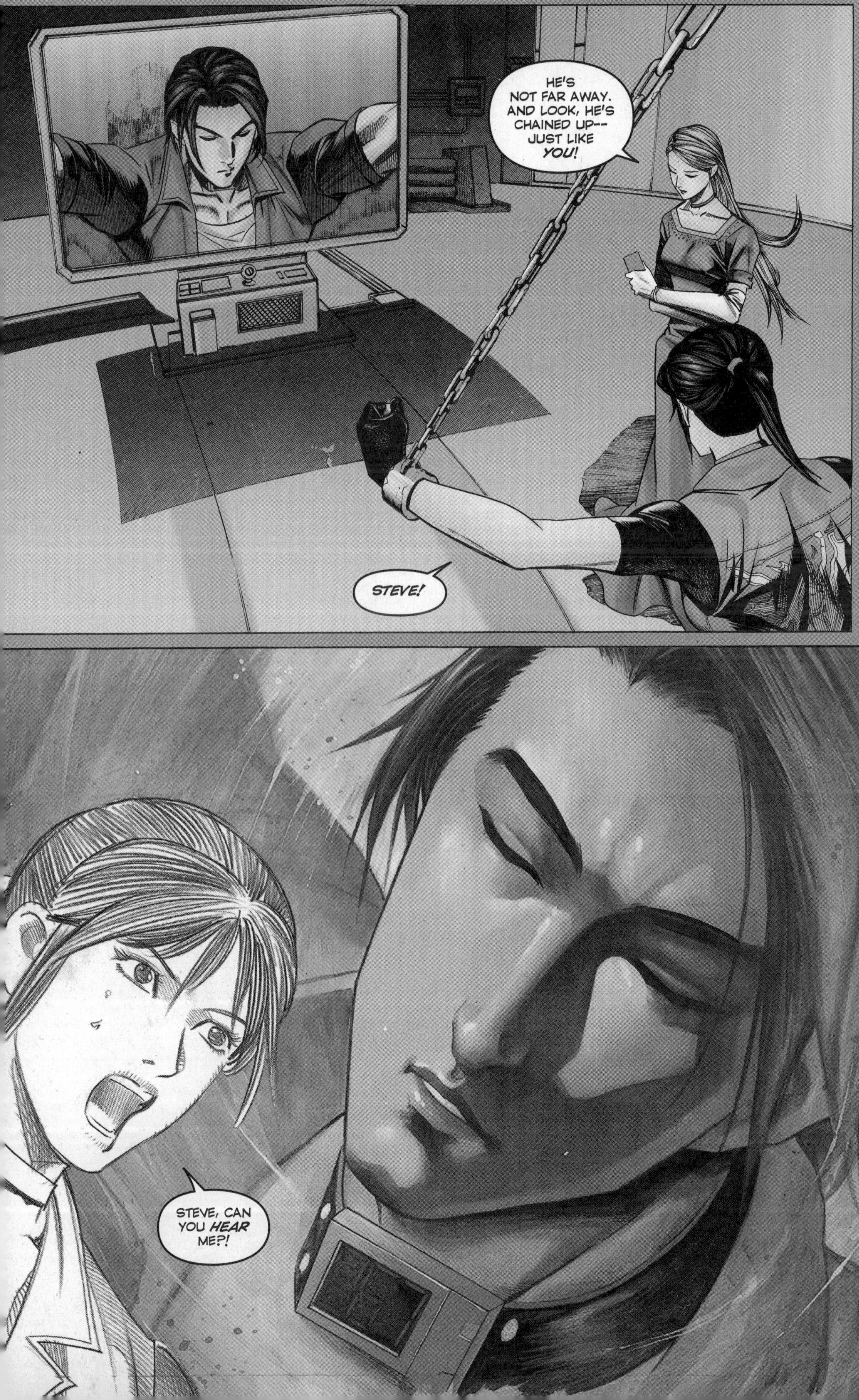
HE'S NOT FAR AWAY. AND LOOK, HE'S CHAINED UP-- JUST LIKE *YOU*!
STEVE!
STEVE, CAN YOU *HEAR* ME?!

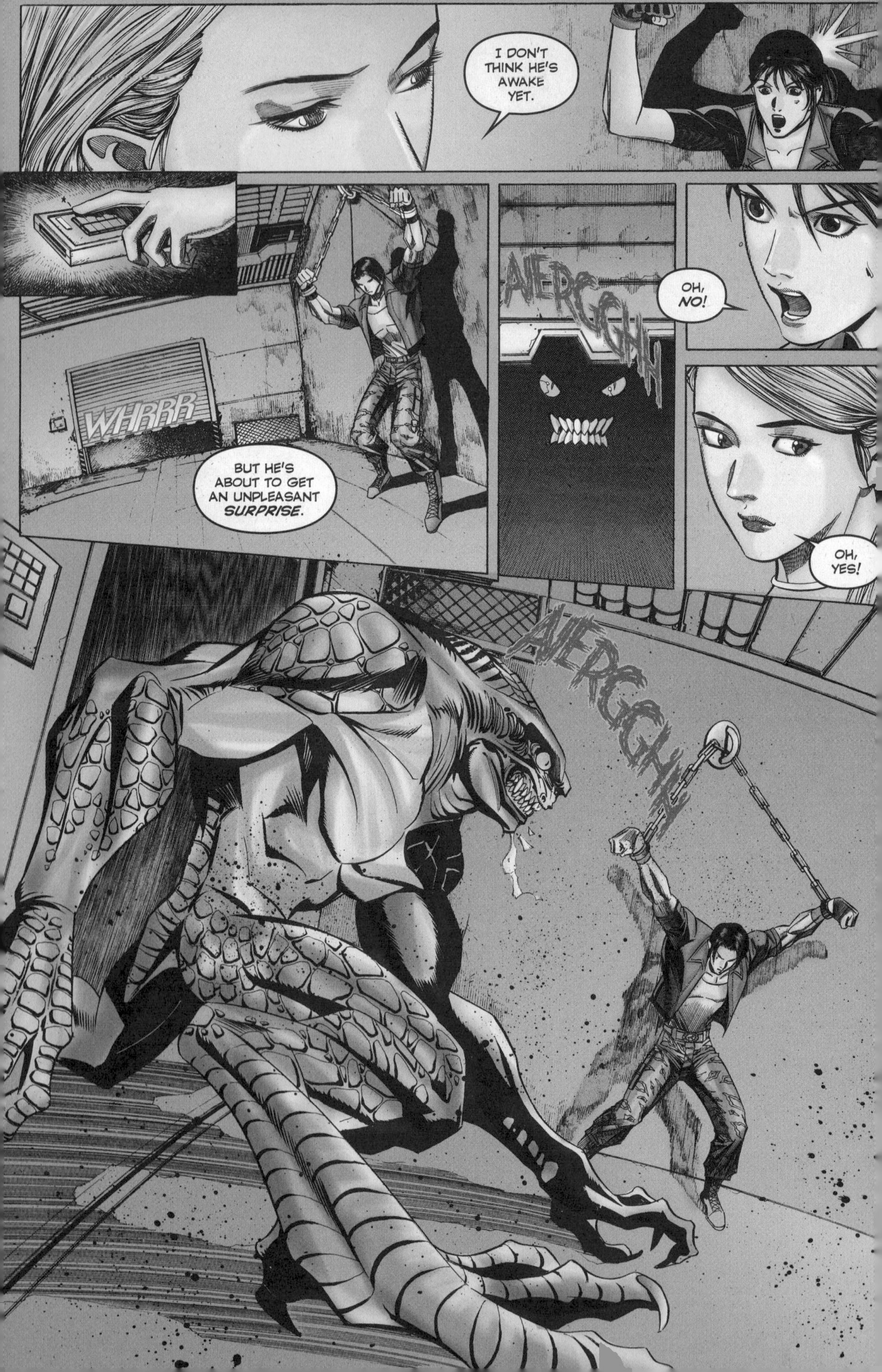

I DON'T THINK HE'S AWAKE YET.
WHRRR
BUT HE'S ABOUT TO GET AN UNPLEASANT SURPRISE.
AIERGGHH
OH, NO!
OH, YES!
AIERGGHH

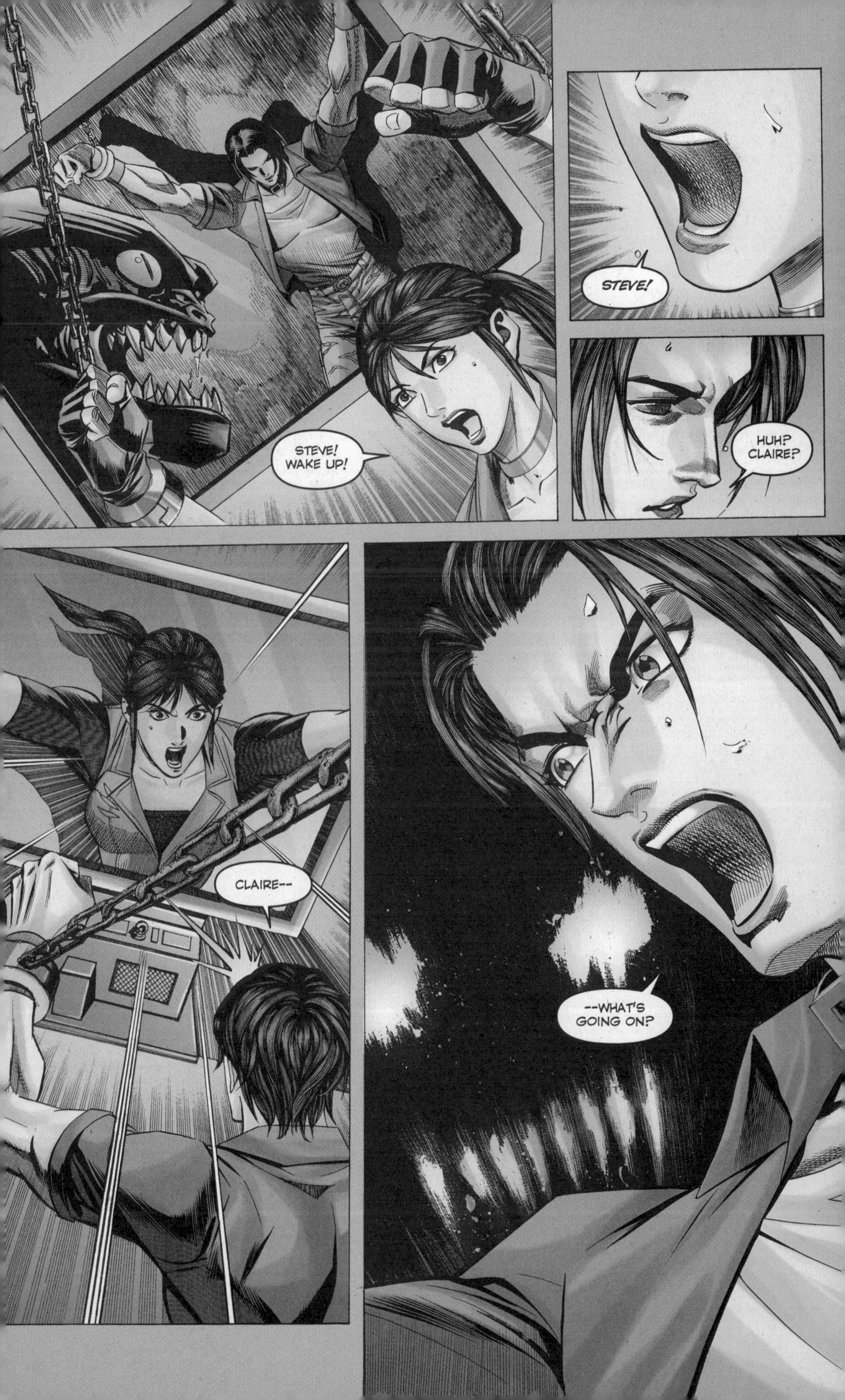
STEVE! WAKE UP!
STEVE!
HUH? CLAIRE?
CLAIRE--
--WHAT'S GOING ON?

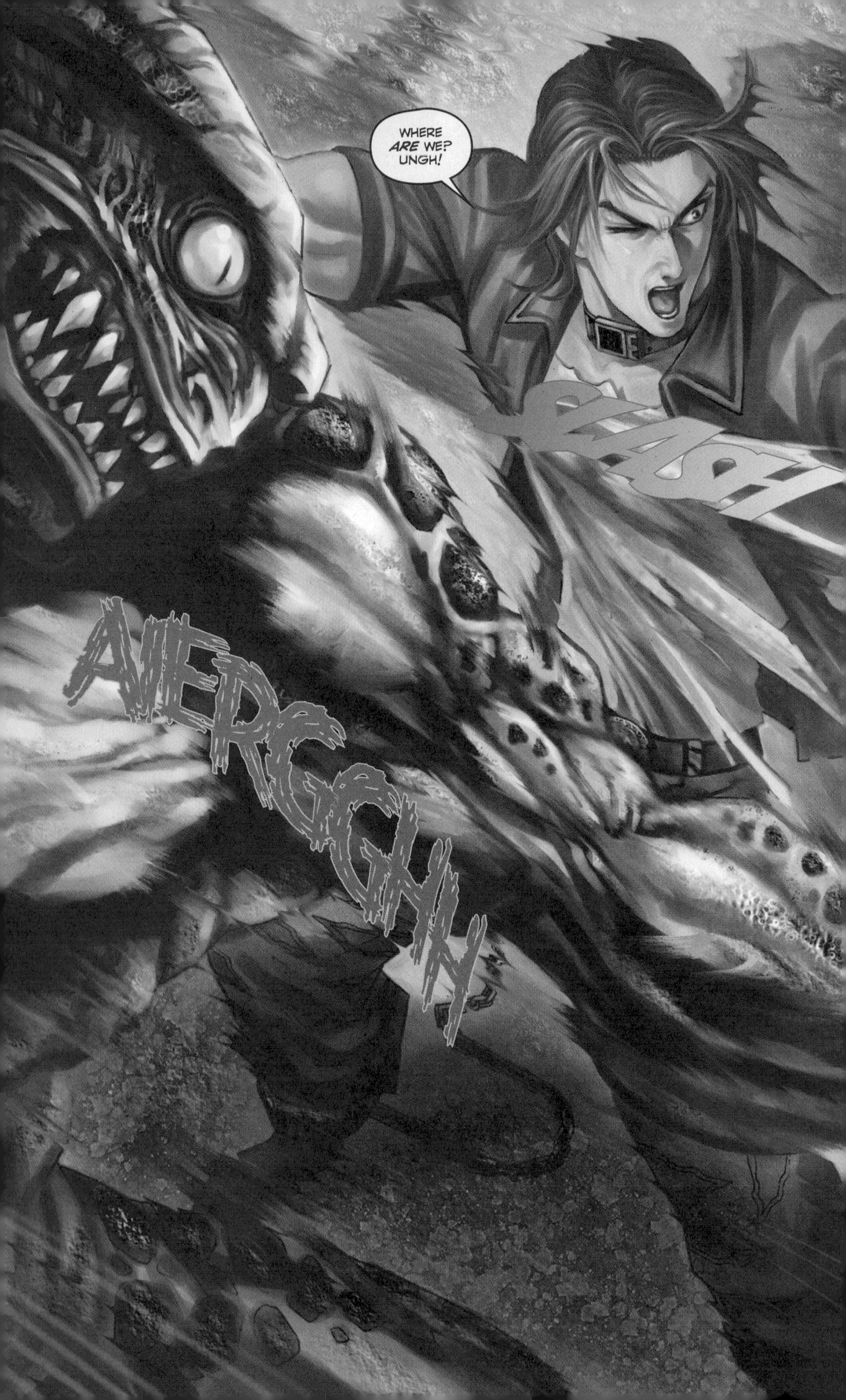
WHERE *ARE* WE? UNGH!
SLASH

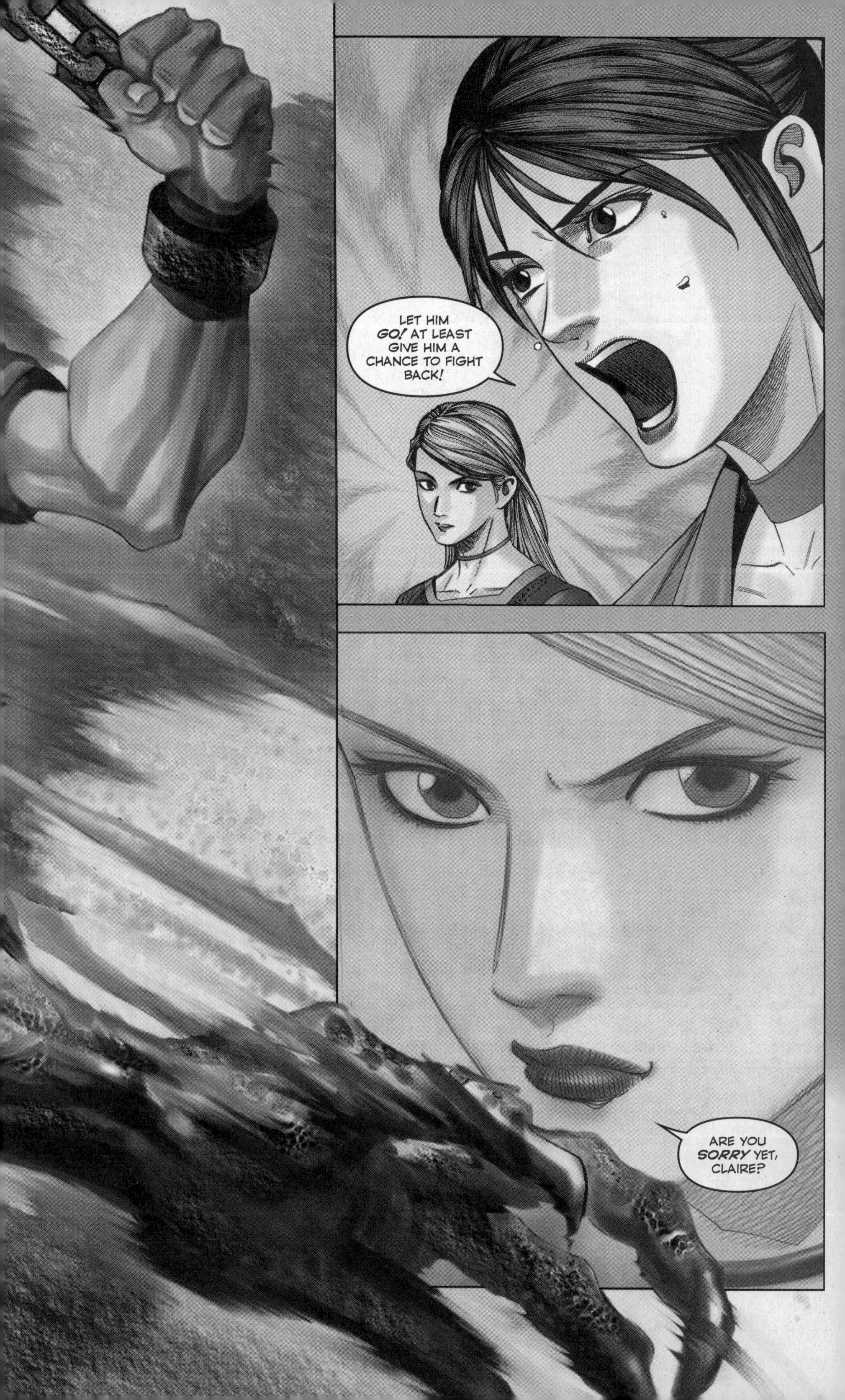
LET HIM GO! AT LEAST GIVE HIM A CHANCE TO FIGHT BACK!
ARE YOU SORRY YET, CLAIRE?

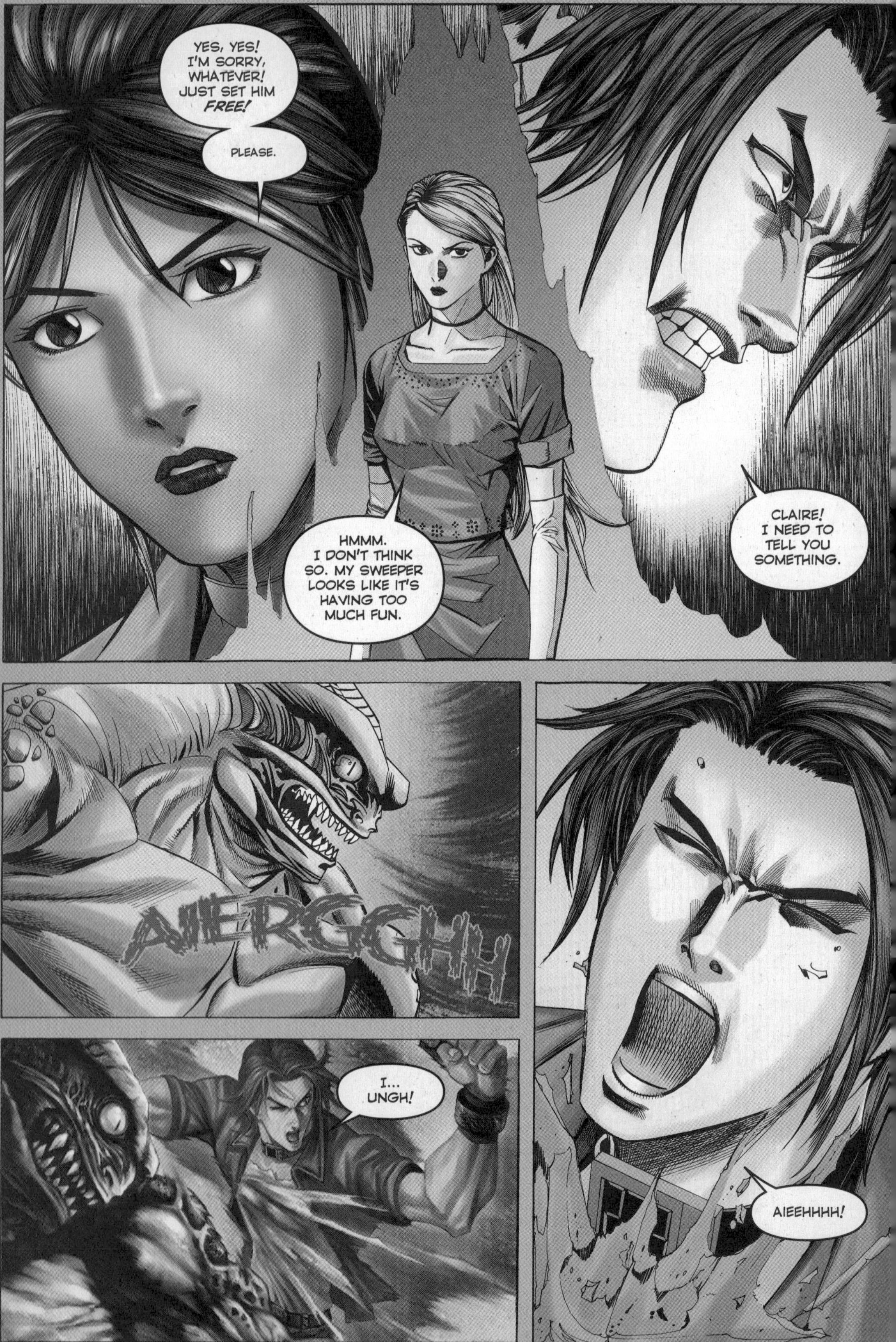
YES, YES! I'M SORRY, WHATEVER! JUST SET HIM *FREE!*
PLEASE.
HMMM. I DON'T THINK SO. MY SWEEPER LOOKS LIKE IT'S HAVING TOO MUCH FUN.
CLAIRE! I NEED TO TELL YOU SOMETHING.
AIERGHH
I... UNGH!
AIEEHHHH!

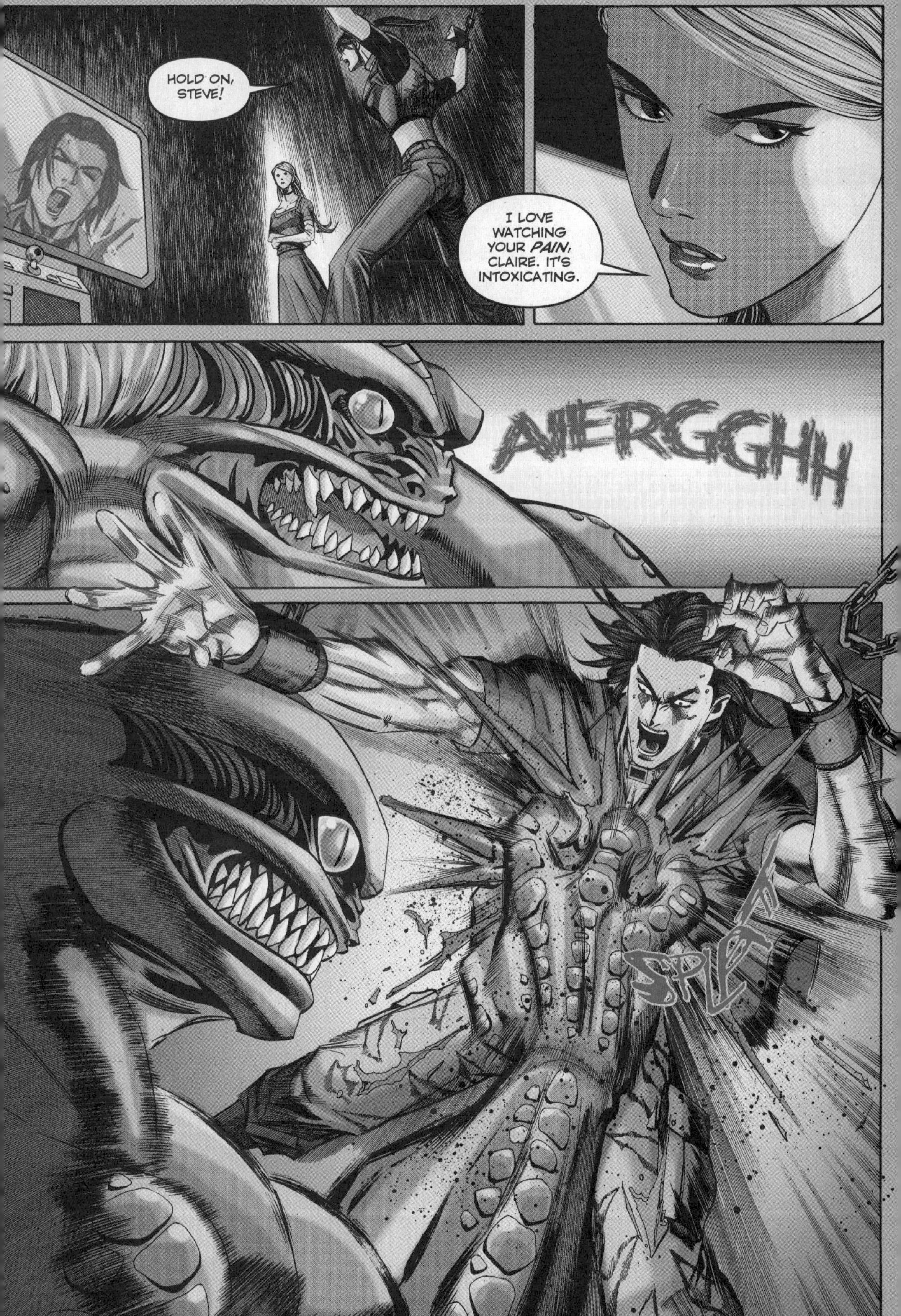
HOLD ON, STEVE!
I LOVE WATCHING YOUR *PAIN*, CLAIRE. IT'S INTOXICATING.
AIERGGHH
SPLAT

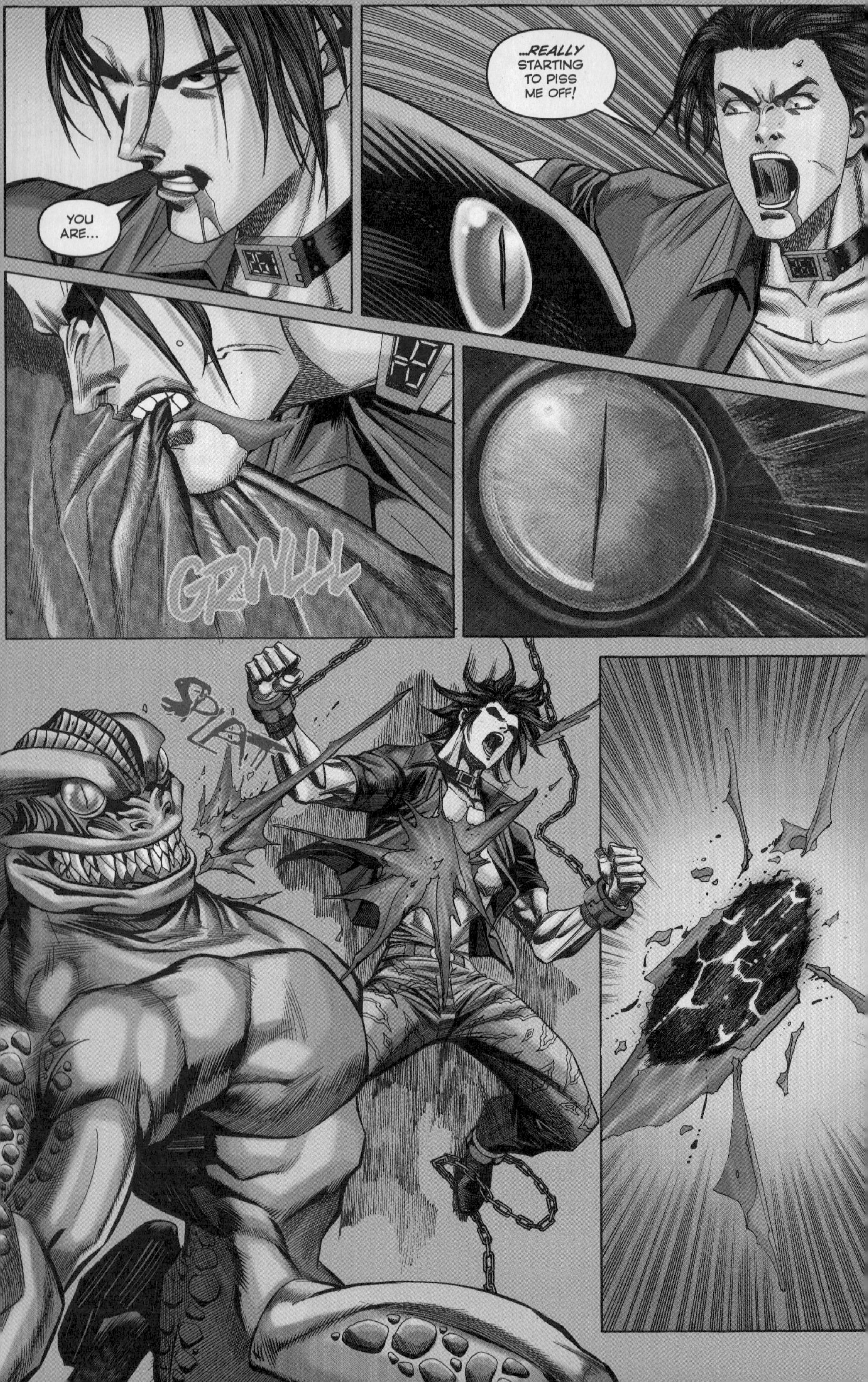
YOU ARE...
...REALLY STARTING TO PISS ME OFF!
GRWLLL
SPLAT

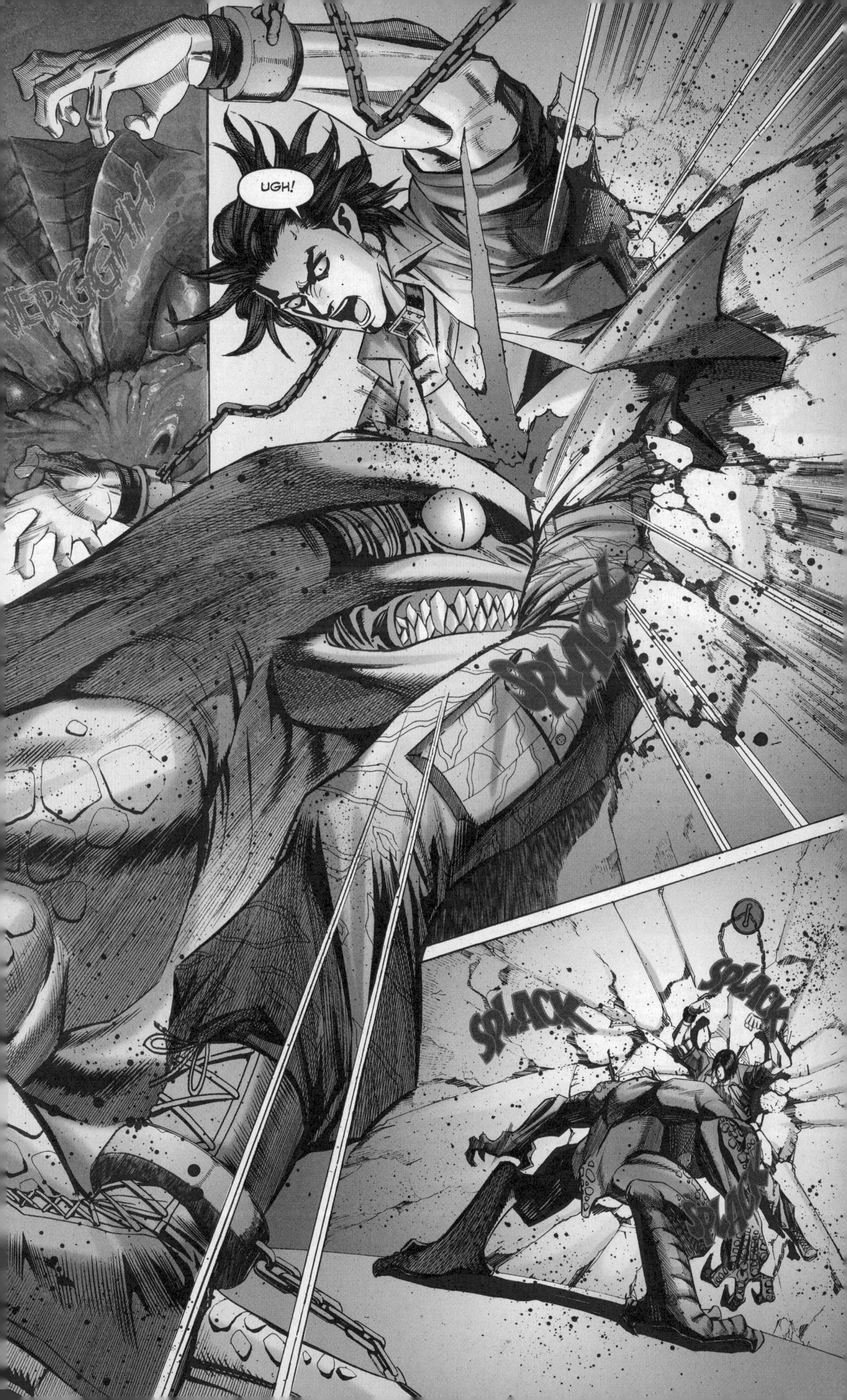

ERGGHH
UGH!
SPLACK
SPLACK
SPLACK
SPLACK

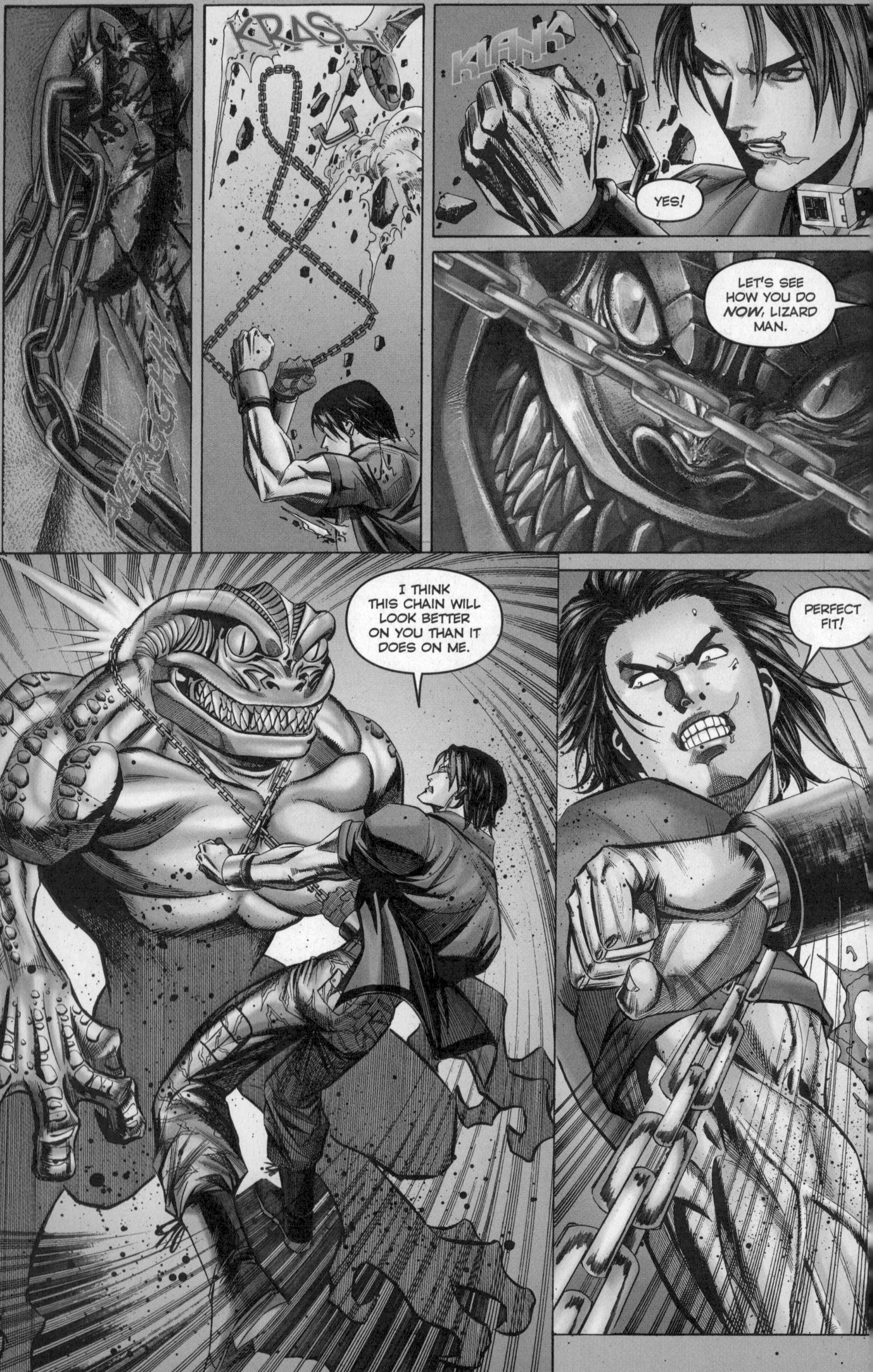
KRASH
KLANK
YES!
LET'S SEE HOW YOU DO *NOW*, LIZARD MAN.
I THINK THIS CHAIN WILL LOOK BETTER ON YOU THAN IT DOES ON ME.
PERFECT FIT!

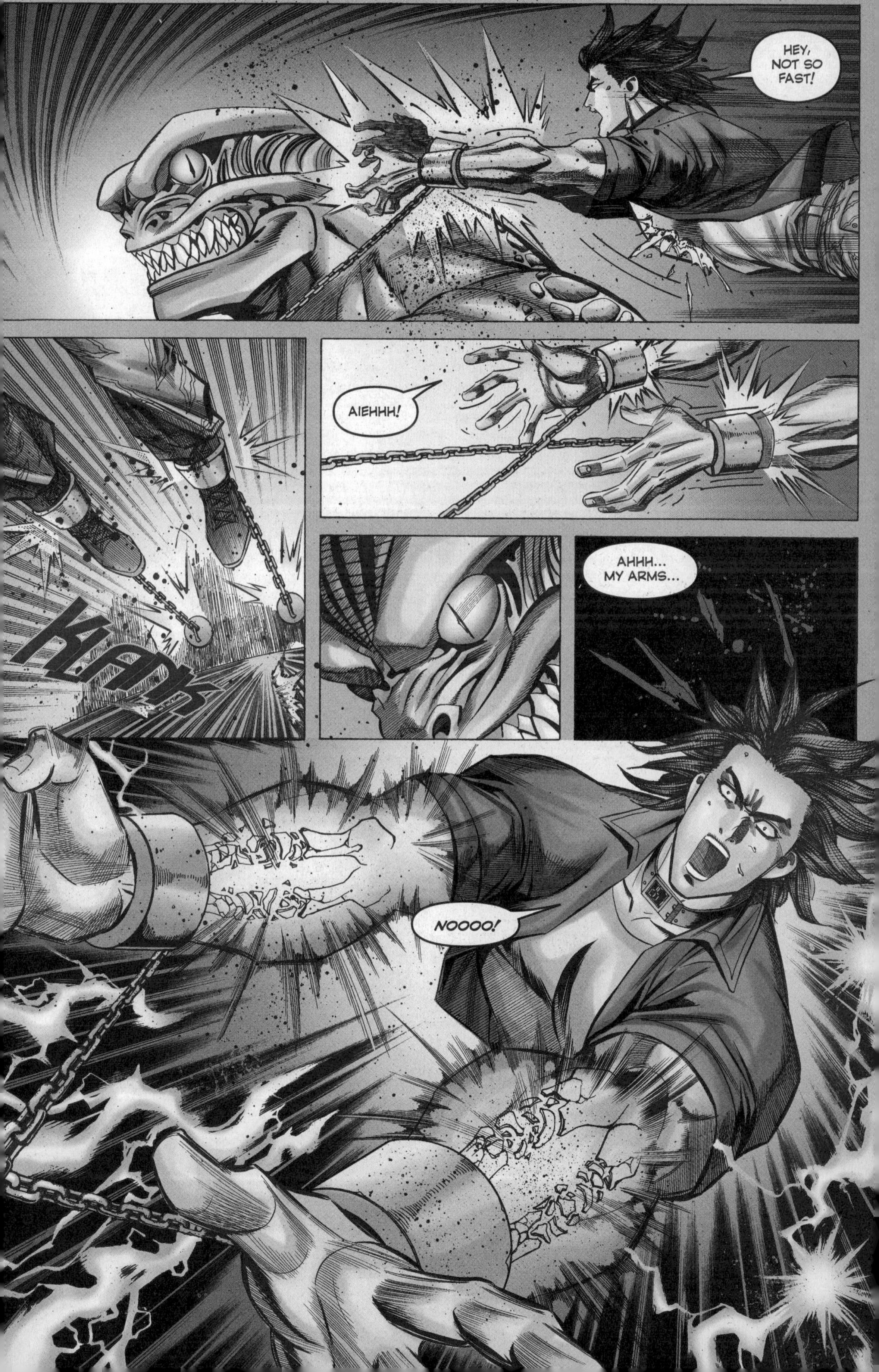
HEY, NOT SO FAST!
AIEHHH!
KRAK
AHHH... MY ARMS...
NOOOO!

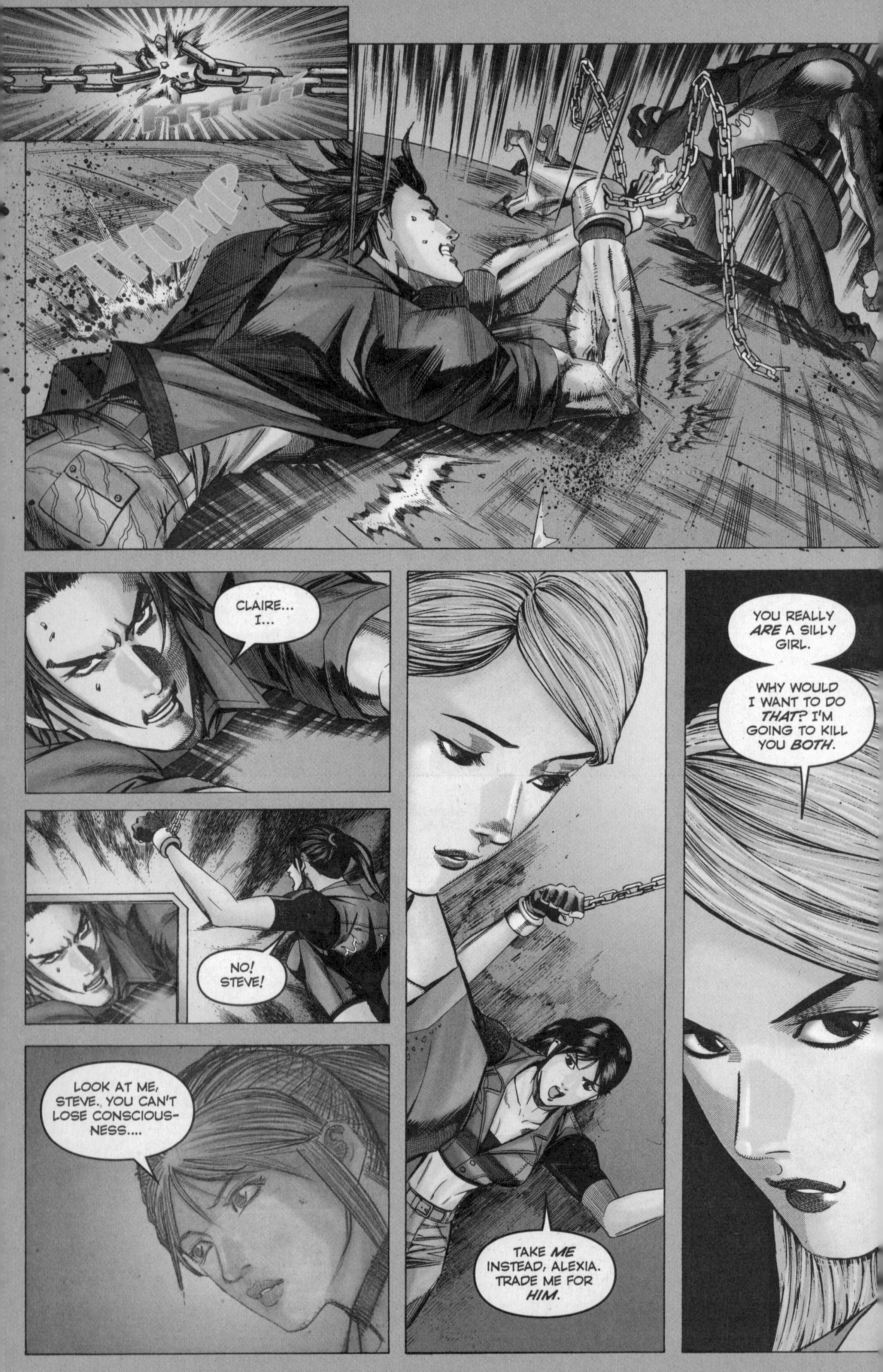
THUMP
CLAIRE... I...
NO! STEVE!
LOOK AT ME, STEVE.. YOU CAN'T LOSE CONSCIOUS-NESS....
TAKE *ME* INSTEAD, ALEXIA. TRADE ME FOR *HIM*.
YOU REALLY *ARE* A SILLY GIRL.
WHY WOULD I WANT TO DO *THAT*? I'M GOING TO KILL YOU *BOTH*.

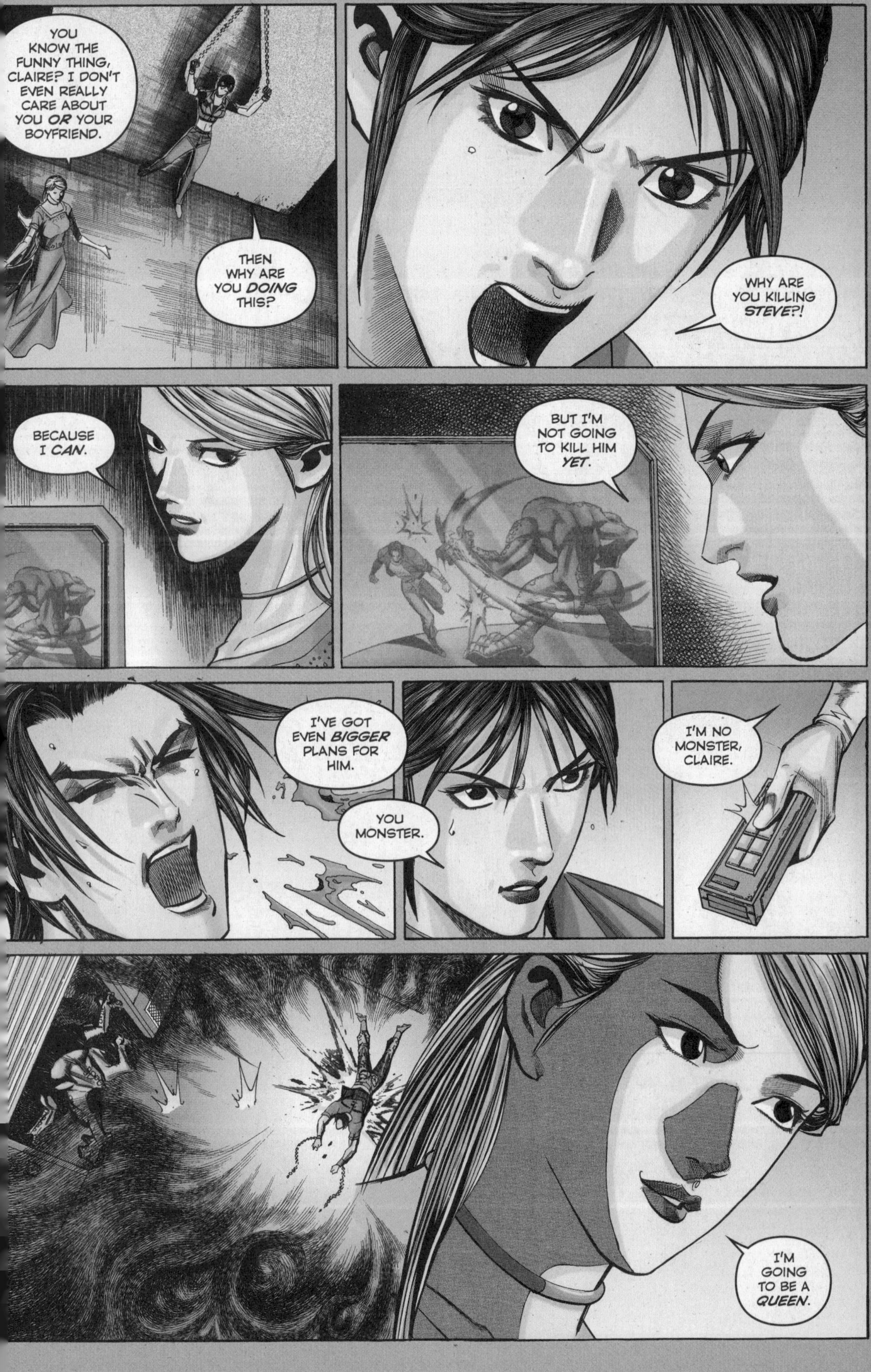
YOU KNOW THE FUNNY THING, CLAIRE? I DON'T EVEN REALLY CARE ABOUT YOU *OR* YOUR BOYFRIEND.
THEN WHY ARE YOU *DOING* THIS?
WHY ARE YOU KILLING *STEVE*?!
BECAUSE I *CAN*.
BUT I'M NOT GOING TO KILL HIM *YET*.
I'VE GOT EVEN *BIGGER* PLANS FOR HIM.
YOU MONSTER.
I'M NO MONSTER, CLAIRE.
I'M GOING TO BE A *QUEEN*.

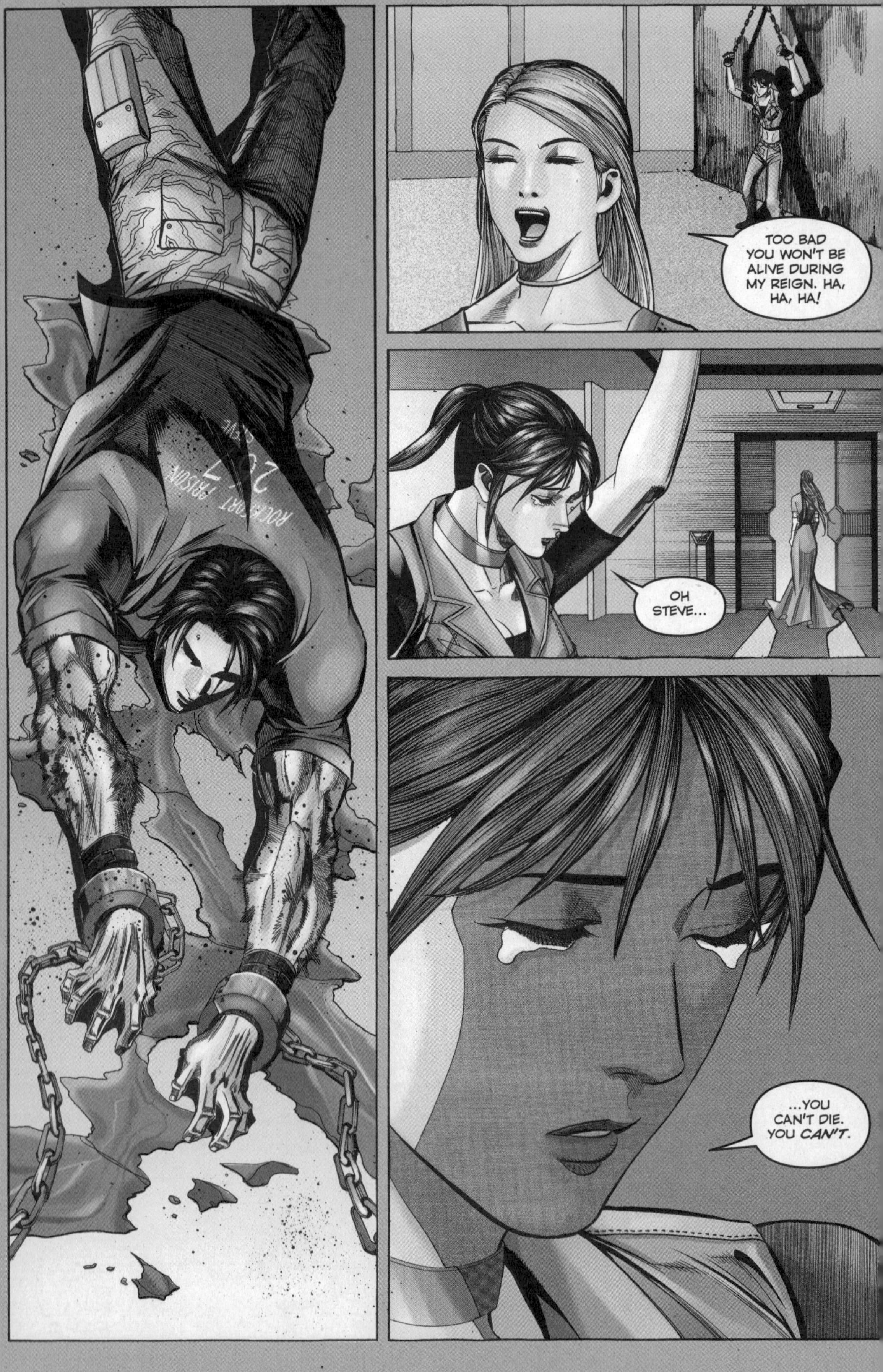
TOO BAD YOU WON'T BE ALIVE DURING MY REIGN. HA, HA, HA!
OH STEVE...
...YOU CAN'T DIE. YOU *CAN'T*.

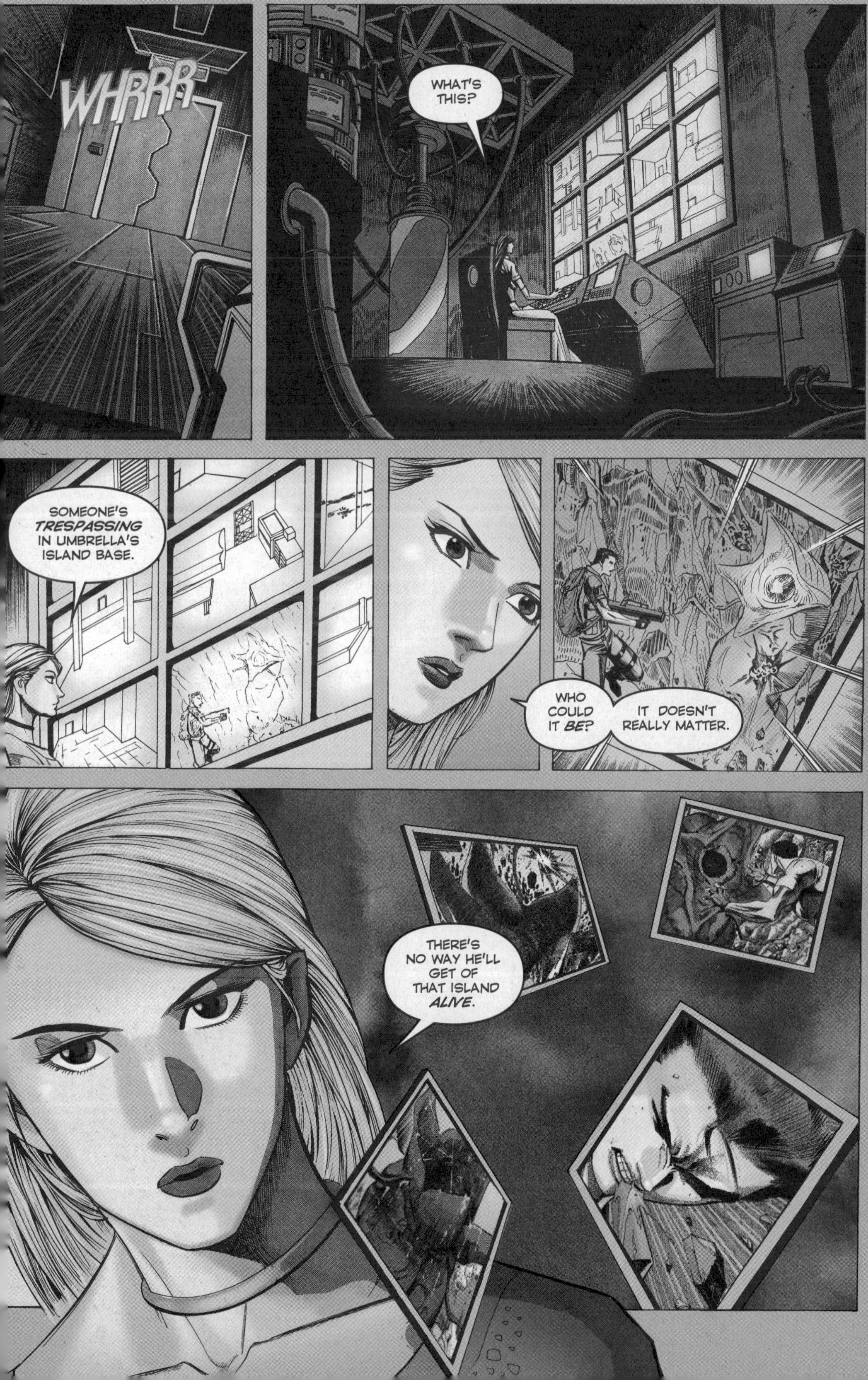
WHRRR
WHAT'S THIS?
SOMEONE'S TRESPASSING IN UMBRELLA'S ISLAND BASE.
WHO COULD IT BE?
IT DOESN'T REALLY MATTER.
THERE'S NO WAY HE'LL GET OF THAT ISLAND ALIVE.

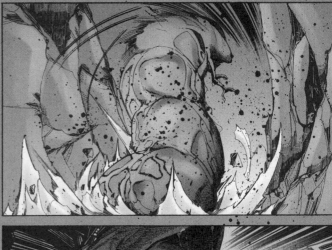

WHILE ALEXIA WATCHES ON HER VIDEO MONITOR, CHRIS MAKES A DRAMATIC EXIT.

BLAM

SPLAT

GROSS, BUT *EFFECTIVE!*

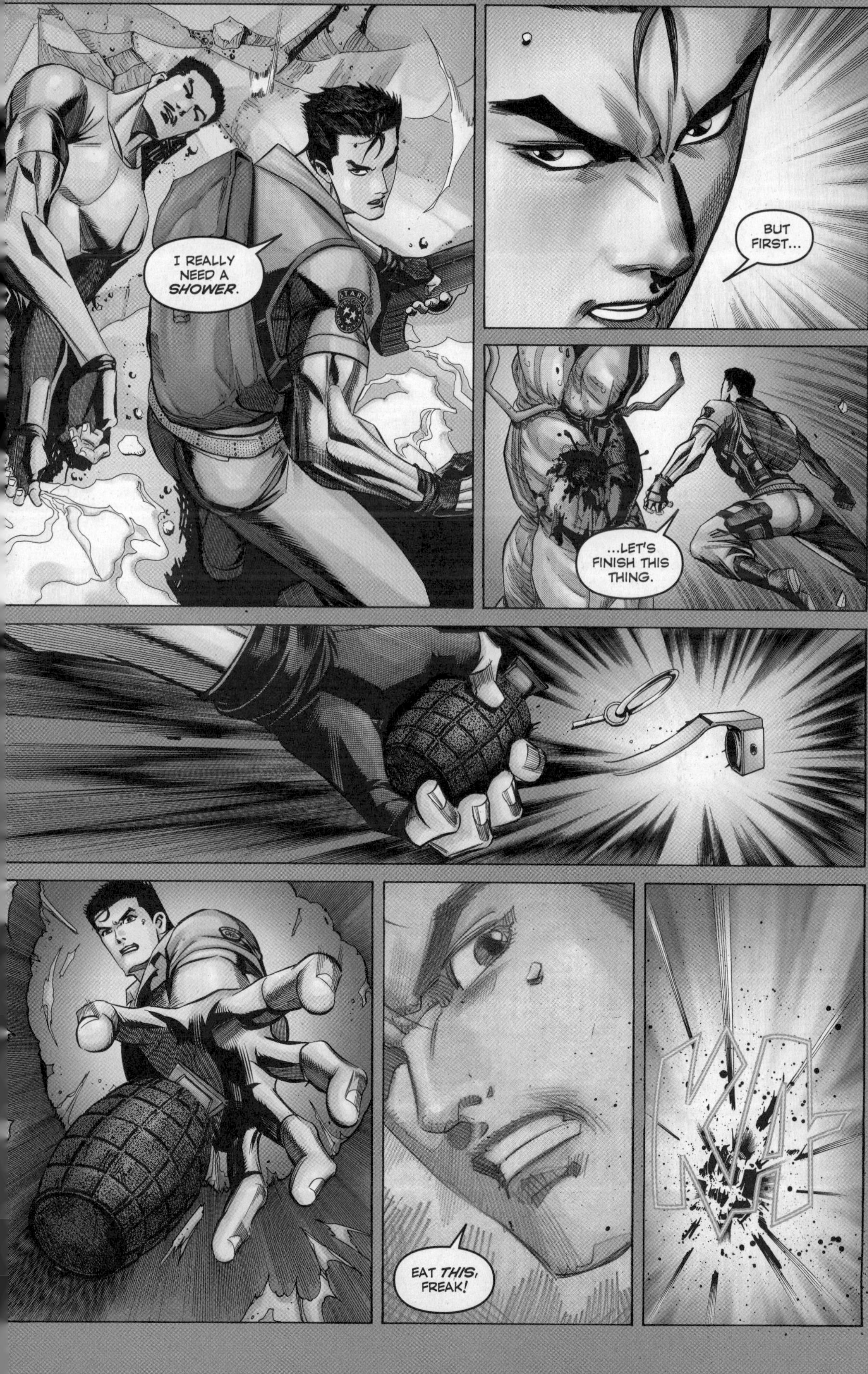
I REALLY NEED A *SHOWER*.
BUT FIRST...
...LET'S FINISH THIS THING.
EAT *THIS*, FREAK!

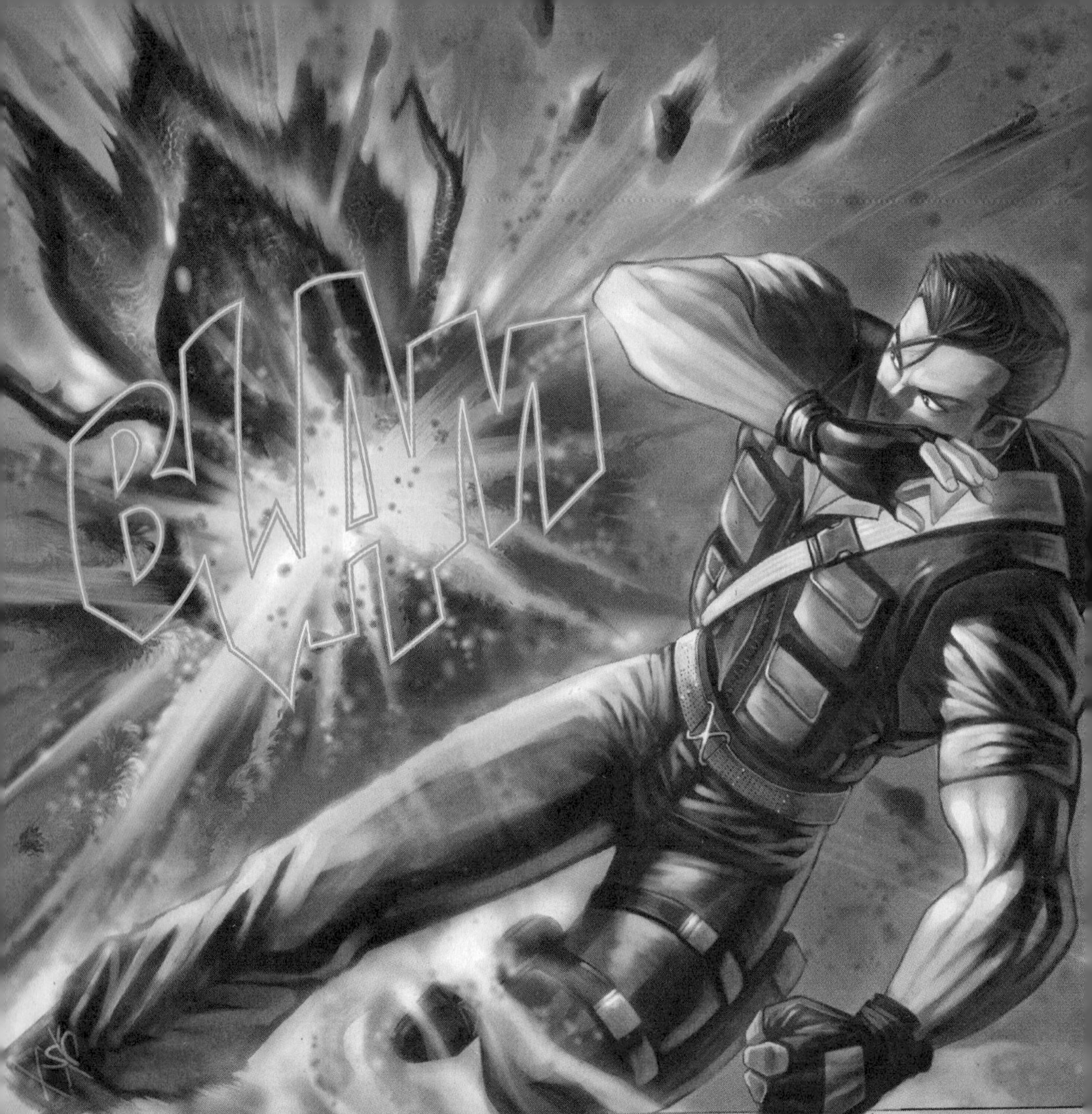
BWM

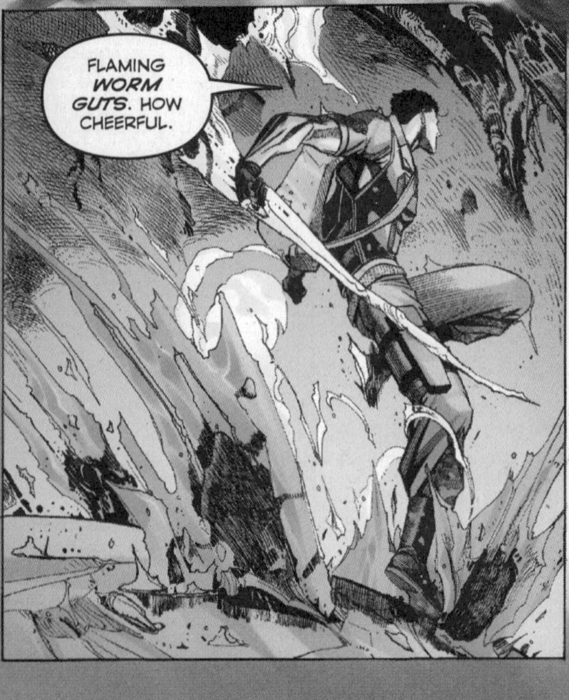
FLAMING WORM GUTS. HOW CHEERFUL.

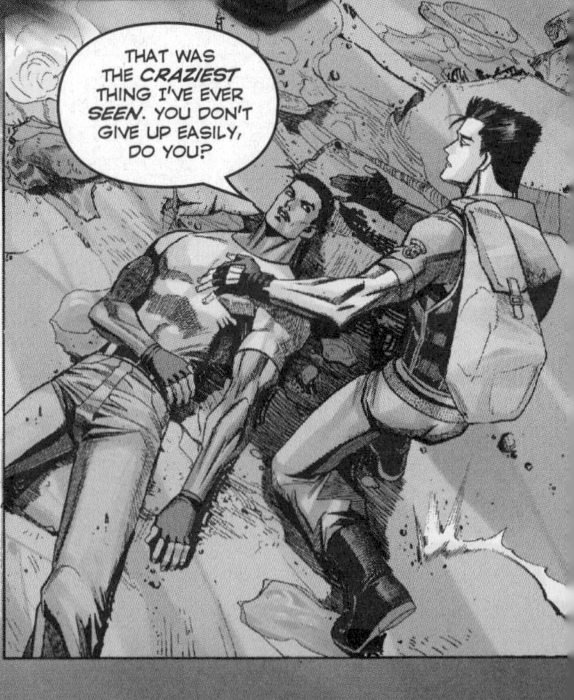
THAT WAS THE CRAZIEST THING I'VE EVER SEEN. YOU DON'T GIVE UP EASILY, DO YOU?

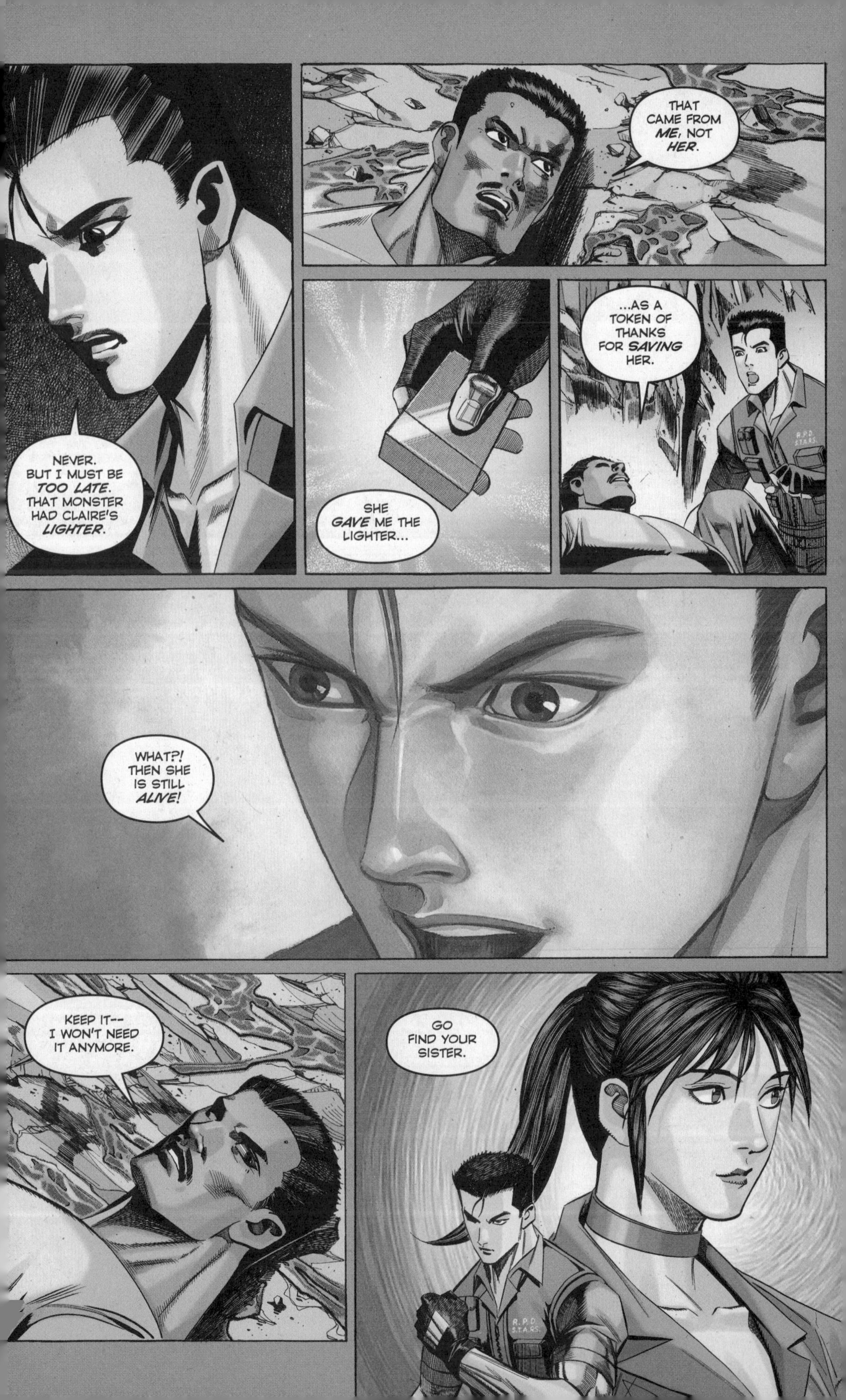
NEVER. BUT I MUST BE TOO LATE. THAT MONSTER HAD CLAIRE'S LIGHTER.
THAT CAME FROM ME, NOT HER.
SHE GAVE ME THE LIGHTER...
...AS A TOKEN OF THANKS FOR SAVING HER.
R.P.D. S.T.A.R.S.
WHAT?! THEN SHE IS STILL ALIVE!
KEEP IT-- I WON'T NEED IT ANYMORE.
GO FIND YOUR SISTER.
R.P.D. S.T.A.R.S.

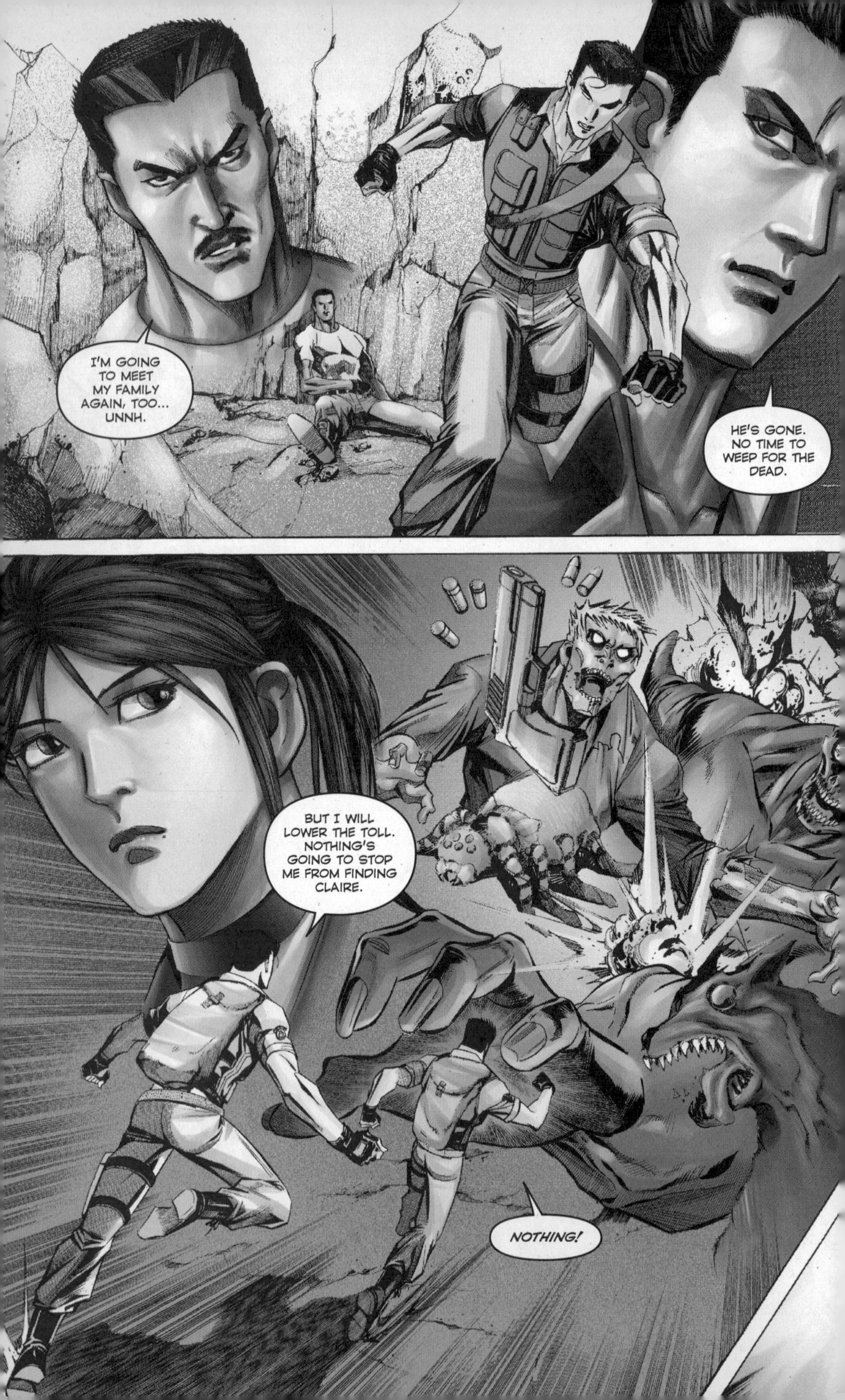
I'M GOING TO MEET MY FAMILY AGAIN, TOO... UNNH.
HE'S GONE. NO TIME TO WEEP FOR THE DEAD.
BUT I WILL LOWER THE TOLL. NOTHING'S GOING TO STOP ME FROM FINDING CLAIRE.
NOTHING!

AS CHRIS CONTINUES HIS SEARCH...

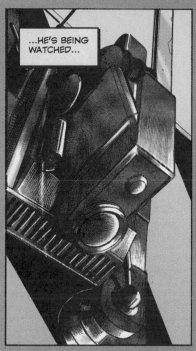

...HE'S BEING WATCHED...

...BY A PERSON HE THOUGHT WAS *DEAD*.

CHRIS REDFIELD. YOU'RE *HERE*. WHAT A PLEASANT *SURPRISE*.

I'M GOING TO SEND SOME COMPANY TO KEEP YOU ENTERTAINED.

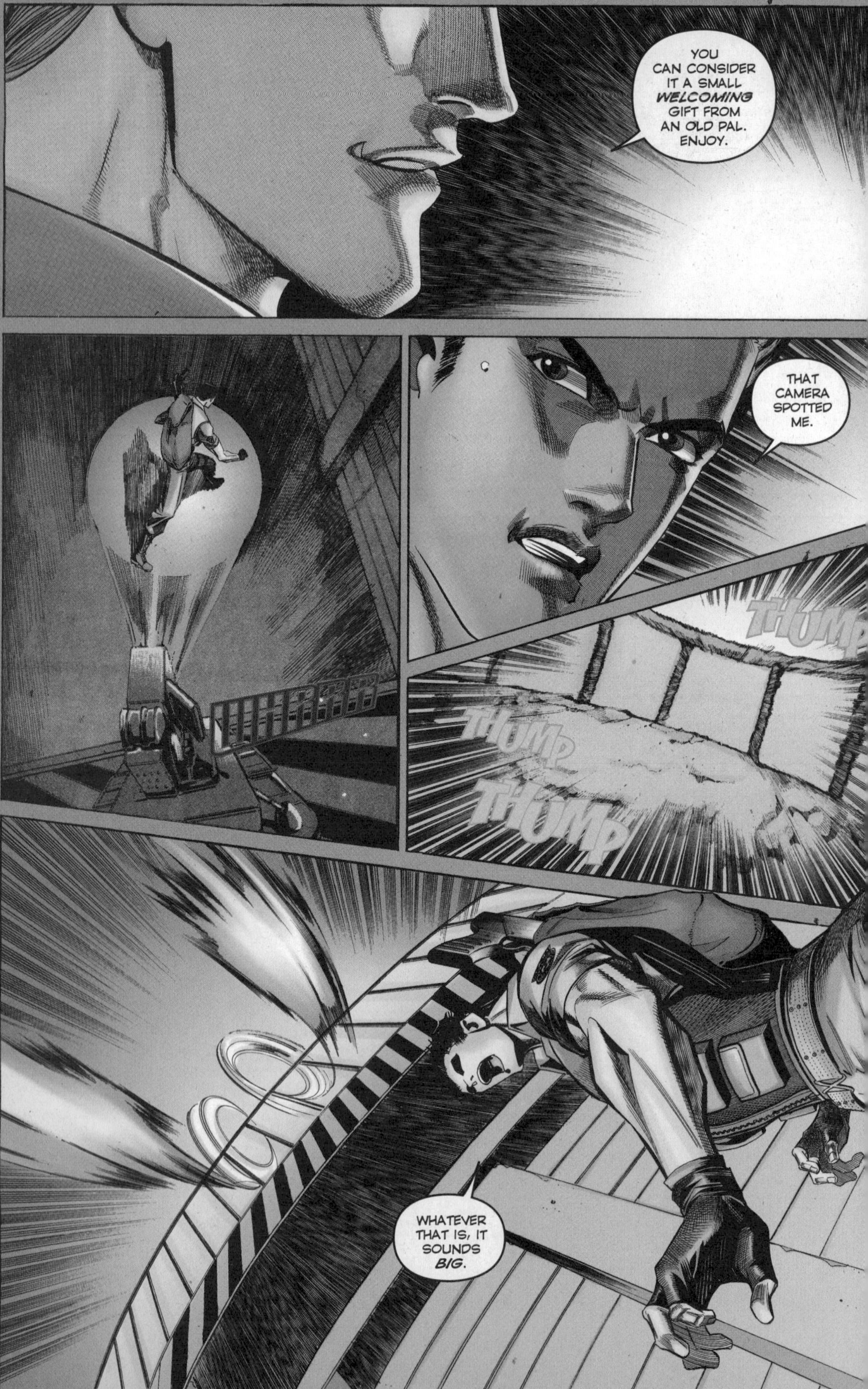
YOU CAN CONSIDER IT A SMALL WELCOMING GIFT FROM AN OLD PAL. ENJOY.
THAT CAMERA SPOTTED ME.
THUMP
THUMP
THUMP
WHATEVER THAT IS, IT SOUNDS BIG.

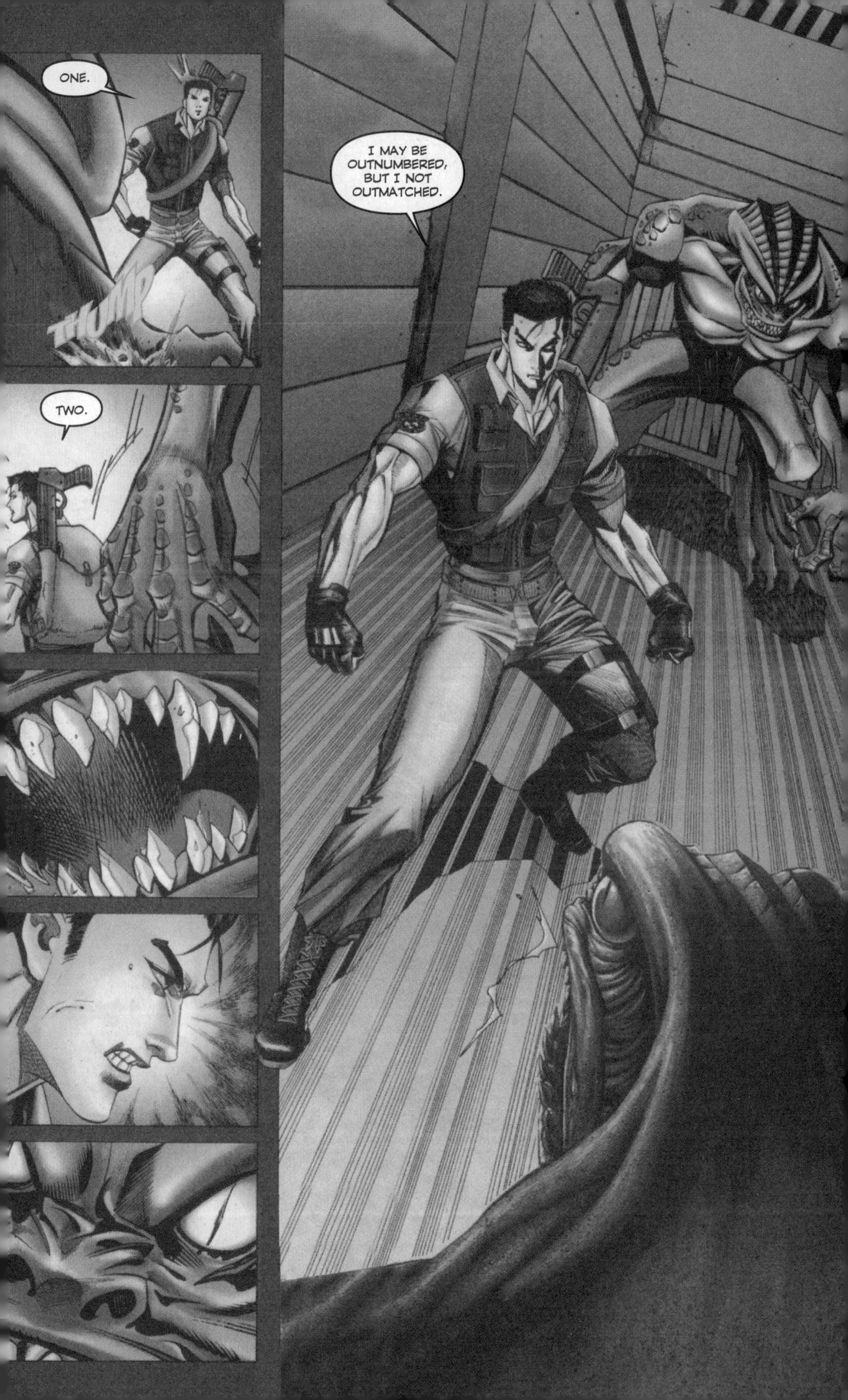
ONE.
THUMP
TWO.
I MAY BE OUTNUMBERED, BUT I NOT OUTMATCHED.

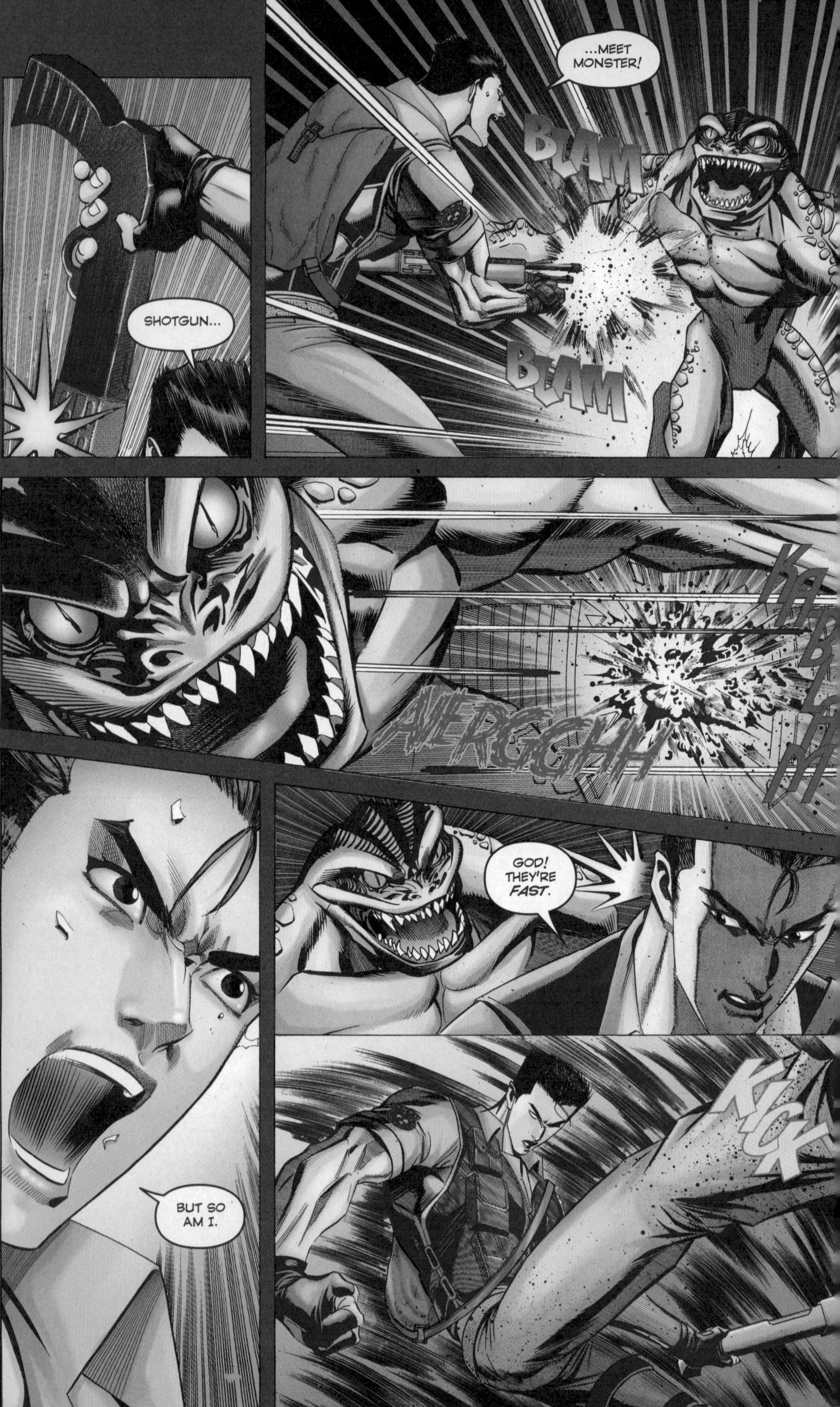
SHOTGUN...
...MEET
MONSTER!
BLAM
BLAM
AIERGGHH
KABLAM
GOD!
THEY'RE
FAST.
BUT SO
AM I.
KICK

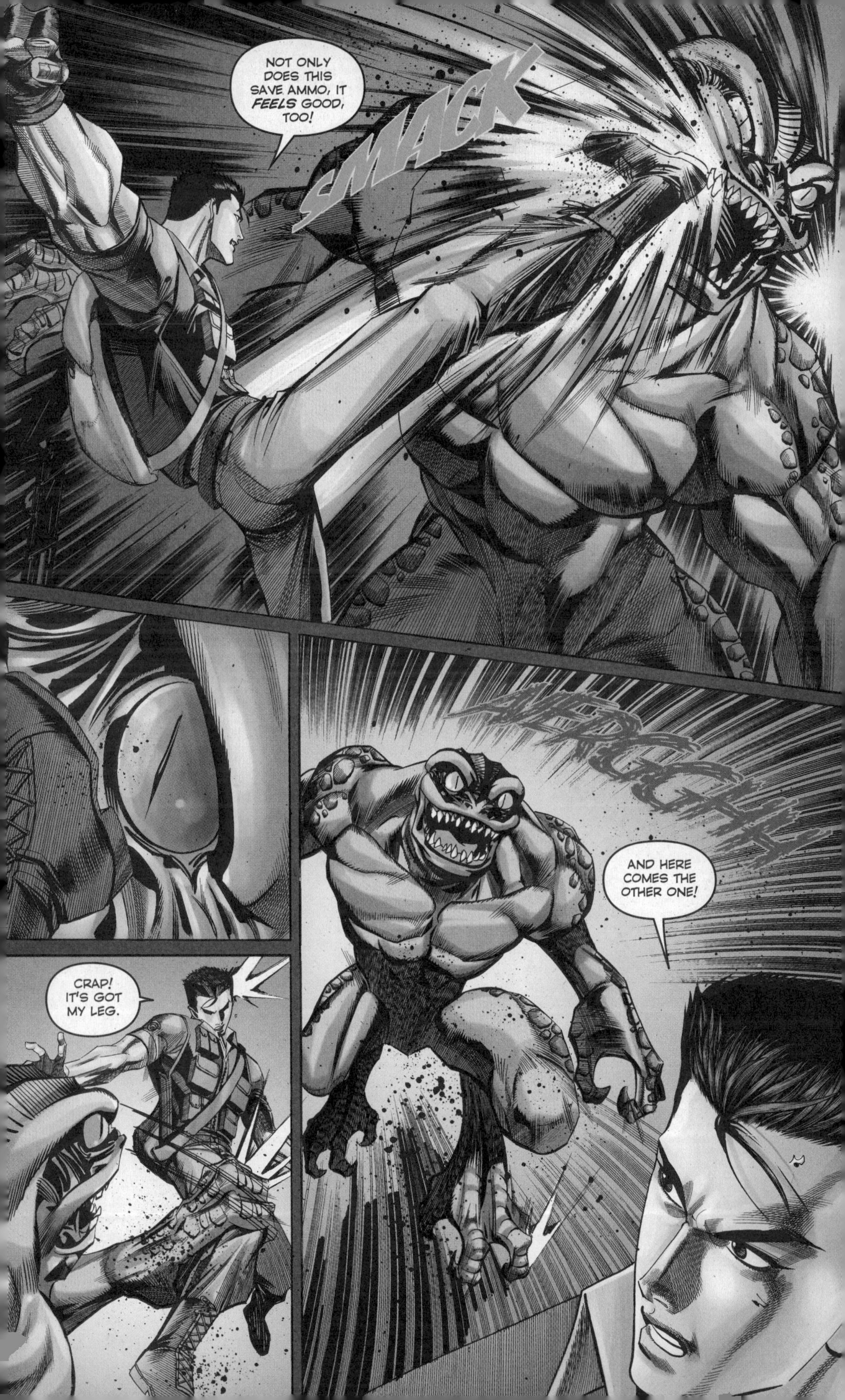
NOT ONLY DOES THIS SAVE AMMO, IT *FEELS* GOOD, TOO!
SMACK
CRAP! IT'S GOT MY LEG.
AND HERE COMES THE OTHER ONE!

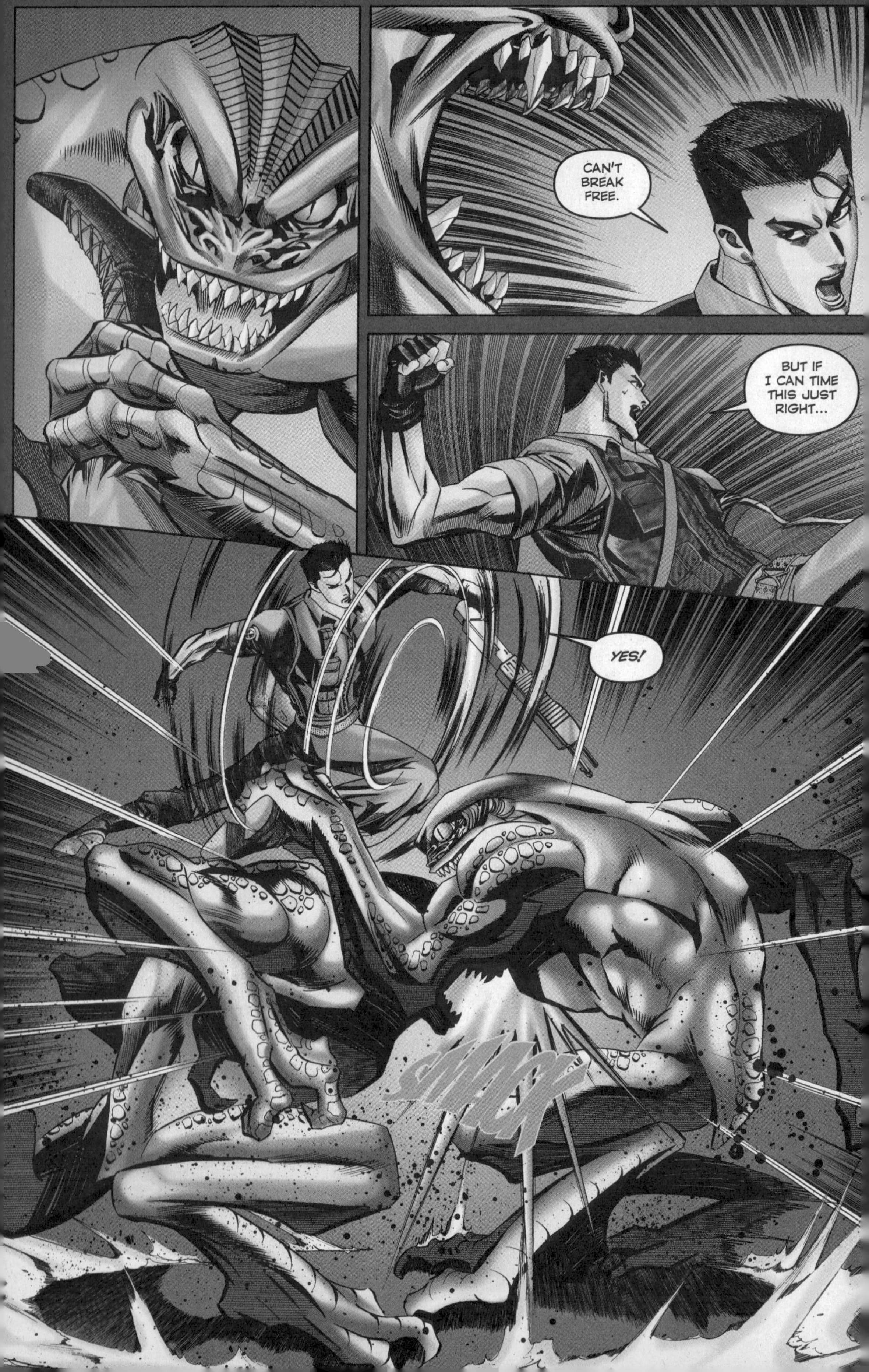
CAN'T BREAK FREE.
BUT IF I CAN TIME THIS JUST RIGHT...
YES!
SMACK

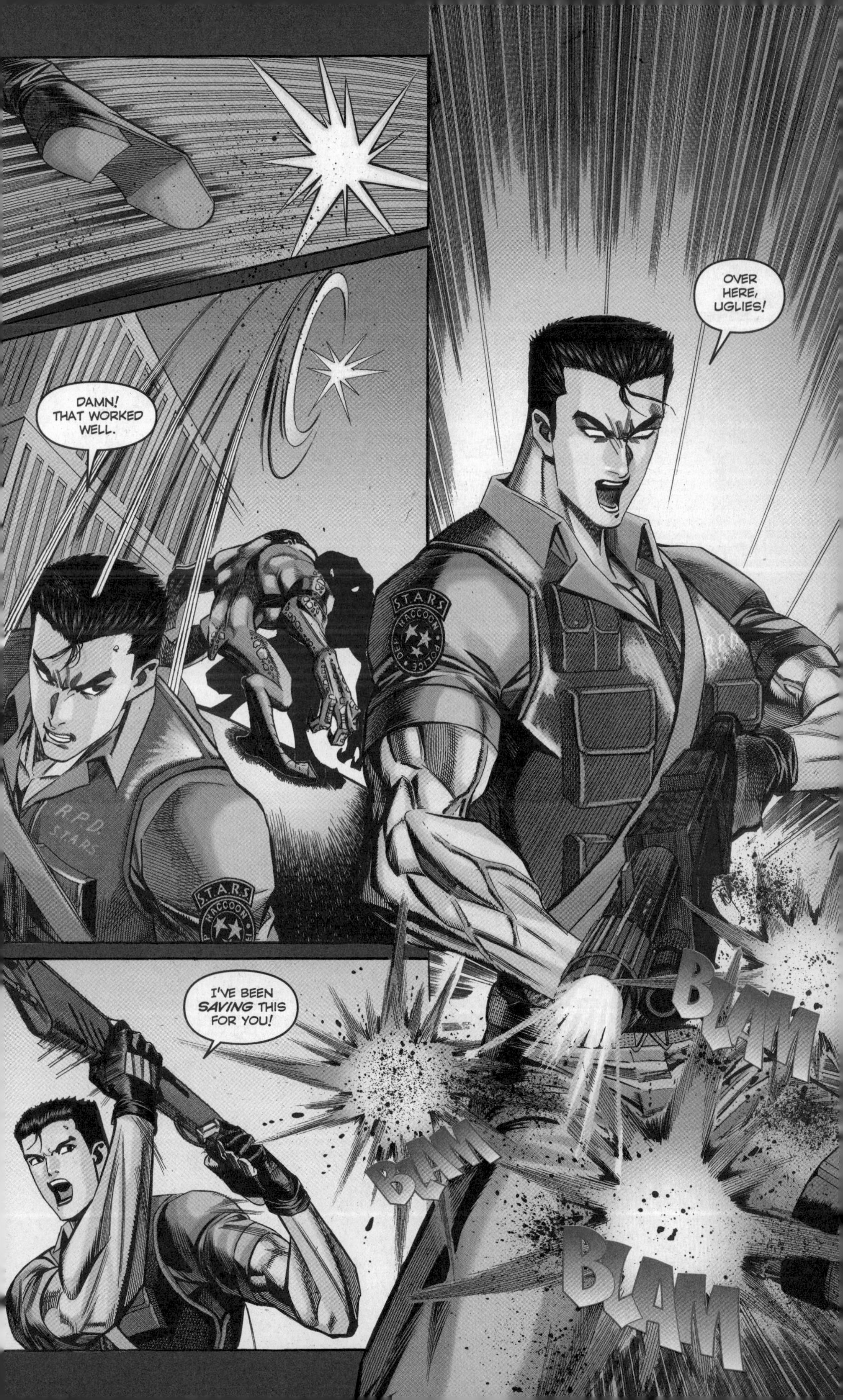

DAMN! THAT WORKED WELL.
OVER HERE, UGLIES!
S.T.A.R.S. RACCOON POLICE DEPT.
R.P.D. S.T.A.R.S.
I'VE BEEN *SAVING* THIS FOR YOU!
BLAM
BLAM
BLAM

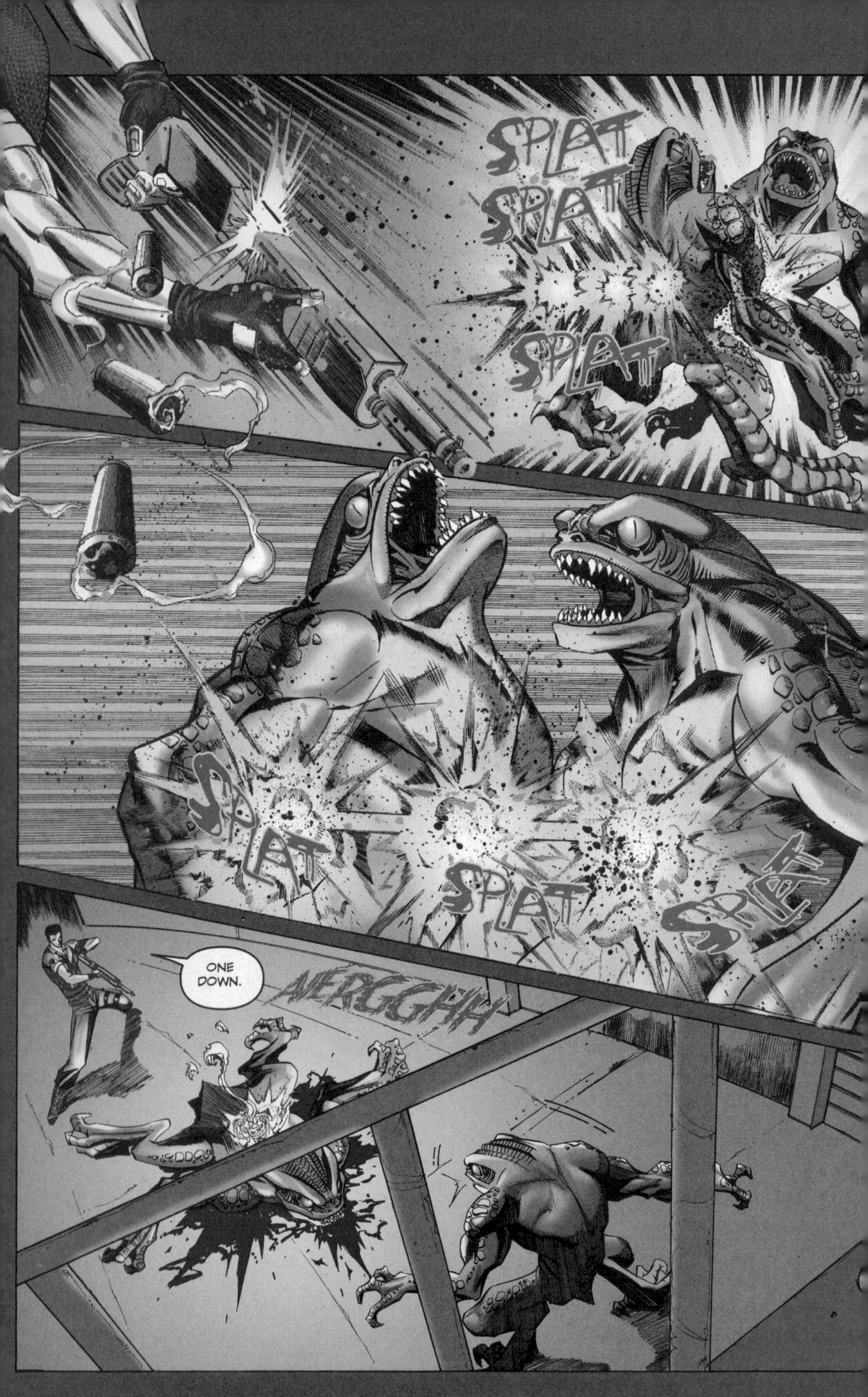
SPLAT
SPLAT
SPLAT
SPLAT
SPLAT
SPLAT
ONE DOWN.
AERGGHH
!!

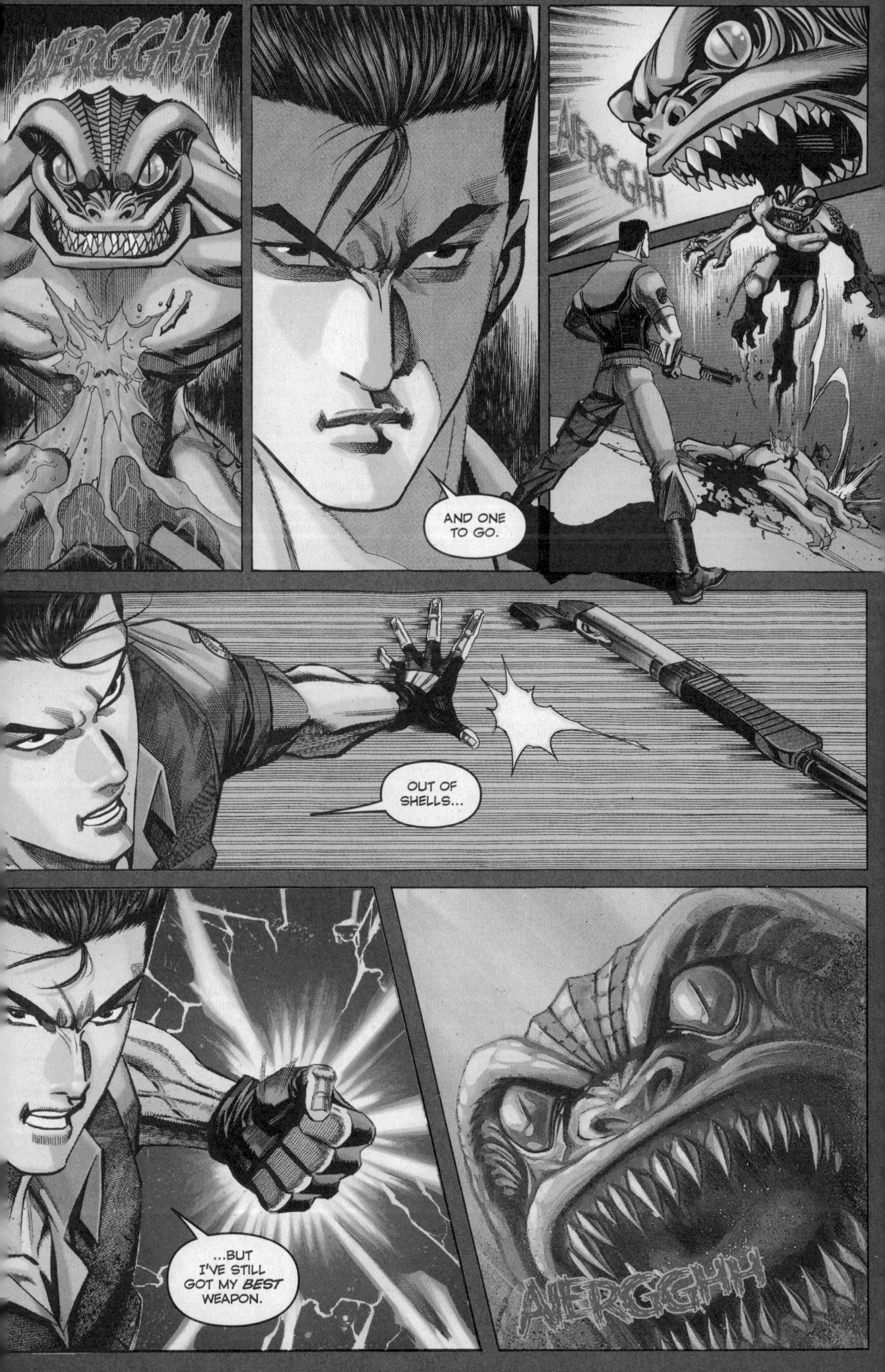
AERGGHH
AERGGHH
AND ONE TO GO.
OUT OF SHELLS...
...BUT I'VE STILL GOT MY *BEST* WEAPON.
AERGGHH

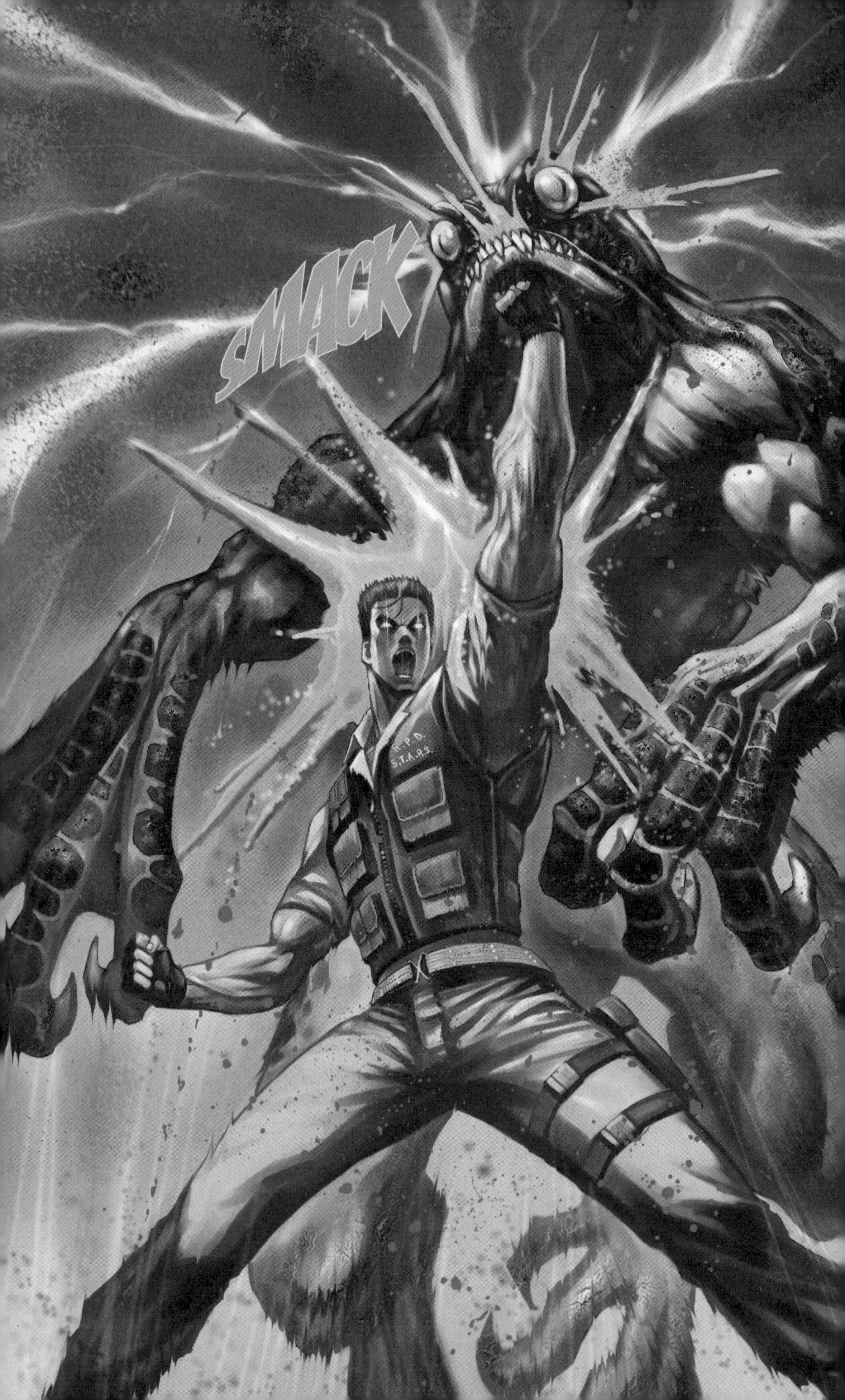
SMACK

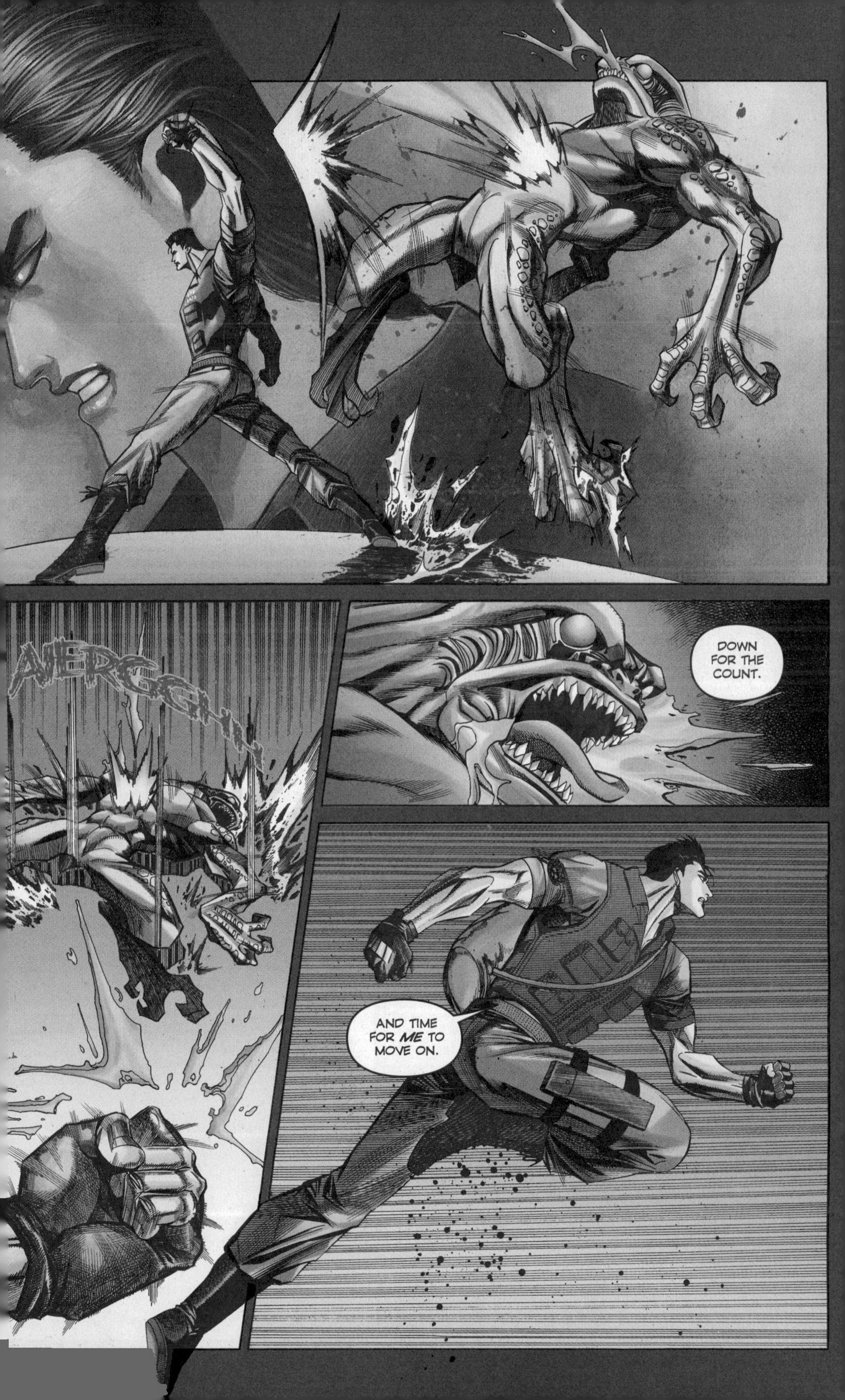
AIERGGHHH
DOWN FOR THE COUNT.
AND TIME FOR *ME* TO MOVE ON.

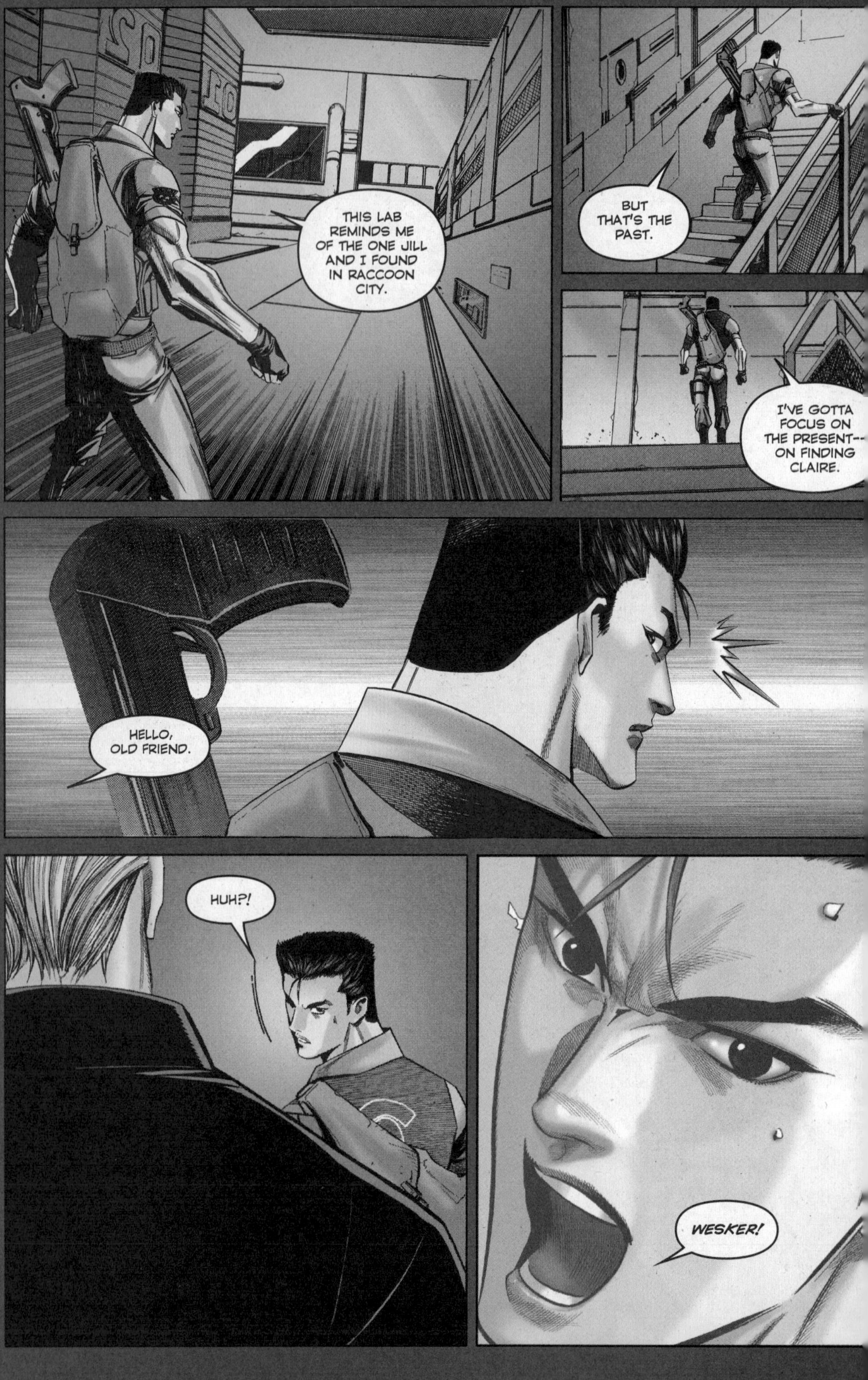
THIS LAB REMINDS ME OF THE ONE JILL AND I FOUND IN RACCOON CITY.
BUT THAT'S THE PAST.
I'VE GOTTA FOCUS ON THE PRESENT-- ON FINDING CLAIRE.
HELLO, OLD FRIEND.
HUH?!
WESKER!

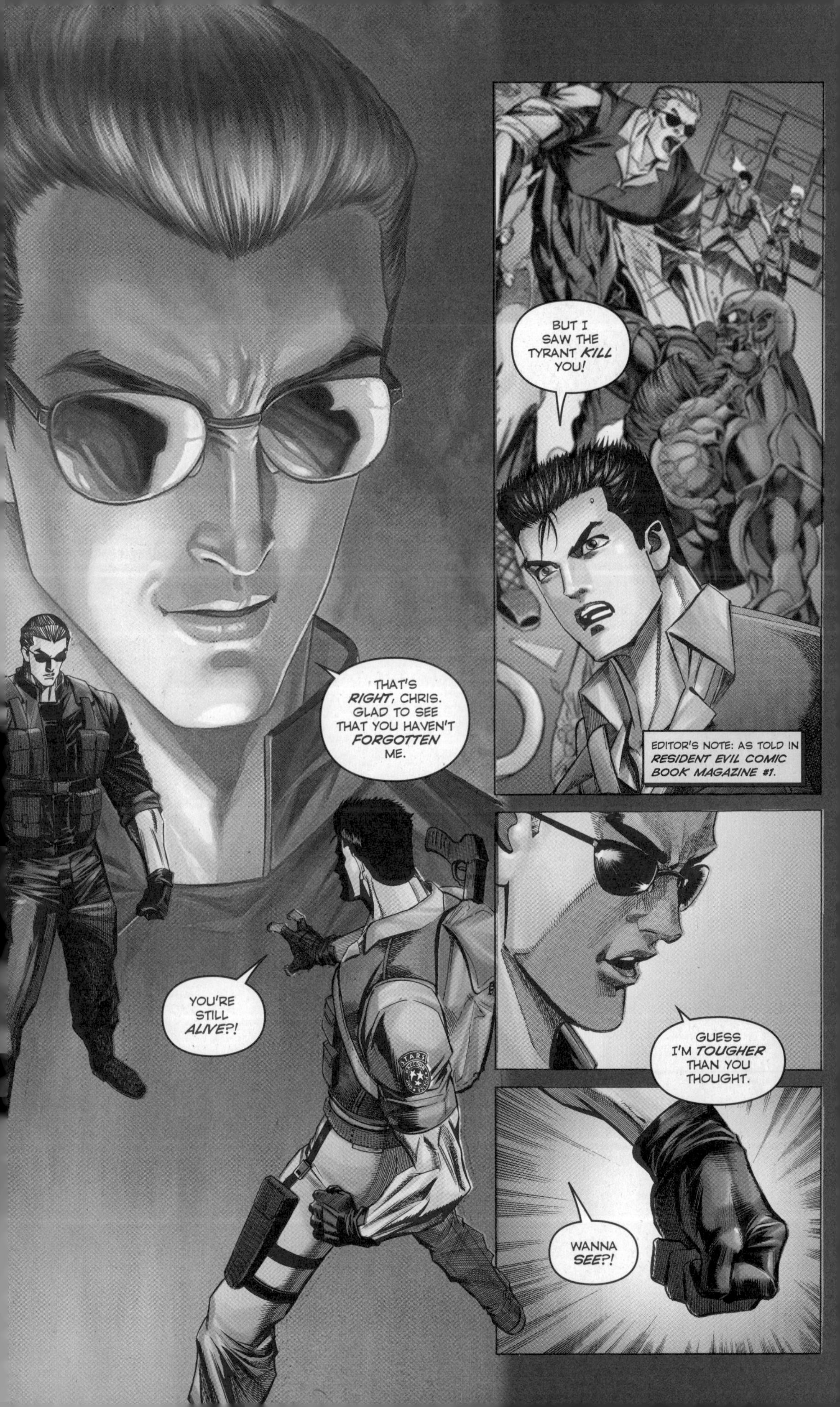

THAT'S *RIGHT*, CHRIS. GLAD TO SEE THAT YOU HAVEN'T *FORGOTTEN* ME.
YOU'RE STILL *ALIVE*?!
BUT I SAW THE TYRANT *KILL* YOU!
EDITOR'S NOTE: AS TOLD IN *RESIDENT EVIL COMIC BOOK MAGAZINE #1*.
GUESS I'M *TOUGHER* THAN YOU THOUGHT.
WANNA *SEE*?!

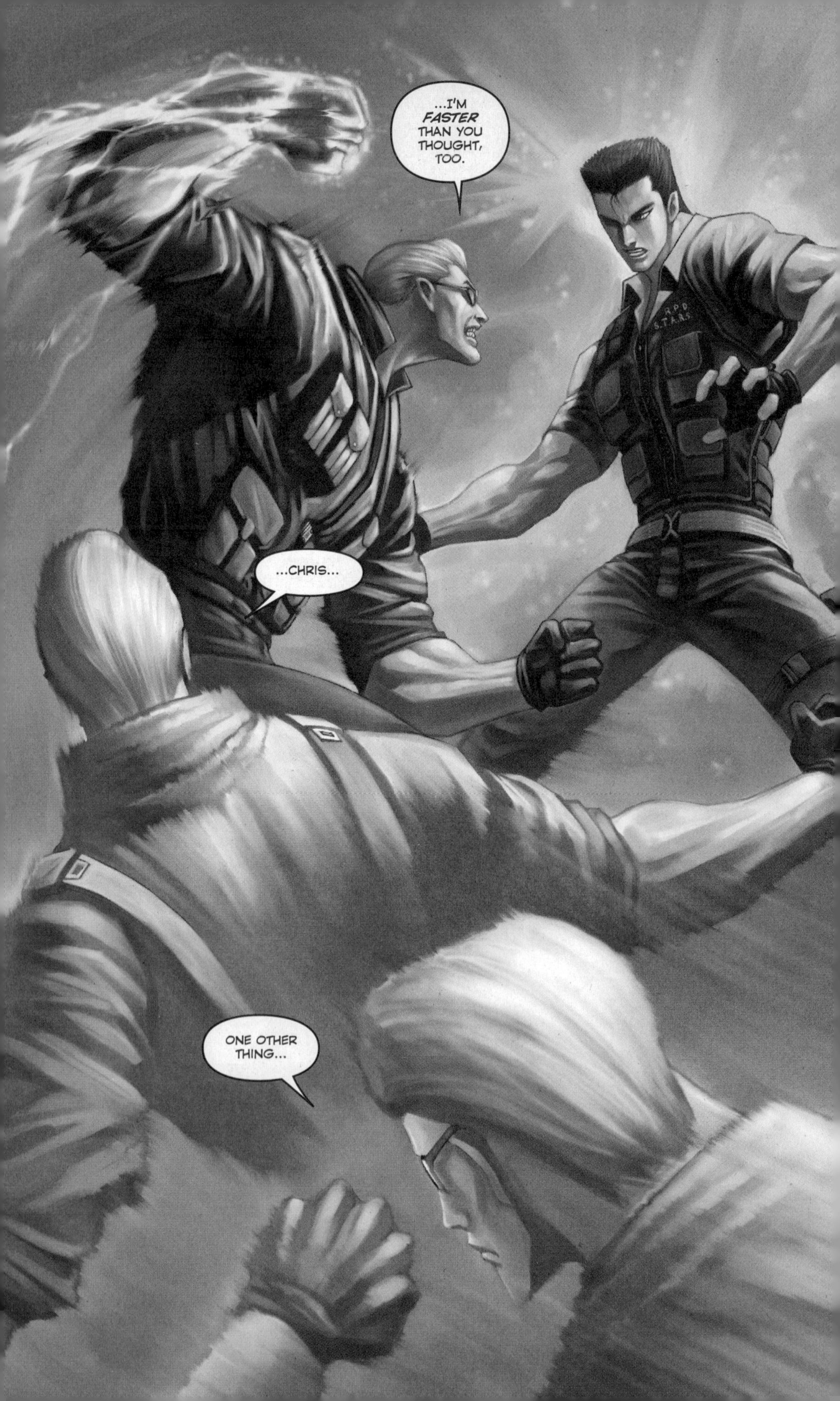

...I'M *FASTER* THAN YOU THOUGHT, TOO.
...CHRIS...
ONE OTHER THING...

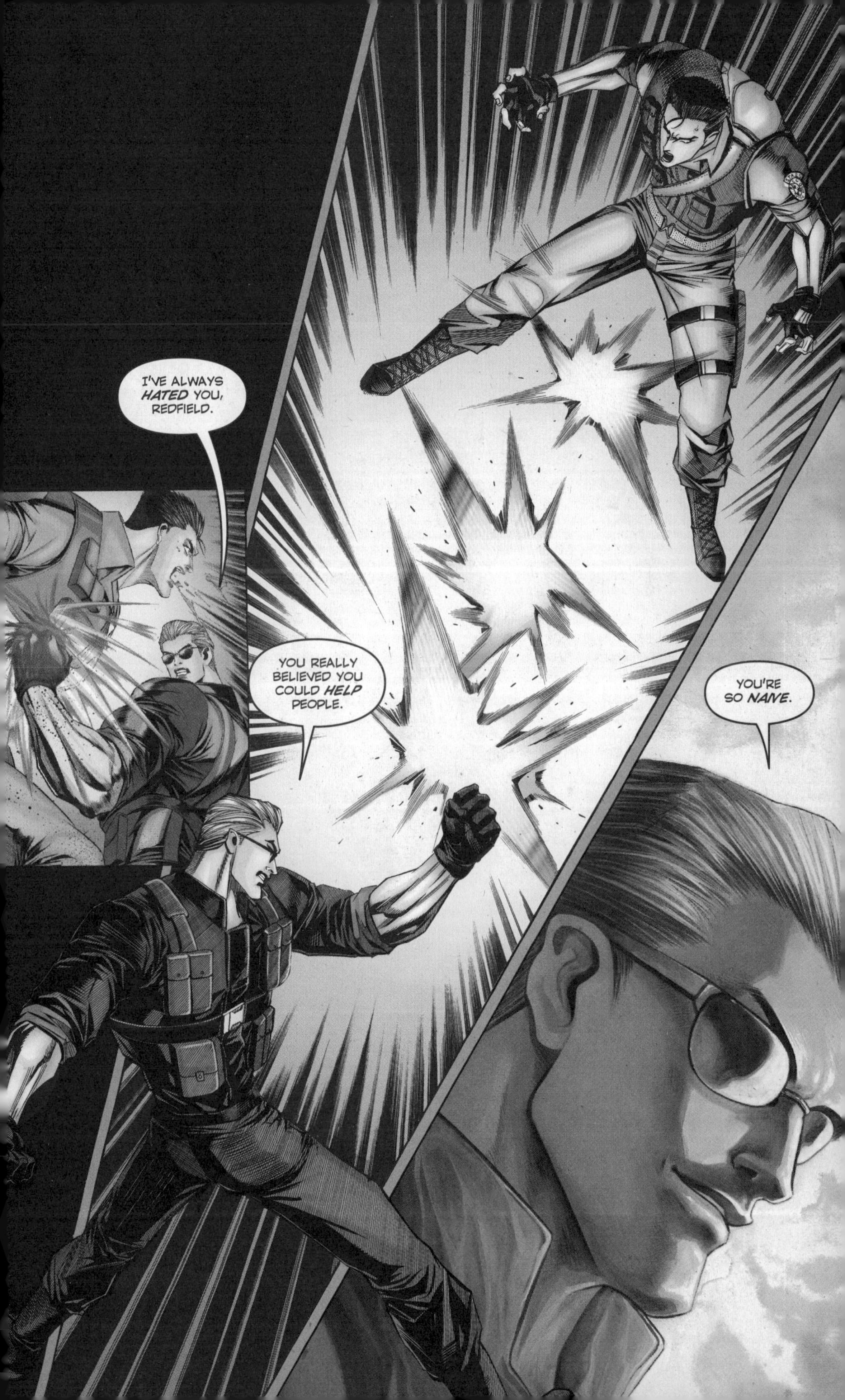
I'VE ALWAYS *HATED* YOU, REDFIELD.
YOU REALLY BELIEVED YOU COULD *HELP* PEOPLE.
YOU'RE SO *NAIVE*.

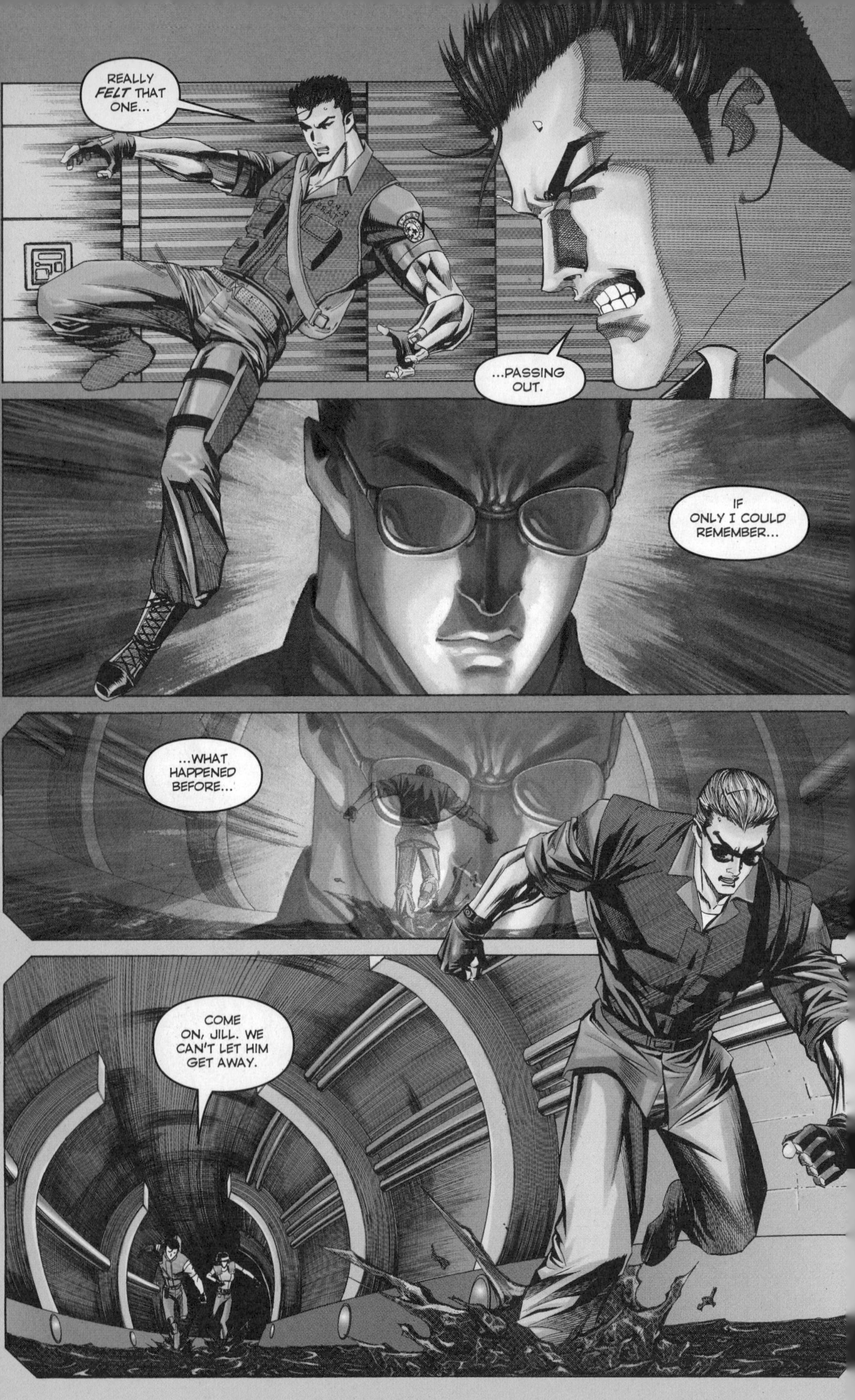
REALLY FELT THAT ONE...
...PASSING OUT.
IF ONLY I COULD REMEMBER...
...WHAT HAPPENED BEFORE...
COME ON, JILL. WE CAN'T LET HIM GET AWAY.

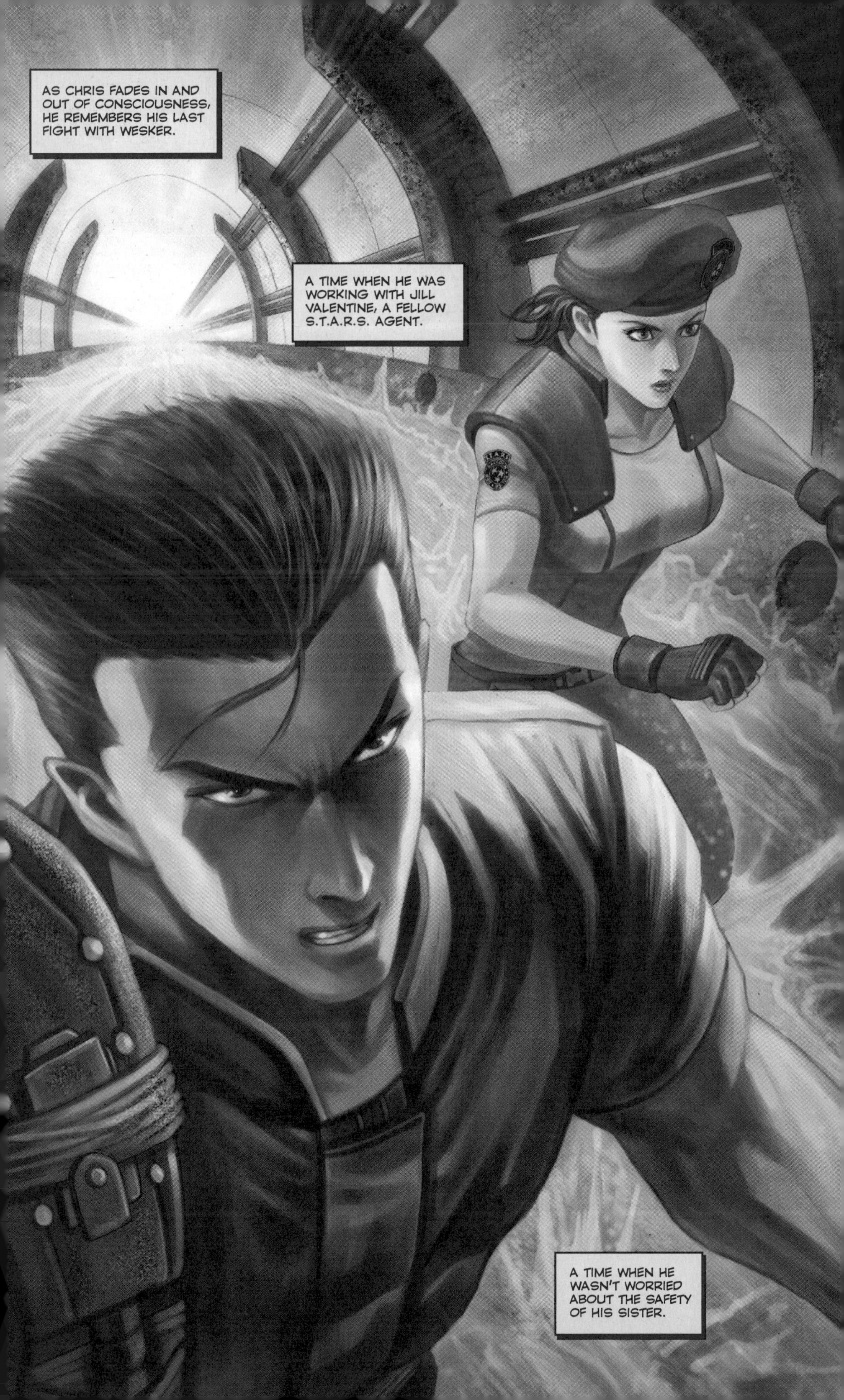
AS CHRIS FADES IN AND OUT OF CONSCIOUSNESS, HE REMEMBERS HIS LAST FIGHT WITH WESKER.
A TIME WHEN HE WAS WORKING WITH JILL VALENTINE, A FELLOW S.T.A.R.S. AGENT.
A TIME WHEN HE WASN'T WORRIED ABOUT THE SAFETY OF HIS SISTER.

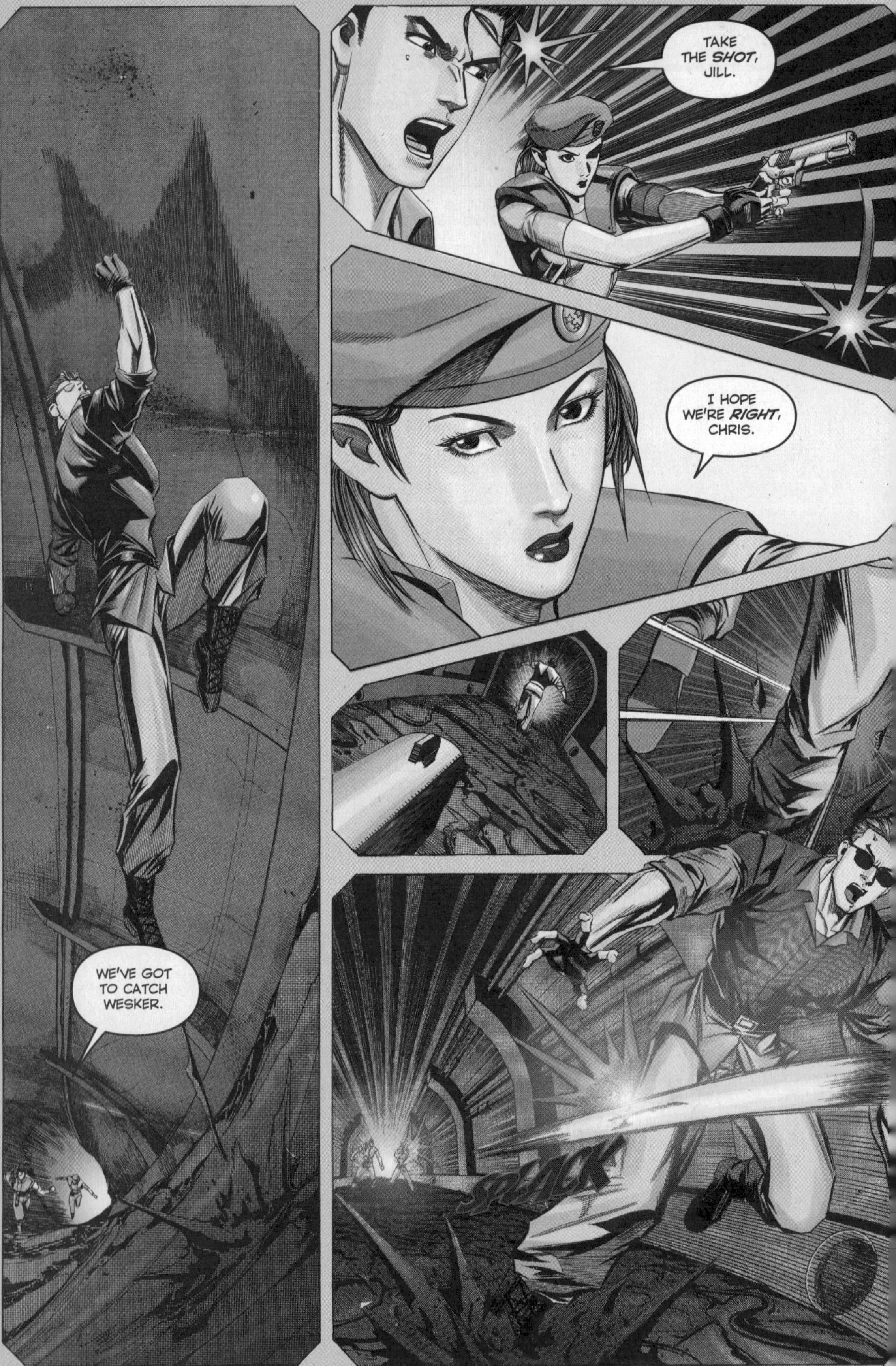
WE'VE GOT TO CATCH WESKER.
TAKE THE SHOT, JILL.
I HOPE WE'RE RIGHT, CHRIS.

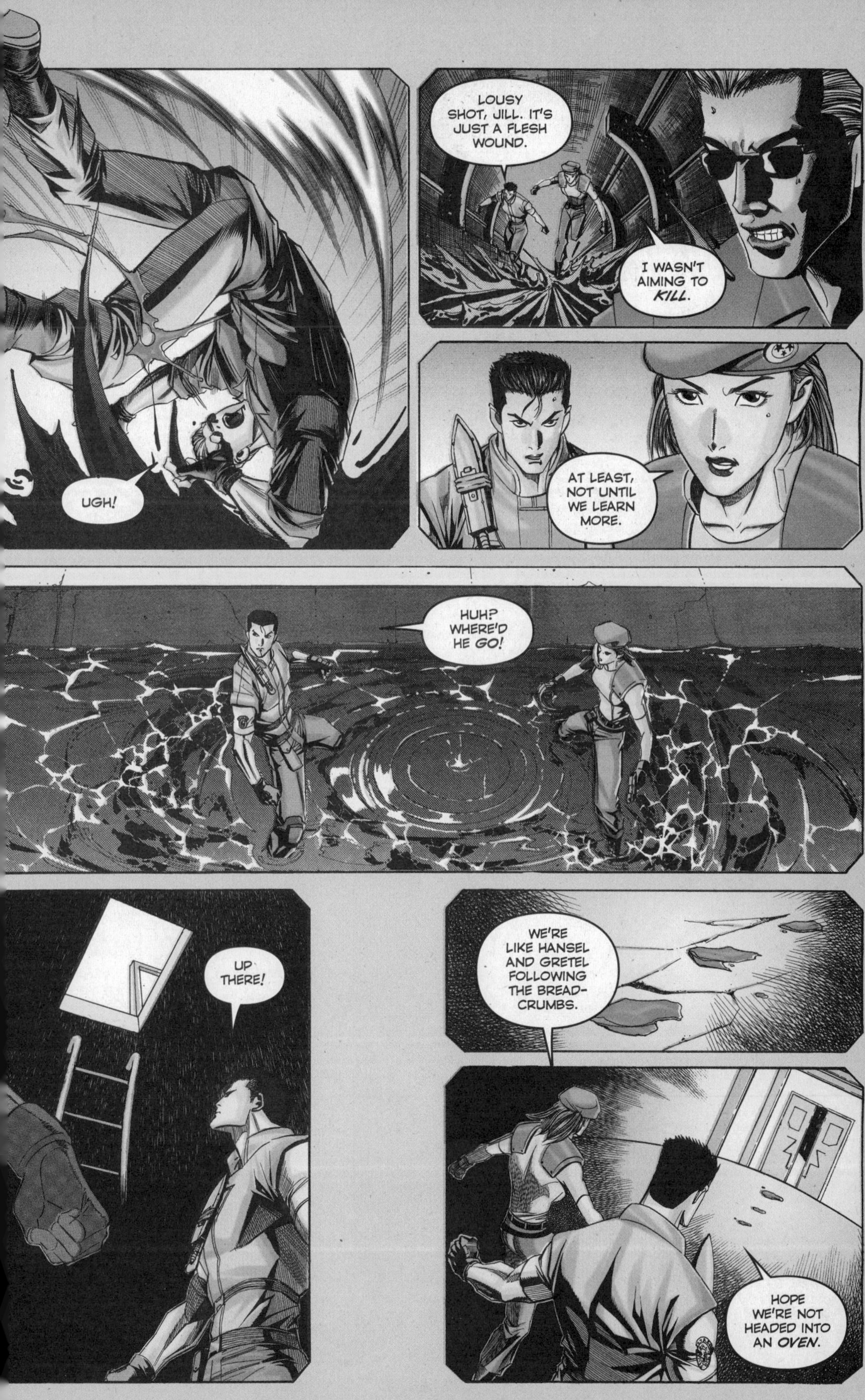
UGH!
LOUSY SHOT, JILL. IT'S JUST A FLESH WOUND.
I WASN'T AIMING TO *KILL*.
AT LEAST, NOT UNTIL WE LEARN MORE.
HUH? WHERE'D HE *GO*!
UP THERE!
WE'RE LIKE HANSEL AND GRETEL FOLLOWING THE BREAD-CRUMBS.
HOPE WE'RE NOT HEADED INTO AN *OVEN*.

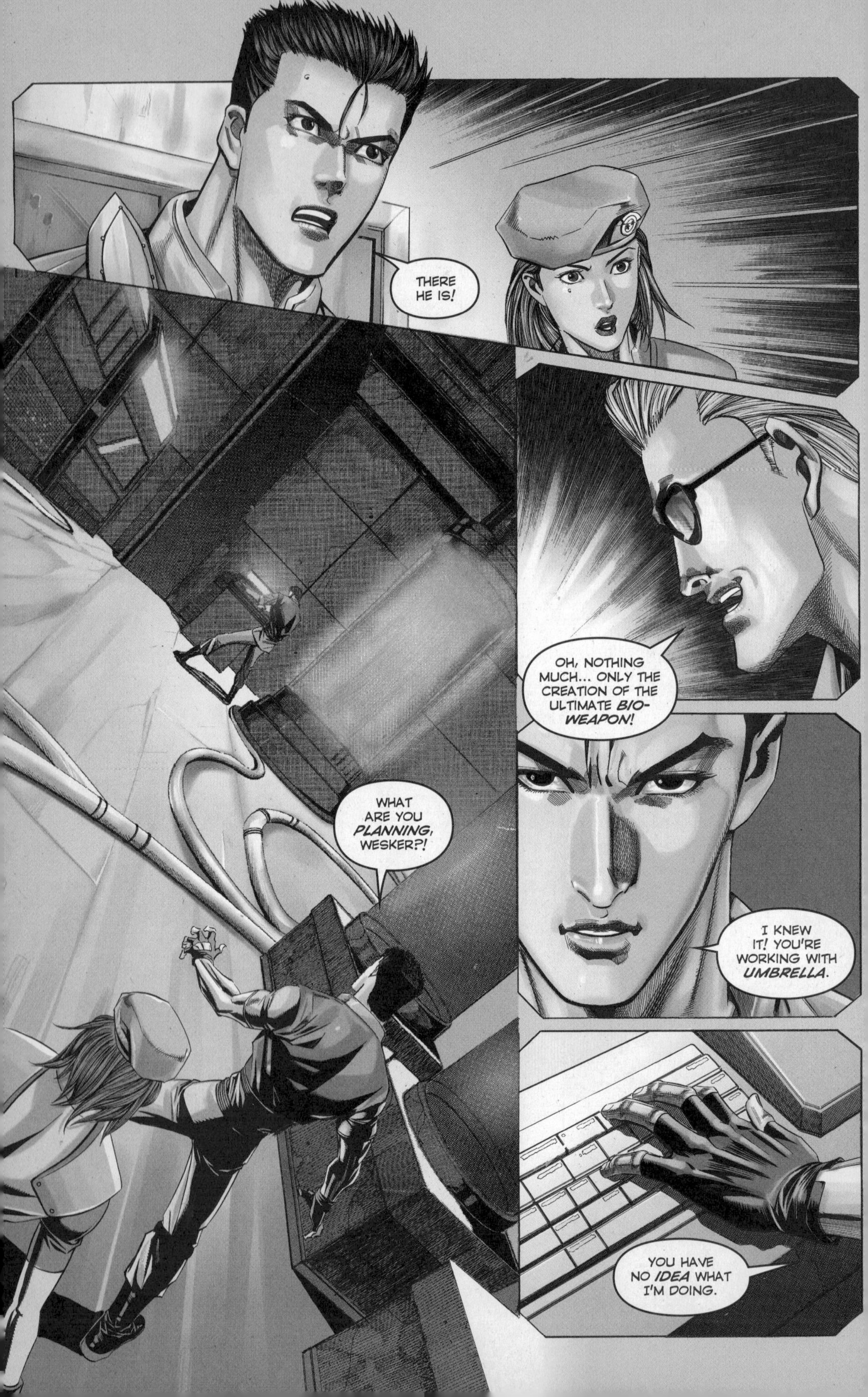

THERE HE IS!
WHAT ARE YOU PLANNING, WESKER?!
OH, NOTHING MUCH... ONLY THE CREATION OF THE ULTIMATE BIO-WEAPON!
I KNEW IT! YOU'RE WORKING WITH UMBRELLA.
YOU HAVE NO IDEA WHAT I'M DOING.

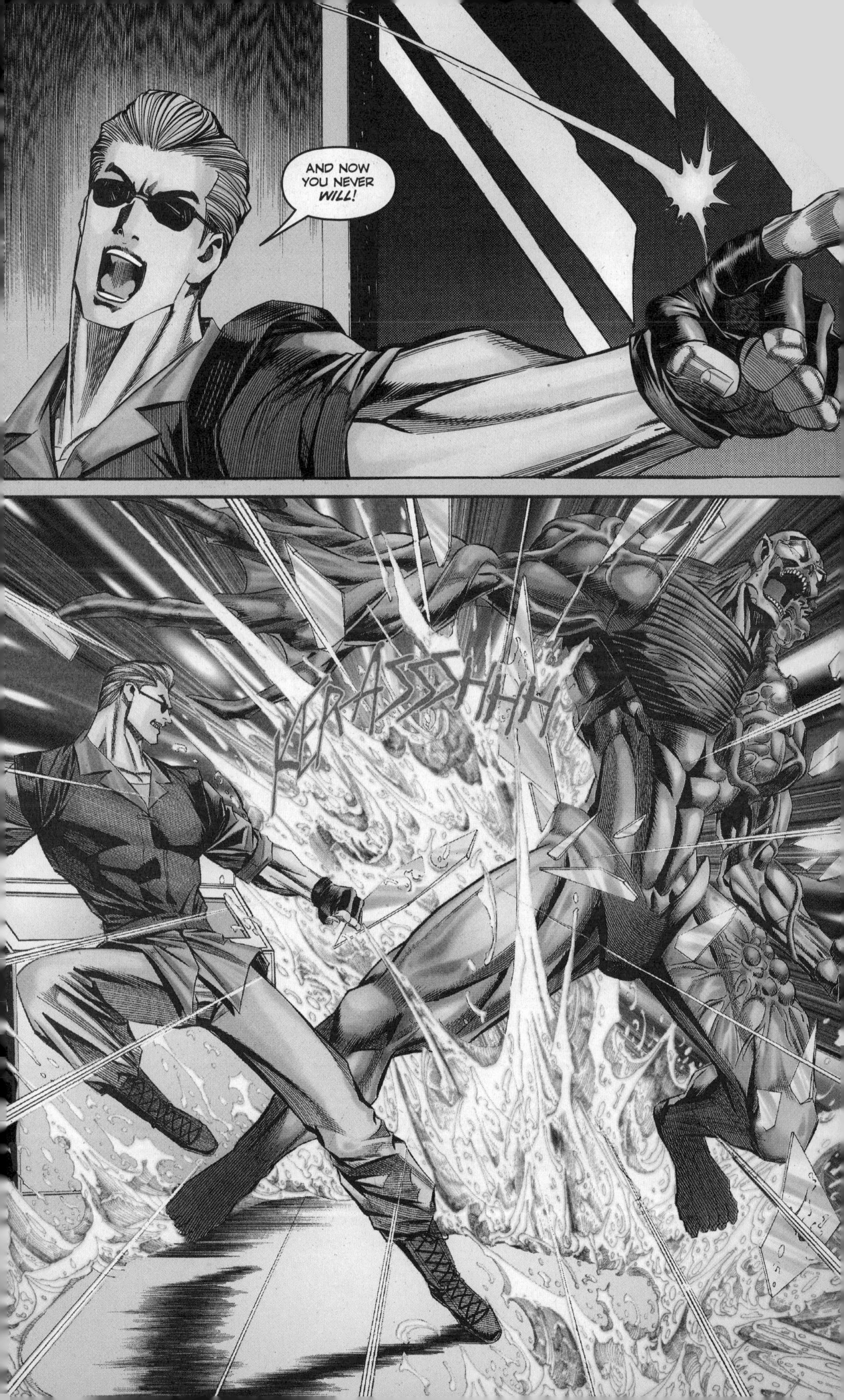
AND NOW YOU NEVER WILL!
CRASSSHHH

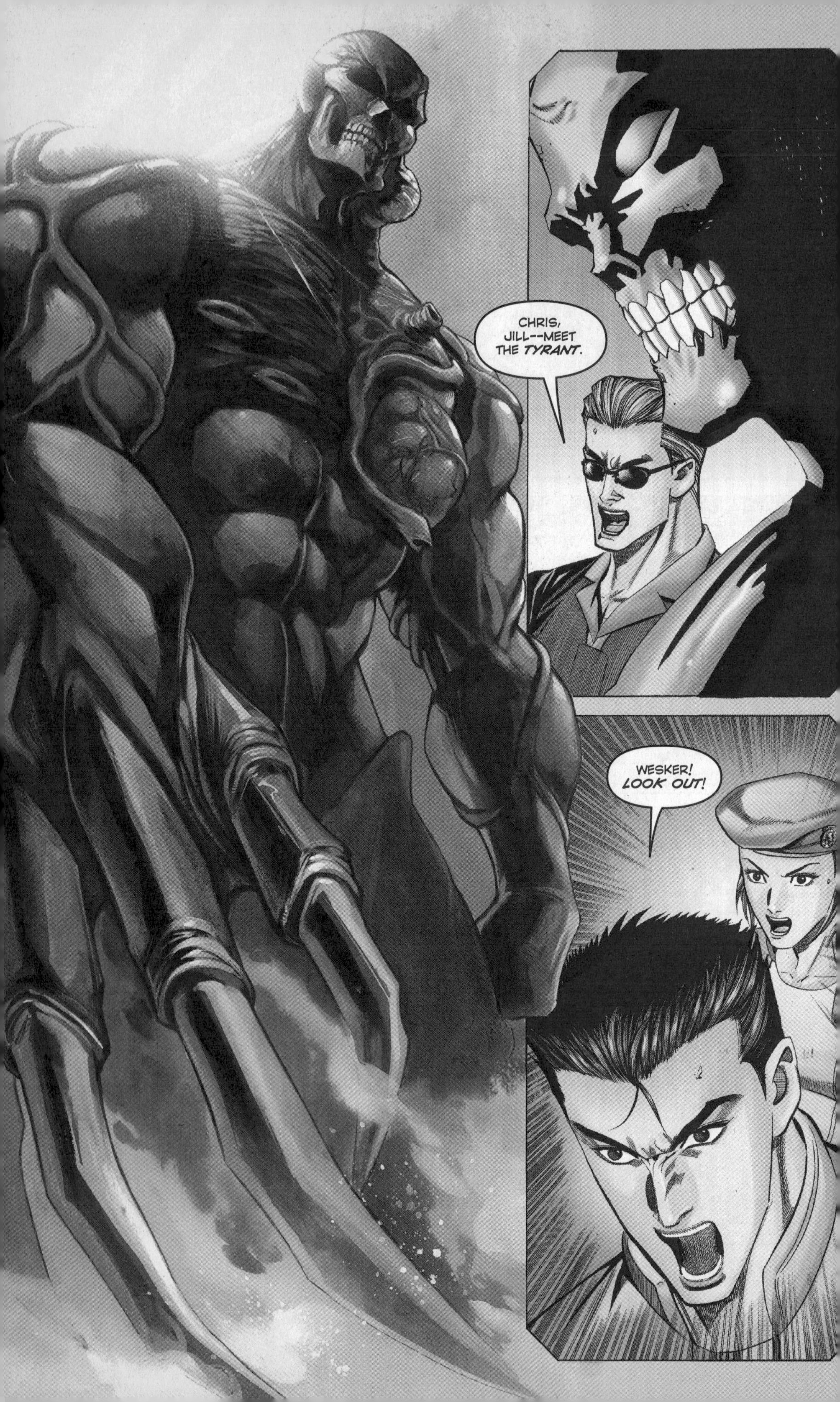
CHRIS, JILL--MEET THE TYRANT.
WESKER! LOOK OUT!

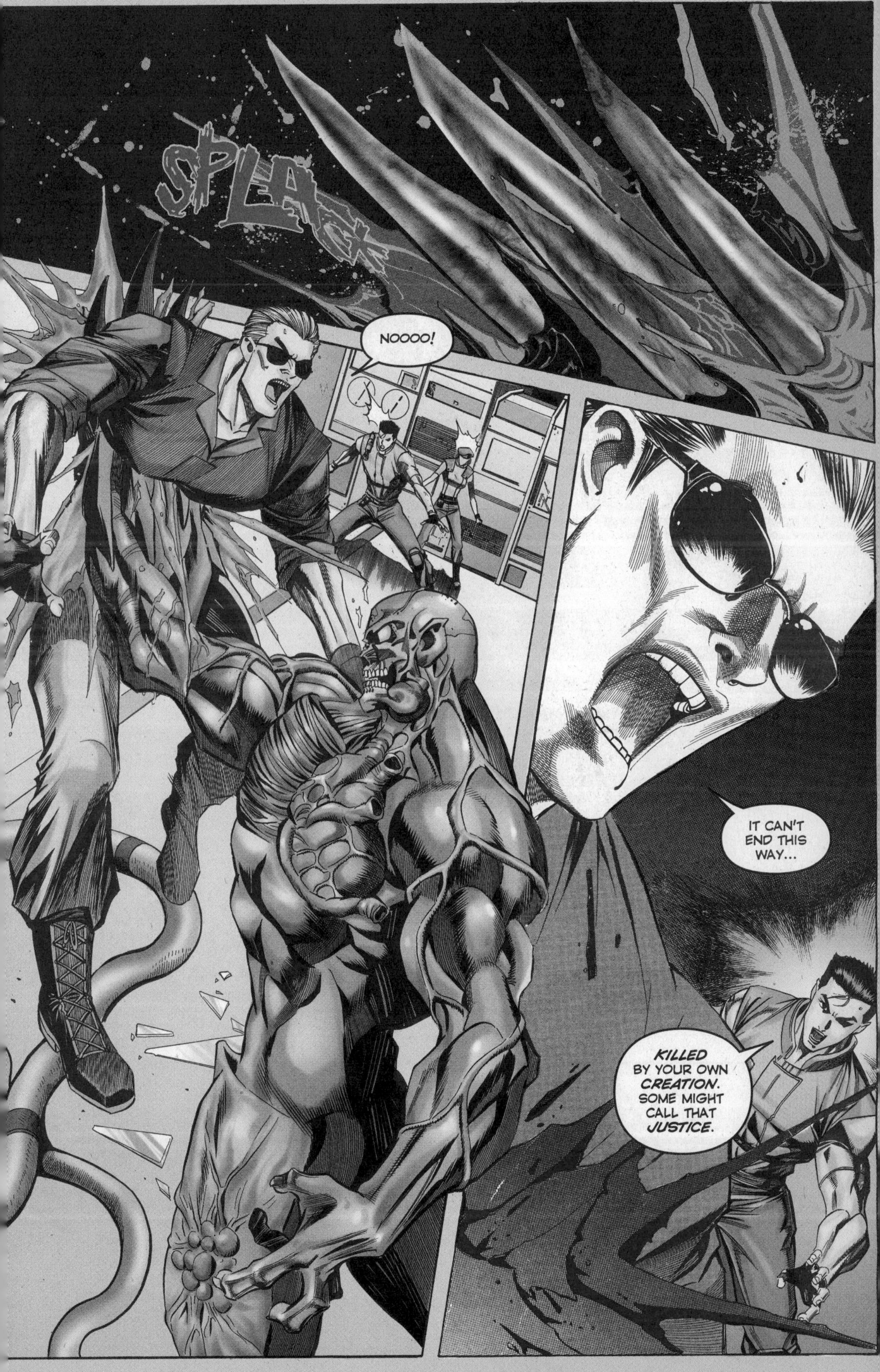
SPLATCK
NOOOO!
IT CAN'T END THIS WAY...
KILLED BY YOUR OWN *CREATION*. SOME MIGHT CALL THAT *JUSTICE*.

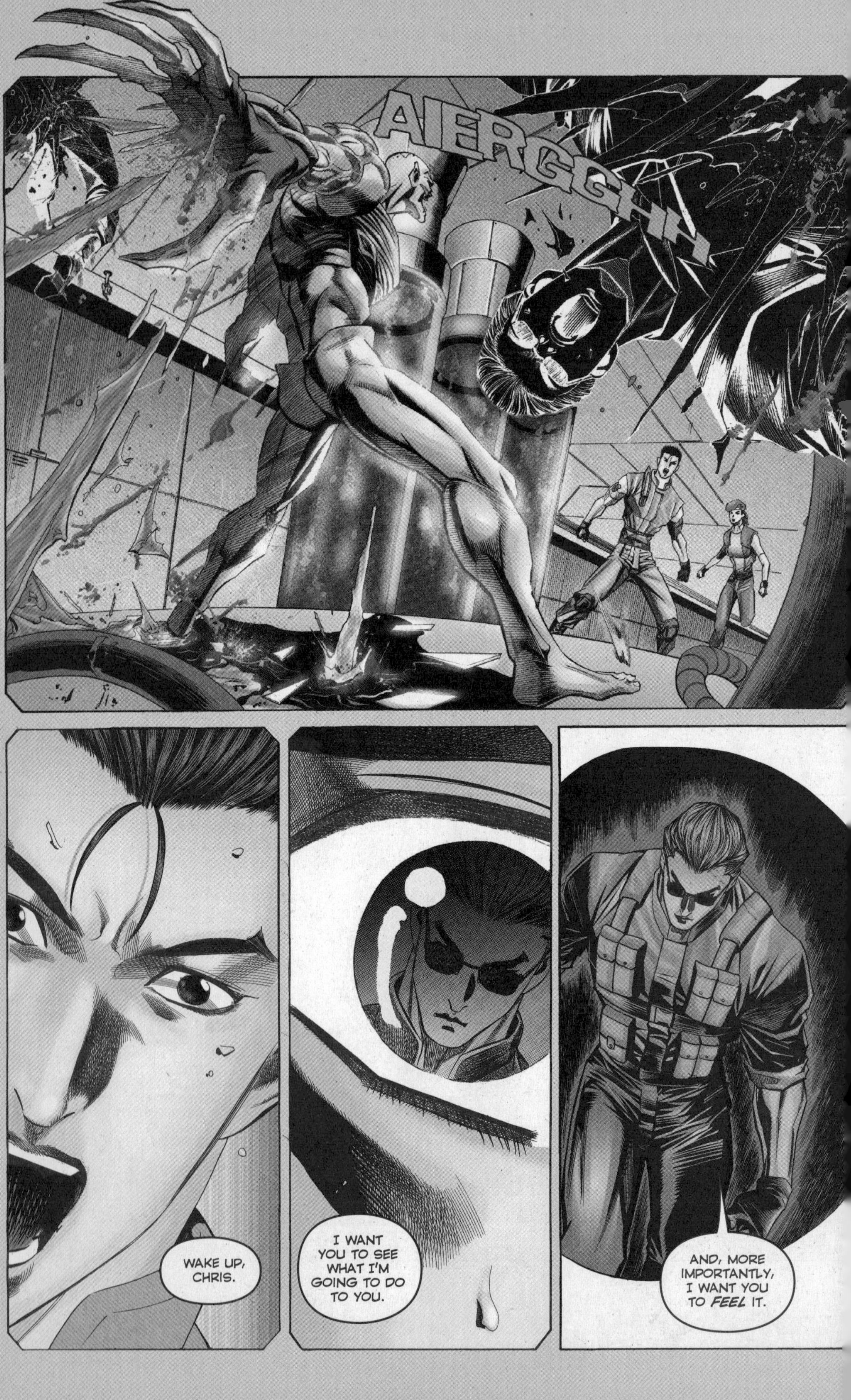
AIERGGHH
WAKE UP, CHRIS.
I WANT YOU TO SEE WHAT I'M GOING TO DO TO YOU.
AND, MORE IMPORTANTLY, I WANT YOU TO *FEEL* IT.

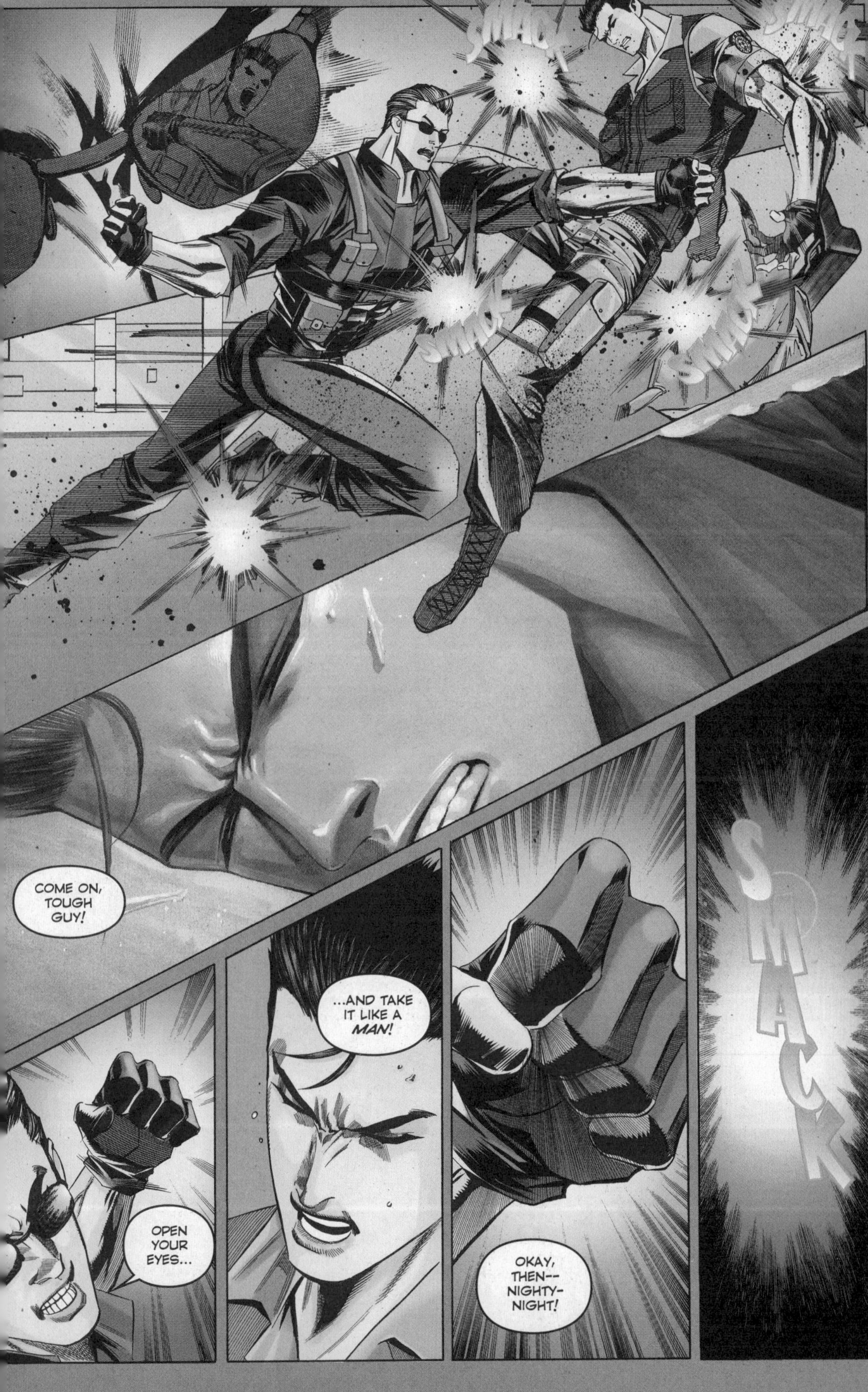
SMACK
SMACK
SMACK
SMACK
COME ON, TOUGH GUY!
OPEN YOUR EYES...
...AND TAKE IT LIKE A *MAN*!
OKAY, THEN-- NIGHTY-NIGHT!
SMACK

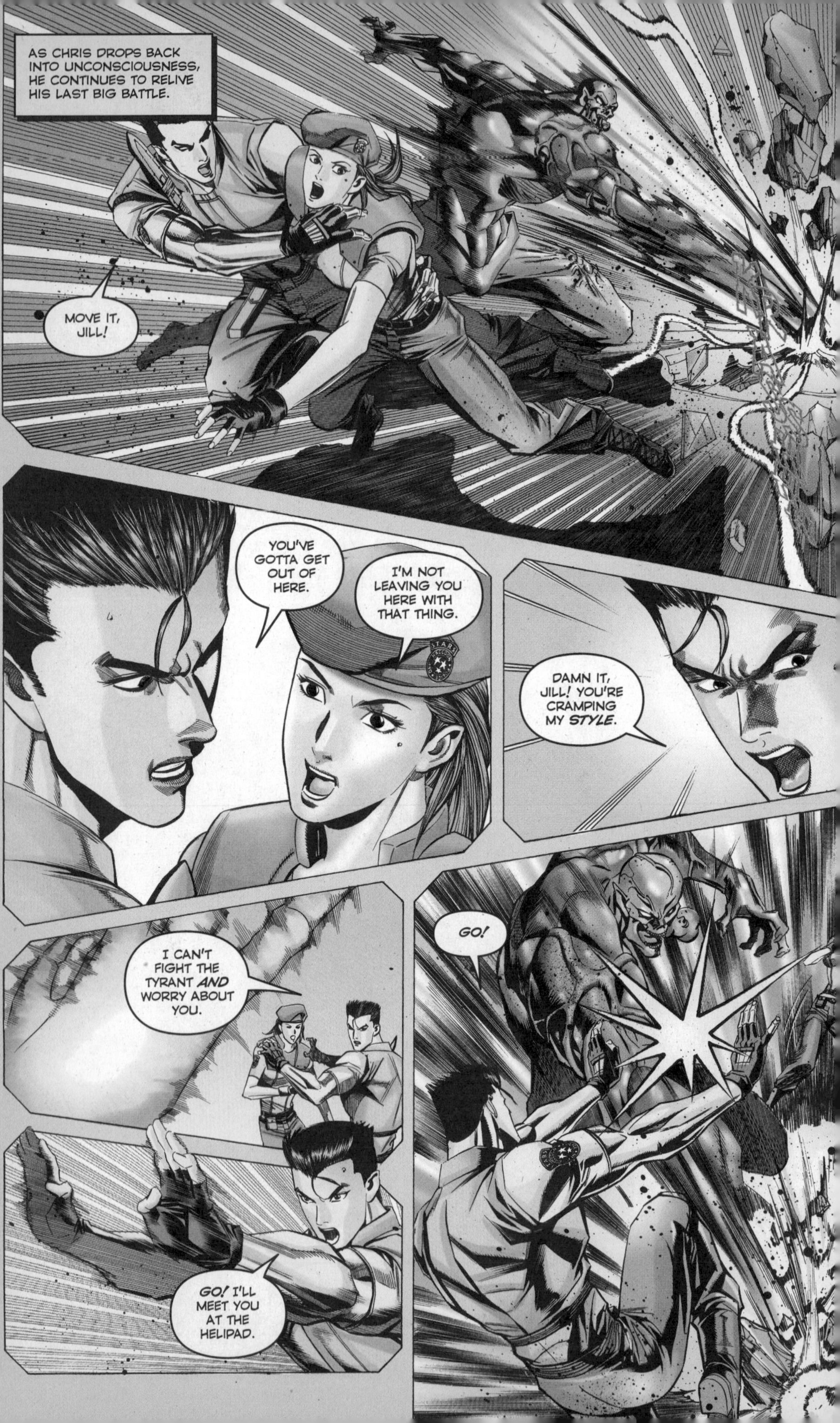
AS CHRIS DROPS BACK INTO UNCONSCIOUSNESS, HE CONTINUES TO RELIVE HIS LAST BIG BATTLE.
MOVE IT, JILL!
YOU'VE GOTTA GET OUT OF HERE.
I'M NOT LEAVING YOU HERE WITH THAT THING.
DAMN IT, JILL! YOU'RE CRAMPING MY *STYLE*.
I CAN'T FIGHT THE TYRANT *AND* WORRY ABOUT YOU.
GO! I'LL MEET YOU AT THE HELIPAD.
GO!

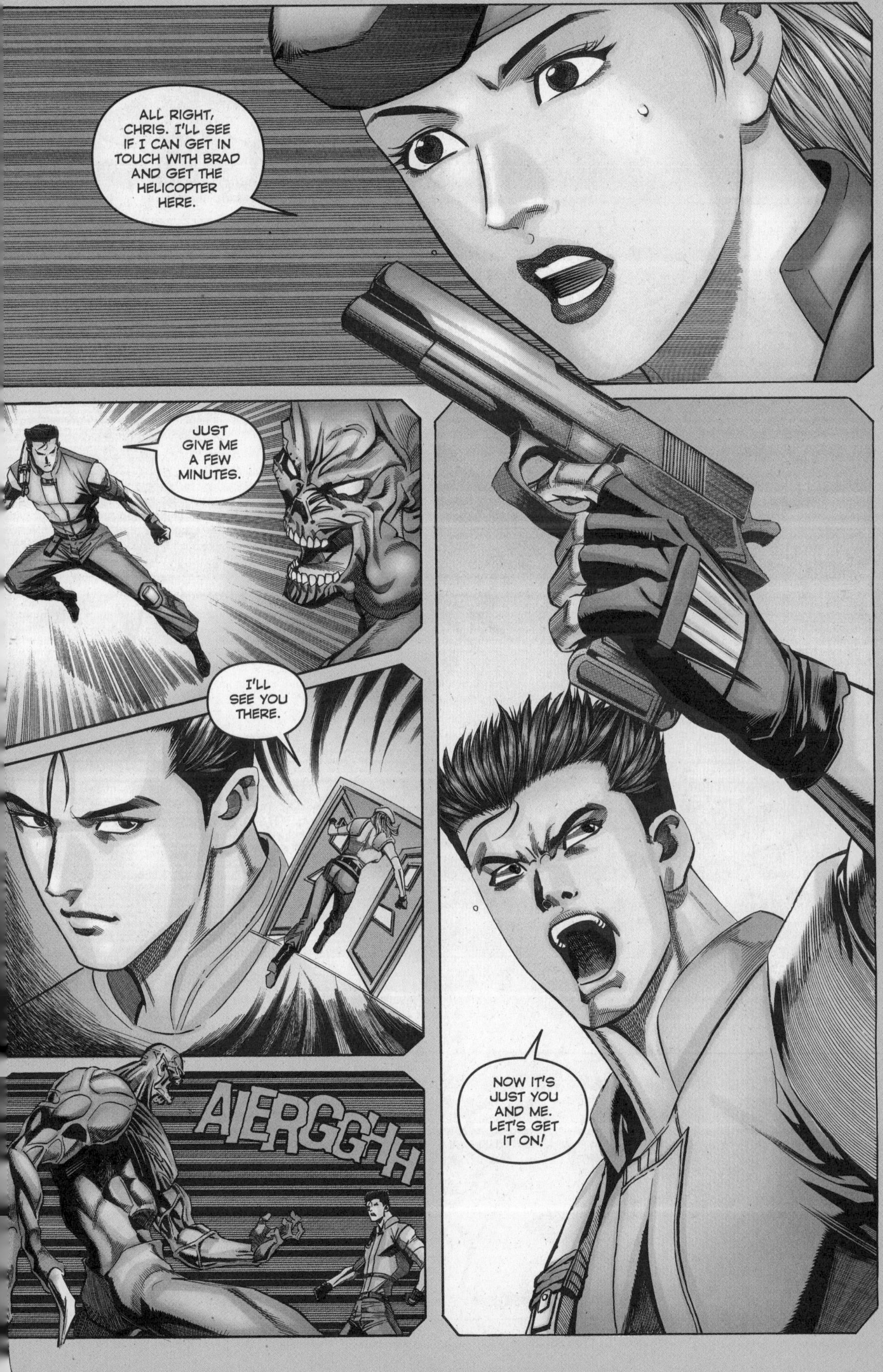
ALL RIGHT, CHRIS. I'LL SEE IF I CAN GET IN TOUCH WITH BRAD AND GET THE HELICOPTER HERE.
JUST GIVE ME A FEW MINUTES.
I'LL SEE YOU THERE.
NOW IT'S JUST YOU AND ME. LET'S GET IT ON!
AIERGGHH

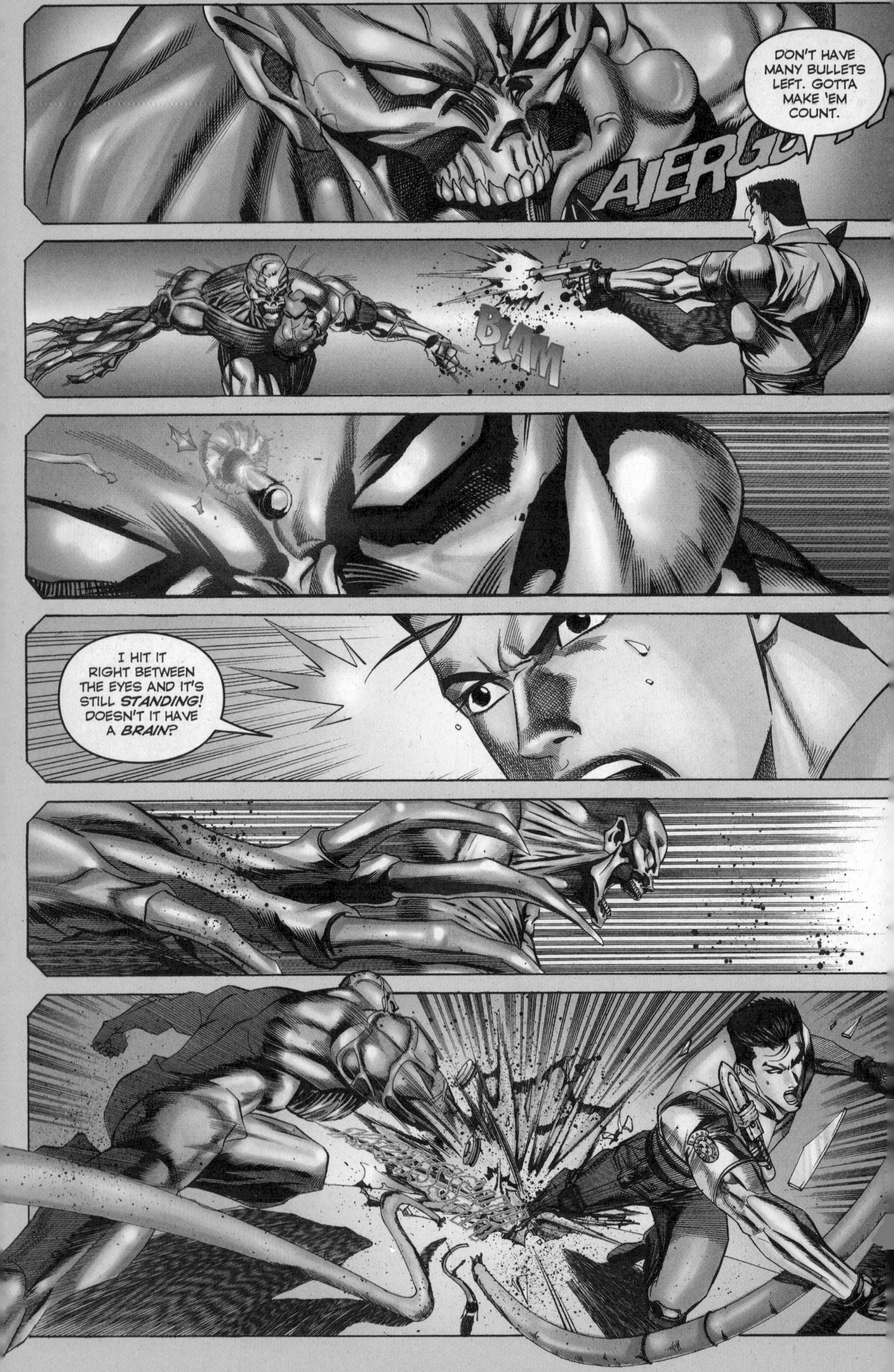
DON'T HAVE MANY BULLETS LEFT. GOTTA MAKE 'EM COUNT.
BLAM
I HIT IT RIGHT BETWEEN THE EYES AND IT'S STILL STANDING! DOESN'T IT HAVE A BRAIN?

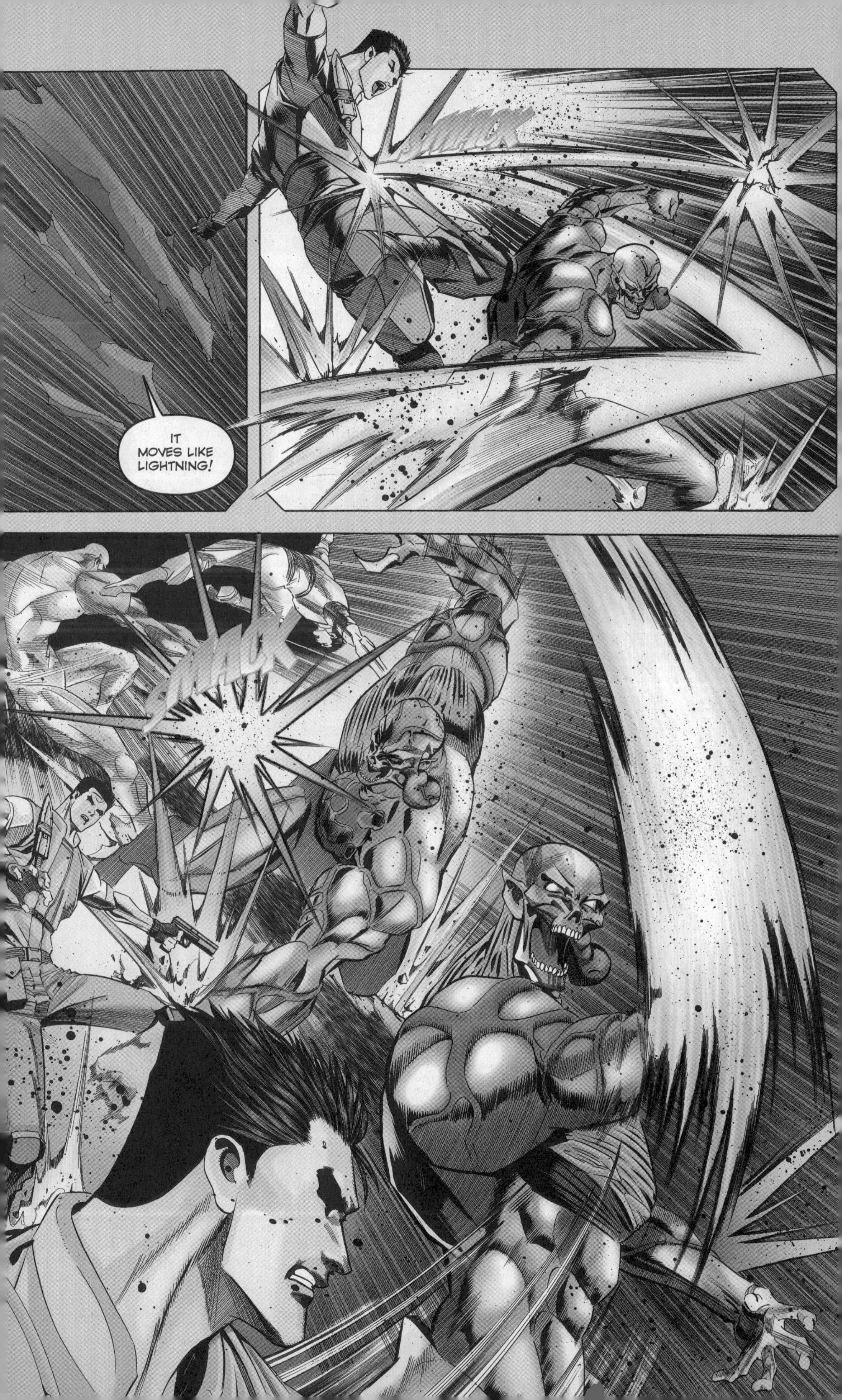
SMACK
IT MOVES LIKE LIGHTNING!
SMACK

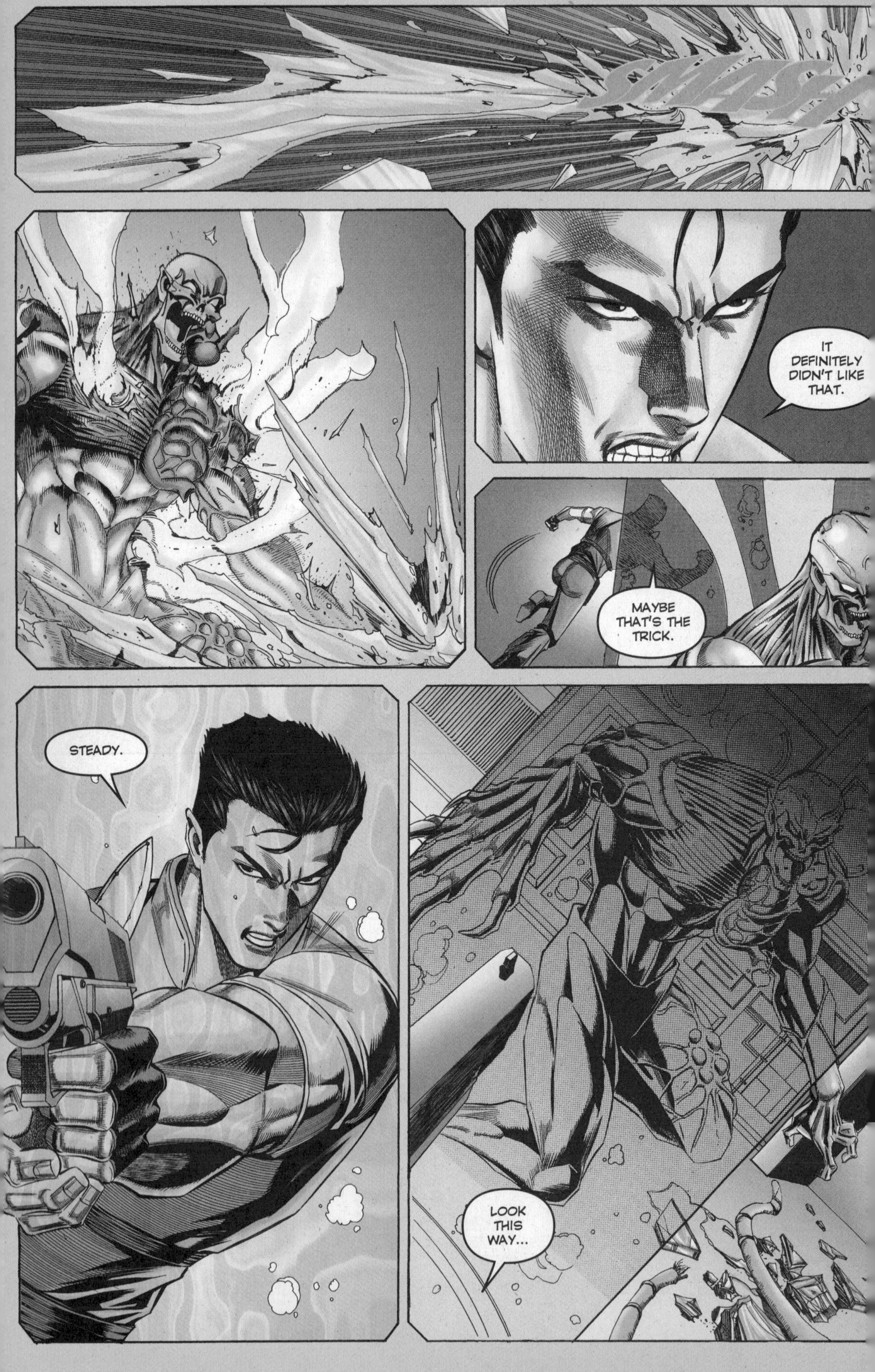
SMASH
IT DEFINITELY DIDN'T LIKE THAT.
MAYBE THAT'S THE TRICK.
STEADY.
LOOK THIS WAY...

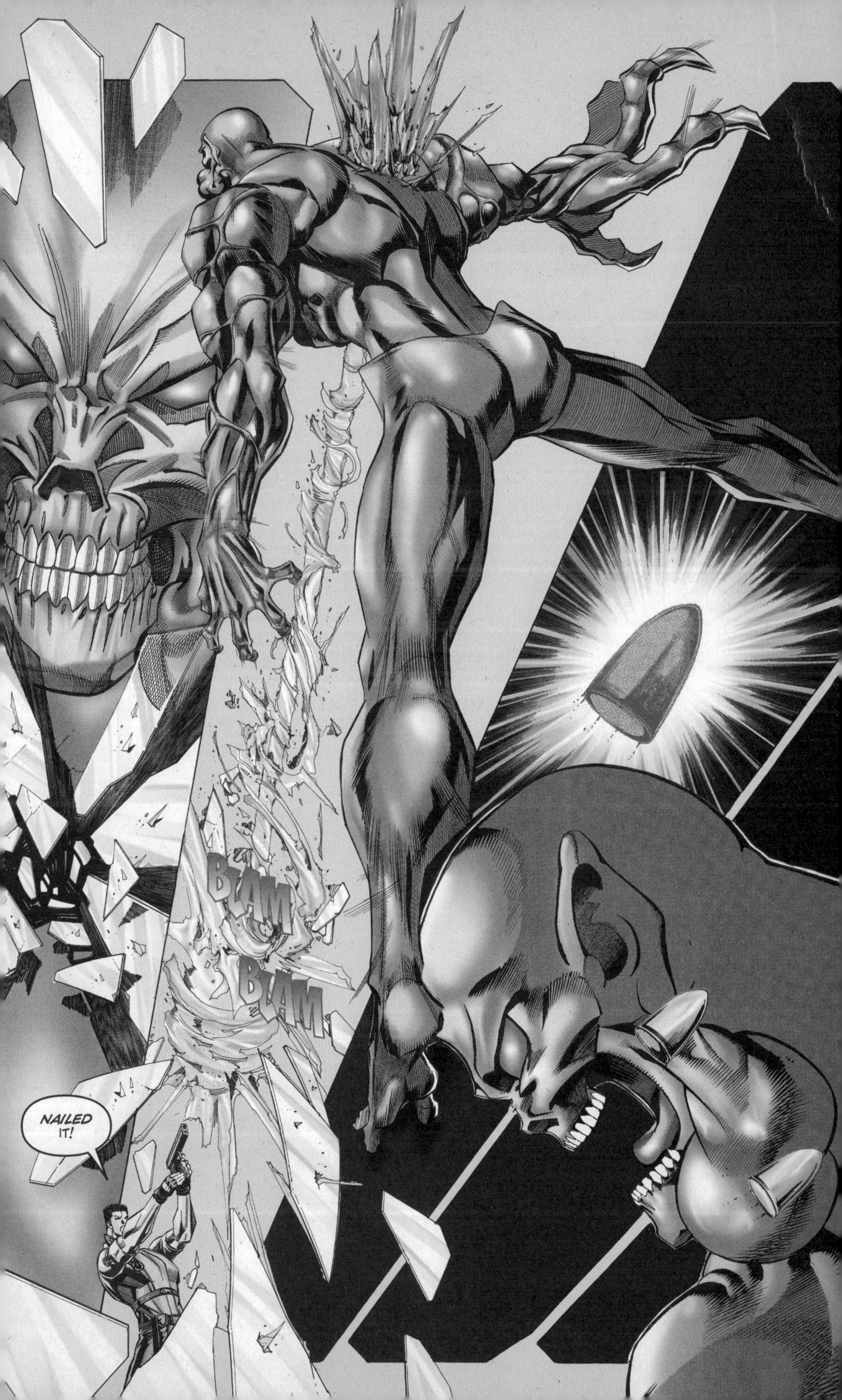
BLAM
BLAM
NAILED IT!

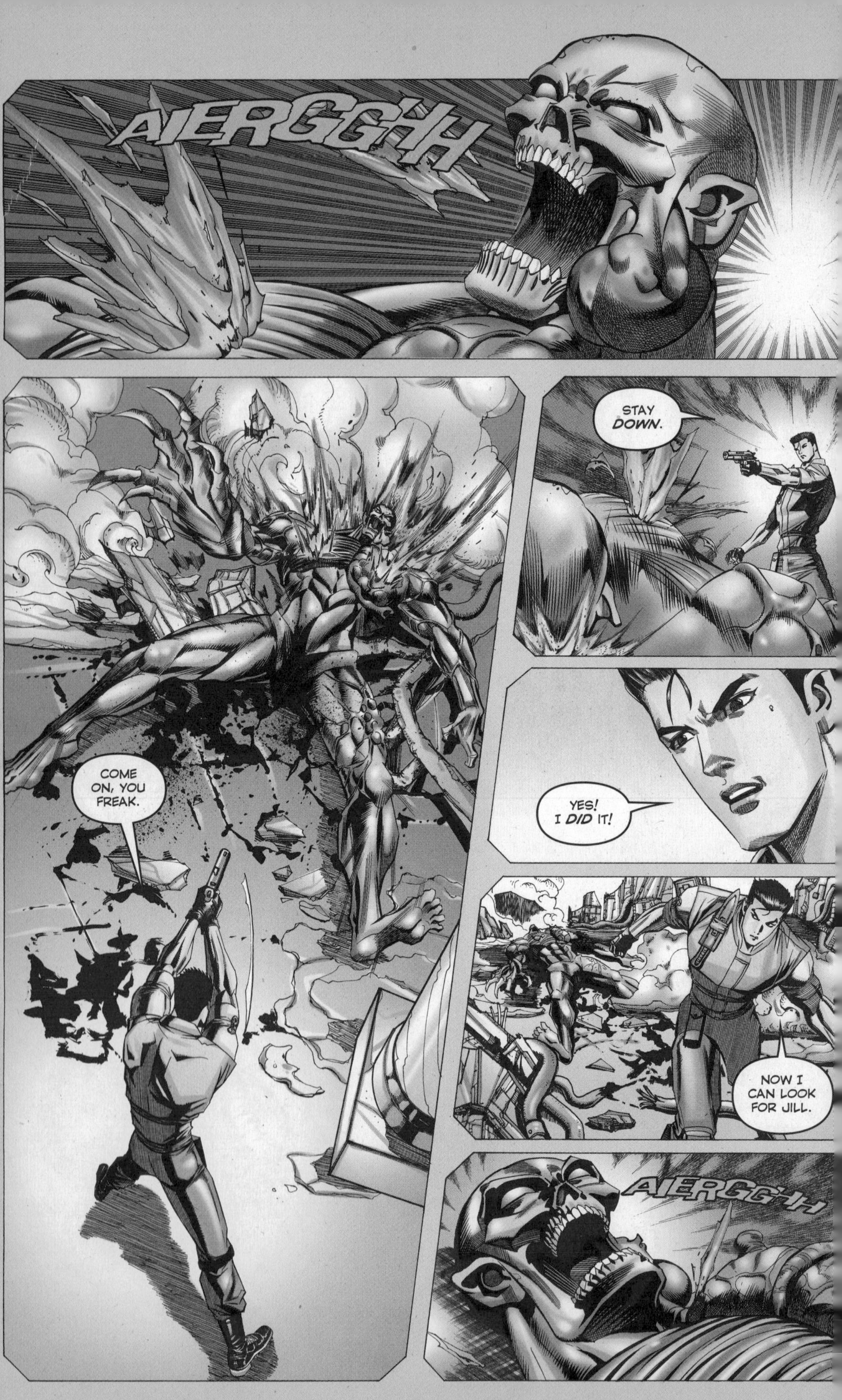
AIERGGHH
STAY DOWN.
COME ON, YOU FREAK.
YES! I DID IT!
NOW I CAN LOOK FOR JILL.
AIERGGHH

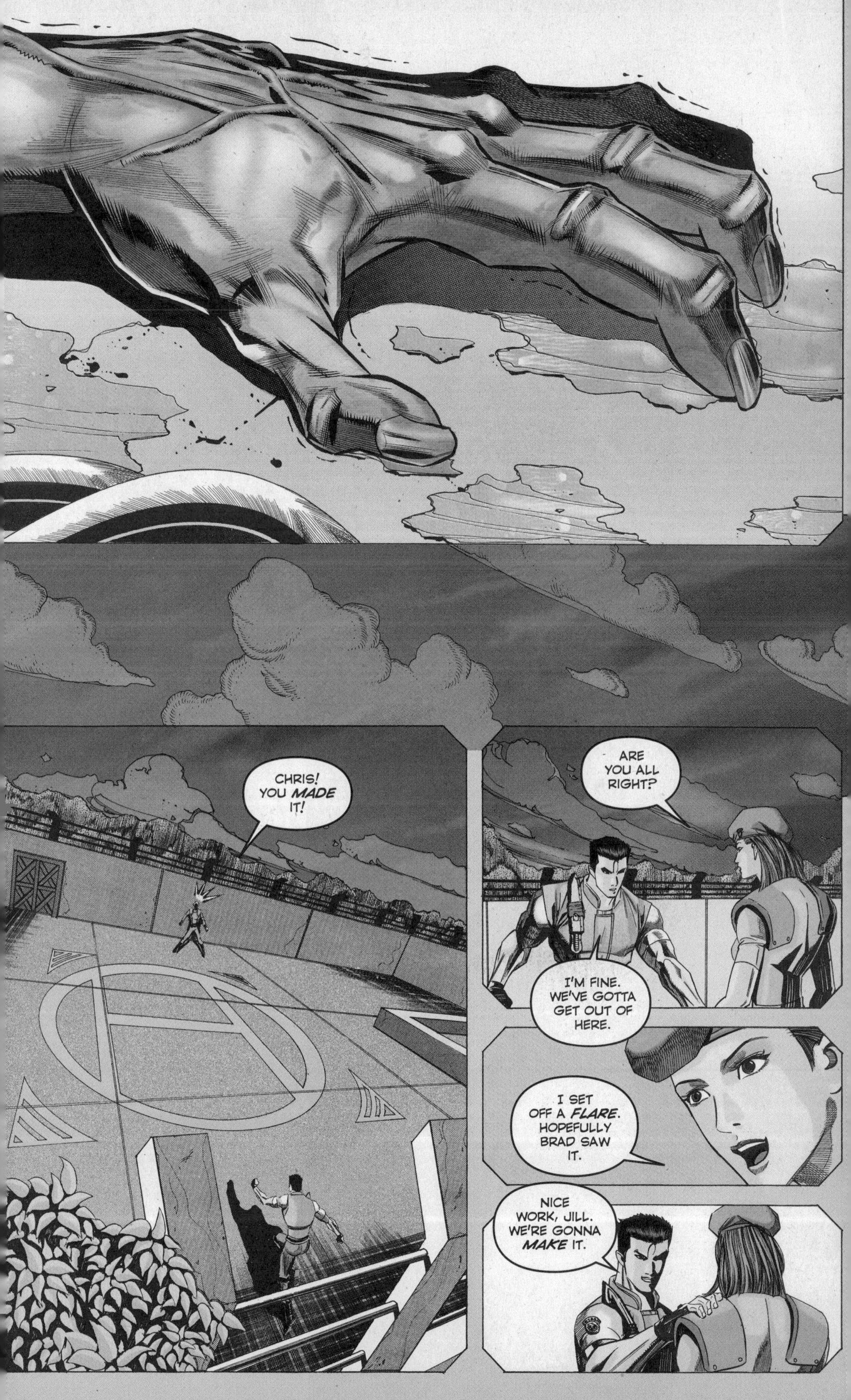

CHRIS! YOU *MADE* IT!
ARE YOU ALL RIGHT?
I'M FINE. WE'VE GOTTA GET OUT OF HERE.
I SET OFF A *FLARE*. HOPEFULLY BRAD SAW IT.
NICE WORK, JILL. WE'RE GONNA *MAKE* IT.

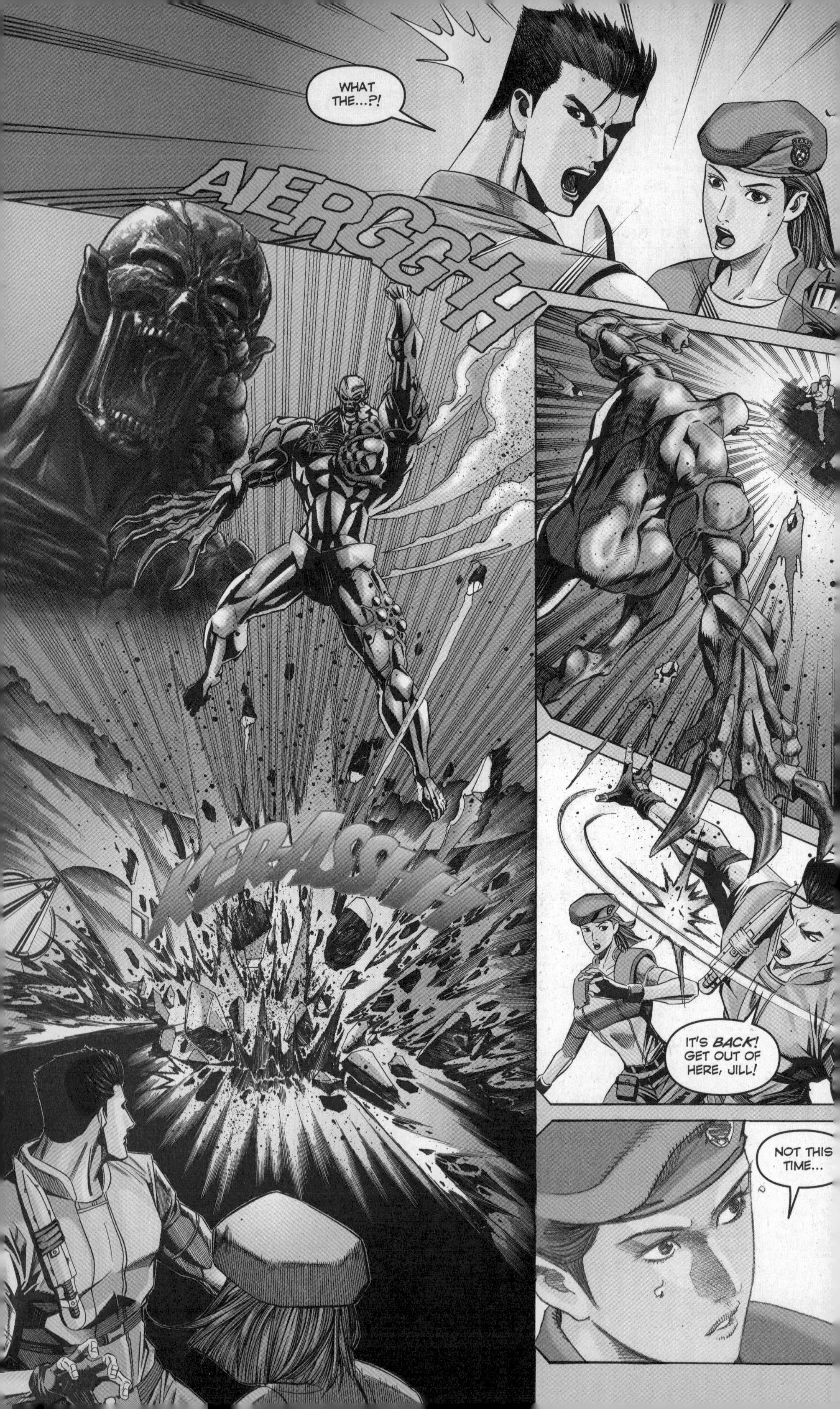
WHAT THE...?!
AIERGGH
KERASSH
IT'S BACK! GET OUT OF HERE, JILL!
NOT THIS TIME...

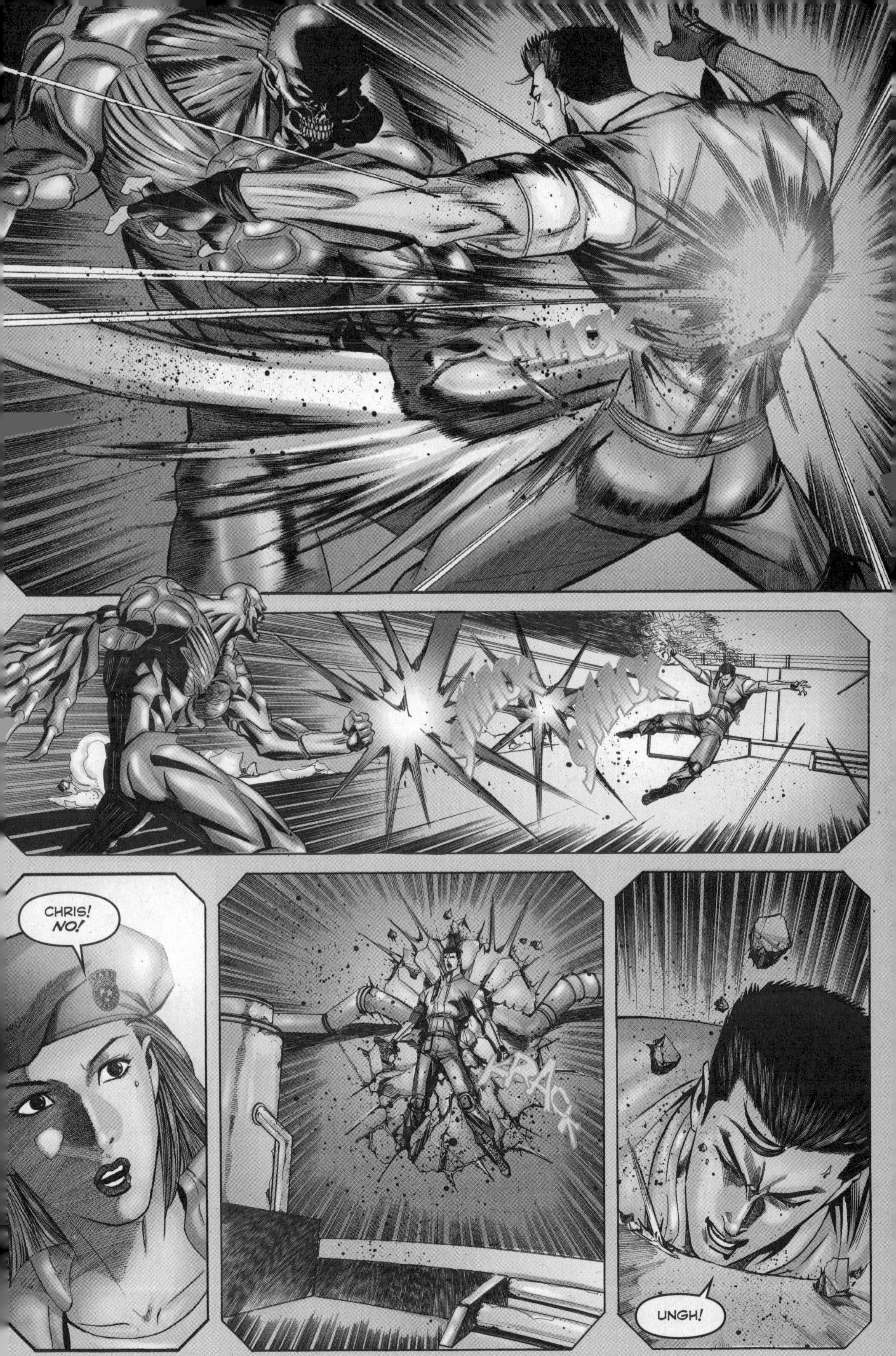
SMACK
SMACK
SMACK
CHRIS!
NO!
KRACK
UNGH!

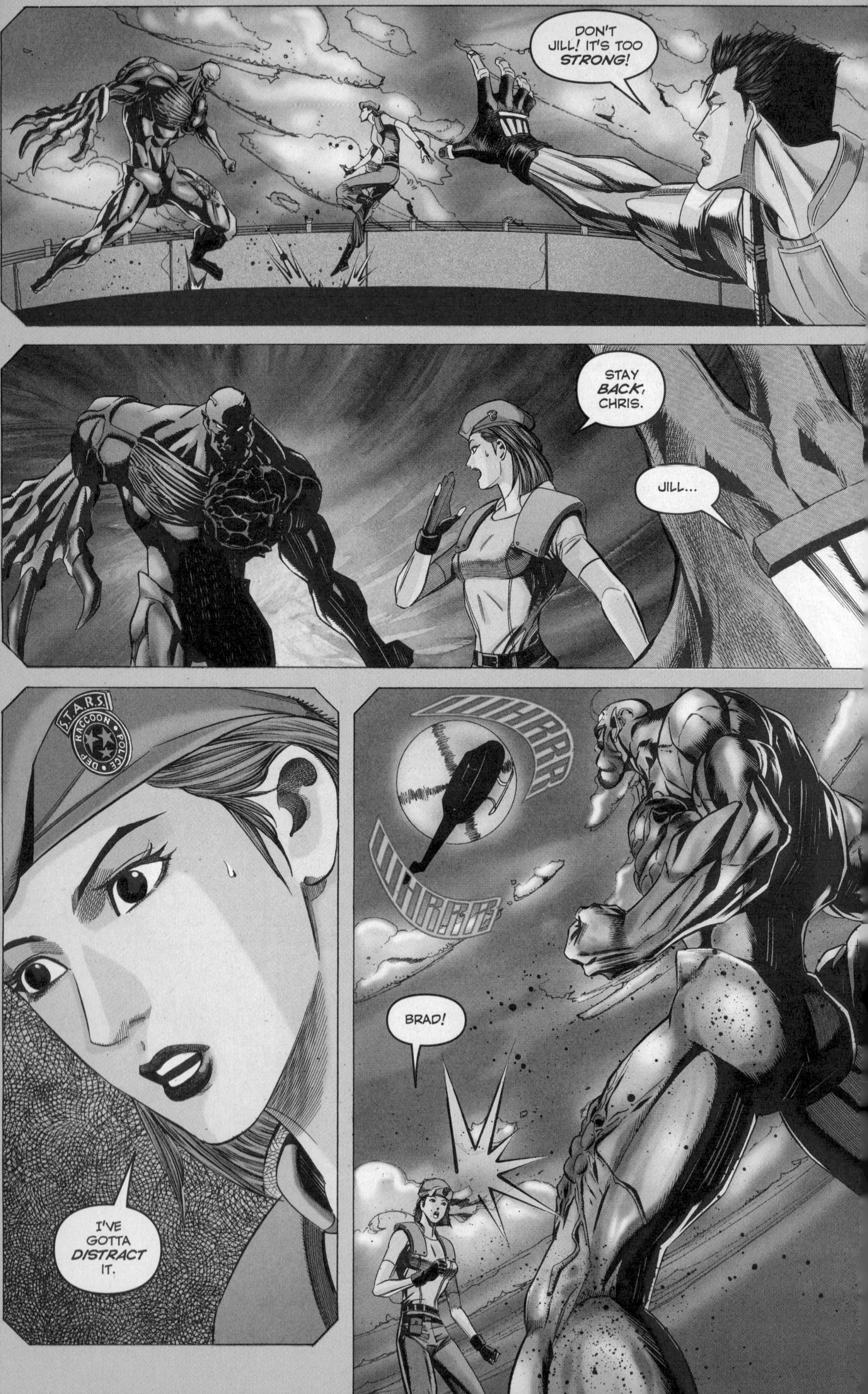
DON'T JILL! IT'S TOO STRONG!
STAY BACK, CHRIS.
JILL...
S.T.A.R.S.
RACCOON POLICE DEP
I'VE GOTTA DISTRACT IT.
WHRRR
WHRRR
BRAD!

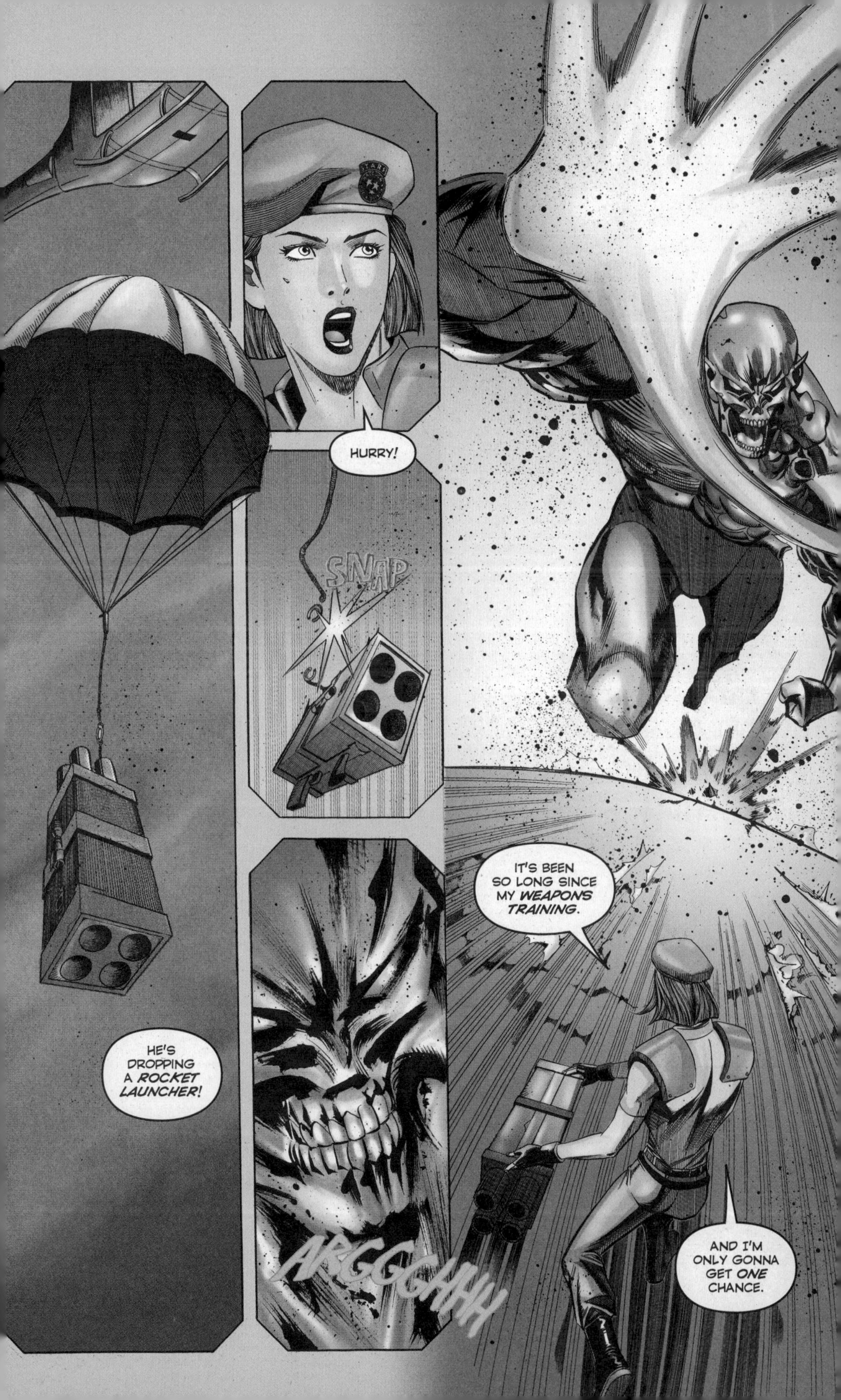
HE'S DROPPING A *ROCKET LAUNCHER*!
HURRY!
SNAP
ARGGGHHH
IT'S BEEN SO LONG SINCE MY *WEAPONS TRAINING*.
AND I'M ONLY GONNA GET *ONE* CHANCE.

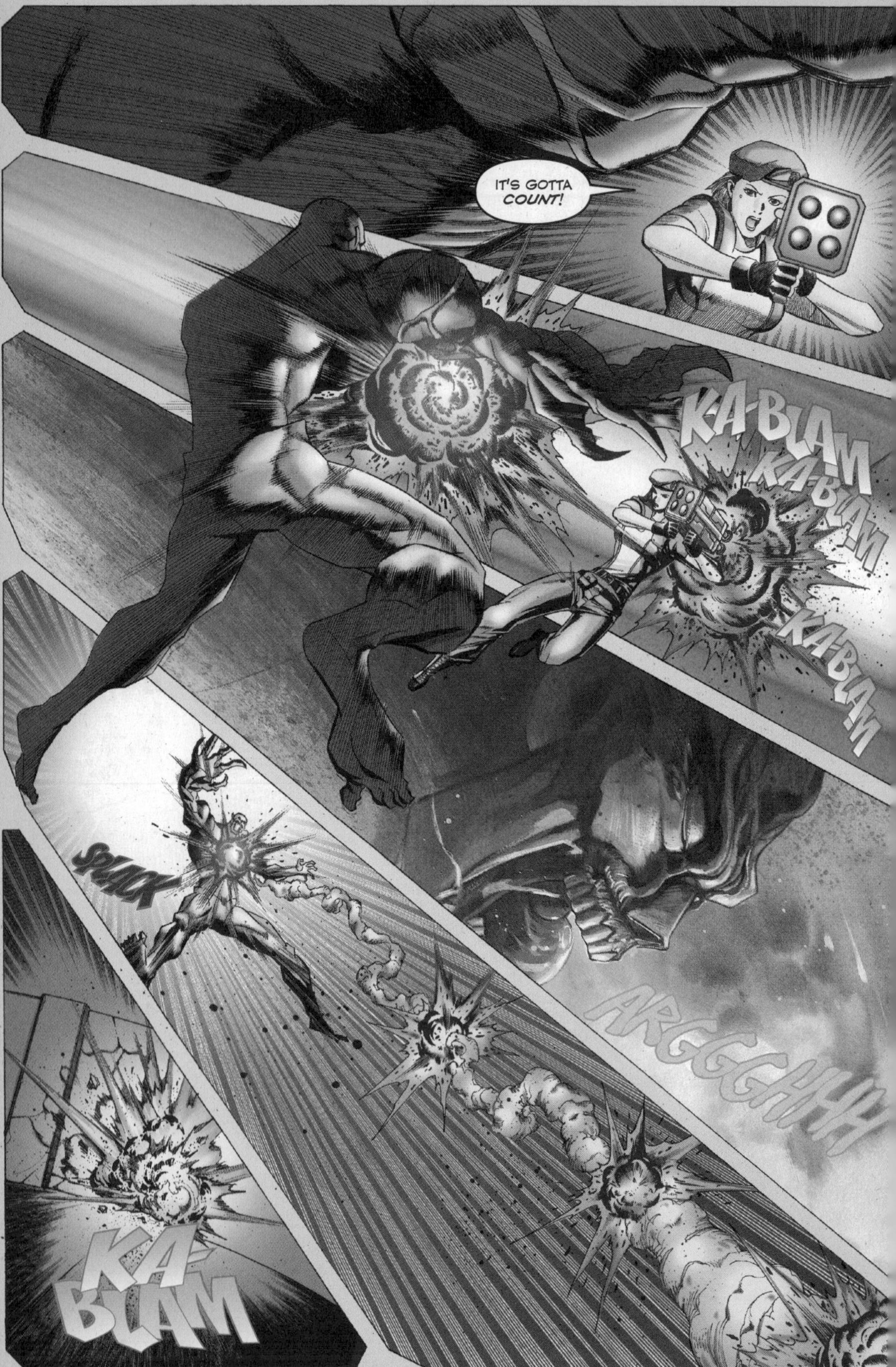
IT'S GOTTA COUNT!
KA-BLAM
KA-BLAM
KA-BLAM
SPLAK
ARGGGHHH
KA-BLAM

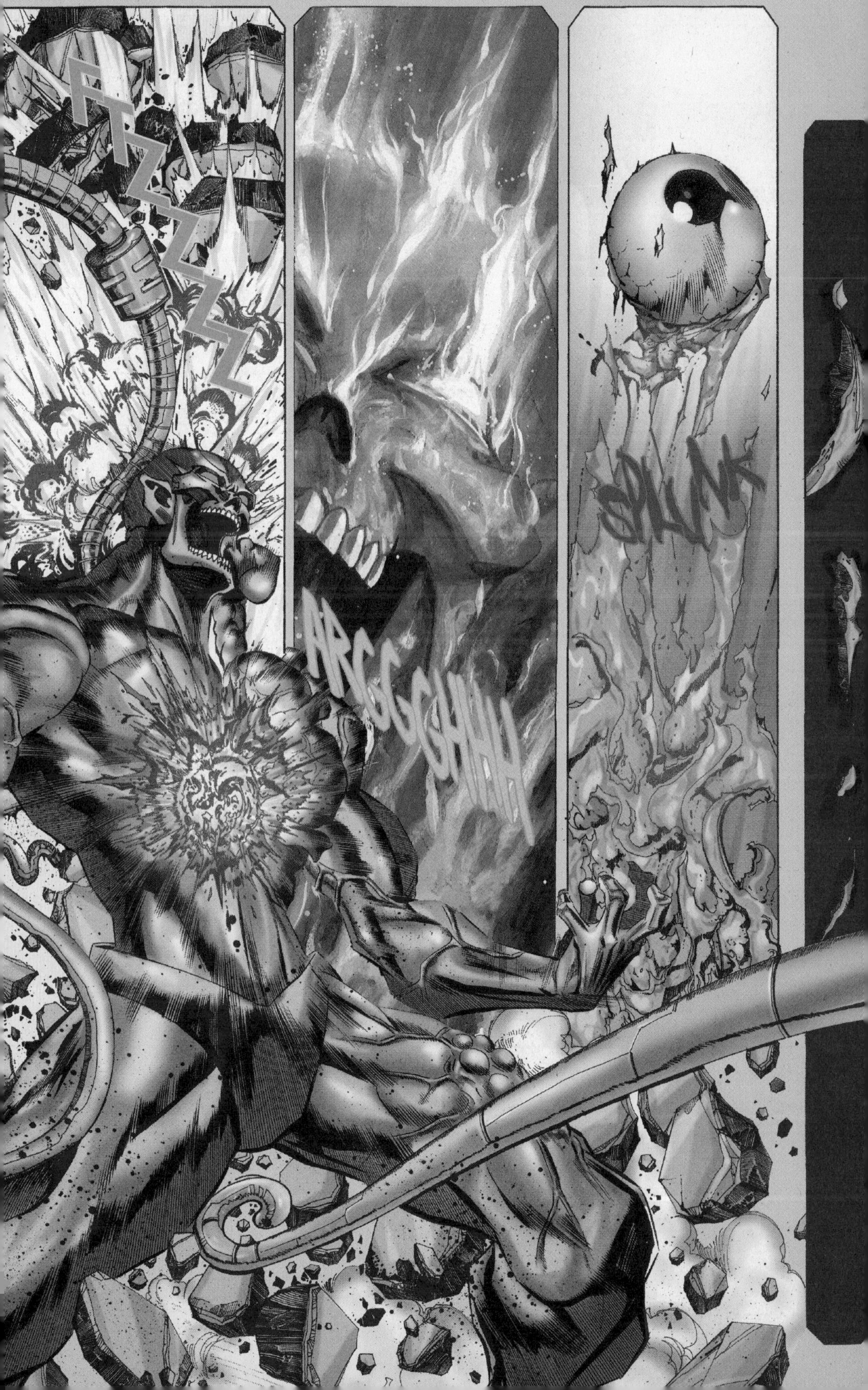
FTZZZZZ
ARGGGHHH
SHLUNK

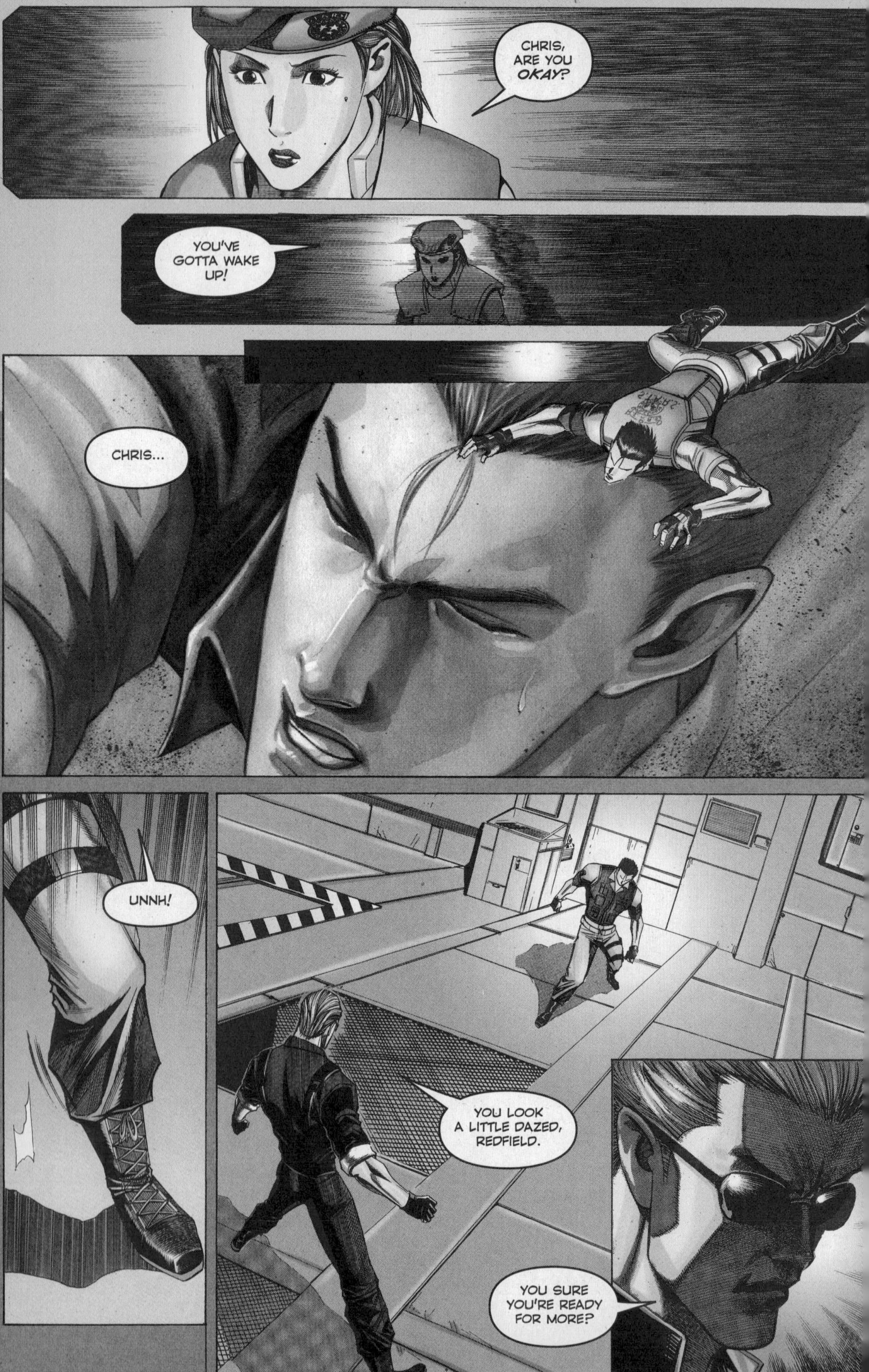
CHRIS, ARE YOU *OKAY?*
YOU'VE GOTTA WAKE UP!
CHRIS...
UNNH!
YOU LOOK A LITTLE DAZED, REDFIELD.
YOU SURE YOU'RE READY FOR MORE?

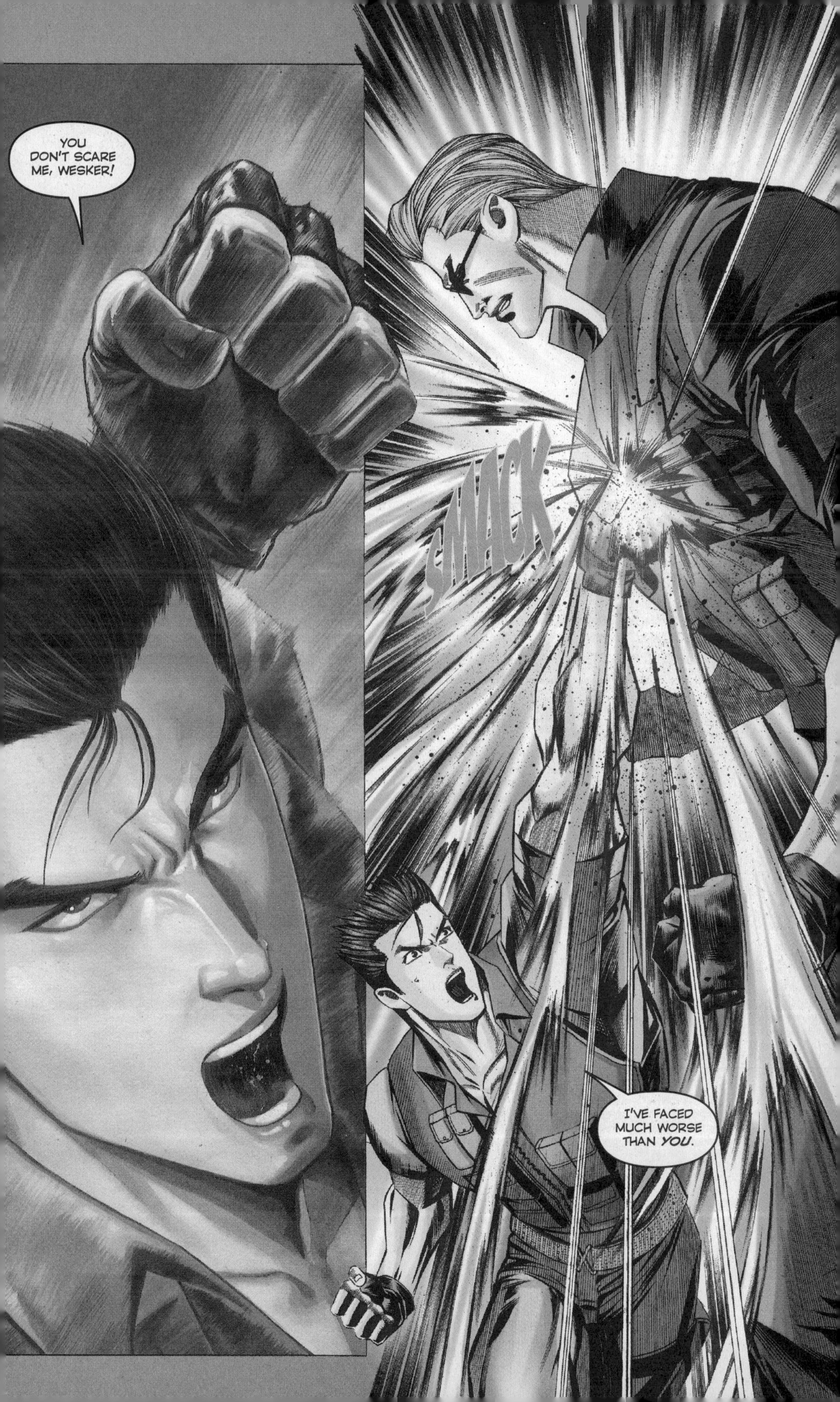
YOU DON'T SCARE ME, WESKER!
SMACK
I'VE FACED MUCH WORSE THAN YOU.

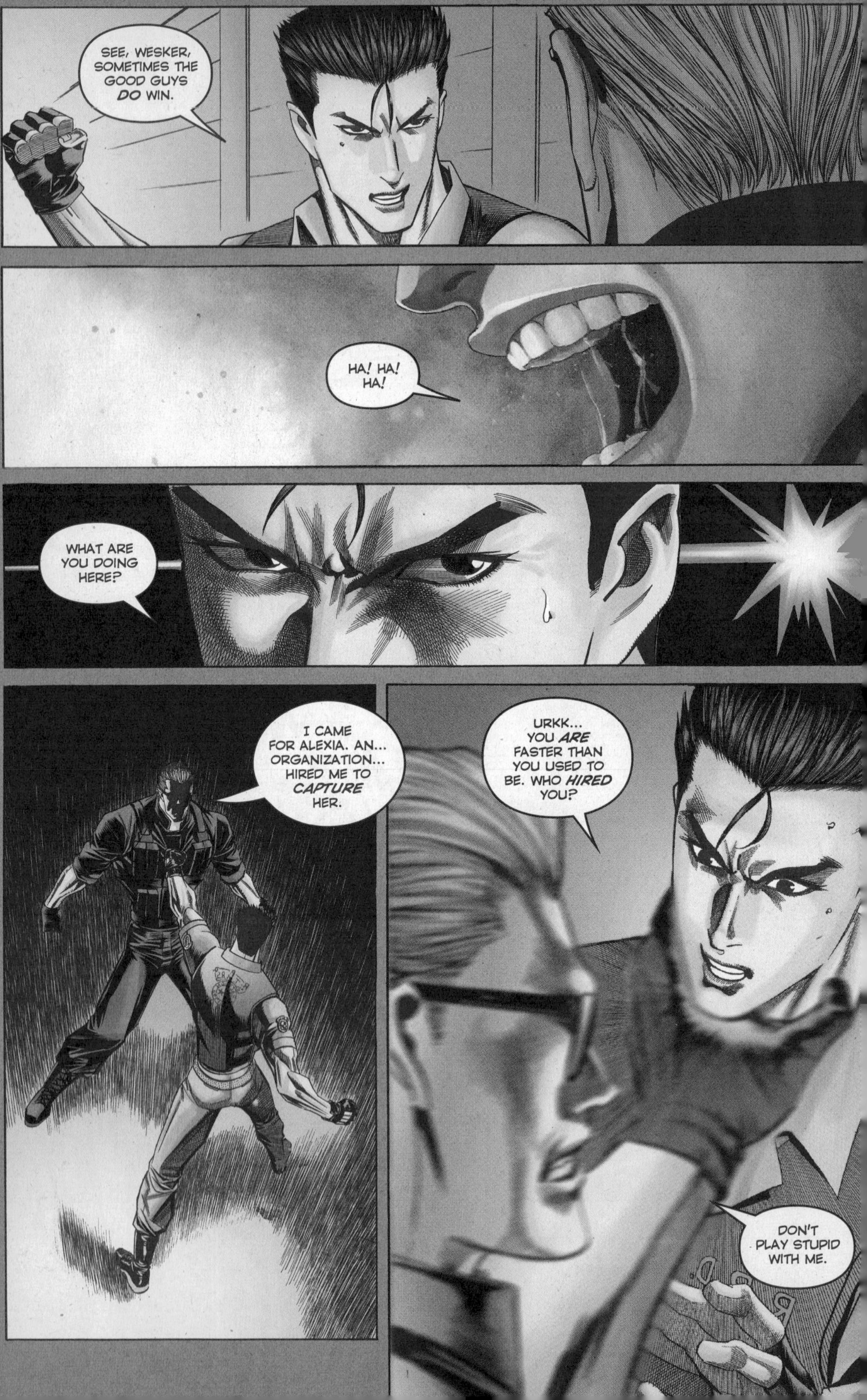
SEE, WESKER, SOMETIMES THE GOOD GUYS *DO* WIN.
HA! HA! HA!
WHAT ARE YOU DOING HERE?
I CAME FOR ALEXIA. AN... ORGANIZATION... HIRED ME TO *CAPTURE* HER.
URKK... YOU *ARE* FASTER THAN YOU USED TO BE. WHO *HIRED* YOU?
DON'T PLAY STUPID WITH ME.

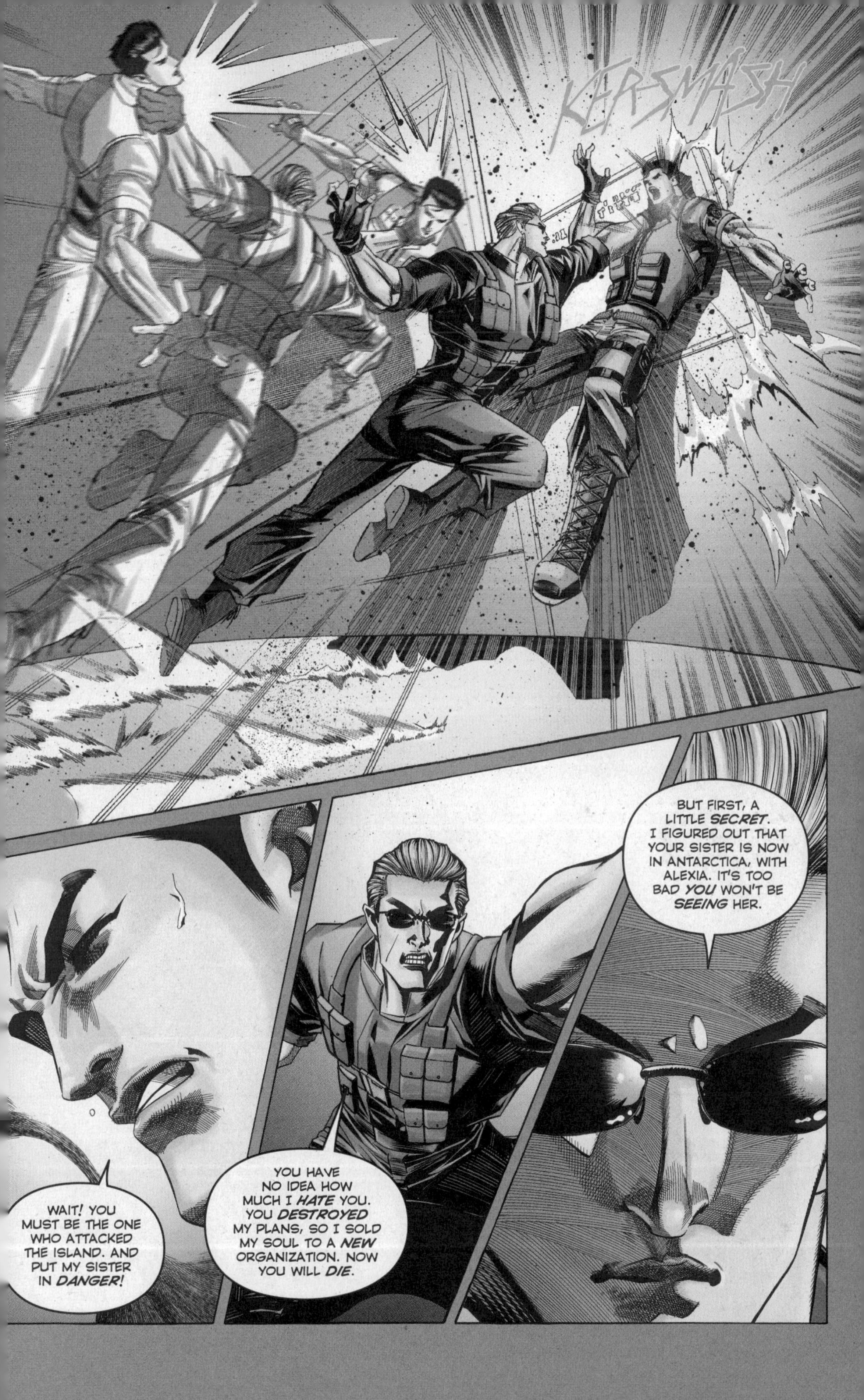
KER-SMASH
WAIT! YOU MUST BE THE ONE WHO ATTACKED THE ISLAND. AND PUT MY SISTER IN DANGER!
YOU HAVE NO IDEA HOW MUCH I HATE YOU. YOU DESTROYED MY PLANS, SO I SOLD MY SOUL TO A NEW ORGANIZATION. NOW YOU WILL DIE.
BUT FIRST, A LITTLE SECRET. I FIGURED OUT THAT YOUR SISTER IS NOW IN ANTARCTICA, WITH ALEXIA. IT'S TOO BAD YOU WON'T BE SEEING HER.

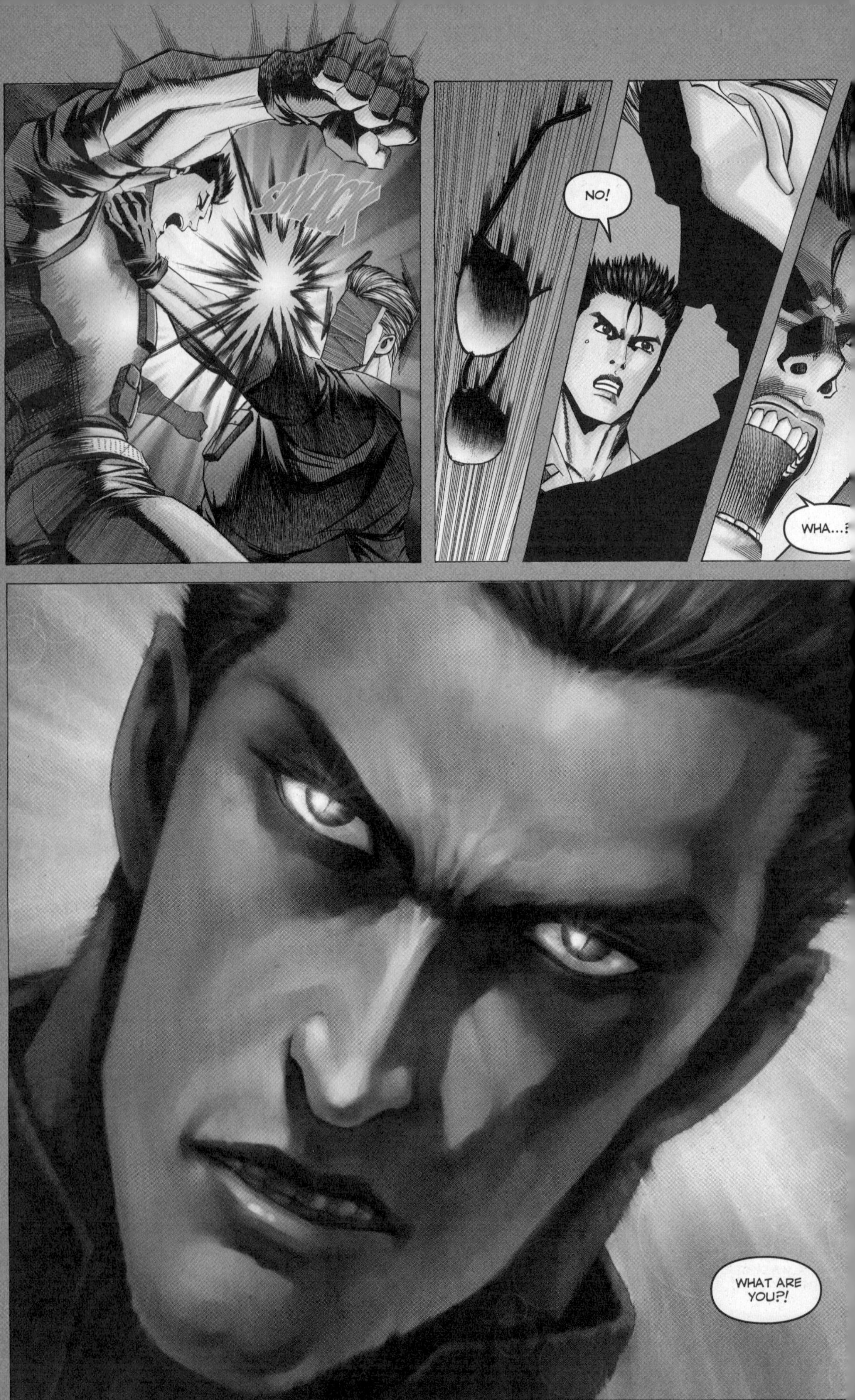
SMACK
NO!
WHA...?!
WHAT ARE YOU?!

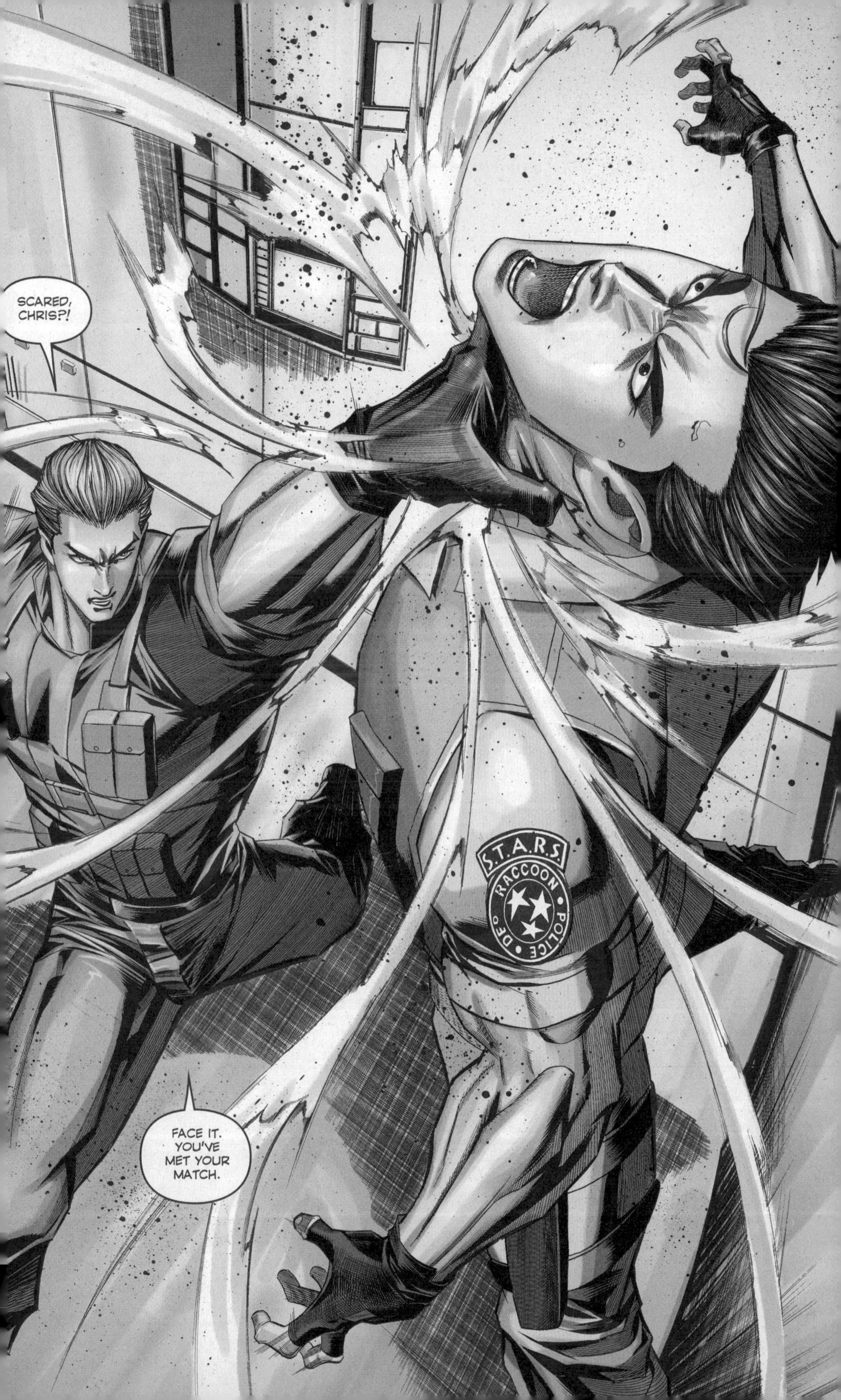
SCARED, CHRIS?!
FACE IT. YOU'VE MET YOUR MATCH.
S.T.A.R.S.
RACCOON POLICE DEPT.

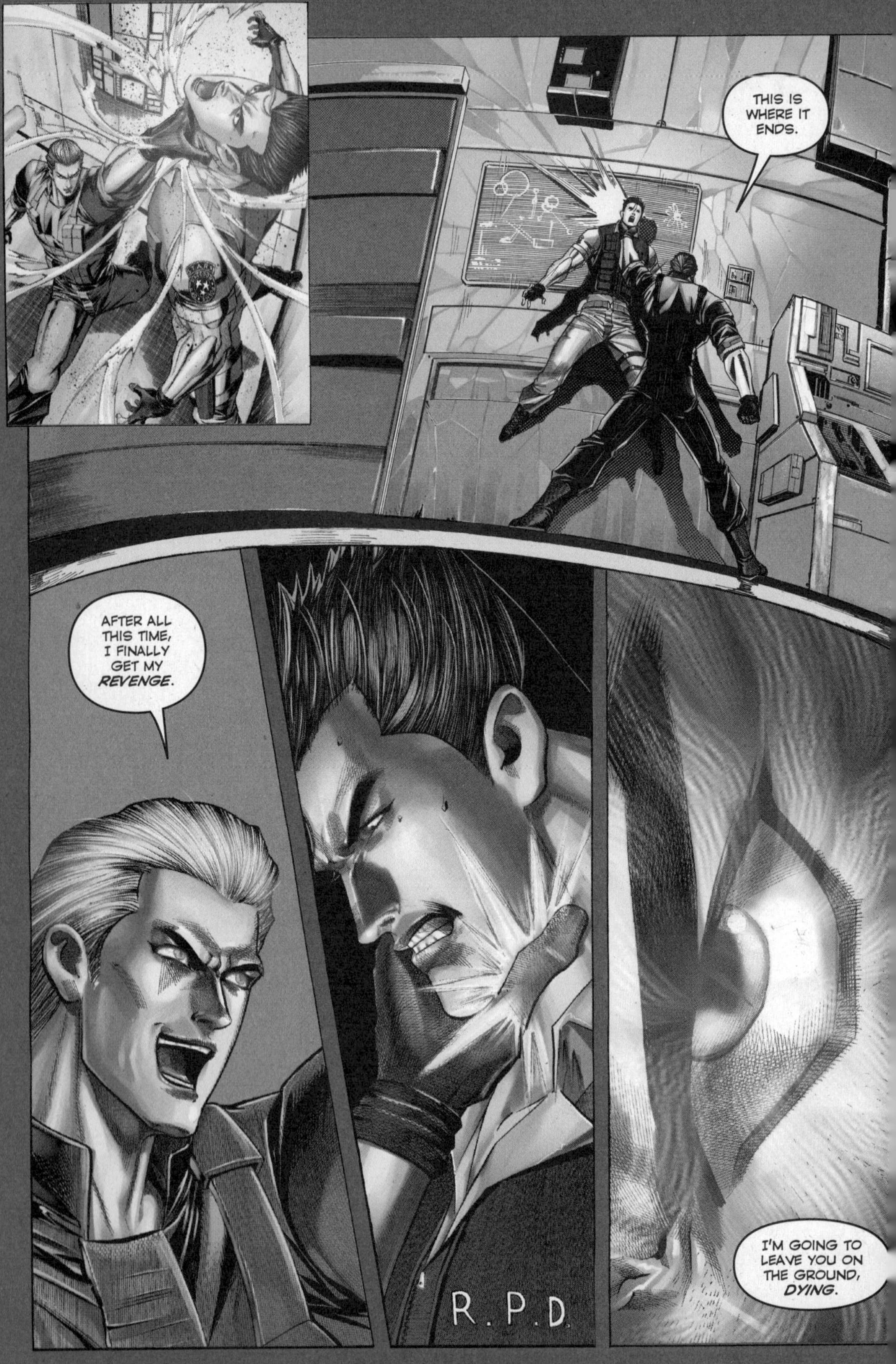

THIS IS WHERE IT ENDS.
AFTER ALL THIS TIME, I FINALLY GET MY *REVENGE*.
R.P.D.
I'M GOING TO LEAVE YOU ON THE GROUND, *DYING*.

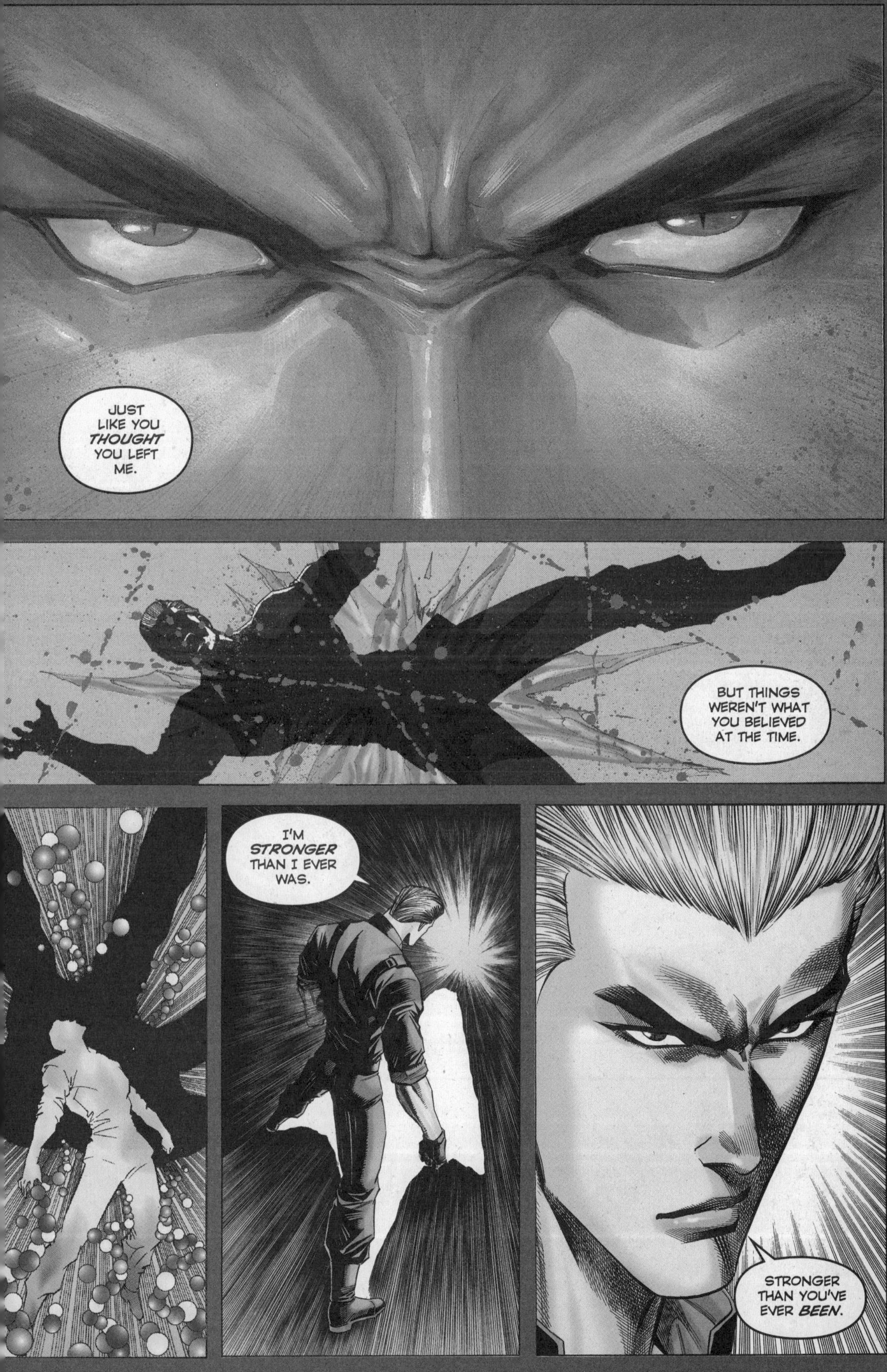
JUST LIKE YOU *THOUGHT* YOU LEFT ME.
BUT THINGS WEREN'T WHAT YOU BELIEVED AT THE TIME.
I'M *STRONGER* THAN I EVER WAS.
STRONGER THAN YOU'VE EVER *BEEN*.

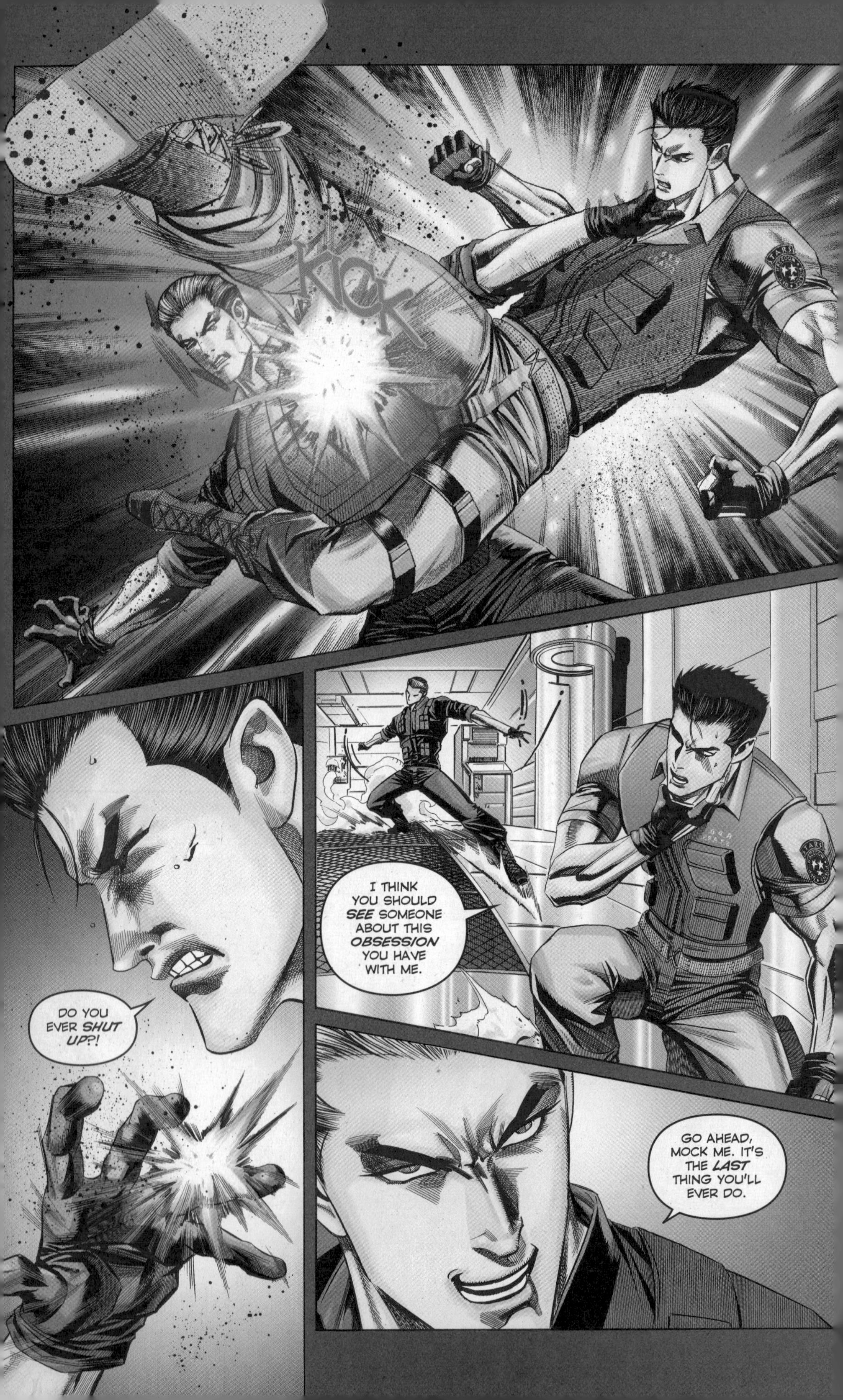
KICK
I THINK YOU SHOULD SEE SOMEONE ABOUT THIS OBSESSION YOU HAVE WITH ME.
DO YOU EVER SHUT UP?!
GO AHEAD, MOCK ME. IT'S THE LAST THING YOU'LL EVER DO.

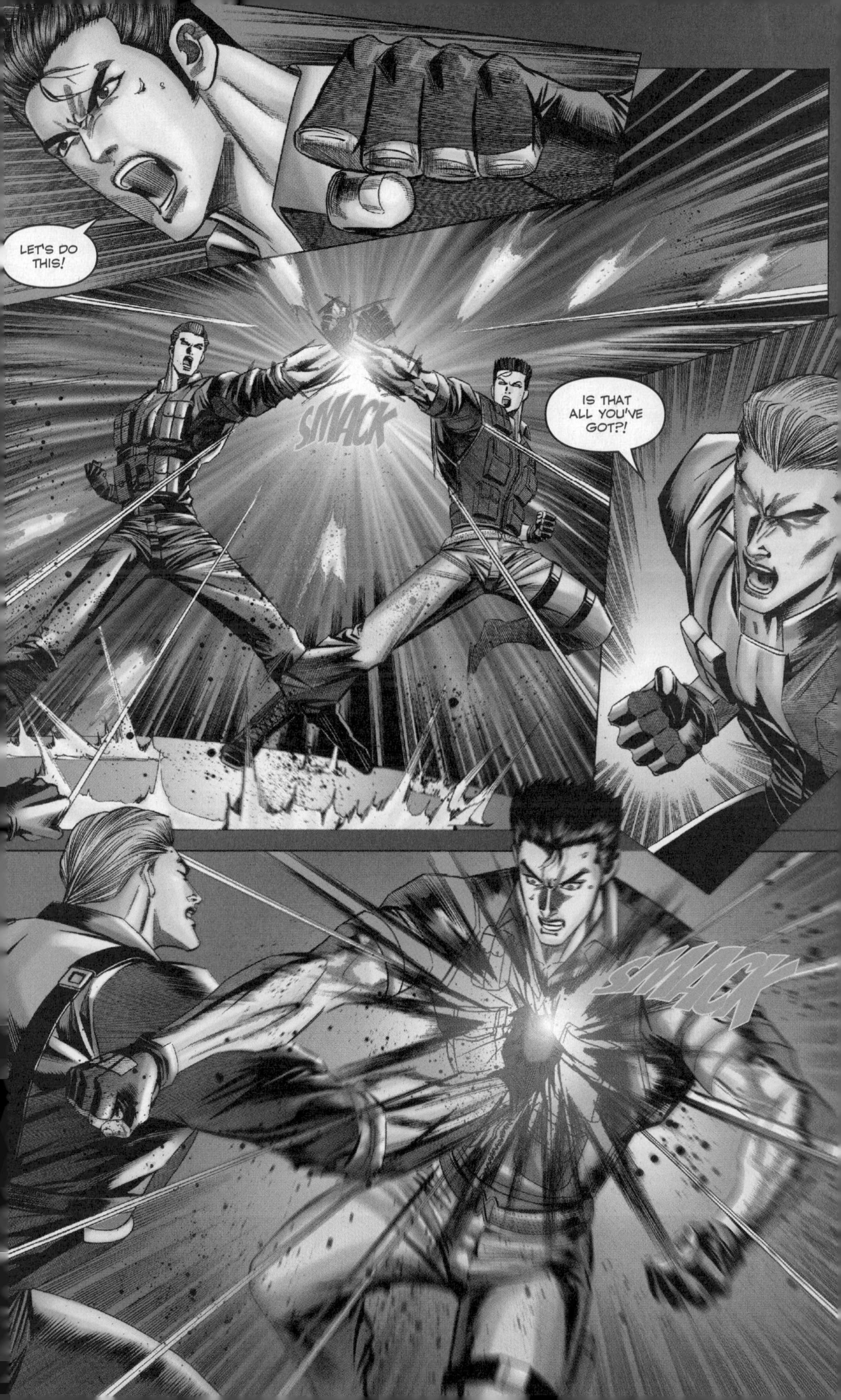
LET'S DO THIS!
SMACK
IS THAT ALL YOU'VE GOT?!
SMACK

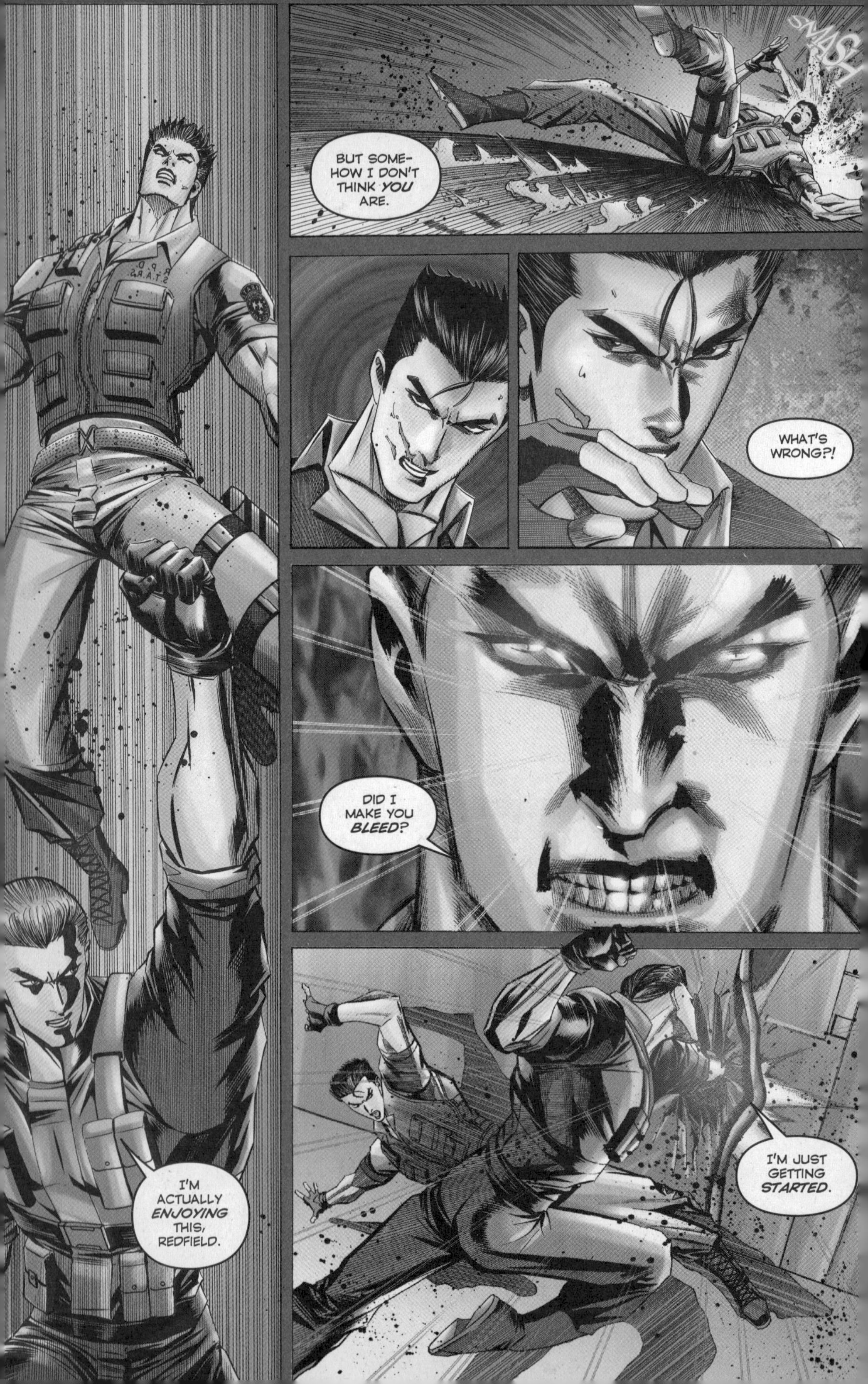
I'M ACTUALLY ENJOYING THIS, REDFIELD.
BUT SOME-HOW I DON'T THINK YOU ARE.
SMASH
WHAT'S WRONG?!
DID I MAKE YOU BLEED?
I'M JUST GETTING STARTED.

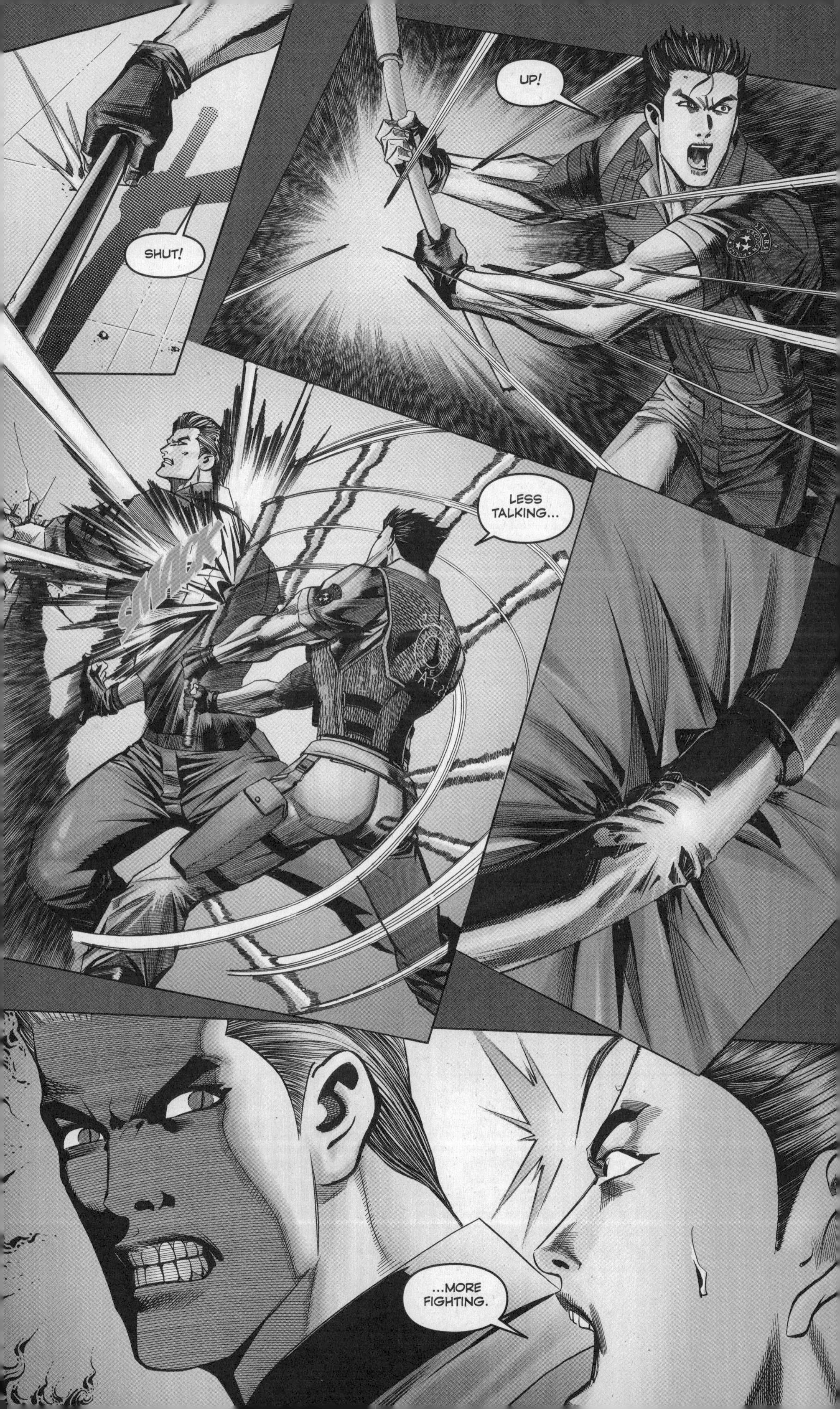
SHUT!
UP!
LESS TALKING...
SMACK
...MORE FIGHTING.

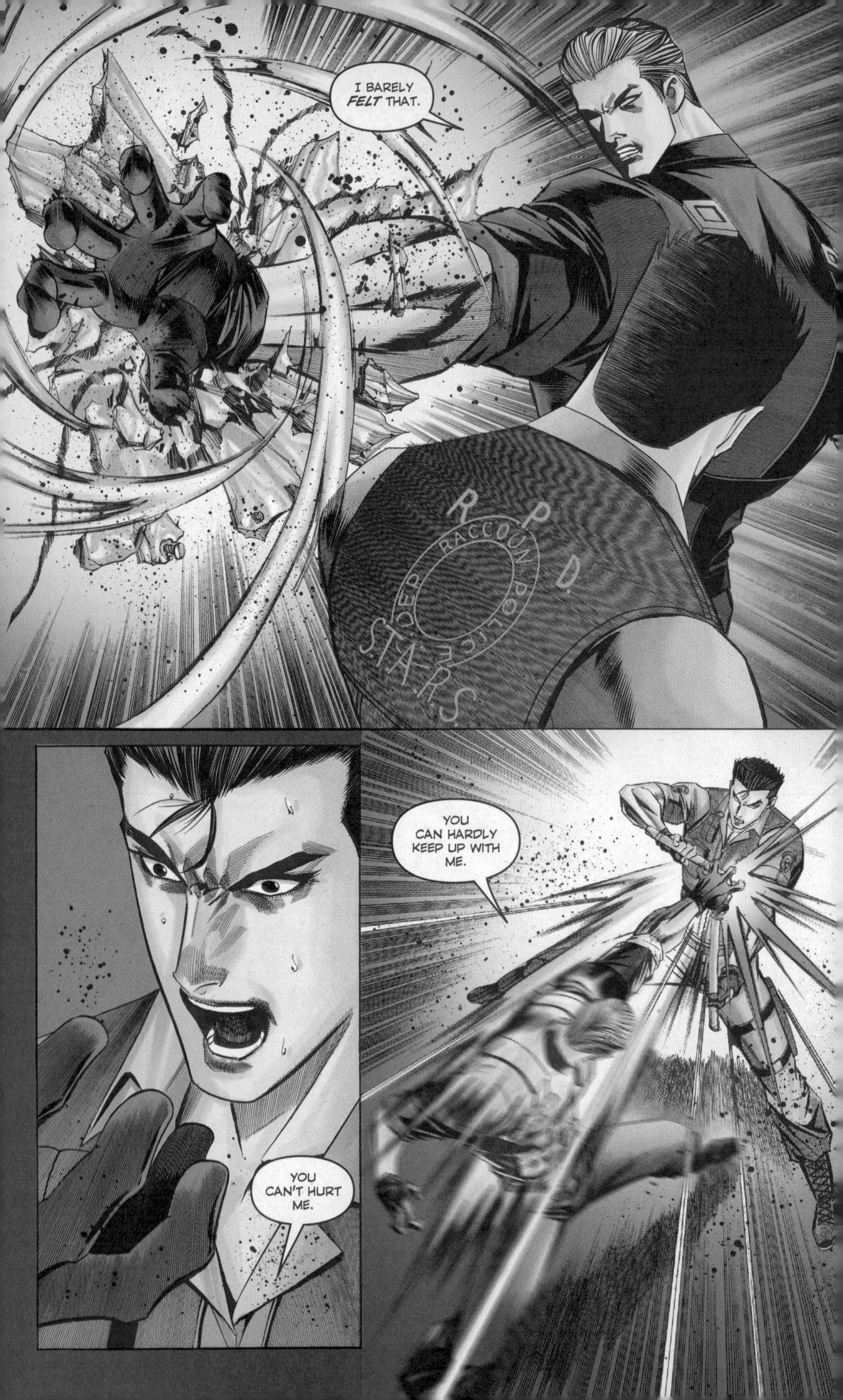
I BARELY *FELT* THAT.
R.P.D.
RACCOON POLICE DEP.
S.T.A.R.S.
YOU CAN'T HURT ME.
YOU CAN HARDLY KEEP UP WITH ME.

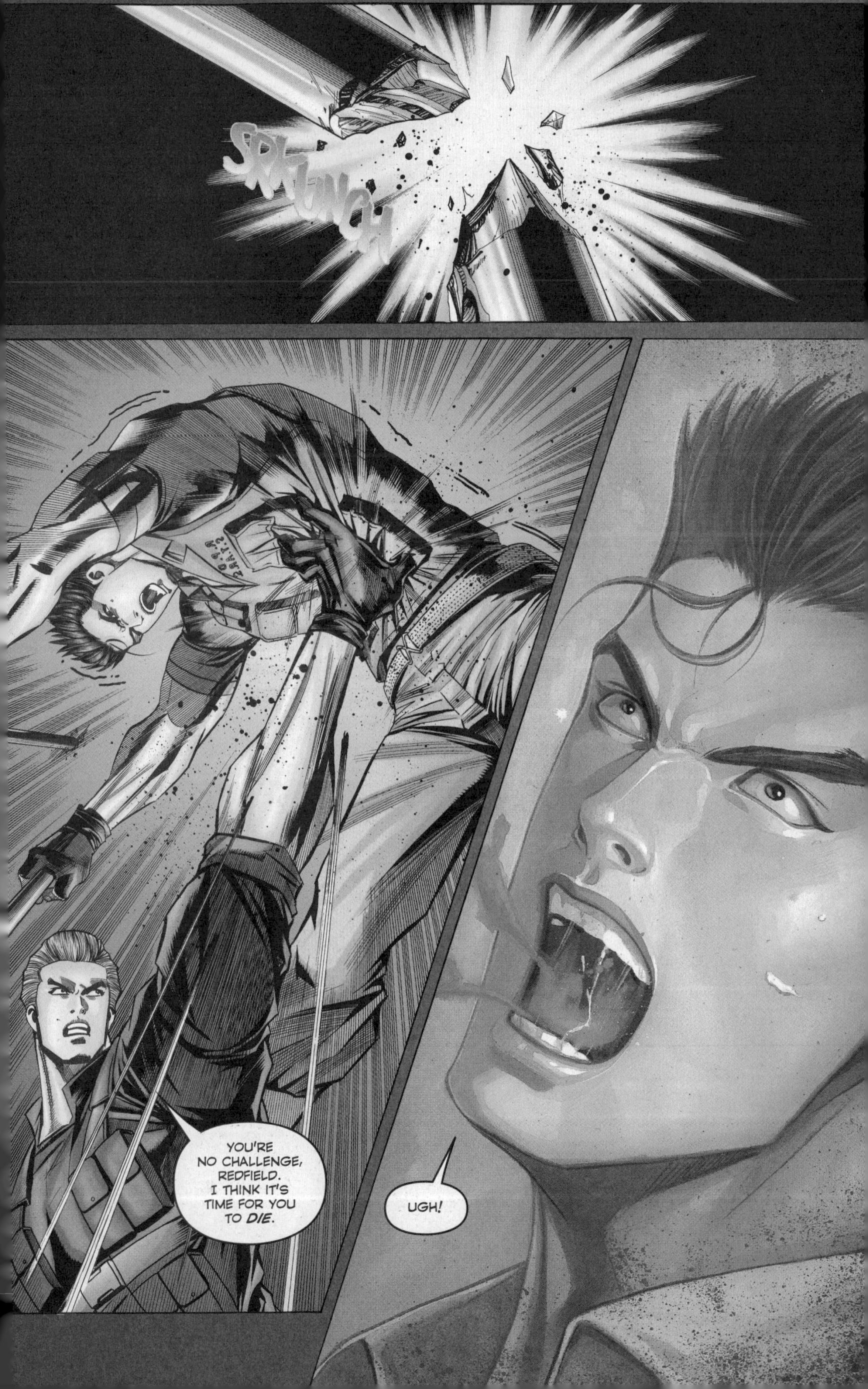
SPKLUNCH
YOU'RE NO CHALLENGE, REDFIELD. I THINK IT'S TIME FOR YOU TO *DIE*.
UGH!

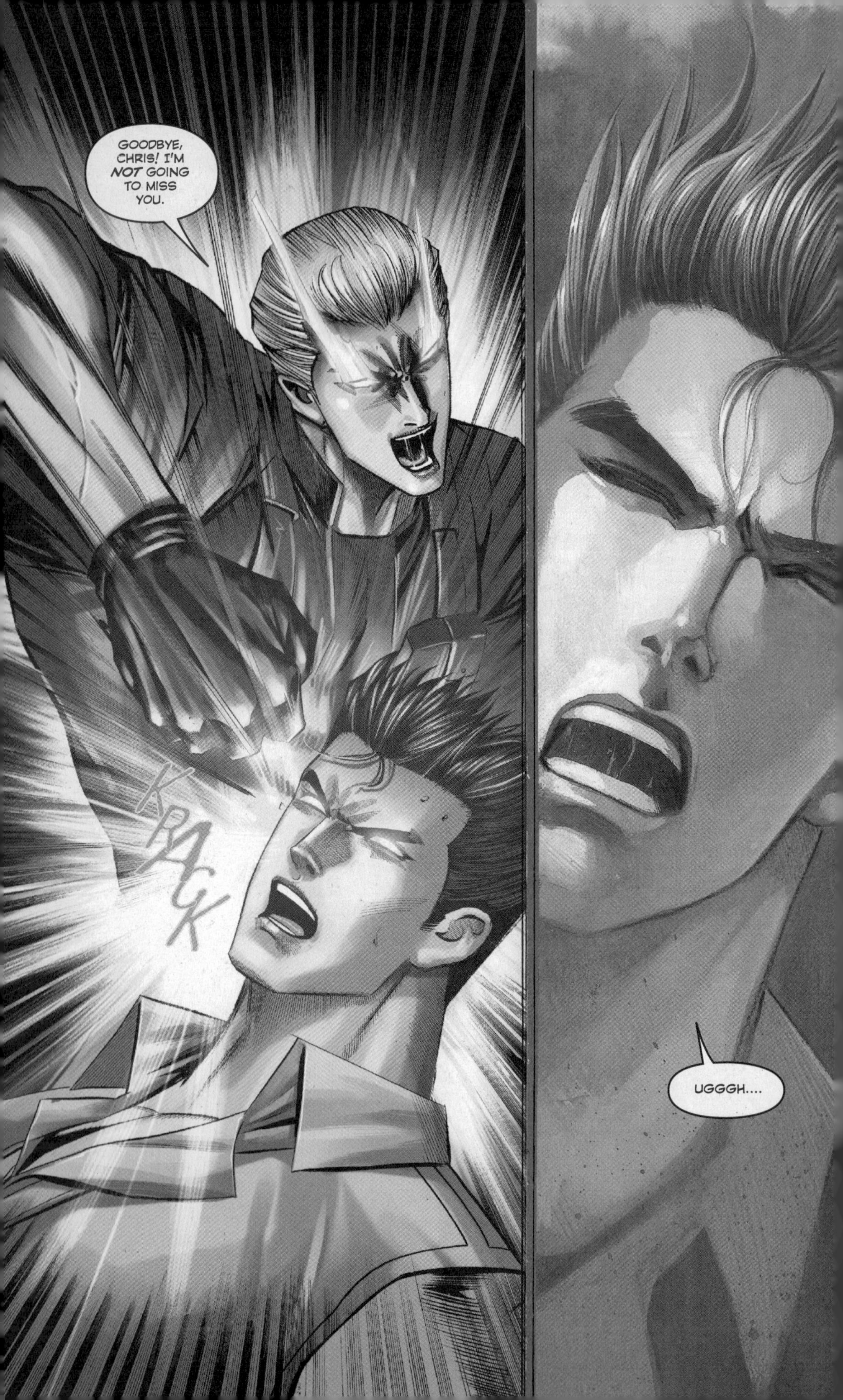

GOODBYE, CHRIS! I'M *NOT* GOING TO MISS YOU.
KRACK
UGGGH....

CHRIS ISN'T THE ONLY ONE WHO LOOKS LIKE HE'S IN TROUBLE.

BACK IN ANTARCTICA, STEVE REMAINS UNCONSCIOUS.

HOPEFULLY DREAMING OF A BETTER TIME.

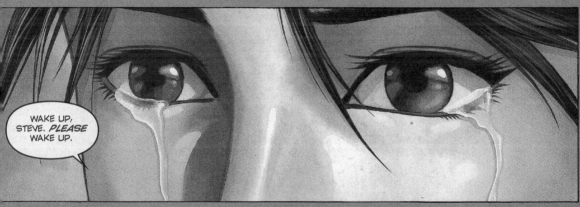

WAKE UP, STEVE. *PLEASE* WAKE UP.

I CAN'T LOSE YOU THIS WAY.

WE'VE COME TOO FAR.

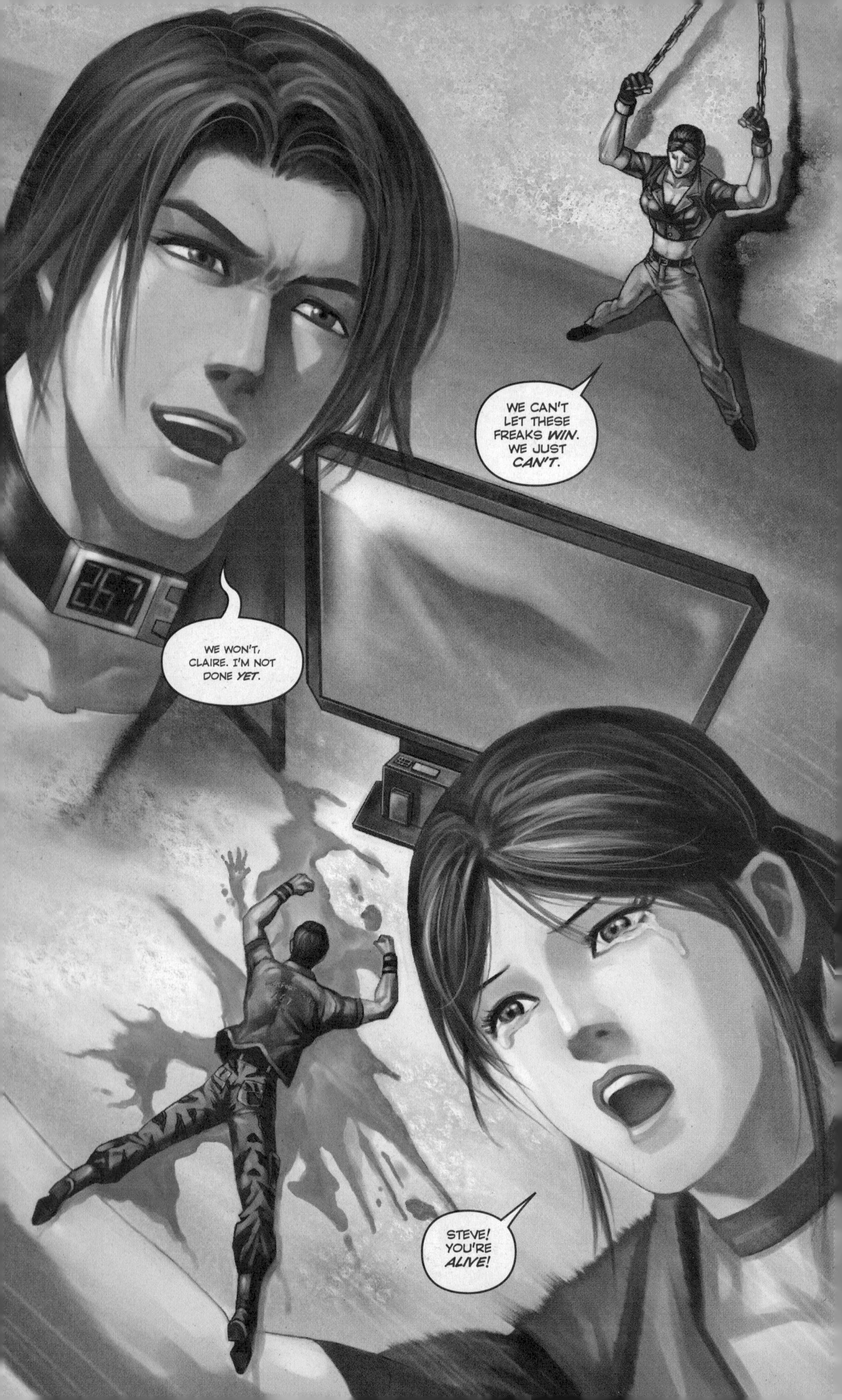
WE CAN'T LET THESE FREAKS WIN. WE JUST CAN'T.
WE WON'T, CLAIRE. I'M NOT DONE YET.
STEVE! YOU'RE ALIVE!

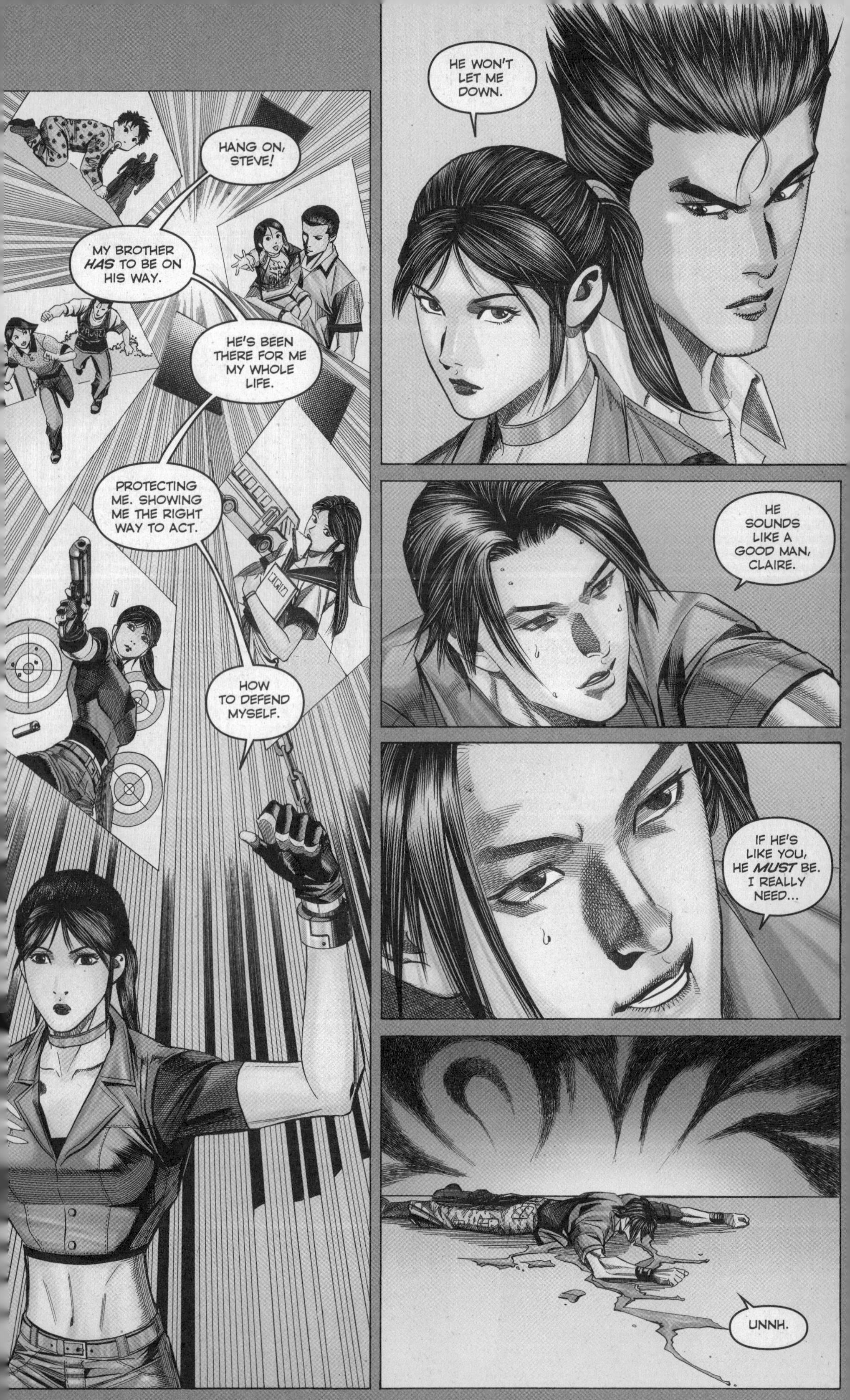
HANG ON, STEVE!
MY BROTHER *HAS* TO BE ON HIS WAY.
HE'S BEEN THERE FOR ME MY WHOLE LIFE.
PROTECTING ME. SHOWING ME THE RIGHT WAY TO ACT.
HOW TO DEFEND MYSELF.
HE WON'T LET ME DOWN.
HE SOUNDS LIKE A GOOD MAN, CLAIRE.
IF HE'S LIKE YOU, HE *MUST* BE. I REALLY NEED...
UNNH.

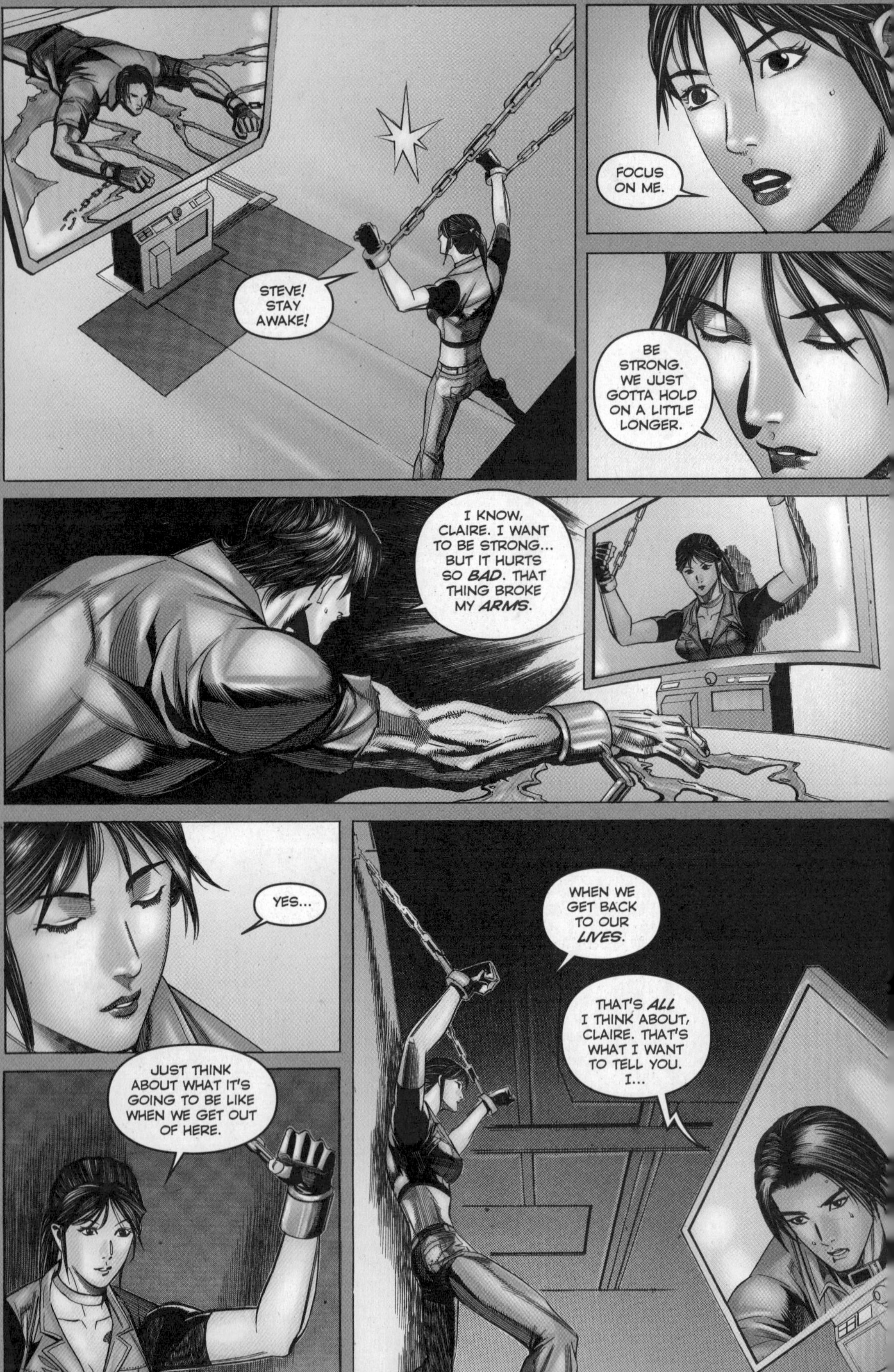

STEVE! STAY AWAKE!
FOCUS ON ME.
BE STRONG. WE JUST GOTTA HOLD ON A LITTLE LONGER.
I KNOW, CLAIRE. I WANT TO BE STRONG... BUT IT HURTS SO BAD. THAT THING BROKE MY ARMS.
YES...
JUST THINK ABOUT WHAT IT'S GOING TO BE LIKE WHEN WE GET OUT OF HERE.
WHEN WE GET BACK TO OUR LIVES.
THAT'S ALL I THINK ABOUT, CLAIRE. THAT'S WHAT I WANT TO TELL YOU. I...

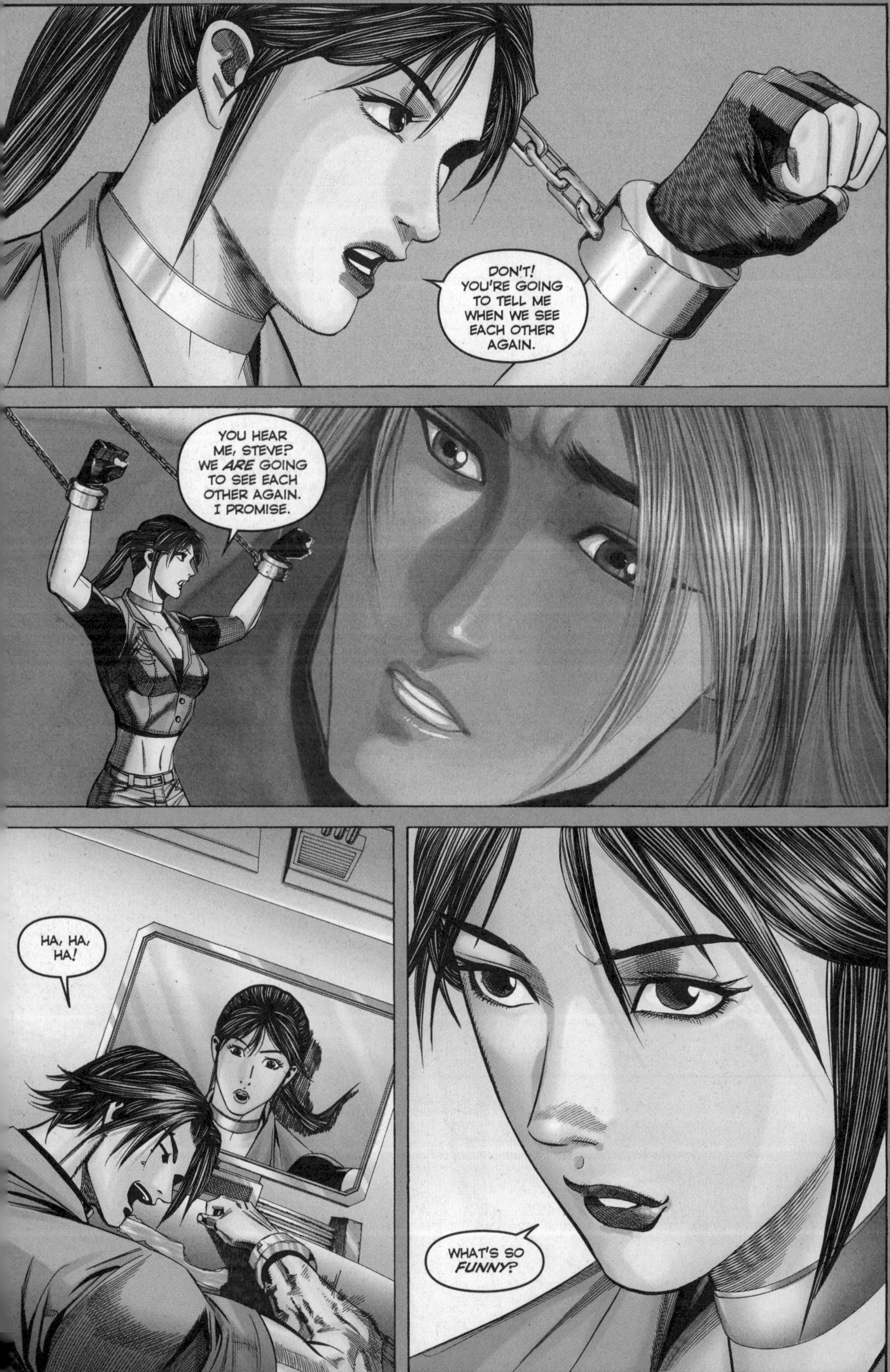
DON'T! YOU'RE GOING TO TELL ME WHEN WE SEE EACH OTHER AGAIN.
YOU HEAR ME, STEVE? WE *ARE* GOING TO SEE EACH OTHER AGAIN. I PROMISE.
HA, HA, HA!
WHAT'S SO *FUNNY*?

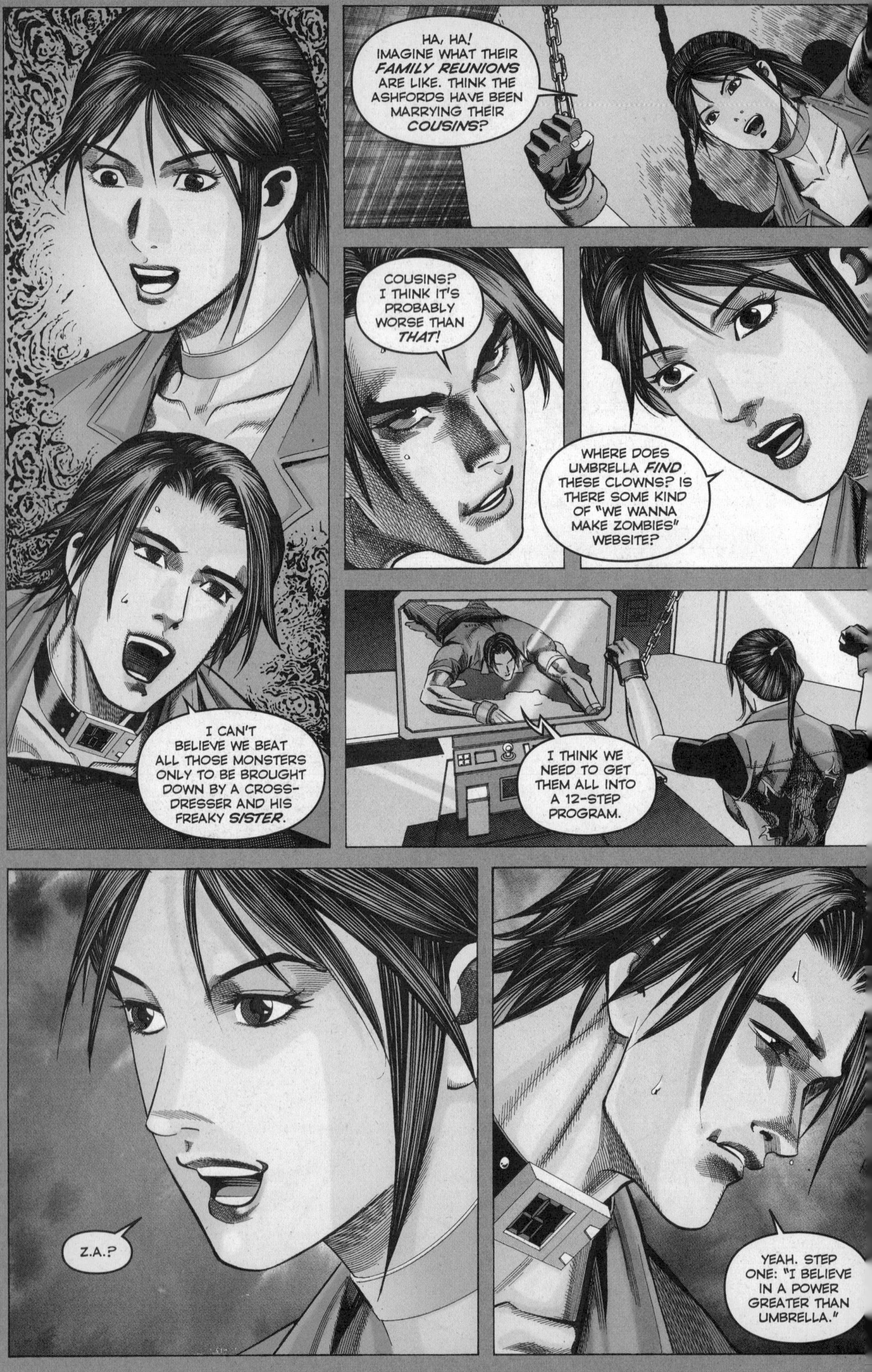
HA, HA! IMAGINE WHAT THEIR FAMILY REUNIONS ARE LIKE. THINK THE ASHFORDS HAVE BEEN MARRYING THEIR COUSINS?
COUSINS? I THINK IT'S PROBABLY WORSE THAN THAT!
WHERE DOES UMBRELLA FIND THESE CLOWNS? IS THERE SOME KIND OF "WE WANNA MAKE ZOMBIES" WEBSITE?
I CAN'T BELIEVE WE BEAT ALL THOSE MONSTERS ONLY TO BE BROUGHT DOWN BY A CROSS-DRESSER AND HIS FREAKY SISTER.
I THINK WE NEED TO GET THEM ALL INTO A 12-STEP PROGRAM.
Z.A.?
YEAH. STEP ONE: "I BELIEVE IN A POWER GREATER THAN UMBRELLA."

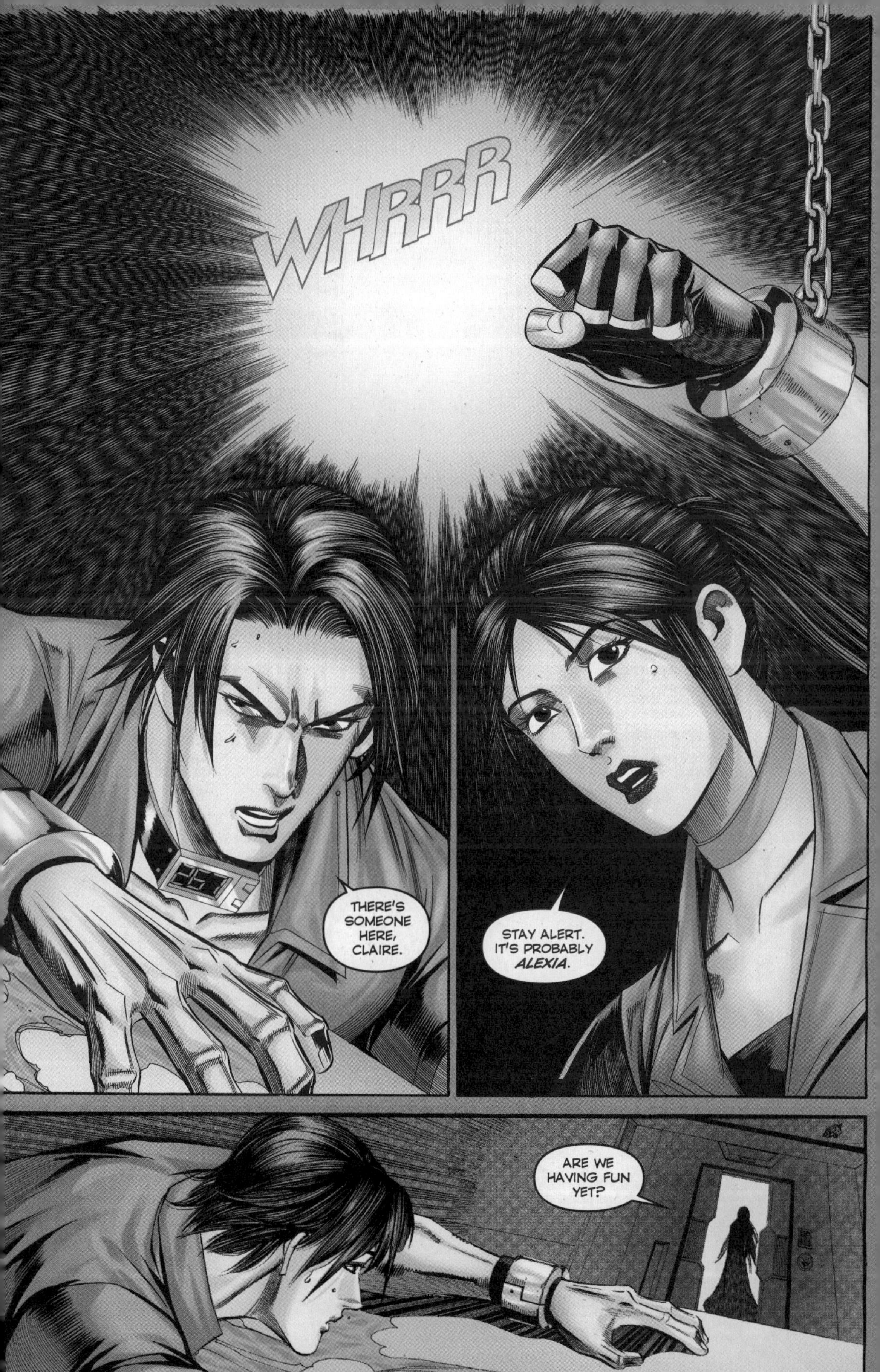
WHRRR
THERE'S SOMEONE HERE, CLAIRE.
STAY ALERT. IT'S PROBABLY *ALEXIA*.
ARE WE HAVING FUN YET?

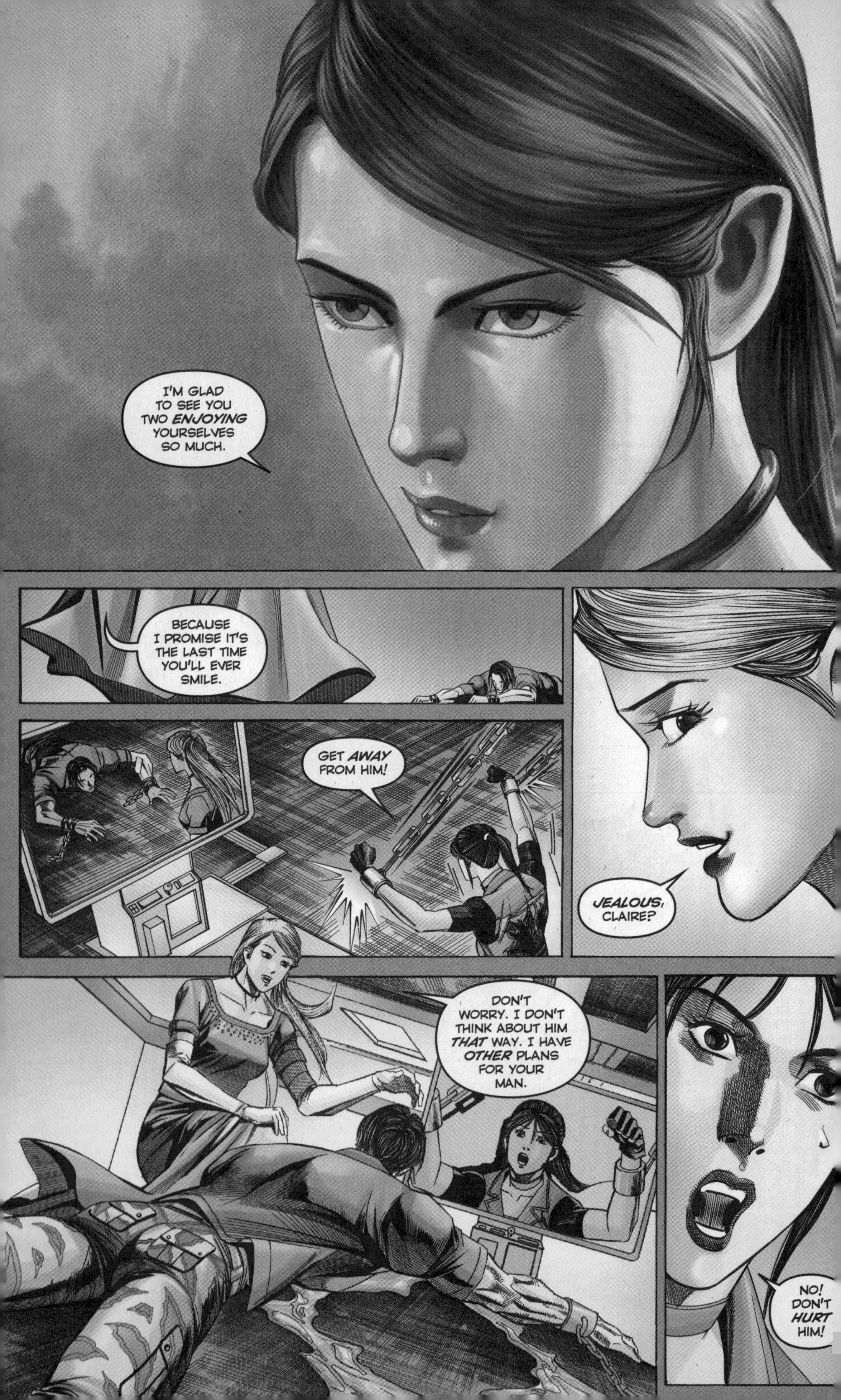
I'M GLAD TO SEE YOU TWO *ENJOYING* YOURSELVES SO MUCH.
BECAUSE I PROMISE IT'S THE LAST TIME YOU'LL EVER SMILE.
GET *AWAY* FROM HIM!
JEALOUS, CLAIRE?
DON'T WORRY. I DON'T THINK ABOUT HIM *THAT* WAY. I HAVE *OTHER* PLANS FOR YOUR MAN.
NO! DON'T *HURT* HIM!

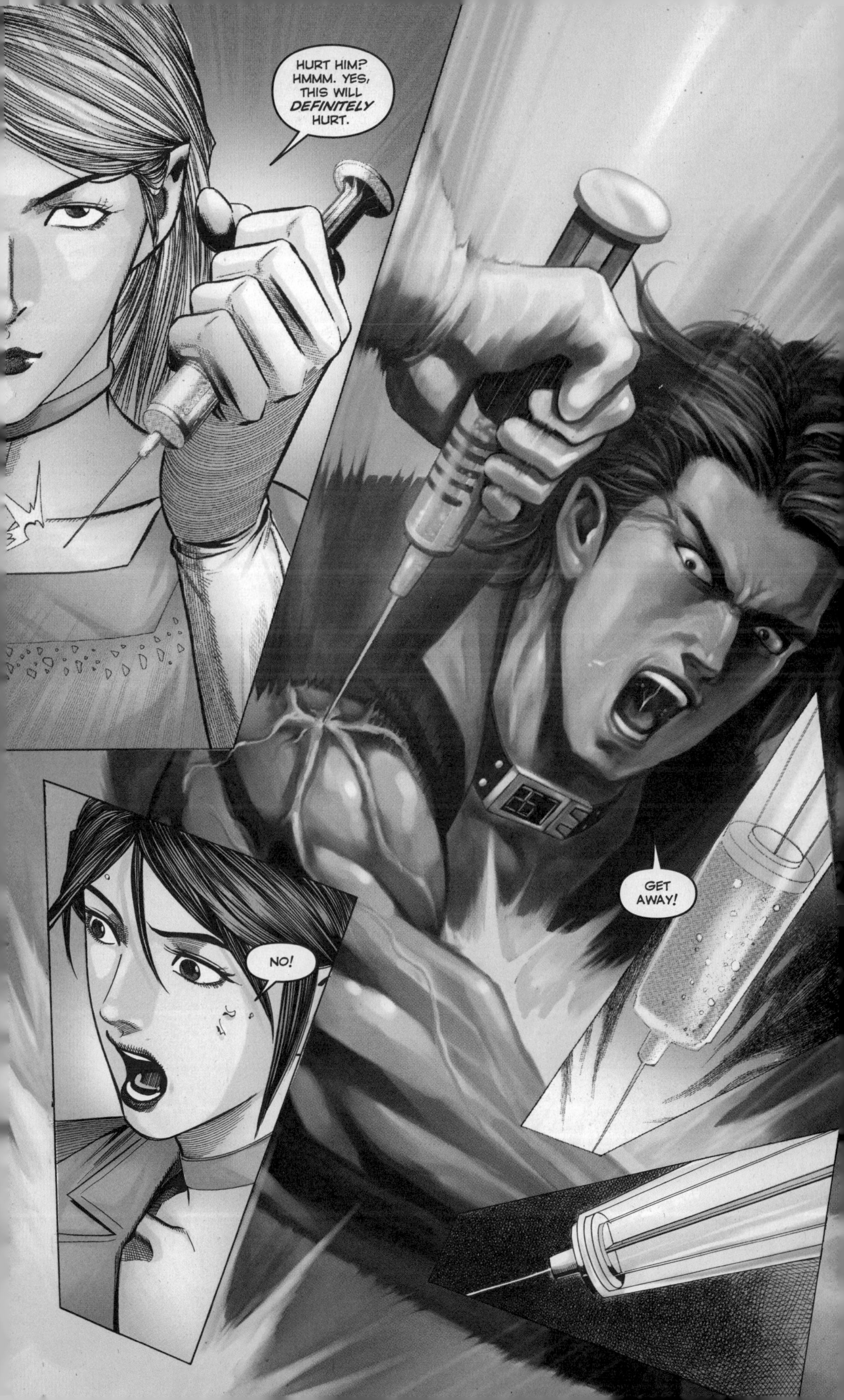
HURT HIM? HMMM. YES, THIS WILL *DEFINITELY* HURT.
GET AWAY!
NO!

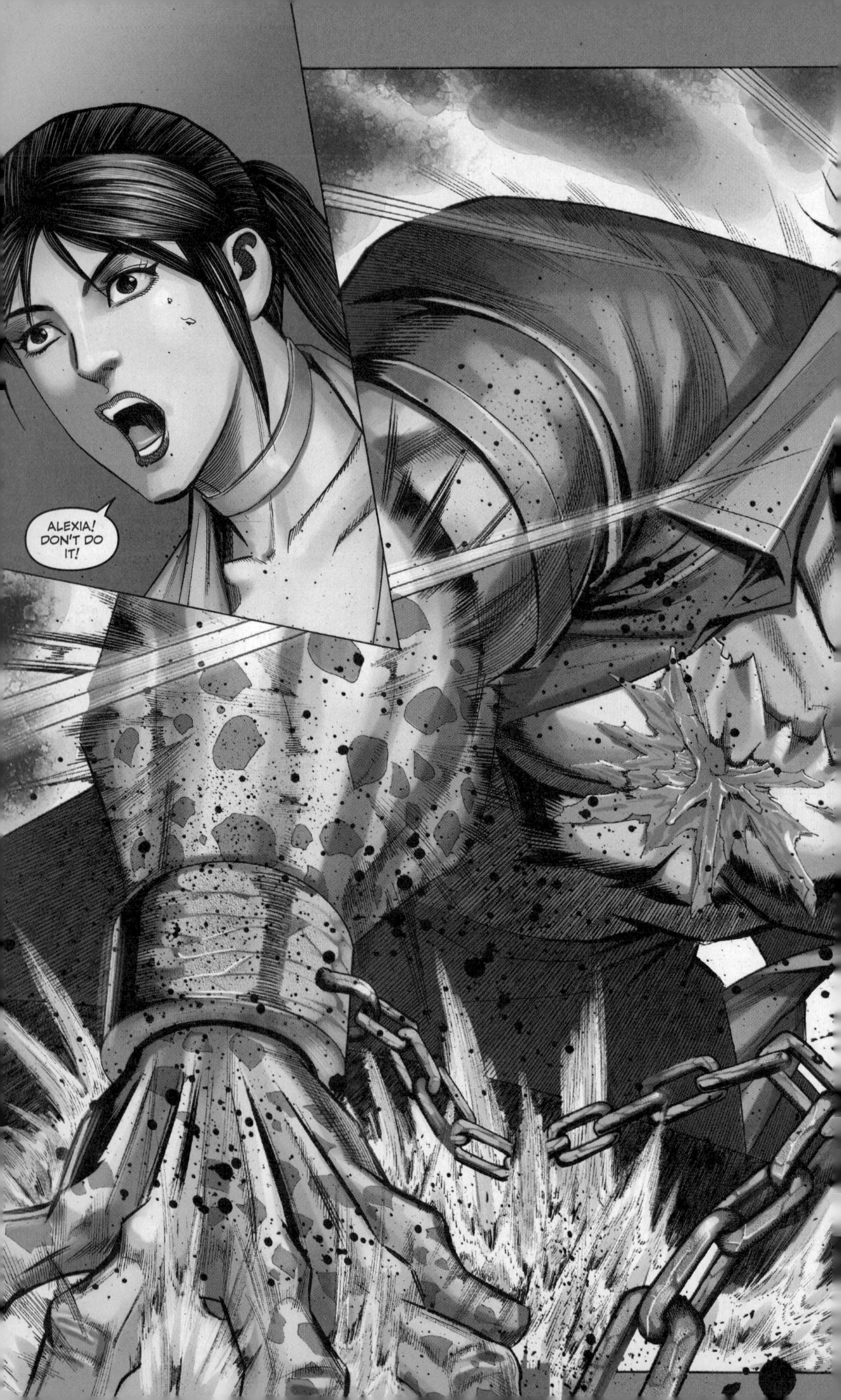
ALEXIA! DON'T DO IT!

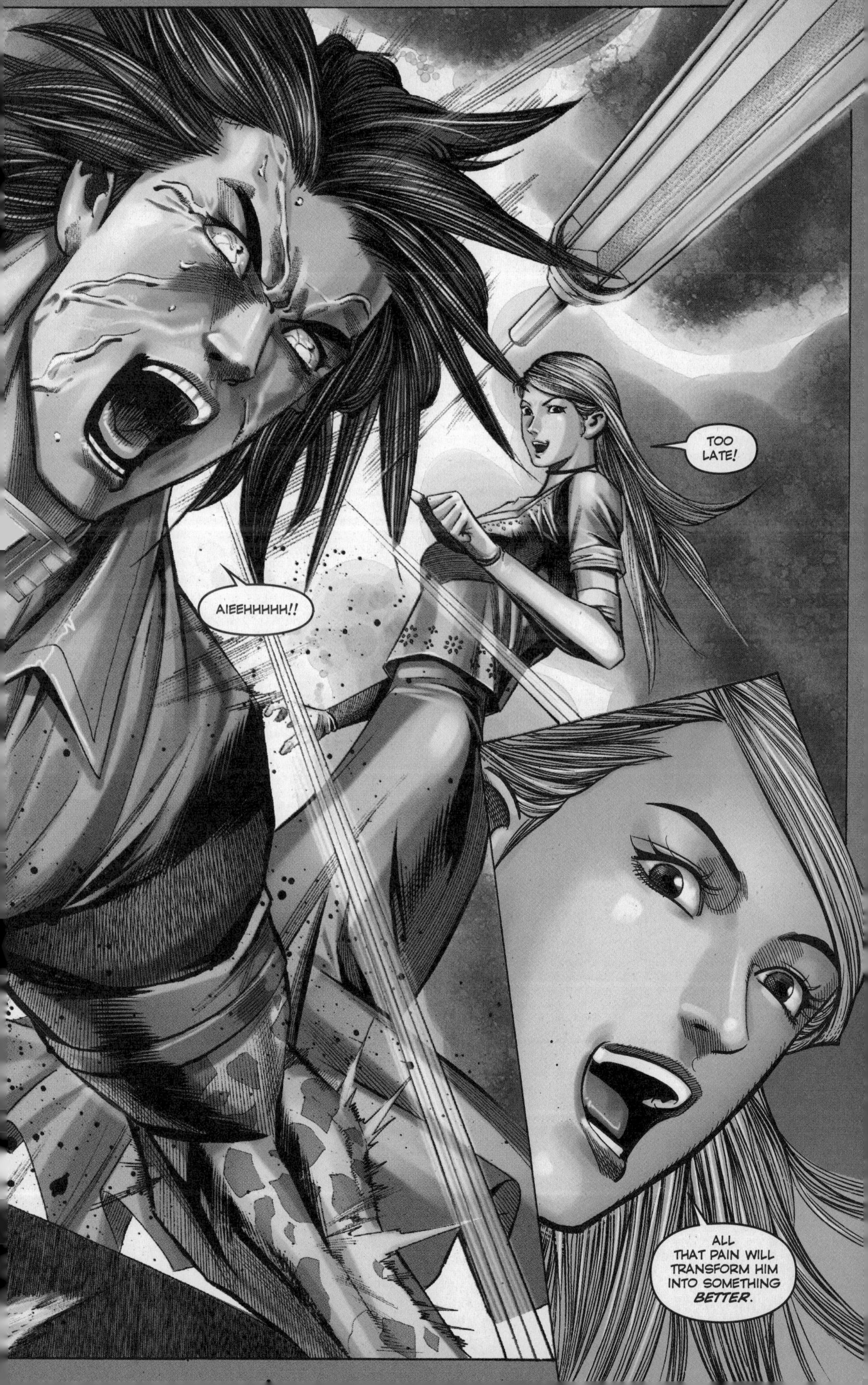
TOO LATE!
AIEEHHHHH!!
ALL THAT PAIN WILL TRANSFORM HIM INTO SOMETHING *BETTER*.

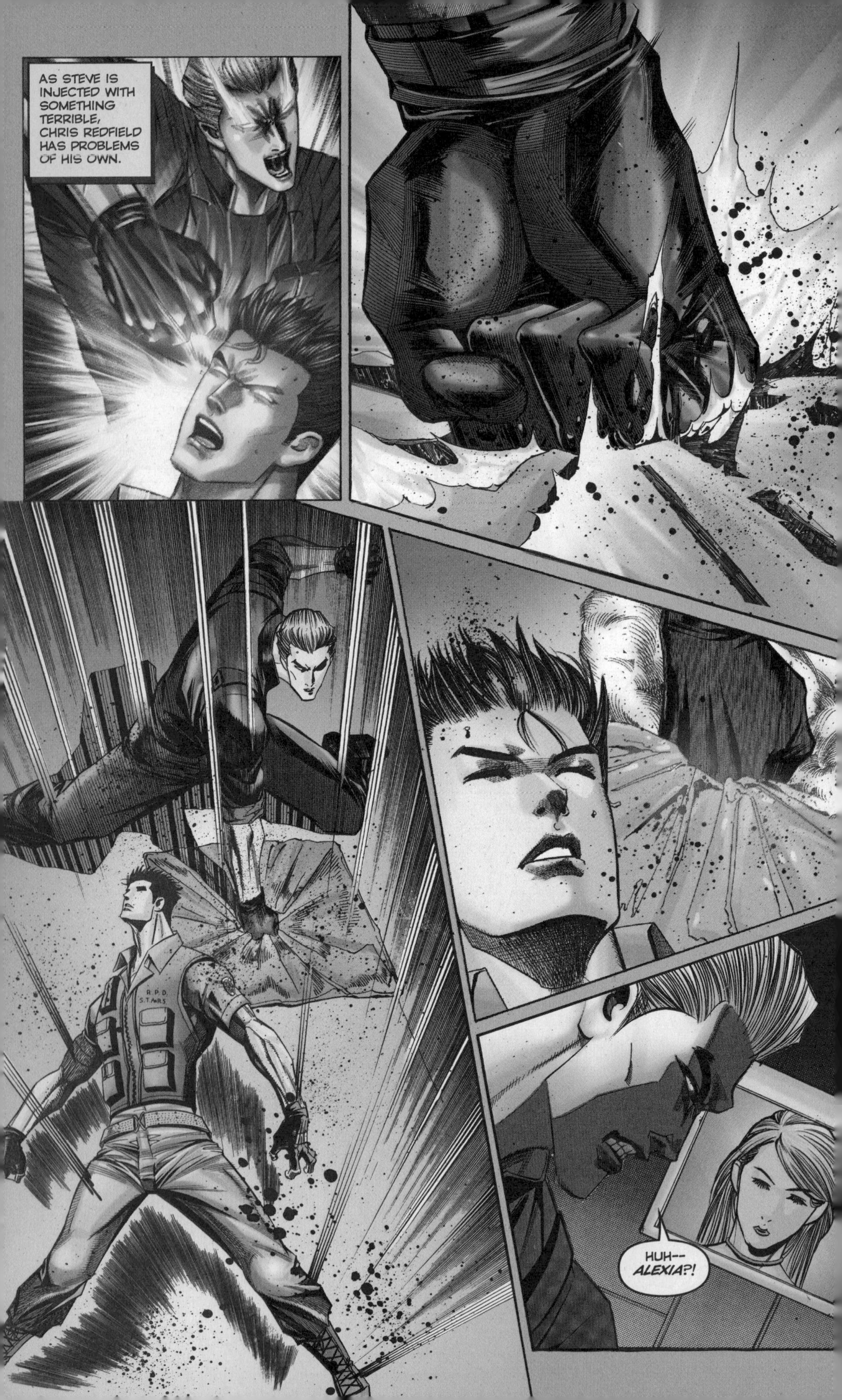
AS STEVE IS INJECTED WITH SOMETHING TERRIBLE, CHRIS REDFIELD HAS PROBLEMS OF HIS OWN.
R.P.D. S.T.A.R.S.
HUH-- ALEXIA?!

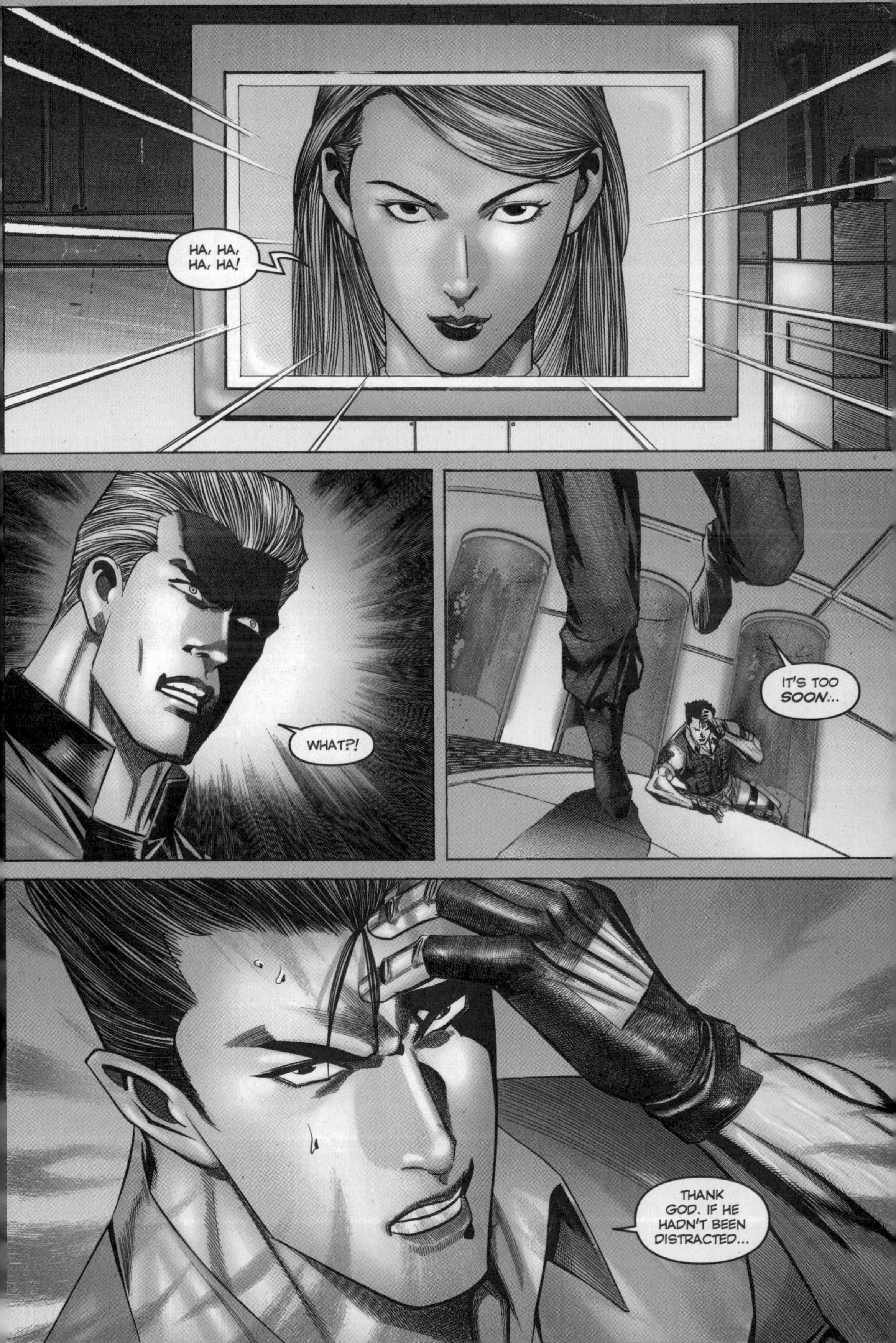
HA, HA, HA, HA!
WHAT?!
IT'S TOO SOON...
THANK GOD. IF HE HADN'T BEEN DISTRACTED...

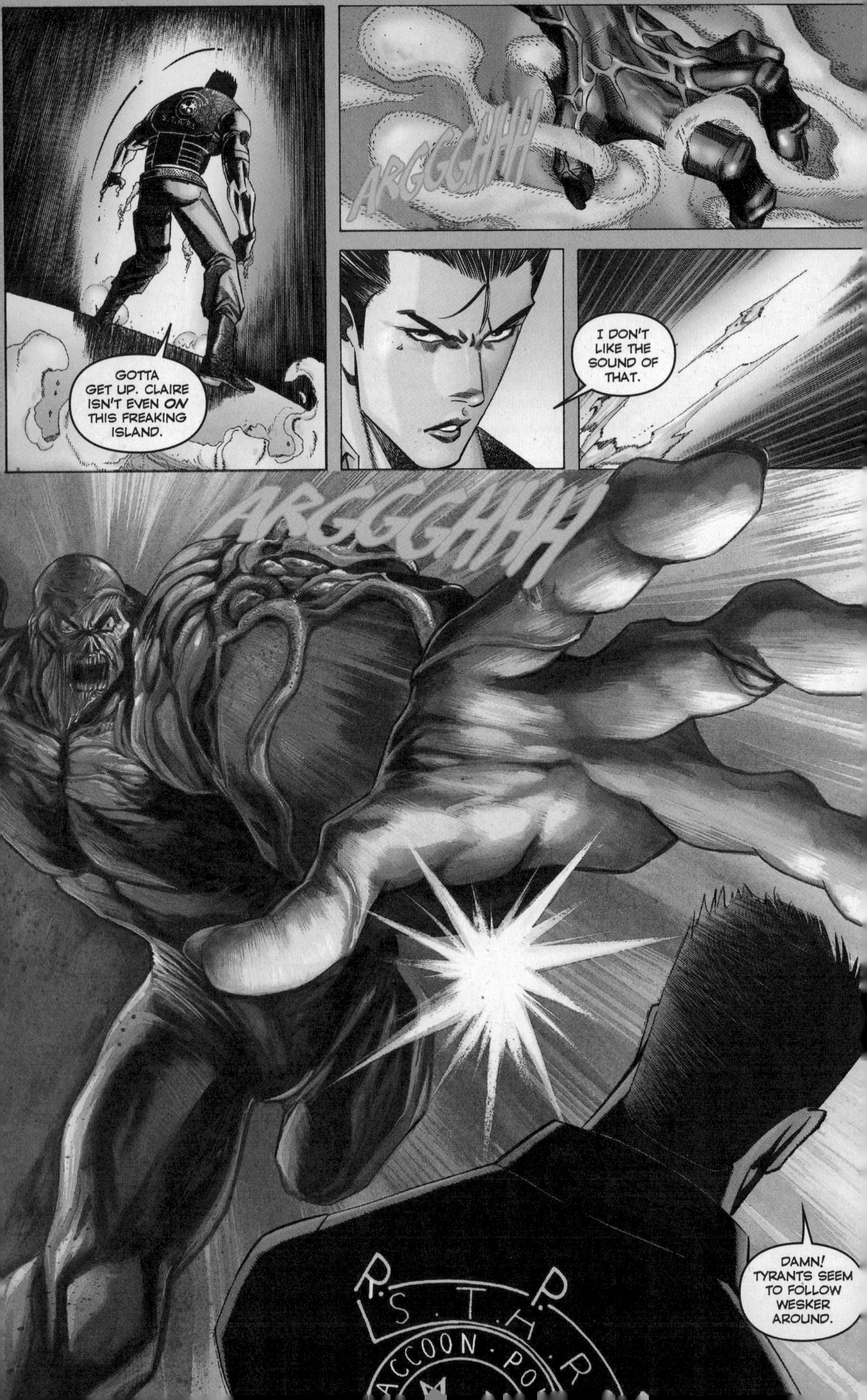

GOTTA GET UP. CLAIRE ISN'T EVEN *ON* THIS FREAKING ISLAND.
ARGGGHHH
I DON'T LIKE THE SOUND OF THAT.
ARGGGHHH
DAMN! TYRANTS SEEM TO FOLLOW WESKER AROUND.
R.P.D.
S.T.A.R.S.
RACCOON POLICE

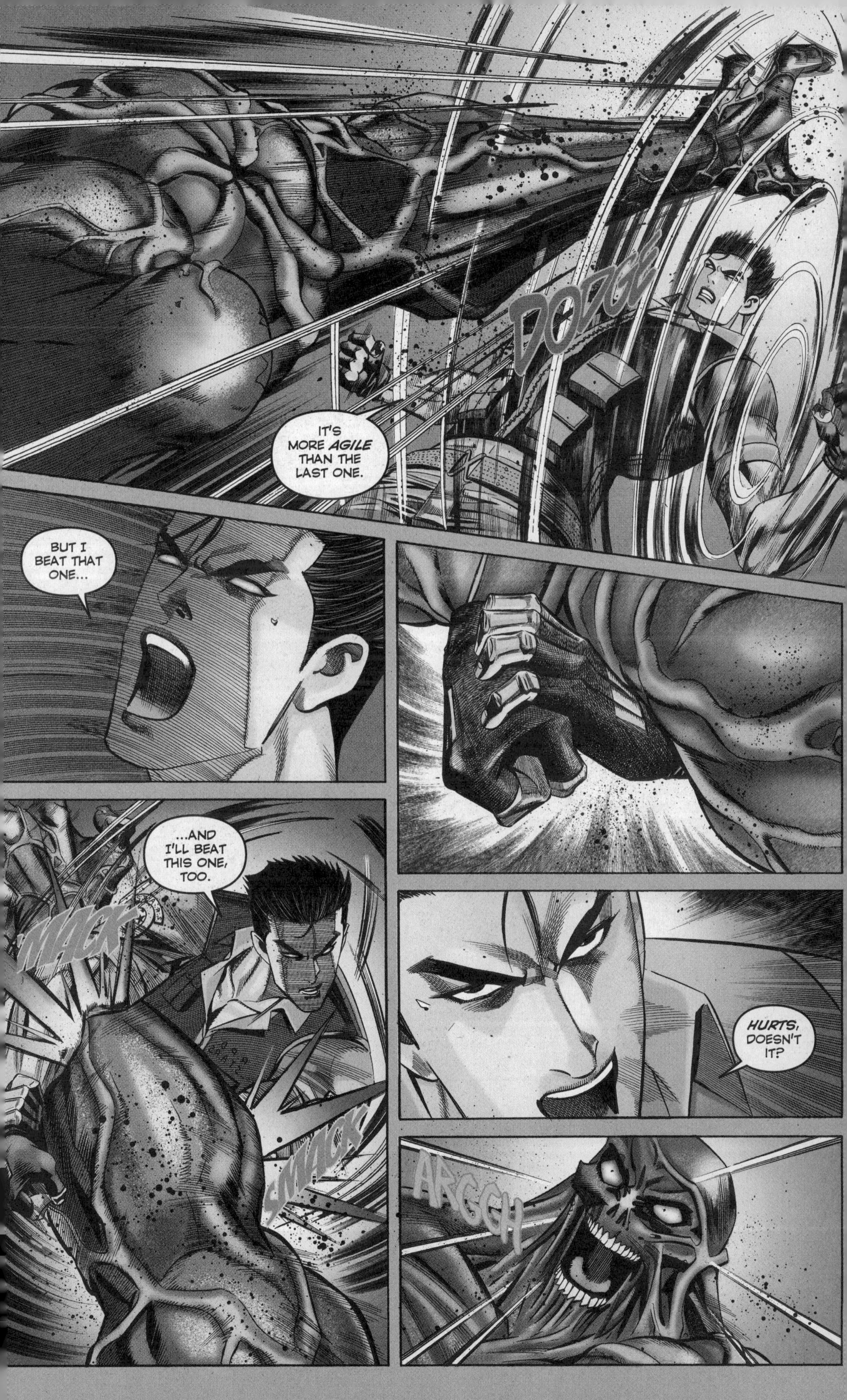
DODGE
IT'S MORE *AGILE* THAN THE LAST ONE.
BUT I BEAT THAT ONE...
...AND I'LL BEAT THIS ONE, TOO.
WHACK
SMACK
HURTS, DOESN'T IT?
ARGGH

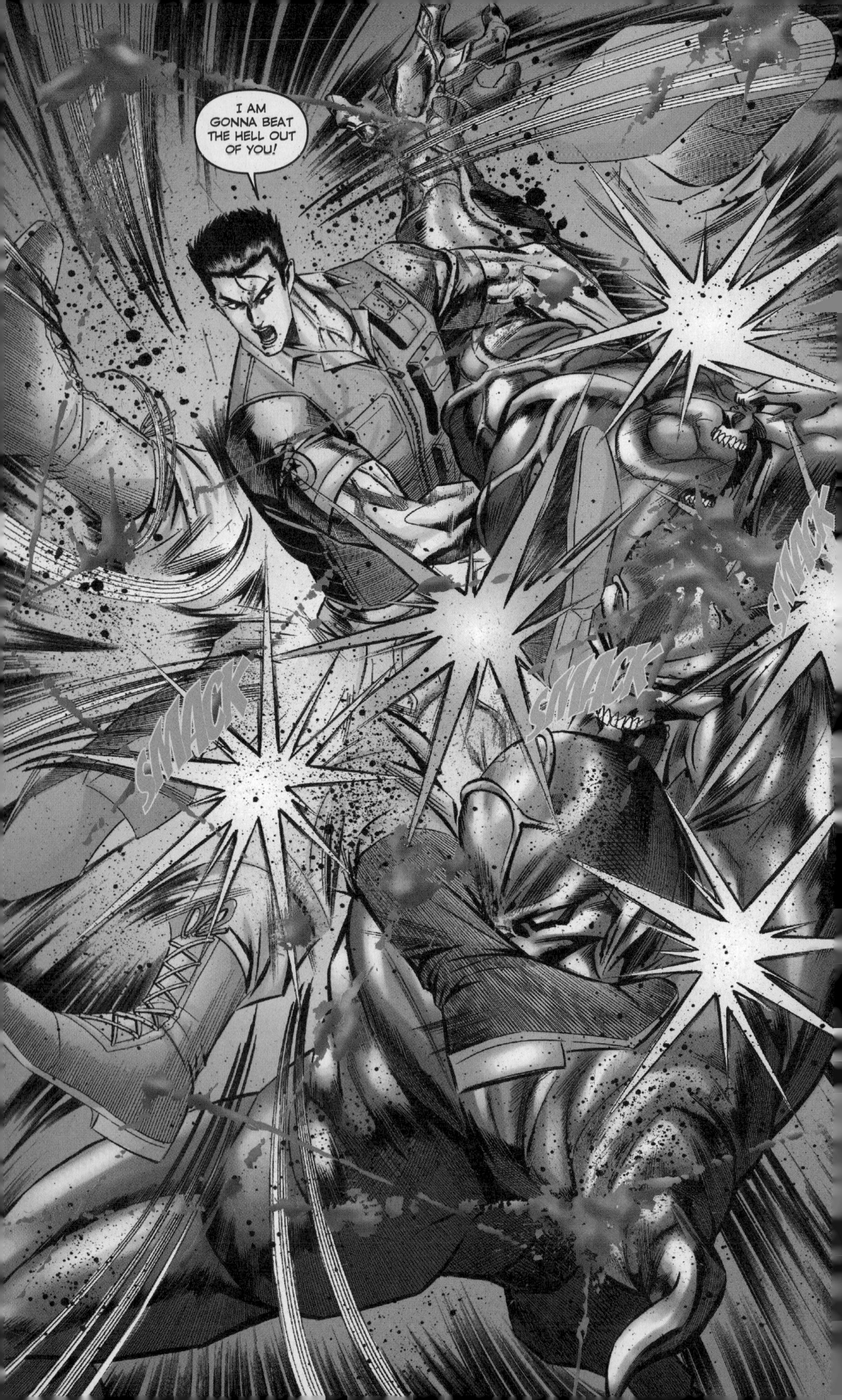

I AM GONNA BEAT THE HELL OUT OF YOU!
SMACK
SMACK
SMACK

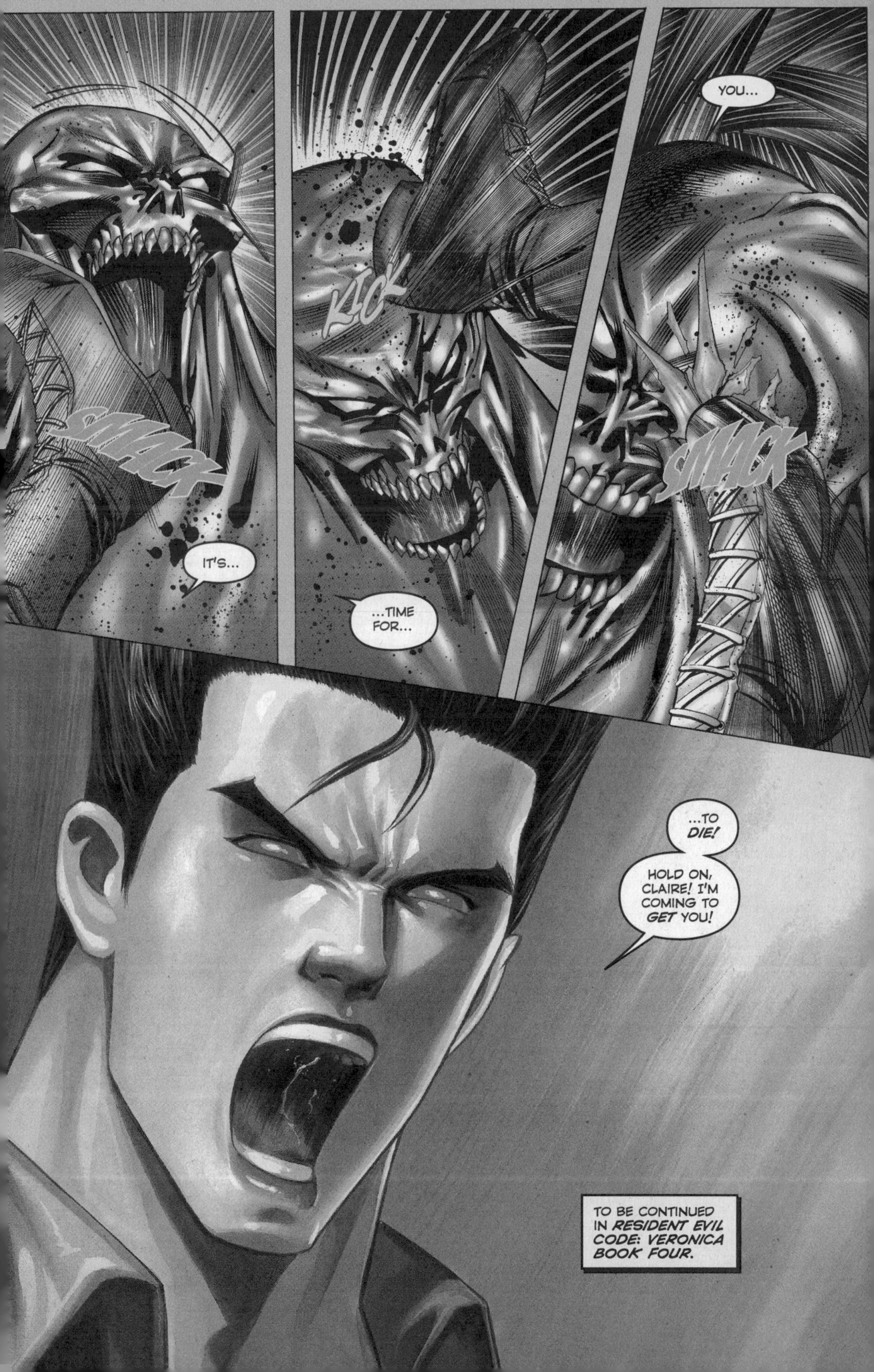
SMACK
IT'S...
KICK
...TIME FOR...
YOU...
SMACK
...TO *DIE!*
HOLD ON, CLAIRE! I'M COMING TO *GET* YOU!
TO BE CONTINUED IN *RESIDENT EVIL CODE: VERONICA BOOK FOUR.*

WILDSTORM COLLECTIONS

The Authority:
Relentless
Ellis/Hitch/Neary

The Authority:
Under New Management
Ellis/Millar/Hitch/Quitely

The Authority:
Earth Inferno and Other Stories
Millar/Quitely/Weston

The Absolute Authority Hardcover
Ellis/Hitch/Neary

Crimson: Loyalty & Loss
Augustyn/Ramos/Hope

Crimson: Heaven & Earth
Augustyn/Ramos/Hope

Crimson: Earth Angel
Augustyn/Ramos/Hope

Crimson: Redemption
Augustyn/Ramos/Hope

Deathblow:
Sinners and Saints
Choi/Lee/Sale/Scott

Danger Girl:
The Ultimate Collection
Campbell/Hartnell/Garner

Divine Right:
Book One
Lee/Williams

Gen13
Choi/Lee/Campbell/Garner

Gen13: #13 ABC
Choi/Lee/Campbell/Garner

Gen13: Bootleg Vol. 1
Various writers and artists

Gen13:
Grunge the Movie
Warren

Gen13:
I Love New York
Arcudi/Frank/Smith

Gen13:
Interactive Plus
Various writers and artists

Gen13: Starting Over
Choi/Lee/Campbell/Garner

Gen13:
We'll Take Manhattan
Lobdell/Benes/Sibal

Gen13/Superman
Hughes/Bermejo/Nyberg

Kurt Busiek's Astro City:
Life in the Big City
Busiek/Anderson

Kurt Busiek's Astro City:
Confession
Busiek/Anderson/Blyberg

Kurt Busiek's Astro City:
Family Album
Busiek/Anderson/Blyberg

Kurt Busiek's Astro City:
Tarnished Angel
Busiek/Anderson/Blyberg

Leave It to Chance:
Shaman's Rain
Robinson/Smith

Leave It to Chance:
Trick or Threat
Robinson/Smith/Freeman

The Monarchy:
Bullets Over Babylon
Young/McCrea/Leach/Pleece

Mr. Majestic
Casey/Holguin/McGuinness/D'Anda

Out There:
The Evil Within
Augustyn/Ramos/Hope

Planetary/Authority:
Ruling the World
Ellis/Jimenez/Lanning

Planetary:
All Over the World and Other Stories
Ellis/Cassaday

Planetary:
The Fourth Man
Ellis/Cassaday

StormWatch:
Force of Nature
Ellis/Raney/Elliott

StormWatch:
Lightning Strikes
Ellis/Raney/Lee/
Elliott/Williams

StormWatch:
Change or Die
Ellis/Raney/Jimenez

StormWatch:
A Finer World
Ellis/Hitch/Neary

StormWatch:
Final Orbit
Ellis/Various

Wetworks: Rebirth
Portacio/Choi/Williams

WildC.A.T.s: Gang War
Moore/Various

WildC.A.T.s:
Gathering of Eagles
Claremont/Lee/Williams

WildC.A.T.s: Homecoming
Moore/Various

WildC.A.T.s/X-Men
Various writers and artists

Wildcats: Street Smart
Lobdell/Charest/Friend

Wildcats:
Vicious Circles
Casey/Phillips

Wildcats:
Serial Boxes
Casey/Phillips

Zero Girl
Kieth

AMERICA'S BEST COMICS

ABC SKETCHBOOK
Various

ABC Special
Moore/Various

League of
Extraordinary Gentlemen
Moore/O'Neill

Promethea: Book One
Moore/Williams III/Gray

Promethea: Book Two
Moore/Williams III/Gray

Promethea: Book Three
Moore/Williams III/Gray

Tomorrow Stories: Book One
Moore/Nowlan/Veitch/Baikie/
Gebbie/Barta

Tom Strong: Book One
Moore/Sprouse/Gordon

Tom Strong: Book Two
Moore/Sprouse/Gordon

Top Ten: Book One
Moore/Ha/Cannon

Top Ten: Book Two
Moore/Ha/Cannon

STAR TREK COLLECTIONS

Star Trek:
Other Realities
Various

Star Trek:
The Next Generation
Enemy Unseen
Various